Kvithavet

Nafraim Sai

DAUVRÅK

KISTESTIK

Ringmark

Nákla-zing

NÁKLA-WALL

Brenn-Torget

HÆRGATA

Florian's Parlors

Náklav College

PRØF. DOLG'S VEI

GE RUNAS VEI

RINGKOLLEN

BODSRABBEN

Vinter-hagen

MYNTSLAGET

Herad

Skodda

Corpse Bay

Tysna

Kleft

an Askran

GUDEBRO BRIDGE

LYKTELØKKA

Matlagap

Náklaborg

SKJEPNASNARET

The Sannseyr home

Sölshov

hill

STEINNLEIA

Varghelling

Kvalbukt

SVEITA

Blögge

Slogness

tan

Náklav

SILVER THROAT

VARDARI — PART 2 SIRI PETTERSEN

SILVER THROAT

Translated by Tara Chace

Arctis

This translation has been published with the financial support of NORLA, Norwegian Literature Abroad.

W1-Media, Inc.
Imprint Arctis
Stamford, CT, USA

Visit our website at www.arctis-books.com
Author website at www.siripettersen.com

1 3 5 7 9 8 6 4 2

Library of Congress Control Number: 2024940551

ISBN 978-1-64690-016-9
eBook ISBN 978-1-64690-616-1

Printed in Germany

To my grandmother,
who may manage to read this
even though she has seen her last night, every night,
for three years.

And to you. You who are angry.
You with the knot in your heart, pulled inextricably taut
from sheer rage, because you have encountered injustice
that no words can make right.
You who must sacrifice all your strength to defeat toxic anger,
each and every time you wake up. This is your book.

IN THE CELLAR

Juva pulled the lever and heard her crossbow span with a reassuring click. She braced the butt against her chest, ready to react, and listened.

The Dead Man's Horn sounded its gloomy warning over Náklav, and just behind her, the men caught their breath, but otherwise, the street was unnervingly quiet. No crying, no terrified onlookers, no one shouting from the windows, not even drunk people on their way home in the semidark summer night.

The magnificent stone walls jockeyed for space along the top of Kingshill, as high as they could get without interfering with Náklaborg. There was no indication that this lovely neighborhood had ever been plagued by wolf-sickness.

She sensed Skarr gazing up at her with those fearless yellow wolf eyes, but she felt no threat other than an awareness that something was coming. The heartbeats beat their eternal warning: *just wait . . . just wait . . . just wait . . .*

Juva leaned closer to Nolan.

"Are we in the right place?"

"Upper Kingshill 9," Nolan replied, pulling out the overly simplistic map of the city. "The runner came straight from the guard booth, first warning. They rarely mess up before the third."

She looked at the imposing house in front of them. A magnificent, old building, shielded behind a wall with an arched gateway. They even had a courtyard in there. She snatched the map from Nolan and turned it over in her hand. The name and location had been hastily scribbled on the arch.

"Girding?"

Nolan looked at her as if she had forgotten her own name.

"Gisting," he said. "Hjarn Gisting. The state councilman, Juva."

"There you go," mumbled Lok.

Juva peered in the gateway. If the councilman had someone with wolf-sickness in there, then it was unusually quiet.

"False alarm?" she asked, even though she doubted it. Those were rare.

Hanuk laughed the hoarse laugh that always reminded her of a magpie.

"Or maybe they bribed the sick person to go somewhere else?" he suggested.

"Or gave him a seat in the State Council," Lok chuckled. "It's not as if anyone could tell the difference."

Juva glared at him. Lok was always ready to criticize his superiors for their money and power, but it's not like either could slow wolf-sickness. She felt increasingly uneasy.

"Or maybe they're all dead," she said.

The seriousness closed in on them again, like they were at a sepulture. Nolan looked back.

"Where the Gaula are they?" he asked.

"I can't believe Muggen hasn't moved in with us or Broddmar," Lok said, rubbing his eyes with his knuckles. "That would have simplified everything."

"Blame his sister," Nolan replied. "She thinks we worship the devil."

"*We* do?" Juva looked at him. "Wasn't she seeing that fool who came to Svartna with us at midwinter? The blood smuggler with the flask strapped around his lower leg?"

Nolan smirked and drew a Jól-ring on his chest.

"I hear she's born again," he said. "Took the water all over again and was cleansed of her sins."

Juva rolled her eyes and saw someone peek out a window just above her. A door was locked. Someone knocked nervously on their neighbor's door. It was the sound of the nighttime peace being broken. The rumor of the hunters would spread down the street, along with the distressing realization that *this time it's us.*

She heard footsteps running and grabbed her crossbow with both hands, but it was just Broddmar and Muggen approaching them, panting. Muggen wiped the sweat off his shiny bald head and gasped for breath.

"This is really . . . at the very top . . ."

"Too many stairs?" Nolan asked with feigned innocence.

Broddmar scowled at him.

"I climbed every step in Náklav before you were born, boy."

Juva slipped in the gateway and looked around in the courtyard. She pulled her fingers over her jawline and checked that her bolt was straight in the groove. Broddmar came over to her.

"Have you sensed anything?"

"I wouldn't have waited if I had." She walked over to the front door and knocked using the knocker. A man in a double-breasted vest opened it, clearly relieved. She knew the look well, the false sense of security he clung to, as if her outfit alone had the power to save him from wolf-sickness. A thin, worn layer of leather against utter lunacy.

He stepped to the side and let them in.

"Welcome! The master will receive you shortly."

Shortly?

"Dead or injured?" she asked, stepping inside.

"Good heavens, no. It's not that bad!" His eyes roamed over her red outfit. "Not yet, anyway."

Juva pulled off her hood and looked around. A staircase curved down from the floor above, and multiple archways made it clear there were more than enough places to attack from. The room was expensively furnished but not with anything big enough to hide behind. There was a testament to prosperity against one wall, a wooden cabinet containing a clock. It featured a built-in hourglass, as if the owner didn't trust the clockworks alone.

Hanuk raised his hand to touch it. Juva cleared her throat, and he refrained. She gestured to them, and they spread out to make sure no sick people were waiting in the shadows of the archways.

A man in a white shirt walked into the room. His hair was streaked with gray, and he was clutching a fireplace poker.

"Praise Jól, it's you!"

He held out his hand to a woman and a girl who hesitated in the opening. They were well dressed, clearly ready to leave the house in short order.

"I'm Hjarn Gisting. This is my wonderful wife, Auga, and my granddaughter, Brina. And you're the famous hunters? Náklav's bleeders, or is it just the two of you in red who . . ."

He looked alternately from her to Broddmar as if expecting an introduction. Juva felt her patience running thin.

"Are you wolf-sick, Hjarn?" she asked, hoping to elicit some sensible action from him.

"No! No, of course not," he replied, embarrassed, and pointed the poker at a door underneath the staircase. "She's locked in the wine cellar. She can't do any harm."

"To people," the wife clarified. "The wine is worth a fortune."

Juva walked over and put her ear to the wooden door. She didn't hear anything but knew the silence was a lie. Something crept around her heart, like breath visible in the frosty air. The men gathered around her, and she gave them a discrete nod to confirm what she sensed.

"Who is she?" Broddmar asked.

Auga covered the girl's ears with her hands before answering.

"No one has ever used blood pearls in this house! We would never have hired her if we had suspected . . . Mildre is the cook. She came with the finest credentials and makes the most delightful palace cake with a meringue base, topped with lemon mousse—"

"Is she alone?" Juva interrupted. She didn't want the details. The more she knew, the worse it was. Now she had to kill Mildre who made palace cake, not just someone with wolf-sickness.

Hjarn leaned his poker against the wall.

"There's no one else down there. I worked late. These are . . . tough times. The Ring Guard is hemorrhaging money and people, and the city council recently lost a member to wolf-sickness. There are barely any boundaries anymore."

Juva read a silent accusation in his eyes before he continued.

"I heard a bunch of noise and came out of my office, and . . . Well, I could tell right away that something was wrong. She was sweating and . . ." He gulped, then continued. "The teeth, right? She was tugging on the door like someone possessed, so I slid her the key, across the floor. It seemed like that was all she wanted, to get down there. It was the oddest . . . Well, as soon as she was down there, I locked the door again right away."

"What does it look like down there?"

"Oh, you know, the cellar itself sits in the actual Kingshill wall. So it's old. It dates back to the tenth century, actually, with very striking vaulted ceilings that—"

"Rooms! How many rooms? Are there windows to escape through? Anything to hide behind? Anything that could be used as a weapon?" Juva was on the verge of giving up.

"Oh, I see . . . There's a hallway at the end of the stairs, with the pantry on one side and the wine cellar on the other. The wine cellar is about the size of this foyer here but divided into bays. I like to sort the wine based on the regions they . . ." He met her gaze and added hurriedly, "But no weapons, of course."

11

Except for the bottles.

Skarr scurried past the servant, who jumped out of the way with a hiccup.

"I'll fetch the lanterns," the servant squeaked. The most sensible thing said thus far.

The young girl took a couple of steps toward Juva.

"Are you going to kill Mildre?"

"No, of course not!" Auga replied, wrapping her arm around the girl's chest. She gave Juva a warning look. "Are you?"

Juva glanced down at Brina. The lie would have been easy for most people, she knew that. But they hadn't grown up with blood readers and been lied to their whole lives.

"Your grandmother's right," Juva said. "Mildre doesn't exist anymore. What we're going to kill is something else entirely."

The girl stared up at her grandmother as if waiting for her to correct the undisguised truth, but that didn't happen.

The servant returned, taking a detour around Skarr, and handed two lanterns to Nolan and Lok.

Juva turned the key and opened the door. Skarr stared down into the darkness and started to growl. She didn't need him to locate people with wolf-sickness. She was better at that on her own now, but he was proof that people understood. And a loyal friend who had hardly left her side since the Yra Race. Since *him*.

She secured the leash to his harness and passed the hand loop to the servant.

"Hold him while we're down there. And—he's strong . . ."

The man paled as if she had asked him to dive off Gudebro Bridge, but he accepted the leash and held it out at arm's length.

Juva took a few steps down. The stairs formed a narrow curve that swallowed the light from the lanterns. She raised her crossbow out in front of her. The motion made her chest feel tight, in the scar that he had gouged into her before he vanished forever.

She gritted her teeth and focused on her fear. It was welcome; she could depend on it. A pulsing sign of life in the abyss she lived in otherwise. She continued downward noiselessly, listening. The uncertainly was always the most unsettling. Never knowing what was waiting. It could be old, young, confused, or beastly . . .

"Expect the worst," she whispered. Nolan was so close to her that she could feel him steel himself. A warm, safe wall of men behind her. The best.

It grew chillier with every step, until she reached the bottom of the stairs. She stepped over a broken wine bottle and turned toward the only sound she heard. A quiet smacking sound, like someone stepping in mud. But there was no one to be seen in the maze of shelves. Wall upon wall of bottles gleamed around her, and the cellar was filled with an intense smell of sour berries. She gestured for them to split up, and the guys spread out on either side of her.

The room seemed to narrow before her, as if the walls were closing in around her crossbow. It was the only thing that existed. Her finger on the trigger. The tip of the bolt. The heart trembling in her chest, as if it were naked against the cold. The feeling was nowhere near as strong as when warow were nearby, but it was more unsettling.

The sound grew louder. She was close.

Juva stopped in front of a tipped-over rack that lay in her way on a pile of bottles. Many were broken. A couple of small casks had cracked like skulls. She barely avoided tripping on one of them. A muffled sound, very nearby, revealed that Muggen had not managed to do the same.

The smacking sound stopped abruptly. A lone empty bottle rolled across the floor.

Juva nodded for Broddmar to come with her and pointed for the others to go the opposite way. They rounded the shelf from either side and almost walked right into her.

Mildre . . .

The woman sat on the floor in a puddle of wine, chewing on a bone. Her wild, wary gaze wandered between them, but she didn't move. The food was more important. Evidently she had tried to drink half the cellar without it soothing her hunger.

She was in her fifties, wearing an apron soaked through with wine. Juva suddenly realized that what she was gnawing on was her own hand.

Broddmar grabbed hold of Juva, as if to support her, or maybe himself. "What the Drukna . . ." Muggen whispered. Lok backed away and vomited. Mildre kept gnawing on her knuckle, sucking it like a baby on a breast, seemingly numb to the pain.

Juva felt cold and aimed her crossbow at Mildre. The bolt trembled as she took aim, and then she fired. Her blood pounded in her ears, and she didn't hear her own shot. But she saw the bolt pierce Mildre's chest. Mildre jerked backward and lay disfigured, sprawled over a barrel. The blood from her hand dripped into the wine on the floor, making it look as if she had lost an incredible amount of blood.

Juva inhaled, her lungs burning. She had forgotten to use them for a while. Her heart shook off the last of the frost from the sick person. She folded up her crossbow, hooked it into place in her harness, and took the bloodskins off her back.

"She's alive!" Muggen yelled.

Juva looked up and saw the bloody hand grab Broddmar's calf. She dropped the bloodskins and threw herself on top of Mildre, who flailed and fought beneath her. Broddmar kicked frantically. A Gaula's roar came from the stairs. Something broke. Someone screamed. Juva fumbled for the knife in her belt while keeping her weight on Mildre, who struggled to get free. For a second, she thought Mildre was growling, but it was Skarr. A mountain of fur and muscles rushed over, knocking them both down. Juva got to her feet and stared at the wolf. He had bitten onto Mildre's throat and was holding on. The skin of his muzzle curled as he waited for her to succumb. He stopped growling, then let go and sat down as if nothing had happened. His tongue swept over his teeth.

Juva picked up the bloodskins again, quickly, to keep the trembling from starting, and Nolan came over to help. Broddmar pretended he was busy inspecting his calf. As if everyone hadn't already realized he no longer had the stomach for the job. He hadn't been the same since he learned that those suffering from wolf-sickness might have a chance with some blood from that damned devil she had freed from captivity.

Nolan strapped Mildre's feet together and hoisted them up onto his shoulder, holding her as vertically as he could. Juva placed the knife-sharp spout against her neck and drove it in. The bloodskin slowly grew between her fingers.

Lok stood with his hands on his thighs, as if he weren't sure he was done throwing up. He had never had the stomach for this. Wolves were wolves, people were people, and he had never coped well with the transition.

Muggen started pacing like a restless bear. He ran his hand over his bald head. He had had enough. They had all had enough. Juva could feel it coming.

"Is this our fault?" he finally asked. "How much longer can they hold out? The warow should be dead—all of them!"

"Muggen . . ." Nolan's voice was a warning that only seemed to cause Muggen to despair even more.

"We've got to be allowed to ask! Wasn't that the whole point of sending that creature home? To get rid of his blood, so the warow would die out? No warow, no blood pearls; no blood pearls, no wolf-sickness; but there've never been more of them than there are now!"

"It takes time, Muggen. Do you understand?" Nolan groaned, heaving Mildre's legs into a better position. "They won't die overnight, and as long as there's warow blood around, they'll use it for blood pearls. That shit is way too lucrative. And even after the vardari have kicked the bucket, it will take time to drain the black market."

"Still . . ." Lok said, straightening up. "He's not wrong. How long has it been since—"

"I'm going back upstairs to tell them the danger is past," Hanuk said.

Juva had a bitter taste in her mouth at his obvious attempt to zero out the question. They avoided his name like the wolf-sickness, as if it weren't constantly churning in her thoughts.

Since Grír. Since the source of eternal life left Náklav.

She pulled the filled bloodskin out of the corpse's neck and pushed in the next one. She had improved and could swap them out with very little spillage.

"One hundred and two days," she said.

No one responded, there was nothing to say. Muggen was right. Lok was right. Her mother had died on the eighth day of Gyta, and the vardari hadn't had a drop of his blood since then. At most, they had six months left to live, and dying warow should have entirely different things to think about than selling blood pearls.

"So why are there just more of them?" Muggen asked.

Juva put the stopper in and heaved the bloodskins onto her back. The city was so full of wolf-sick people that they didn't even need wolves to operate Nákla Henge. The portals ran on the sick blood alone, a bitter truth now that there would have been enough wolf blood. Nafráim had admitted that himself.

The only consolation was that it spared the wolves, because she was finished as a wolf hunter. The sickness had never had anything to do with them. But she still had a hunting team—not for wolves, but for humans. There were enough humans getting high on blood pearls, even though they knew it could give them wolf-sickness.

16

But not enough of them for it to be like this . . .

She looked into Muggen's pleading eyes and wished she had an answer for him. That she could say it would be over before fall arrived, but she had already promised too much. To the whole city.

"Anyway, it's not our fault, Muggen," Nolan said, loosening the strap around the corpse's feet. "We have to expect it to get worse before it gets better."

Juva thanked him with her eyes, and he rewarded her with a pained smile that reminded her the men usually teased him for being vain. In their world, that meant he smelled good and didn't cut his own hair. But he was anything but vain and had never shied away from hard work. Jól only knew why he did this macabre job, because he didn't need the money. But she didn't either, anymore, so he probably had the same reason. It needed to be done. And now he was better at it than Broddmar.

Juva squatted beside the corpse and unhooked her pliers from her belt. Lok emitted a groan and turned his back to her. She looked up at Broddmar, silently daring him to protest, but it had been many deaths since he had given up protecting her. This was her job now.

She opened the dead woman's jaws to a sick stench of rotten meat and acidic wine. Her tongue was swimming in blood. Nolan held the limp head steady, while Juva snapped out the fangs. One of the fangs hadn't fully grown in yet and took some strength to extract. It had just forced its way in, beneath the canine, which was dangling by a thin thread.

Juva wrapped the teeth in a handkerchief and stuck them in her pocket.

Hanuk came back in and kicked a wine bottle out of the way. "The Ring Guard is here," he said, as if there could be any mistaking the tromping on the stairs. They arrived in force and took over the cellar in an instant.

"We'll take it from here," Broddmar said, giving the back of Juva's neck a pat. "Go home and get yourself a little sleep." She didn't respond. It felt far too little and far too late. A lie Broddmar told himself, that he was still a rock.

Juva swallowed her disappointment. She let the guards clean up and returned upstairs with Skarr at her heels. There was a smashed hourglass and a couple of gears sitting partway up the stairs. She realized the servant had tied Skarr to the clock to get out of holding him. Juva sighed and glanced down at the wolf, who stared back; she could have sworn he would have shrugged his shoulders if he could have.

This was confirmed up in the foyer, a trail of splintered wood from the broken cabinet on the floor. Auga and the girl were nowhere to be seen, but a handful of guards were looking after Hjarn. If they were short-staffed, it wasn't evident here on Kingshill—that was for sure. The state councilman stared awkwardly at them. "I had no idea she even drank . . ."

Juva walked out into the courtyard. In the hazy light that made it impossible to tell what time of day it was in Náklav for all of Heita, in the only month that could be called summer, fewer people were waiting there than she had feared.

They stood in groups murmuring around the black corpse carriage, tired, scared. Their conversations stopped when they saw her. They drew back, letting her through to the gate, staring at her, at the wolf.

Juva pulled her hood farther forward but still felt naked. The bloodskins hung like warm wings on her back. A woman in a nightgown stood with her arms wrapped around herself, as if she were rubbing her upper arms to try to warm up.

"You promised this would end!" she yelled.

Her outburst emboldened the others.

"The vardari are punishing us!" an elderly man yelled.

Juva fought against her nausea. Those words drained her strength, and only now did she realize how little strength she had in reserve. Her feet grew heavier, and she used the last of her energy to get through the door and out onto the deserted street.

Vardari... Oh yeah, they were going to punish people—no doubt about that. Her most of all.

One hundred and two days since she had tricked Eydala up at Nákla Henge. When she had lied and said that the letter to Nafraím showed the way to the devil, the source of eternal life. Gaula only knew what had happened to those two warow since then. Juva hadn't sensed hide nor hair of any of them.

Merciful Jól, may they be dead.

"Juva!" Nolan came running out the gate and came to an abrupt halt when he saw that she wasn't far away. He pulled his hand over his short, freshly trimmed beard. "Are you sure you don't need someone with you until tomorrow?"

"Skarr will keep an eye on me," she said, wiping blood off her hand. "Besides, if she knew what I had done, I'd be dead by now. There's no danger anymore."

He looked puzzled, and she realized he was talking about something completely different from Eydala.

"I meant with the city council," he said. "They're under a lot of pressure. There's no telling what they'll do."

"Oh . . ." She smiled as best she could. "Well, they should be more worried about what *I'm* up to. Good night, Nolan."

She released the wolf and let him lead the way down the street and the endless stairs until she was no longer above the city but trapped within it. The sea disappeared from view, and the sky became streaks visible above the alleyways, broken by the occasional enclosed overhead skywalk. Several were ripe enough to crumble and fall any day now. But they had looked like that for a long time.

Skarr sped up as they reached Lykteløkka. What had been Broddmar's wolf was now hers. Broddmar had tried to take the animal home with him several times, but he had always found a way out and appeared on her doorstep.

As Juva fumbled in her pocket for the key, the door was abruptly yanked open, and Kefla stood before her with her lips pursed.

"You're late," the young girl said, putting her hands on her hips. Juva pushed her way inside past her.

"What are you doing, Kefla?! You can't just open the door to whoever. Are you not thinking?!"

Kefla slammed the door shut so the wrought iron sang through the gloomy foyer.

"Hey, I sensed Skarr, so I knew it was you."

"You can never know that. How many times do I need to tell you that? Am I going to have to throw you out?"

She regretted her words as soon as she had said them. Kefla tightened her lips, but her eyes revealed her fear. Juva undid her harness straps, catching her crossbow and the bloodskins before they hit the floor. She peeled off her red suit and tossed it over the ornate, black banister.

"You're not safe here. You know that."

"You have an iron door!" Kefla scoffed. "You nailed all the windows shut, aside from the ones facing the sea, and you have a wolf. How could it be any safer?"

"You need to be more careful, Kefla. That's what I mean."

Kefla flipped her bangs out of her face and pouted.

"Careful like you? Roaming the city at night, killing the wolf-sick, always alone . . . That kind of careful?"

Juva tried to think of a good retort. Kefla was sharper than a twelve-year-old ought to be, honed by all her years on the streets.

"I'm not alone. I have Skarr and my hunting team. And I've learned to recognize the warow. You haven't yet."

"I have! Just as well as you."

Juva sighed.

"But you can't tell them apart," Juva sighed. "You don't know who's—" she cut herself off.

Who is the beast, Eydala.

Why hadn't that macabre woman come after her yet? Nafraím must have explained everything, about the letter, and about Gríf, whom Nafraím had personally seen leave the world. Had the blood shortage already cost both Nafraím and Eydala their lives? Or had they murdered each other before Eydala learned the truth? Juva clung to that thought but knew that if she had believed that, she would be living a completely different life. And sleeping at night.

She went into the library, filled a glass with rye whiskey, and relaxed on the sofa. Skarr lay down at her feet. His fur glowed in the midnight sun, which cast patches of light through the mullioned windows. The waves struck the cliffs outside, reinforcing the feeling she always had in this room of being aboard a ship.

The corpsewood burned in the fireplace, just beside the table where the dead had sat, like dolls. Solde. Ogny and the other blood readers. Nafraím's misdeed. And on the chimney wall stood the cabinet with the ridiculous stuffed raven that told fortunes in runes. The cabinet that had hidden the shaft that led down to the family's centuries-old sin.

Gríf.

A memorial to deception. To her own idiocy.

Juva drained her glass and pushed it away on the table. She hadn't been down there since he had left. Not a single time. What would she do there? Reminisce like some fool about everything they had discussed? Feel betrayed? Smell the scent of him?

A motion startled her awake, and she realized she had dozed off. She reached instinctively for her crossbow, but it was only Kefla snuggling up next to her on the sofa. Juva put her arm around the girl's skinny body and mumbled, "We can go see the others tomorrow."

"Are you sure? Do you promise?"

"After the meeting. I promise," Juva replied, even though she had promised herself never to make another promise.

SACRIFICIAL LAMB

The chairman of the city council's voice was solemn. Sjur Skattanger was used to being heard, even though everything he said was extraneous.

Juva watched his expressionless face as he chanted his way through the list of the slain as if it bored him. Name after name. The wolf-sick people Juva had killed and bled out. The victims she hadn't been able to save. To him, they were just incidents; to her, they were memories. She didn't need a list of names to remember.

She began to regret her decision to stand by the short end of the laughably long table, but she had expected this to go quickly. Her demands were simple: proper payment for the men and a clean-up of the shadiest places, where blood pearls were still changing hands. That was it. Now it seemed she was there for reasons totally different than she had thought.

This was the first time they had received her in this room, and it was hardly a coincidence. The ceiling was so high that it would make anyone feel insignificant. The columns were decorated with patterns that made it difficult to get one's bearings. The floor gleamed of white veinstone, and every single word echoed. It wasn't the usual committee, either, but close to half of the city council, over twenty women and men with grim faces.

This was no innocuous report. They wanted something, and her uncertainty tingled in the back of her scalp.

She put her hands behind her back to keep from drumming her fingers together. The other city councilmembers sat as if half-asleep over their own reflections in the glossy tabletop. Even Drogg avoided looking at her. The enormous man could have easily warned her what to expect, but she no longer had high expectations of anyone.

Still . . . She had helped him out of the lie her mother had paralyzed him with—the belief that every heartbeat he wasted shortened his life so that the man had hardly dared to move. All to ensure a steady cash flow from a man who needed constant reassurance about how long he had left to live. Heartless, even for Lagalune.

Blood reader. Swindler. Mother.

The city council chairman peeled away the top page and continued with the next.

"Vigda Renne, twenty-seven, Pissveita: broken neck. Kol Herstein Skjegge, forty-two, Tungeskaret: shot by a crossbow . . ." He paused and eyed her over his glasses. " . . . in the throat."

He was trying to put her on the defensive. She would have realized that even if she hadn't grown up with blood readers. Juva reminded herself that he actually needed her recognition to succeed. She raised her chin and added, "And with a knife in his back, if I remember correctly. His own."

The chairman set down his list and let out an elaborate sigh.

"Juva Sannseyr, I would hope and believe that we don't need to point out that you can't go shooting people—"

"Wolf-sickness."

"—with a crossbow in Tungeskaret. That is not a neighborhood where people are willing to get used to that sort of thing."

"Hmm, where are people willing to get used to that?"

The chairman's face pursed up a bit more. The corners of his mouth were so heavy that it was hard to imagine he had ever smiled.

"Young Frú Sannseyr, you stood on the balcony at Nákla Henge—in front of half the city—and promised to end the wolf-sickness.

That was more than three months ago, and it's worse than ever now. Do you think it's strange that people have lost faith in the hunters? In the Seida Guild?"

And in you.

Juva kept that thought to herself. He was right, after all. The city was roiling, and all she could do was wait. And put up with it. Without ever being able to tell anyone why she knew it would pass.

Because wolf-sickness comes from blood pearls, which come from the vardari, who have been living off the blood of an immortal jerk with fangs, whom we sent home, wherever the Drukna that might be.

No one doubted that wolf-sickness afflicted people who used blood pearls. But the rest . . . They would think she was insane, and that was a reality that she and the guys had to live with. They had put an end to the vardari, and no one would ever thank them for it.

Juva braced her hands against the table and leaned forward.

"It's worse than ever because people think wolf-sickness is to blame for everything. Every burglary, every fight, every drunken idiot or poor rambling nut on the streets, it all stems from the sickness. And *you* think you just need to count the dead, but a lot of the fangs we've collected come from warow, vardari killed by other vardari. They know Náklav isn't a safe haven for them anymore, so they're fighting each other, and yes, it's going to get worse before it gets better. In the meantime, we have hunters who—"

"Vardari?!" A woman seated at the middle of the table exclaimed. She rolled her eyes as if seeking strength from above. "So we're talking about the omnipotent, immortal ones again?"

Poorly concealed murmurs spread around the table, but the chairman controlled himself, as he should. He pushed the papers aside.

"Juva Sannseyr, your famous speech during the Yra Race was a disaster. There's no doubt about that. Not only did you confuse Náklav about what the Seida Guild is and should be, you also promised an end to wolf-sickness. You made a bombastic declaration of war against a figment of the imagination, a conspiracy of immortal lawless beings that cannot be detected or recognized—oh, but their consequences can. Your delusions have given the people a taste for the fanatical! Now many of them believe that the vardari exist and that . . ." Sjur turned to the secretary. "Don't record this, man!"

The secretary dropped his pen as if he had burned himself. The chairman sighed and looked at Juva again.

"They believe the vardari exist and that the city council isn't doing anything to get rid of the problem."

"Which you're not."

Juva heard his intake of breath, even though the end of the table was a good distance away, and even though her words were far gentler than they should have been. She burned to list everything they had neglected to grapple with; presumably, that would only make things worse. Self-criticism was rare within these walls.

"You're young," he said. "It's understandable that you don't see the big picture, but you're benefiting from your position. You have been given a tremendous amount of freedom to do this job."

"That no one else wants to do."

"That no one else *wanted* to do. But the city council needs to devote its much-needed time to *real* problems, not your nightmare, Frú Sannseyr. And here I must add that the real problems are the ones you have created."

"Moral panic!" said the woman who had interrupted earlier.

The rest of the city council perked up around the table, nodding in agreement, and Juva had the uncomfortable feeling that they were uniting around this point.

"A moral panic," the chairman said, pointing to the woman. "That's right, Ingra. A nuisance of doomsday predictors, cries for punishment, and insufferable priests. One of them carved out a career for himself by claiming that . . ." Sjur snatched up the lists again and read with raised eyebrows, " . . . that only sinners get sick, that the wolf-sickness is a punishment from God, the *one* God, and that Náklav must become a sin-free city."

He tossed the pieces of paper down again.

"They call themselves *the Hallowed*, and it's a mystery to me how anyone can get a following in this city by urging moderation, but perhaps they have something to teach us."

Moderation . . .

Juva suddenly felt weak. His words pulled her into her memory of that dilapidated hall of mirrors with thousands of candles. Abducted by Eydala, who sat facing her, going on about believers from Undst in a cold, lazy voice.

A mysterious people, don't you think? They came here with their lone god and toothless threats of eternal torment for the greedy. Can you imagine how much conviction it would require to come here, to Náklav, and preach moderation?

Juva could almost feel the strangling cord she had had around her neck, and she couldn't even say that she had been taken against her will. She had allowed herself to be caught, with no inkling of what was coming. To pit the vardari against each other, to make them believe that Nafraím had the devil, not her. All for him. For Gríf.

Juva looked down at her hands, pressing them against the tabletop to keep from shaking. She still had blood under her nails from the night's hunt. Had slept too little.

Never let them see a weak blood reader.

"Frú Sannseyr, do you understand our difficulty?"

She looked up.

"I understand that *I'm* not the one who should be standing here if priests are the problem."

"This priest, this Silver Throat, is using *your* words. He quotes *your* speech and has praised you in the most immodest of terms for revealing the truth about these so-called vardari. And since he has the ability to spread these ideas among fanatics, we feel forced to allow him to continue. Tragically enough, he is providing people a sense of security that they are no longer getting from the Seida Guild."

Juva put her hand to her forehead.

"So you want to replace one lie with another?"

"My dear child, every morning I walk by a guild for Votn, a temple to Muune, and a stall that sells Virriveg runes to travelers, and they're all on the very same street. This is Náklav! The sum of the world. We are home to the godless and to believers, all coexisting beautifully—and above all, lucratively—and I really couldn't care less what lies people profess, as long as it doesn't go to their heads."

"And the vardari go to their heads?"

"*Everything* goes to their heads. All the while, the Dead Man's Horn is going off every week, and red hunters are shooting the wolf-sick in the streets. It spreads unnecessary alarm and it must cease."

She felt a twitch at the corner of her mouth, an intense need to bare her teeth at him.

"I would have thought that that list you just read would have shown that we're doing our best."

Sjur Skattanger pursed his lips in a smug expression that was perhaps meant as a smile.

"Yes," he replied. "That's what we're afraid of."

Juva had an eerie feeling that she had walked into a trap. His words were anything but spontaneous. This was a set-up.

"And your best yesterday," he continued, "was a trashed wine cellar and an irreplaceable clock, smashed to splinters."

Before Juva could respond, Councilor Horski emitted a loud snort, as if he had been holding back his own voice with great effort.

"Relief workers must be the response. What about using volunteers from one of these . . . sects? More red hunters is the best we can do."

Juva stared at the man. He had hectic, red bun-cheeks that gave him a coarse look. Like a screaming newborn. But the worst part was that he appeared to be serious.

"Volunteers?" she asked. "You mean we should hire people who are eager to kill from a group you just described as fanatics, so that it will look like you're doing something about the wolf-sickness? You can—"

"Look like?!" Horski pulled his head back, so offended that it gave him an extra chin. "We've considerably slowed down the wolf hunt to keep the streets free of blood pearls. What could be more important?"

Juva bit her lip. Even if she could have explained how wrong he was, she wouldn't have known where to begin. The pearls contained blood from warow, not wolves. Wolf-sickness never had anything to do with wolves. They had slowed down the hunt for the sake of appearances, and because, these days, the stones in Nákla Henge turned on the blood from the sick. It was as simple and hopeless as that.

She knew that she annoyed them, that was abundantly clear from their faces. They exchanged glances, silently challenging each other to make the next move.

Juva realized that most other people would have been thrown out of here ages ago, but the fear of blood readers ran deep. She was young and did not belong in this room at all, but she was still Juva Sannseyr, and even if Anasolt was doing the work, on paper she was the guild master of the Seida Guild. A thousand years of superstition gave her the freedom to speak her mind. She clung to that hope and continued where Horski had left off.

"Trust me, the last thing we need right now is random idiots hunting for an excuse to murder a neighbor they can't stand. I have a good hunting team, people who are trustworthy. Staffing is not the problem. The problem is stopping the people who are selling the blood pearls, and finding the sick before they do harm."

"I thought you said the vardari are the problem?" the chairman said coolly. "So wouldn't it help to have more people who wanted to kill them?"

Juva would have laughed if she had the strength to spare.

"You want to use volunteers to hunt for something you don't want to acknowledge exists? With all due respect, Councilors, at some point you're going to need to decide whether they exist or not."

A blond woman spoke up abruptly, as if to stave off a fight.

"Frú Sannseyr is right. The wolf-sick aren't the biggest problem. After all, they brought this fate on themselves through their blood use."

Juva shuddered. No one had ever asked to contract wolf-sickness, nor had she ever said anything like that, but she let the woman continue.

"The problem is the panic and the harm the wolf-sick cause others. What if we promise a reward to their surviving relatives in exchange for the sick coming forward before they turn beastly?"

Juva stifled an exasperated moan.

"A reward? Thousands of healthy people would show up tomorrow if they could provide for the rest of their family that way."

The councilors stared at her blankly, as if she had spoken some other language. She flung up her arms.

"Haven't you ever needed money? Haven't you ever cared about someone who did? Haven't you ever gone hungry?"

Sjur gathered his stack of papers as if the matter had been resolved, but clearly it hadn't.

"Juva, your dedication is . . . touching. But it seems to me that *you're* the one who doesn't want to do anything here. You're not even twenty, right? Such incredibly young hunters and guild masters border on irresponsibility; obviously, we have demanded too much of you. You have been through the sepultures of dead relatives and friends, your own mother and sister. And you worked for someone who came down with wolf-sickness, isn't that so?" He glanced at the papers again. "Ester Spinne. But it says here that she had a regular sepulture? I thought the wolf-sick were fed to the stones . . ."

Juva stared at him in disbelief. Was this a threat? Ester . . . Wonderful, old Ester, whom she had been forced to kill. And now she was being used in a game of politics.

Juva nodded to the empty chair she guessed had belonged to Olm Fennar and still would if he hadn't caught wolf-sickness and tried to set fire to his own living room.

"I thought so, too," she responded. "But I know people in the Seida Guild who were at Olm's sepulture."

The councilor pretended not to have heard her.

"And in the middle of all this," he said, "we hear rumors that you've adopted a child?"

"Several, I've heard," Ingra mumbled.

"I don't have any kids, and I don't have any plans for them," Juva said.

"No," the chairman said, scrutinizing her. "That's not exactly compatible with your job, I'd say."

There it was . . .

Juva felt her despair grow at the realization. They wanted her out as guild master, a job they had begged her to take because no one else had dared. A job she had never wanted. And she had become a bleeder to help Broddmar and to hunt warow. But the vardari were living on borrowed time. In no time at all, she would stand here listening to extravagant praise because the city was safe again, because wolf-sickness had been eradicated. Half a year, at the most. Until then, she couldn't lose anything or anyone, least of all the possibility of protecting Kefla and the others.

This meeting was purely laying the groundwork, a warning. The Council had found the easiest way to make it look like they were doing something, and that was by replacing her. Of course. But when?

"Good," the chairman said, thumping his papers against the table as if they had both agreed on something. "Then you have one month. If things haven't improved by then, we'll have to take action."

Juva glanced at Drogg, but he didn't notice her. He was looking at the chairman with what she read to be genuine confusion. Was it because he didn't know or was he playing along, too?

"Take action?" she asked, even though she feared the answer.

Sjur pretended he hadn't heard the question and waved her away without looking at her. Juva turned her back and left them. Only now did she notice that her shoes had left muddy tracks on the way in. She walked down the wide staircase and avoided making eye contact with anyone. Her body felt pursued and shaky, as if she were hungover.

Get a grip! Kefla is waiting for you!

She came out onto the street and walked straight toward Nákla Heng, fighting her anger in vain. Kefla stood leaning against the massive ring wall right by the north gate and lit up when she spotted her. The girl started running to meet her, as if she were half her twelve years.

Juva clenched her teeth and shook her head.

It's not safe.

Kefla slowed down and her smile faded. She stood there in the middle of the street as young porters pulled carriages of travelers. They rattled over the cobblestones but were smiling all the same, delighted to be in Náklav, the city of all cities.

Juva turned and walked in a different direction. Kefla's gaze burned through her back and came to rest in her stomach in a knot. Juva could hear fragments of an argument that hadn't happened yet. About the promise she had made that she could no longer keep.

I've turned into Lagalune.

That thought was agonizing. Was she doomed to turn into her own mother, to be equally despised?

No! This would be over in half a year. No more wolf-sickness, no more vardari, and no more danger for a young blood reader like Kefla. She just had to hold on and let time do its thing.

The waiting was the worst part, but she had promised Broddmar not to do anything else. He had been a warow himself, so she couldn't blame him. She had shot one of them, at Haane's house, and even though he was a vardari, she had blood on her hands.

Five months, maybe six.

Then she could explain everything to Kefla and live a normal life.

But she knew she was lying to herself. She had met Grif. She had freed a monster, and nothing would ever be normal again.

FALL FROM GRACE

His forearm was covered in gashes. Open from the thumb to well over halfway to the elbow. Nafraím tried moving his fingers, but they might as well have belonged to someone else. He had no power over them, felt no pain, not even when Seire dabbed an already soaked cloth against the open wound to absorb the blood.

She squeezed his wrist, holding him together while she pulled the stopper out of the bottle with her teeth. This was nothing; she had both seen and done worse, but he felt her hand trembling against the wound all the same, and he had an overwhelming feeling that he genuinely meant something. For the first time.

She hesitated with the bottle in her hand.

He looked into her eyes and smiled. "You could also just let me bleed to death . . ."

Seire rolled her eyes and spat the stopper out into the fresh snow.

"I'd rather Sekla devour me than have to listen to them paying tribute to your memory. You're bad enough alive. You'd be insufferable dead."

She emptied the liquid from the flask over his wound. Blood from the beast mixed with his own, filling his body with an intense tingling, as if he were awakening from the icy cold. Burning. Heat. Power. His skin felt alive, demanding. The edges of the wound gathered themselves closed and he could see it happening, see with his own eyes—he now knew for certain that the injury was no longer incurable. He had life in his veins, more than any human before him, and they were witness to it, all three of them.

"This won't change anything," Faun said. Those blue eyes contained nothing but innocence.

"Wrong." Seire smiled broadly and beautifully like a piece of jewelry. "This is going to change everything."

Nafraím stared at his own skin as it crept over flesh and bone, fusing into an uneven, bloody landscape. He reached for water, thirsty.

Thirsty . . .

Nafraím jumped, not sure if he had fallen asleep or lost consciousness. His back was numb against the cold cellar floor. His tongue was raw and meandering, as if it wanted to crawl out of his throat on its own. Was this the first spasm? How long did he have until his organs failed?

He suppressed the cough that would have made a bad situation worse and forced his eyes open. Daylight cut in at an angle from the opening to the floor above, like a toppled pillar, making the motifs on the floor glow. Tongues of flame, set in fingernail-sized tiles, of which he had come to know every detail. A burning ring of red and yellow and the only thing with any color in the entire crypt.

The sound of footsteps from above revealed what had awakened him. Nafraím struggled to his knees and leaned his back against the wall. The pain left no doubt that this was the closest he would come to dignity today.

The cold usually completely paralyzed him, but summer was at its warmest now, if his scratch marks on the wall were an accurate tally. Still, Náklav never truly got hot, so this heat came from within. A smoldering sign that his body was losing its battle with the thirst.

He had been close to the darkest of all possible thoughts: saving himself from the agony. Opening a vein, lying down between two of the massive stone coffins in this godforsaken vault, and bleeding out. Disappearing. Many centuries late.

Borrowed time. Stolen time.

It wouldn't cost him a thing. He had been ready for death for a generation. Had planned it, for himself and every single vardari, ever since the Witness had come back to life in Nákla Henge, with its greenish-blue gears, warning of the wolves on the other side. The only thing that had kept him alive was the need to see *her* die first.

He looked up. Eydala came into view by the edge of the gaping hole in the ceiling above him, standing by the wreckage of a lost spiral staircase. Only the attachments were left, jutting down like broken bones. She watched him for a while. Then she tossed a waterskin down into his lap.

The weight was so intensely promising, but he had learned to rein in his expectations. It was impossible to predict what she would do, what she would try, and her mood swings had gotten steadily worse since she had realized he wasn't going to help her.

She sat down by the staircase attachments on the floor above him, like a stubborn teenager, and pulled the blood reader card out of her pocket. She felt it with her discolored fingertips, as if the devil could tell her where he was, if she just paid especially close attention.

Nafraím pulled the stopper out of the waterskin. Smelled it. Nothing.

The still-thinking part of his brain begged him to test the contents first, but he could no longer override his instincts. He consoled himself with the knowledge that she needed him alive, after all, and gulped down the water. Pure, wonderful water, as much as he dared to avoid cramps. Those few sips were exhausting. He leaned his head against the wall and looked up at Eydala. The woman who was his second biggest mistake in an incomprehensibly long life.

Eydala studied him with her lethargic gaze.

"Where's the letter?"

He had heard the words so many times they had lost their meaning. He could sense that she didn't expect an answer, either. It wasn't a question anymore. It was the quiet beginning of an angry outburst.

"I've done everything, Nafraím," she said, turning the card over in her hands. "Everything there is to do and still you have nothing to say?"

He felt a twitch at the corner of his mouth. *Everything*. That little word contained an ocean of pain. She had starved him, kept him awake, drugged him, and let him wake up with broken bones. Everything she could do without laying a hand on him herself. And without letting him bleed. It was tempting to think it came from some shabby vestige of respect, but it was more likely a practical consideration. She didn't know how much of a bleeder he was. Some warow could bleed to death from a harmless scratch, if it wasn't seen to, and she wasn't the type to have remedies like ringborre.

Nafraím took another swig of water, enjoying the cool relief as he waited for her to continue.

"Why won't you just tell me where he is? I don't understand you. It's as if you *want* to die! What could be more important than your own life?" Her eyes wandered between him and the devil on the card, as if she were looking for similarities. Her cheekbones cut down toward the corners of her mouth. She had grown thinner. "Don't you understand that I'm going to find it? We're going to take your place apart, stone by stone, and when I find the letter . . . When I find *him* . . ."

She let the word hang there for a moment, in her theatrical way.

"You think you can hold out longer than me? That all you need to do is wait? No . . . no, Nafraím. I'm going to find him, and once

I have the blood, I can watch you suffer for all eternity. Don't you see?"

Nafraím couldn't help but smile. This warped woman had no idea that the devil was lost. Gríf had left this world, condemning every single warow to death. If that thought had so much as crossed her mind, it had been smothered by a morbid motivation that had to do with more than thirst.

She put her hand on her chest and looked at him with false compassion.

"You must be exhausted, frozen, and thirsty. You don't need to end your days here, Nafraím, in this undignified way. You could have left here today if you wanted to, gone home. You must be unbearably tired . . ."

Nafraím rested the waterskin on his chest, gathering his strength to speak.

"Everything . . ." he began and swallowed to lubricate his voice. "Everything we are and have is based on a nearly seven-hundred-year captivity. It seems unreasonable for me to complain after a hundred days."

Eydala tossed her head and laughed silently. It was an eerie habit, as if she had learned to laugh by watching others do it without hearing them.

"You think someone is going to save you," she said dryly. "But that's not going to happen. No one cares anymore, Nafraím. No one knows where you are, not even *you*."

"Not even me?" He began to laugh. A hoarse laugh that cost him energy, but the reward was the uncertainty that flitted across her face. "You are a Thervian tragedy, Eydala, a narrow-minded fool unable to grasp your own limitations—and the gods know they are manifold. Less than two hundred years on Earth, and yet you know what there is to know? You are a child, a historyless child. I know more about where I am than *you* do."

Eydala stared at him. The card with the devil trembled in her hand. Nafraím continued while he still could.

"I can tell you where the veinstone in these coffins comes from. I can tell you why the floor is a burning wheel. I'm in a crypt. I share my days with bones in stone coffins, even though Náklav sepultures its dead. We give them to the sea and to Gaula, not to wood and stone. The names on the lids are carved in Heino, but I suppose it's too much to expect that you would be fluent in languages other than your own. This crypt belongs to a family from Undst that built its fortunes on the art of mirrors. I knew these people before you were born."

"You?" Eydala suddenly stood up and hissed at him. "You're calling *me* a narrow-minded child? You, a man who has a house full of toys. Models, machines, and drawings . . . It doesn't make it more mature just because it's *you* who's doing it. You always think you're so fucking much better than everyone else, so smart, so noble . . ." She spat out the word. "You talk about history, knowledge, and science as if they were gods, but the greatest invention is mine." She tapped her own chest with her index finger. "You're not the genius here—I am."

"You mean your father?"

His words seemed to drain the last of her will to maintain her straight face.

"I could have changed the world," she screamed. "I could have! But you stopped it. You stole the chance I had to become . . ."

Immortal.

The word was left unsaid, which seemed to make it resonate all the more. Immortality came in many forms. He had taken one away from her and given her another. Because it was necessary. So infinitely much had been necessary in his life.

Her rage was justified, and she continued with the strength of someone who knew that.

"You dare to call yourself a scientist? You who took the progress from me and from the humanity you claim to serve?"

"One of my many mistakes," Nafraím said, looking at her.

"Keep your sentimentality, you damned weakling. I don't want that. I want the *devil*! I know you have the letter. The girl never opened it, Nafraím. I was there. I saw it with my own eyes. She gave you a sealed envelope, without so much as squeezing it. And all that's left is this." She flicked the card with her fingernails. "The devil, Nafraím. He was in your own pocket. It couldn't have been any clearer what the letter was about. The girl was telling the truth, so where's the letter?"

Nafraím suppressed a smile he could not afford to show. Juva had grown up with liars, an art she intensely despised and yet had exquisitely mastered. She had tricked them both. But how long could it last? Sooner or later, it would occur to Eydala that there had never been any letter in the envelope, that both it and the card had come from Juva herself. And then . . .

The thought sent a shiver through him. Eydala would tear her to shreds, and Juva must have known that, too. Even so, she had made up the story about the letter that would lead the way to the devil. Bought herself time so she could send him home in secret. All to put an end to the vardari. He didn't want to think about the hatred that must underlie her willingness to take that chance.

"Are you going to faint again?" Eydala's contempt roused him from his thoughts. She smiled, clearly pleased to have an audience again. "Did you hear her speech?" she asked, with feigned shock, as if they were sitting in a parlor, gossiping together. "She has made it hopeless for us; the city is terrified of warow. She really hates us." Eydala tossed her head in one of those noiseless laughs again. "She should be whipped, that girl. Although you've already seen to that since you killed her family in their own home."

Nafraím fought a spasm of nausea, which could be due to the cold water or the way she had said that. As if she admired him.

"She can sense, the girl. Did you know that?" she said, and her lazy gaze held a rare trace of interest. "That would have been damned useful now, for sniffing out warow."

He tried to make himself more comfortable, without revealing how taxing that was.

"Do you need to hunt for company? Doesn't anyone want to spend time with you, Eydala?"

"*With* me? Why in Drukna would I want anyone *with* me? So there will be more people to share the blood with when I find him?" She chuckled. "No, spare me! But someone out there must have set a little aside. Stashed away some blood for hard times, right? Maybe they even have the letter. I intend to find it, and since *you* won't help..."

Nafraím looked at her and felt the cold creeping in. A fear of a completely different sort than he had experienced in these last few months. The smugness lay thick on her.

"You're finally realizing that I'm not an idiot, Nafraím. I've understood that you don't care about yourself any longer. But you care about what you've created." She smiled contemptuously, then raised her hands and drew a semicircle in the air in front of her. "Náklav. Your magnificent construction."

Anxiety grew in his chest, chasing the blood through his body until he could feel that he was alive again. The pain that had slumbered lashed out again.

She backed away, disappearing from sight. Nafraím held back his relief, far too aware that this was not over.

An unsettling sound drew nearer. Something was being dragged across the floor above him. Something heavy. A dark outline appeared and grew into the pale beam of daylight. A head tipped backward, and it occurred to him that it was a dead body being pushed over the edge. He felt a twitch, an instinctive urge to prevent the fall, even though there was no life left to save. The body smashed onto the floor in front of him with an unpleasant sound and lay there in the middle of the patterned mosaic, surrounded by flames.

Yrgen . . .

Nafraím inhaled a breath that stung with grief. He had been dead for a while but was just as beautiful. Handsome, pleasure-crazed Yrgen. The blond hair, those full lips. He was pale as a statue. A rusty line along his wrist showed why. She had let him bleed to death, pressing him for answers that he had never had.

Nafraím looked up. Eydala stared shamelessly back.

"Yrgen here didn't want to share blood with a poor thing, but fair is fair. I don't think he had any saved up, either."

She put her fingers together, creating a square which she viewed him through, a frame, as if he were a painting.

"You think you've built something strong, Nafraím Sai, but I am infinitely stronger. You haven't created a single thing I can't tear down. I will kill every single vardari, until there's no memory of you left." She pouted repulsively. "Unless you tell me where the devil is, of course. I'll let you think that over, overnight."

Nafraím closed his eyes and heard her shoes clicking across the floor. He waited until he was sure she had left the room before he defied the pain, crawled over to Yrgen, and closed his wide-open eyes.

"You are the luckiest of us," he whispered and knew that it was true. Yrgen wouldn't need to fight the thirst and the pain that would kill them all before winter. Eydala, too. She would never be able to do much damage beyond taking lives that had already been taken. The world would endure that; he had built it to endure that. The wheels would keep turning, the medical, the financial, the political . . . The Might would run the gates, and the best out there would drive the future. Those who would not allow themselves to be bought. People with hearts and minds, power and will. People like Juva.

Gríf was gone, his oldest sin, and if there were any gods with a vestige of grace left, he would never return.

Nafraím could die in peace.

A RUMOR

Juva crossed Brenntorget and did her best to rein in her dislike of the massive ring wall that towered up as if the gods had planted it there. Nákla Henge was an eternal, unwavering center. Densely built stone buildings swarmed around it, conforming to its shape like ripples. The city hadn't built the henge; it was the henge that had built the city.

She felt smaller the closer she came to the weathered copper gate. There were three of them, and it was said they were the biggest in the world—as if coming in second was ever an option for Náklav. But they were also the world's most unusable gates—huge as they were—so at some point, smaller doors had been installed to serve the constant stream of people.

They crowded through the doors like ants, slower now that the gate guards were checking the teeth of everyone with a travel card. That measure did little beyond provide the illusion of control, and the routine nature of it had made the guards sloppy. People barely had to yawn before they were shuffled along. But wolf-sickness could be dormant and undetectable in their gums.

Juva showed the woman behind the window her hunting pass and proceeded to the gate guard. The guard recognized her and waved her on, but she stopped anyway and bared her teeth to him—a reminder of the seriousness of his job.

"You're a bleeder!" he said, as if that was supposed to explain his laxness.

She stuck her hunting pass back in her pocket.

"Anyone can catch wolf-sickness."

The man cast a concerned look at her jaw.

"You don't have a travel card, and you're the one hunting them," he muttered. "That's all I'm saying. I mean . . . Who would we send after *you*?"

Fanatical volunteers?

The thought was a bitter echo from her meeting with the city council. She had taken it for granted that they would be desperate enough to listen. That they would strengthen the hunting team. Or at least the notification procedures. She had gone in with demands and come out with a one-month deadline to improve something they knew she had no power to improve.

Why?

The question was all she was left with once the worst of her anger had subsided. She was doing a job that few other people could do or wanted to do. Were they really willing to change that to look like they were taking action?

Juva left the gate guard and entered the busy square around the henge. Visitors appeared and disappeared between the stones in an erratic pulse. The city's beating heart pumped people like blood through seven towering pairs of stones. The eighth pair had never been used, so those two might as well have been demolished. They were probably there for symmetry's sake. And for the stories, of course. Mysticism was a commodity in Náklav, which presumably explained the myths about the dead stones leading straight to Drukna. A shortcut to death and Gaula's insatiable tentacles.

The stones were bathed in the glow of enormous lanterns that burned corpsewood as if it were free. The light stretched up and disappeared between the grooves in the wooden dome. It made the roof look like a ribcage. A chest that protected the city's most important organ, weakened only by the opening in the middle. Pale daylight pointed down at the Witness, which she avoided looking at. She had no time for self-pity.

She slipped through the crowd over to the Ring Guard office and knocked on the old iron door. No one answered, even though the red pennant flag was flying, which meant the spigot was on inside and the blood was flowing in the gutter between the stones. There should be people in there.

She knocked again and leaned against the brick wall while she waited. Her eyes were inexorably drawn to the Witness, the blueish-green monster of grinding gears in the middle of the henge. Sprawling walls, as if a giant had pierced the ground with a three-edged sword and broken it off crosswise.

She had heard it called many things—a sculpture, a clockwork, an ancient treasure—but never what only she and the guys knew: the Witness was a gateway to a world that didn't exist on any map. And it had swallowed Grif.

In the middle of the Yra Race, as half the city had run in the traditional jubilant parade around the stones wearing furs and fake fangs, he had left this world. He should have done it in silence. Unnoticeable in the maelstrom of people. That had been the agreement, the plan they had so painstakingly come up with. But Grif had had other intentions the whole time. He had appeared too early to see Nafraím, the man who had held him captive. Not even *once* had it occurred to her that Grif's hatred of the warow would be stronger than any plan, stronger than any bond she had been foolish enough to believe he had with her.

It had become painfully obvious when a member of the Ring Guard spotted him outside the race route and hurried over with a crossbow. Then he had shown who he was, maybe for the first time. He used her as a shield and dug his claws into her chest. She still felt the pain as if it had just happened.

46

. That was the last thing he had done before he left.

Time was useless. It didn't heal anything, neither the betrayal nor the scar. She would have to live with both forever. That was the price of trust, of relying on someone.

She had been so naïve that the shame bothered her more often than the pain. How in Gaula could she have believed she had meant anything to him? He was an immortal creature with fangs and claws! The source of eternal life, held prisoner by the vardari for more centuries than she could comprehend, right up until she had stumbled upon him in the shaft below her house.

She had never been anything to him but the key to freedom, a tool. And she hadn't realized it until she saw him standing in the henge, staring at Nafraím with a promise of all the torments of the world. His white eyes had blackened to ink. She had kissed this man! And he had kissed her, with a hunger and intensity she would never get to experience again.

"Blood and teeth?"

Juva jumped. Klemens's deep voice had woken her from her nightmare, and she nodded gratefully.

"Yes, blood and teeth."

He opened the iron door and let her into the office, a tactful word to use for this primitive room in the ring wall. It was a crawlspace that suited him. Rough and sparse, and marked by the drudgery of the job. The head of the Ring Guard was a man she would have trusted if she hadn't given up that sort of thing. Maybe that's why she liked him; she didn't think he trusted anyone, either.

He went over to the desk with the limping gait she had heard came from an injury, and he unlocked the drawer with the money-box.

"It's not getting any better," he grumbled through his full, dark beard.

"No . . ." Juva pulled the bloodskins out of her backpack and lifted them on the desk along with the fangs. He recorded the details about the deceased, set the coins on the desk, and pushed them toward her. It was thirty runes, but there was still a look of pity in his eyes.

"If this keeps up, you'll be able to support more than the five guys."

Juva smiled weakly. She already supported far more, but he couldn't and shouldn't know that. She waited while he went into the back room and drained the bloodskins. When he handed them back to her, they were flat. Ready for the next guy.

She thanked him and left the office. She nearly walked right into a man in front of the door and apologized before she recognized him. Black-haired with narrow, dark eyes. He probably had roots in Aura, like Hanuk. He was well dressed and freshly shaved, nervous.

"Pavl Ringmark," he said, clearly to jog her memory. It came to her, abrupt and dishonorable. The house up in Kistestikk. A girl with black hair who had climbed up inside the chimney, hiding from the wolf-sick Vera. Pavl had locked himself in and was pounding on the door to distract the wolf-sick woman from his daughter.

Vera had been heavy with child, and yet demented. Broddmar had paled, hesitating too long with the knife, which could have cost everything. Ever since then, he had been losing his stamina. Now it was gone.

"I remember," Juva said.

"You look . . . different," Pavl said, his eyes wandering uneasily over her face.

Juva smiled bitterly, aware that that was a polite way of saying *haggard*. She had met him at her baptism by fire as a red hunter, the first time she bled a human being, before she had any idea what she was in for.

Juva felt an urge to ask how it had gone with the little girl but realized she didn't know her name. The shame crept back in, but when would she have asked her name under those circumstances?

Pavl's eyes wandered, as if he were searching for words that would keep her there. Juva sensed that he had been waiting for her.

"Thank you for coming," he said.

Juva was surprised by his words, which reinforced her sense that this wasn't a chance encounter.

"Back then," he added.

"Oh . . ." She shrugged. Her back was weighed down by all the things she could never set down: the suit, the bloodskins, the crossbow . . . "That's what we do," she said more casually than she felt.

He nodded, as if he were embarrassed about having thanked her.

"Noora's struggling," he said. "She has . . . fits, Frú Sannseyr. They come on without any warning, and they've gotten worse since—"

"What sort of fits?"

"Well, if we knew that . . ."

Juva chewed on her lip. She knew she was about to cross a line, that almost imperceptible point where she cared more than she could afford to, unable to turn back. But she already had plenty— more than enough—to think about.

"I'm sorry to hear that, Pavl. Ask the nurses out at Hylberg." She turned around to go.

"It's her heart, Frú Sannseyr."

Juva stopped. His words came too quickly to be small talk, and he said them as if he knew they carried weight. She put her hand on his back and led him into the shadows below the balcony. He continued, eager now that he had her attention.

"She panics sometimes, clutches her chest, it's . . . We've tried everything. Hoggthorn and berka-brew, but that sort of thing is in short supply these days. And then we heard that . . . They say you can help girls like her."

Juva cast a furtive glance around, but the only company was a dull plinking from a music box in the shop next door. She couldn't afford for that rumor to spread, but at the same time, she depended on it doing just that. It was a dilemma with no way around it.

"This is Náklav," she said. "You shouldn't believe everything you hear."

"I never have," he replied. "And I wouldn't have asked if Noora hadn't wanted me to. You said something to her, back then."

Juva thought back. The black-haired girl who had crawled down from the chimney. Her bare feet in the ashes. Those skinny arms clinging around Juva's neck.

I'm Juva Sannseyr, and if anyone tries to tell you that you didn't see what you saw tonight, then come and find me.

The image seemed clearer than before as the truth dawned on her. Noora could sense. That's why she had hidden in the chimney. She had known what was coming.

Juva stifled a burgeoning worry she was familiar with. A well-known fear of promising more than she could deliver. Of being needed by others when she was barely keeping it together herself.

"We're afraid fanatics will find her," Pavl said. "We can't talk to nurses or doctors. We don't dare ask anyone. They might say she has wolf-sickness. It doesn't take anything anymore, people see the devil everywhere!"

"And you think *I* don't? Me, who's hunting them?"

"You've seen it, Frú Sannseyr. You know what wolf-sickness is and what it isn't. *They* don't."

Juva followed his gaze toward the henge. In the middle of the crowd of travelers, two women had sat down on the pavers in the square. They were kneeling right next to the dead pair of stones.

One of them had lit a candle, which she set next to the stone towering over them. Juva could see the silver ribbons gleam around their necks.

The Hallowed.

Pavl shook his head in exasperation.

"They come here all the time. They believe the Drukna stones go to the gods. You would think they lived before the brightening, I mean . . . people have been traveling as long as the stones have been standing, without any divine intervention. They only need to look around to realize that."

"The priest comes from Undst, they say," Juva said with a shrug. "They don't have a ringed city, so I suppose it must seem like witchcraft."

"Exactly." Pavl ran his hand over his face. "*Everything* is the devil's work to them, including the sick, like Noora. I dare not think what they would have done if they . . . One of our neighbors went to them, and now he wears that grotesque nail around his neck, too. It's sick. They're not . . ." He cast a quick glance at Juva and seemed to remember that she was a Sannseyr. "But I'm not a believer, so what do I know," he added without conviction.

"That makes two of us then," Juva replied, fully aware she could tell him things that would cause him to doubt. She pinched the bridge of her nose, feeling the beginnings of a headache. She needed something to drink, preferably a beer. That liberating thought was followed by a double heartbeat.

Warow. At least two of them!

The fear grabbed her like a claw. Had Eydala finally sent someone to kill her? Or were there other warow who knew she was the way to more blood readers? Juva pressed herself back against the wall and pulled Pavl in close.

"Stay still," she whispered. "You don't want to be seen with me."

She heard him gulp. From inside the shop came the tones of

another music box, seemingly random notes without a melody. Juva tried to block out the disturbing rhythm and locate the source of the danger. Her heart revealed that the warow were on the move, whoever they were. It wasn't anyone she had sensed before, as far as she could tell. But they had appeared so abruptly that they must have come through the stones. From where? And what were they doing here?

What if they were all over the world, and the blood shortage had brought them all here, to Náklav?

That was a scary thought, an ice-cold reminder of how little she could control.

I need to know who they are!

"Is it someone with wolf-sickness?" Pavl gasped, muffled. Juva closed her eyes for a second, weighed down by all the things only she knew. Pavl believed his daughter might arouse the rage of fanatics, but the vardari were the real threat.

She summoned up a mask of calm and shook her head.

"No, no, nothing like that. Listen, Noora can stay with us until she's better. A woman will come to get her. Her name is Heimilla. I have to run, but first, promise me you won't share her name with anyone. Do you understand?"

Pavl nodded, looking bewildered, but she didn't have time to explain. Juva turned her back to him and let her heart lead the way down the gallery. She jogged until she located the heartbeats again, knowing they were close.

A sudden commotion by the gates made her sensing unnecessary. Some people were hitting each other in what appeared to be a brief fistfight. Someone yelled. Someone ran.

They were running away from the guards!

The guard who had checked her teeth lay floundering on the ground. He put his hand to his jaw and struggled to get back up again as people rushed over to help. Juva ran past them, through the gate and out onto the street, searching desperately with her eyes but with no idea who she was looking for.

She slowed down, coming to a stop by two Ring Guardsmen who had also clearly given up the chase. Her heart pounded in her chest and told her she had already lost her chance.

A TREASURE

Juva warmed her hands around the teacup and watched while Kefla gobbled down the rest of the porridge. Sure, it was more jam than porridge. The girl still ate as if she were expecting a famine, but if nothing else, at least she had stopped hiding food in her bag. A fragile sign of trust that would be shattered before the day was done.

Guilt clawed at her diaphragm, and Juva strained to keep it at bay. Kefla couldn't keep living here; it wasn't safe. It never had been.

She could always deal with the city council's involvement, but not the death spasms of the vardari. The two she had sensed by Nákla Henge were strangers, new ones. Was Eydala gathering forces? Or were all the warow in the world heading here, searching for the last drops?

Just thinking about that seemed to evoke the smell of blood, but then it dawned on her that it was real. Skarr stood in the corner by the stairs wolfing down raw meat, as unconcerned with table manners as Kefla. He could consume a bucket full of offal a day, which would cost a fortune if Olaf the butcher in the food halls wasn't so honest.

Juva caught herself wondering what would happen if Skarr went hungry. What did wild animals do when they got hungry? What about the vardari?

Scatter blood pearls like hail to take the whole city with them when they die?

The thought sent a shiver through her, a fear that Nolan was right. It had to get worse before it got better. Náklav bore the burden of a hidden war, and all she and the guys did was clean up. She could feel the price for that in her body. Her bones felt heavy. The pressure in her chest that usually came and went with her anxiety had clearly decided to stay. Perpetual anxiety.

What makes you think you can take care of other people?

"What's she like," Kefla asked, licking jam off her fingers. "This new girl?"

Juva pictured Noora climbing out of the chimney, smeared with soot.

"She's smart, like you. And has black hair, like you, only long. But she's a little younger, and . . . nervous. She's going to need you."

You're going to need to stay with the girls now.

The words wouldn't come out, but all indications were that Kefla heard them in her thoughts. Her eyes were dark and distrustful beneath her bangs, before she turned the conversation in a completely different direction.

"Was it bloody yesterday?"

"It's always bloody." Juva got up and rinsed Skarr's bowl in the water barrel. She had promised herself she would never lie to Kefla, but that didn't mean she needed to paint the full scene. The girl knew they hunted wolf-sick people, and that was enough to bear.

"Which way are you going?" Juva asked and received an expected groan in response.

"A different one than last time," Kefla said as if imitating her. "Can I go now, or what?"

Juva waved her away.

"I'll catch up. Take a new route and feel it in your heart, right? Stay back if you notice them."

Kefla rolled her eyes.

"If I feel them, I'll stab them!" She ran up the stone stairs, two at a time. Juva took a deep breath and looked at the empty bowl she had left behind. It was completely cleaned out, as if there had never been anything in it.

You need to tell her. Today.

The wolf licked blood from his muzzle, pacing by the stairs, aware they were about to go out. Juva closed the oven door to put out the flames, then she followed Skarr up the stairs. She strapped the harness onto him, hoisted on her backpack, and fetched the surprise for the girls from inside the stall. It was a big box, but it had a practical handle on the lid, so she could carry it with one hand.

Outside, Lykteløkka glowed in the strange light only found during Heita, the last days that could be called summer in this city. The cobblestones changed colors with the sun's low angle. The windows were ajar in the alleyways, letting out the scents of bread and fish. Beer taverns and teahouses had their doors open, as if they knew summer would be over soon. She could hear the guests chatting away, sounding so carefree that it grated on her nerves. They had ordinary lives. A normal life meant not waking up with blood under their fingernails.

Normal had never been an option for her. That opportunity had vanished the second she was born a Sannseyr. She could have had another chance, nineteen years later, when she was the only Sannseyr left. Instead, she had found *him*.

Juva immediately shut down that thought, knowing it would become an abyss if she let it. She rounded the corner into Myntslaget, past Agan Askran, whom she very surely had to thank for her still being alive. His crossbow had cost her an arm and a leg, but it had never failed her.

She looked around, even though her heart told her she was alone. The vardari could have hangers-on, regular people, and they must never find out . . .

Juva walked into the Vinterhagen guesthouse and steeled herself against the feeling of being exposed. Naked, in a way. It was a lovely space, but the walls were steeped in grief. Memories of Ester, wolf-sick bordering on madness but strong-willed enough to die before she had hurt anything other than the birds who had lived here.

I killed her . . .

That was how she had wanted it, the old woman. Making Juva her heir seemed like a gloomy thank-you, but she had left behind enough wealth to save lives. Hidehall, Vinterhagen, and Ester's own home in the same stone building, which now housed Hanuk as well as Lok's family of five children. They were packed in there, right next door, but it was easier to have the guys together when the Dead Man's Horn sounded. She would have preferred to have Muggen there, too, but his sister insisted. Newly converted, she was convinced that the hunting team was a bad crowd.

Juva left her boots on the porch and barely made it halfway up the stairs to the living rooms before Tokalínn came running to meet her.

"Juva, Juva, Juva!" she cried, as if it were a song. She was the youngest of the girls, barely six winters old, but she had a strong sense for wolves and knew best of all when Skarr came, but the wolf was smart enough to let Juva go ahead and take the brunt.

Tokalínn flung her arms around Juva's thighs, unable to reach any higher. Juva barely managed to save the box by hoisting it up out of the way.

"Careful! You don't want to ruin the surprise, do you?"

"Surprise?"

The word held a magical appeal. Suddenly, she was surrounded by girls following on her heels into the great room. She set the crate down and carefully took out the box. She had wrapped it in a table-cloth to protect it, one of many she was sure her mother had never used.

Juva set the box on the table and removed the tablecloth with a tug, which she realized she did with an intentionally dramatic flair, the impulse to excite. It felt strange and was followed by a sense of danger. A threat that came from within. She let her thoughts turn briefly to blood and teeth, to remember who she was.

Juva Sannseyr. Juva the Hunter.

The girls flocked around the mysterious box.

"What is it?" Tokalínn asked wide-eyed, but then again, she was always wide-eyed. The blond girl mostly looked like she had seen a ghost no matter what she was doing.

"Something expensive . . ." Kefla folded her arms across her chest. Her boyish voice was deep with suspicion. Juva avoided her wary gaze. Kefla was right; it was expensive, but it wasn't just to entice her to stay. The girls needed it. Most of the people who had been to Vinterhagen had only needed a day or two. An explanation of what caused the palpitations and a reassurance that it was harmless before they could return to their safe homes. But these girls . . . They were here because they needed to be.

They ranged from ages six to fourteen and everywhere in between. A couple of them had no other home. Others had homes Juva wouldn't have allowed an enemy to go back to. But they had two things in common: hearts like hers, and a life with far too few good surprises.

Tokalínn raised her hand to touch the box but stopped before she got that far and looked up at Juva with fearful, blue eyes.

Juva nodded and stepped back so the girls could figure out what they were dealing with. They found the crank handles quickly, and a jumble of messy notes spread through the room. The girls squealed, and Skarr shuffled out of the room with his ears down. He passed Heimilla in the doorway, and the woman flinched out of the way. She came over to Juva, smoothing her apron unnecessarily.

"A music box? You bought them a music box? Holy Jól, what a present!"

"It's not a present; it's a tool."

Heimilla raised an eyebrow.

"That wasn't an accusation . . ." Her eyes were warmer than Juva remembered them from her childhood, and she felt only gratitude in her chest. It was good to have people she could trust to run this place. Heimilla, Ive, and the cook, Gomm, had worked in the Sannseyr home without suspecting the darkness the house hid. They would never find out, either, that the devil had lived and breathed just beneath them as they puttered around doing the most mundane things.

"How is Noora doing?" Juva asked, following the new girl with her eyes. She seemed to be more captivated by the others' excitement than by the music box itself.

"She's coming around. She was uneasy all yesterday, but Ulie gets everyone to open up. It's just . . ." Heimilla hesitated. "They're so young. They didn't need to know."

"I'm not going to lie to them, Heimilla."

"No, ugh. I would never ask you to lie, but they really don't need to know the whole truth now. Imagine being in your seventh summer and finding out that your heart races because you can sense evil people."

"That's better than *not* knowing it. Trust me."

Heimilla looked down. Her face seemed to wilt for a second, as if she were also remembering old times.

"Is Vamm out?" Juva asked.

"Yes, I sent him on an errand to the food hall. He doesn't like idleness." Heimilla pursed her lips without managing to hide the smile that revealed what she thought about that trait. She stood watching the girls for a bit before she sighed. "Other people's heartbeats . . . I wouldn't have believed it if I hadn't heard them say it with my own ears. It's . . ."

"Ungodly?" Juva smiled.

"It's not good or right, at any rate!" Heimilla said, raising her chin.

Juva didn't respond. She had not seen much that was good or right, but if anything was, it was Vinterhagen. The guesthouse was the exact opposite of the Sannseyr house, colorful and full of life, sumptuously decorated in greens and blues. Painted fruit trees bloomed on the walls, and ornate chairs drowned in embroidered pillows. It had become an unlikely refuge, bearing traces of the girls. The exquisite cages that dangled from the ceiling were decorated with folded paper birds, drawings were pinned to the silk wallpaper, and someone had hung a collar of dried flowers around the neck of a sculpture that was surely a priceless piece of art from Thervia.

Juva watched the girls bickering around the instrument. Vinterhagen had never been a place for children. Ester had never had any, and Juva had sworn she never would.

But here they were. Lost blood readers, five girls just like her, who had never understood why their hearts raced. They struggled with their own pulse as much as they did the music box. No matter what they did, it was a chaotic mess of sounds.

The sight made her feel fragile. It ate away at her shell, which she couldn't live without, and suddenly she felt restless. She had wolf-sickness, blood pearls, and warow to worry about. She needed to finish up here.

Juva walked over to them and took over the box.

"The secret is that it can be played by multiple people," she said and turned one of the cranks. Inside the box, one of the three brass rollers began to rotate slowly. Tiny spikes, hardly bigger than a grain of sand, forced a row of thin keys to plink out notes into the air.

"Do you see that little mark on the roller?" Juva pointed and the girls craned their necks. "That's the beginning of the melody. You need to start in the same spot."

The girls stared open-mouthed as if a light had come on for them. Juva handed her crank handle to Noora, who was so intent on doing it right that she scarcely dared breathe. The notes were clear and pure, but still monotonous. Tokalínn shifted from foot to foot and Juva let her hold the other crank.

"You see? When Noora's mark appears, you begin. Then, try to turn them at the same speed."

The girl nodded eagerly and started turning the handle. The notes were different than Noora's, but in perfect harmony. Ulie took the next crank and turned it as soon as she saw the other two's marks. The melody became rich and perfect, with low and high notes. Even Syn, the pretty, redheaded girl of fourteen, had tears of wonder in her otherwise far too blank stare.

Juva stopped the youngest two and asked Noora to keep playing on her own. The intricate melody reverted to its solitary beginning. Juva had explained to them what caused the heart palpitations, but now she had an example to demonstrate it in a completely different way.

"Imagine that the notes Noora is playing are a heart. Do you hear it? A totally normal beating heart. When everything is as it should be."

Dark-haired Ulie stared at the floor, and Syn chewed on her lower lip. Kefla folded her arms across her chest as if that would convince anyone that this topic bored her. Juva couldn't blame them. She had never talked about it herself. But then she hadn't known what it was, either.

"But then one day, when you're not expecting anything, out of the blue comes a warow. Maybe walking by outside, and maybe there are a lot of people out there, so you have no idea who it is. But you feel it."

Juva started turning the second crank handle, and the notes blended.

"Your heart is suddenly playing for two, right? Or even three." Then she turned the last crank and realized she was making her point more clearly than she had expected since the three parts of the melody no longer harmonized.

"That's creepy!" Tokalínn said.

"Yes, it is creepy. I think so, too. But it isn't dangerous."

"You said before that they *are* dangerous!" Ulie protested.

"Yes," Juva said, letting go of the crank. "*They are.* Your heart will never hurt you, but the warow can. That's why you need to tell each other where you've felt them, right? Then it's easier to go a different way. But sometimes you'll still notice them, and what do we do then?"

"Stab them!" Kefla declared defiantly.

Juva didn't take the bait. She felt sure Kefla knew what was coming. That she needed to live here with the others, and that the revenge had already begun. Syn corrected her.

"We pretend not to notice because they mustn't ever know that we can sense them."

Noora let go of the last crank handle, and the notes died away. The silence sucked the life out of the room. Juva felt a great anger awaken again. Why were the warow still around? Couldn't they just die, all of them? How long did she need to go on counting the days?

"But what if they catch us? What then?" Tokalínn blurted out, sensitive to the mood.

"Then we escape," Ulie said, putting her arm around her.

"And if we can't escape, then we stab them," Kefla said defiantly.

"If anyone can escape," Juva said, looking into Kefla's eyes, "it's you."

"Not if we're on top of a cliff!" Tokalínn raised her arm as high as she could. "Then we can't escape!"

"Then you'll have to make a rope out of your clothes!" Juva touched the tip of Tokalínn's nose. "And climb down the underwear!"

Tokalínn laughed until she was hiccupping.

"What if Skarr's with us? He can't climb down. And he's not evil, either, even though I can feel him here." Tokalínn patted her hand over her heart.

Juva smiled regretfully, thinking of the wolves she had hunted, all for nothing."

"No, Skarr isn't evil. The wolves aren't like in the fairy tale."

"Will you read it? Please, Juva? Juva, Juva, will you read it?"

Juva cast a pleading glance at Heimilla, who was struggling to suppress a smile.

"Don't look at me. We have food to prepare and bedding to wash!" she said and disappeared so fast that her skirt whipped the gilded doorframe.

Juva was groping for excuses, surrounded by expectant eyes, but she knew the battle was lost. She sighed and sat down. The girls cheered and crawled over each other to sit next to her like kittens, wild and out of place on the blue silk sofa. A few weeks ago, anyone would have thought they were squatters, but with Heimilla on the team, they had clean clothes and combed hair. Now she and Kefla were the ones who looked like runaways in the house.

The youngest girls sat right next to her with their knees pulled up, two on either side. Syn sat down in a nearby chair and handed her the book. Juva swallowed. She wasn't ready for what awaited between the covers, but she opened it anyway and started reading the old fairy tale about the three blood reader sisters who got their powers from the devil in wolf form.

Grif...

The whole fairy tale was based on him, on his destiny.

The words poured out, and she changed her voice depending on which character was talking—another impulse that came out of nowhere—and suddenly, she felt helpless. Her lips went dry. A lump grew in her throat. She had steeled herself against the rage, her anger at his betrayal, but the girls smothered that with their small, clingy bodies. What took its place was worse. An unbearable longing that burned in her chest. He was gone.

He had left her—in a city full of desperate warow, more wolf-sick people than ever, and a bunch of girls who needed protection from both, who needed a family. But all she had learned about family life was how not to do it.

RIDDLES AND LIES

The staircase wound its way down, forever. A dark spiral carved from cold stone, and Juva knew she had gone too far. She turned around and went back, but the stairs turned around with her, and a few steps later, she was still on her way down. There was no going back.

The depths no longer enticed but demanded. She took off her clothes and left them lying on one of the ancient steps. In the abyss, she had to be the way she was born. Protection was a perk for the surface.

The stairs disappeared abruptly right into the rock, and she did the same because she could feel him.

"Juva . . ."

She stood in the mountain, in a grotto that was alive. Pulsating. Beating like a heart, and pebbles slid down from the walls with each beat. Grif sat before her. Pale, naked, and unequaled, with those chiseled muscles, so alien around the shoulders. The black hair stuck to his face as if he had been running, and his chest rose and fell with his breathing. He smiled wryly, revealing a fang. His eyes darkened into wells of ink. No ring, no pupil, no hint of white in the whole eye, and she remembered that that had once confused her, an ocean of time ago. Now he was easier to read than any man.

He got up and gestured with his arms in an invitation she had been accepting her whole life, but all the same, she didn't move, feeling the longing swell too large for her chest. He flicked his claws as if to say that he wasn't going to wait forever, and she went to him. His arms *enfolded her in an embrace she could die in. He smelled of fur and blood.*

His heart beat double, both inside her and against her. She clung to his back and found an opening. A hole by his spine. Her fingers disappeared in a moist warmth, and suddenly her hand was around his heart. She was startled, pulled away. The opening grew in his chest as well, and he dug his claws into it. Tugged out the beating muscle and held it up over her face.

The heart struggled in his grip. Blood ran between his claws and down onto her lips. He wanted her to drink, but she couldn't open her mouth.

"Juva . . ."

He was furious. Turned his back, threw the heart against the rock wall, and snarled like an animal.

"Juva . . ."

The voice didn't belong here. An insistent whisper, a shaking of her shoulder. Juva forced her eyes open and looked right into Lok's brown gaze, sad to be waking her. He stood leaning over her and put one finger to his lips before she had a chance to say anything. It was dark, but through his red braids, she saw the silhouette of the music box, and she remembered where she was.

She sat up and looked around for the girls, but Heimilla must have put them to bed. How deeply asleep had she been? She usually awoke at the slightest sound, if she even slept at all.

Grif . . .

She put her fingers on her chest and felt the scar through her shirt. It hadn't been there in the dream. She had forgotten his betrayal, and remembering it now made it fresh. She was doing it to herself. The scent of him still lingered in her nose, wild and alluring. The price was a fresh pain in a wound that had taken her months to heal.

Damned fairy tale!

Juva pulled her hands over her face and sat there for a moment to gather her energy for what lay ahead. It was quiet, far too quiet.

"Dead Man's Horn?"

"Not yet," Lok whispered, handing her her backpack. He had a fresh inkblot on his arm. The fifth child. The boy was barely six months old, and his name was sharper than the other kids'. Juva clenched her fists and looked away. Red hunter was no job for him. He didn't have the stomach for it, and too many people were counting on him.

"They sent the runner straight to us," he said. "It's right up here, by that rich guy's parlors."

Florian's ...

Juva got to her feet and pulled the suit out of her backpack. She sent a silent thank you to Heimilla who had alerted Lok and Hanuk to the fact that she was here. She should have had the sense to do that herself, but she had only planned to stop by. Not to stay. And certainly not to read any fairy tales that made her weak and useless.

Skarr yawned over by the stairs, and it struck her that they were equally out of place here, wild animals in Vinterhagen. She changed quickly, a rite her fingers knew by heart, always the same. Rolled up the backpack, secured it to her harness under the bloodskins, and strapped the whole thing on. The crossbow in her hand since they weren't going far.

Hanuk was waiting outside, the only person in the dim light. The fog crept in over the damp cobblestones that shone like silver. Myntslaget, the "Coinery," deserved its name tonight.

They hurried up toward Florian's as Juva buttoned her collar. The leather was stiffened with steel stays and might be all that stood between her and fangs.

Nolan came running as they reached Lykksalige Runas Vei. They slowed down to let him catch up.

"The others?" he asked, helping Juva put on her mask, even though it wasn't necessary.

"We were alerted first," Lok replied. "They sent a runner to the guard booth on Kong Aug's."

Nolan let out a sigh. "Then we can expect them sometime around the fall equinox. Maybe they'll make it in time for Heyafest."

Hanuk sniggered, but Nolan didn't look amused. Juva saw that he was trying to catch her eye, but she avoided making eye contact. She knew what he was thinking, but after her meeting with the city council, she couldn't promise them anything. No action to counter the blood pearls, no coins or better warning systems. Quite the contrary, they had complained that—

The Dead Man's Horn—here comes the panic!

Juva put a lid on her worries. Of course they hadn't silenced the warning, that would be unthinkable. Runners were on their way, but it was a long way to Knokle. That took time.

The others ran on, but Juva hesitated. She had felt something, a twitch in her heart. It had vanished again as quickly as it had come, but she had stopped having doubts a long time ago. Too much was at stake. She squatted down and pretended to check something on her shoe as Skarr sniffed around her.

The feeling came creeping back. Nolan noticed her and came running back, and she warned him with her eyes. He squatted down and pretended to help her.

"Vardari?" he whispered.

"Yes," she said. She stood up, letting him retie her boots. "Just one. They're keeping their distance. It's not anyone I know."

Not Eydala.

The fear made its presence felt anyway, but it wasn't the same. It hadn't been since Grif. This was a new fear, as furious as it was afraid. An instinct to protect. This was far too close to Vinterhagen . . .

Nolan eyed her questioningly, a silent *what do we do?* She nodded and they ran on. If someone was out to get the girls, they wouldn't be following her. The thought was a poor consolation. If the rumor of blood readers had spread among the warow, she would need to move them. But where? No one was safe at her house, and Hidehall was no place for children.

The guys spoke in short, winded sentences as they ran. The runners hadn't had much information. Someone with wolf-sickness, at least one person dead, little else. They still didn't know exactly what or where, so they ran toward the unknown, the thing everyone else was running away from. Like always.

The pecking at her heart came and went. Whoever it was, they apparently didn't know she could sense, so not a henchman for Eydala or Nafraím. Who, then? And what were they after?

Juva stayed ahead of the others until they reached Florian's. She stopped and listened. It was as quiet as a sepulture, no signs of violence, barely any signs of life. The guys strolled aimlessly around the square, looking up at the dark windows. The fog crept over the cobblestones as if it were following them. Juva walked to the ornate double doors and peeked into the closed parlors. Not a person to be seen. She recognized the golden lamps and green glass panels from her meal with Nafraím.

This was where she had made him believe he would receive the letter she was expecting. The one that would show the way to the devil, to Gríf. A lie that had left Nafraím at Eydala's mercy, and Gaula only knew what she had done to him.

I don't care. If he's lucky, he's dead.

Of course he was dead. If he was alive, he would have told that damned woman how everything fit together a long time ago. That the devil was gone for good and that she had tricked him, tricked them both.

Maybe that was exactly what had happened? Was it Eydala's revenge she felt pecking at her heart now? A warow sent to kill her?

She was startled by Broddmar and Muggen, who came running into the square. Before they caught their breath again, a yell came from Nolan.

"Here! Skarr found something."

He stood some distance away in a covered arcade walkway that ran through one of the stone buildings. Juva motioned for him to wait and ran toward him. The others followed, and she led the way into the walkway. She raised her crossbow, listened. She could hear Skarr growling somewhere ahead. Water dripped from the ceiling.

The walkway led through the building to an inner courtyard, which had two other exits, obvious hiding places. Skarr stood with his ears flat and his hackles up, growling at a circular depression in the middle of the courtyard.

Juva approached slowly, the guys right behind her. It was a sunken pool, drained, the flagstones lining it were cracked. A man lay on his stomach by the side, motionless. Rainwater had gathered around him and soaked into his clothes. She lowered her crossbow and nudged him with the tip of her shoe. Nothing. Nolan and Muggen rolled him onto his back.

Dead. Fangs.

Juva squatted down and studied the body. The man was around thirty winters old. Someone had killed him, presumably by hitting him on the head with a rock. His hair was caked with dried blood, but apart from a small wound under his chin, there was no other sign of a fight. A stab wound? A nail?

He was moved here.

The guys checked the rest of the courtyard without finding anything. Broddmar knocked on a couple of the doors, but there was no response other than a window slamming shut somewhere.

"No one is going to say what happened here," Nolan said, returning his ax to his belt.

"I don't think it happened here," Juva said.

"But he was wolf-sick?" Muggen asked, chewing on nothing due to his underbite. He looked like he thought it was a sin just to be here.

"Or a warow . . . But sick, judging by Skarr."

"So who is he?" Hanuk eyed the body, his forehead creased. "And who alerted the runners?"

"Could have been anyone here," Broddmar said. "That's for the Ring Guard to find out."

Juva pulled the pliers out of her belt and snapped the fangs out of the rigid mouth. A tingling in her heart revealed that the warow had come closer again.

"We're not alone," she whispered, passing the bloodskins to Nolan. He nodded and quietly passed the news on to the others. Juva backed away and gestured for them to wait. She thought Nolan and Broddmar were going to object, so she stopped them with a silent assurance.

I know what I'm doing.

Nolan and Hanuk started the bleeding, while she moved away from the pool and crept along the building's walls. Her heart led her to the walkway they had entered through, and she realized she was smiling. This was an easy place to capture someone.

She snuck out through a different walkway. Followed a narrow alley back to Florian's with Skarr slinking along behind her.

Approaching the walkway from the outside, she saw the silhouette of a slight figure up against the wall. Her fear had lied to her; she had been expecting someone bigger. The warow stood with its back to her, watching the guys as they worked on the dead body.

I've got you . . .

Juva raised her crossbow in front of her and proceeded into the tunnel without a sound. Skarr growled. The warow was startled, turning around suddenly and flattening itself against the wall. It was a woman. Unexpectedly young, barely more than her early twenties. Juva rushed toward her, pressing the crossbow to her throat.

"Who are you?"

The woman tried to twist free, but the pressure against her throat made her think better of it. Juva remained at arm's length but pushed harder.

"What do you want? Who sent you?"

The woman raised her hands to protect herself. They trembled against the bow of Juva's crossbow, as if she wanted to push it away, but she had the sense not to. Her fangs had clearly been filed down, slightly crookedly.

"Sent?" she swallowed heavily. "No one!"

Juva let out a short laugh.

"You followed us here from Myntslaget, at night, completely randomly? That's what you want me to believe? I'm a Sannseyr!"

The woman tried to shake her head, but the bolt tugged at her skin.

"You," she said. "I followed *you.*"

"Why?"

The warow stared at her. Her appearance was doll-like, cute and dark-haired.

"You're a blood harvester, a hunter. I though you would find . . ." The woman hesitated. A hunted, tired look came into her eyes, as if she didn't actually want to fight for her life.

"Find what?"

"Wolf-sick . . ." The woman glanced at the guys who came running toward the arcade. "I just wanted . . . They say it can help. I never hurt anyone!"

Riddles and lies!

Juva clenched her teeth, fury eating its way through her chest like acid. She had had enough of fear and lies.

"*What* helps? Against what? Answer me!"

Broddmar came over and Juva expected him to make a clumsy attempt to calm her down, but he didn't do anything. He just stared at the woman as if he had seen a ghost.

"Ferkja?" he whispered.

Juva looked at him, gaping. The silence seemed to swell around them, leaving no room for anything other than the hollow dripping from the ceiling.

A jerk of the crossbow, and she realized she had lost the upper hand. The woman was free and had set off running down the walkway. Skarr started barking. Juva raised her crossbow and aimed at the woman, but Broddmar grabbed it before she had time to fire. Her heart pounded in her chest with an echo that vanished with the warow.

Ferkja ... He knows her ...

"Who was that?" Muggen asked, not picking up on the mood.

"A vardari ..." Juva replied, suddenly realizing that she had just seen the woman who had once turned Broddmar into a warow for a short time. Until he realized how foolish he had been and gotten her father's help to knock out his teeth and set aside his thirst for blood.

"And we kill vardari now? Is that how it is?" Broddmar said. "Are we fanatics, Jufa?" His speech impediment gave away how stressed he was, and his eyes burned as if *she* had made a mistake. But *he* was the one who had fallen for a warow. *He* was the one who seemed to care more about the warow's safety than hers.

Juva folded up her crossbow.

"She followed us," she said. "She could have been sent by Eydala, and *we* could be dead now."

Outside Florian's, the Ring Guard arrived—four men tramping along with a corpse carriage—but Broddmar didn't seem to notice them. He was staring at Juva with seething anger, and she knew if she were anyone else, he would have punched her in the face. If he had any strength left in his body or mind at all. He, the mountain that could no longer bleed.

Juva walked up close to him, ready to fight if he perked up.

"What? What the Gaula should I have done, Broddmar? She was spying on us, the gods only know why. Should I just let them keep doing that? It's only getting worse, and there's more and more people with wolf-sickness!"

"What did you think was going to happen?!"

His words thundered down between them like a portcullis. An accusation, spat with a repugnant matter-of-factness, as if he had always understood it would get worse. He had been just as much a part of it; they had sent Grif home together. But he was going to foist the consequences off on her?

"Pull yourself together, man!" Nolan said, pushing Broddmar away from her. "The Ring Guard are here."

Broddmar stared at him, and for a second, Juva thought he would throw a punch. Skarr started howling, as if he thought so, too. A hollow howl, completely out of place in the dark streets. It penetrated through the tunnel walkway and through her skull. A lament for everything she had done and hadn't been able to do. Everything she could never have. It tore at her nerves, and she snapped at him.

"Skarr!"

The wolf abruptly fell silent, taking a few unsteady steps before sitting down, as if she had pushed him. The guys stared open-mouthed. Their eyes alternated between her and the animal, and she saw a pained look flit across Broddmar's face. She knew why. This was a power he had never had over Skarr. Neither had she, but she didn't say anything.

Someone complained from a window that opened onto the courtyard. Hanuk sighed, pushed his way between Broddmar and Nolan, and went to help the guards. That seemed to bring some sense to the other guys, who followed his example.

Juva exhaled and leaned against the wall. The blood was rushing in her ears. The arched ceiling dripped its staccato tears.

Broddmar didn't understand shit. He cared more about a warow they didn't know anything about than about his own people.

No . . . She knew *one* thing about her. That she was following them to find people with wolf-sickness. Something that could help. With what? Juva had an eerie feeling that she wasn't going to like the answer.

The Ring Guard ran past her with a stretcher into the courtyard. People had woken up and were coming outside in their nightclothes, unaware that this had anything to do with wolf-sickness because the Dead Man's Horn still hadn't sounded.

Skarr looked at her and whined.

DEAD BLOOD

Nafraím could feel everywhere in his body that he had been drugged. Sickle flower, no doubt. He would have recognized the smell or taste of anything else. It was strong enough to knock out a horse. It settled in his joints like seaweed liquor, a nagging arthritis from a body finally collecting on his debt from over the centuries.

Eydala hummed next to him without the echo he had grown accustomed to, and the air was fresher than he had felt in months. He wasn't in the crypt anymore.

He kept his eyes closed, buying himself time to feel. Pain? Nothing new, other than the grogginess from the drugs. He was naked, sitting on a hard sofa of some sort with pillows behind his back. His arms wouldn't move. They were tied, one to the armrest, the other stretched out along the back of the sofa. But his feet felt free on the cold floor.

The humming left the room, and he opened his eyes. He was startled by eyes staring into his own. It took him a second to recognize Yrgen. The dead body was slumped next to him, naked and pale against the blood-red silk. The lips that had seduced hundreds of women and men were just as full, only dry and gray. Death had revealed the thirst this beautiful man had spent three hundred years slaking with drunkenness and lovemaking. In vain.

Nafraím took a deep breath, cooling the simmer of sorrow and anger that wouldn't be of any use.

We are dead regardless, every single one of us. Her, too.

Eydala's game didn't mean anything anymore. No matter what perverse torment she was planning for today, she couldn't do any harm.

He looked up and recognized the mirrored ballroom. He had danced here generations ago, when the room had teemed with life. Music, playful laughter, clinking glasses. He remembered painted lips and plunging necklines that glistened with sweat and jewels. The scent of perfume. Hemlines in all the world's colors had swept across the floor.

Now it was a lifeless place, empty and marked by decay. The paint was peeling off the ceiling, excruciatingly slowly, and the luster had blackened in the mirrors. He could see a thousand faded repetitions of himself and Yrgen, like an army of naked men. Half of them dead.

Eydala came sailing back into the room, setting a platter of fruit in front of Nafraím on the tea table without sparing him a glance. She restacked the fruit and stopped humming for a second as she elaborately positioned a rotten apple, as if the exercise required her full concentration.

When the fruit platter finally seemed to be in line with her expectations, she came to the sofa and pushed Yrgen over. The corpse smacked into Nafraím and lay in the crook of his arm, its weight smothering. She repositioned Yrgen's lifeless arm several times, as if everything had to be just right, before she left it draped over Nafraím's waist like a cold belt.

She was close but kept to the side, enough that he couldn't reach her with his legs. An indication of fear that made it hard for him to hide his smile. She noticed that, and it seemed to irritate her for a brief moment.

"Even you can't ruin this day, Nafraím. Because I have something to celebrate." She took a couple of steps back and put her thumbs and index fingers together to create a frame through which she regarded him with a disgruntled expression.

She handed him a cracked wineglass from the table and waited for him to take it before her eyes fell to his bound hands. She cracked her neck in one of those eerily silent laughs as if she had forgotten about his restraints. As if she hadn't just done her utmost to keep him at a safe distance. It was a transparent attempt to regain an imagined upper hand. But she had never had the upper hand. She could tie him up, starve him, drug him, and get other people to break his legs because he knew that she didn't dare do it herself. But she would never have the internal upper hand. That was the true crux of her scorn.

"Maybe just as well," she said and set the wineglass back down on the table. "I'm used to celebrating alone."

He knew she expected him to take the bait, but he didn't need to participate in her play. He was here to die, however long it might take for that to happen.

She framed the scene with her fingers again.

"Aren't you going to ask? You, who like to think you're so curious?"

She peeked at his crotch and wrinkled her nose.

"Cross your legs for me, please. You used to have more to brag about than that."

Nafraím got a bitter taste in his mouth. She was so vulgar, it made him sick. Schadenfreude was an emotion he rarely dealt with, but he had been through enough the last several months to appreciate knowing she was doomed to die, that she would never find the blood she sought. The end couldn't come soon enough.

Impatience, also a rare emotion.

He crossed one leg over the other. Yrgen's arm was squashed against his thigh. Eydala smiled and disappeared behind a tent-like curtain a few paces away. The pungent odor revealed what she was doing in there.

Yrgen's head rested on his chest, a cold weight on his heart. A rust-colored depression on the back of his head showed where it had hit the floor when he had been dumped down into the crypt. Nafraím would have combed his fingers through Yrgen's blond hair if he could have. Reassured him that he was safe now, asked for forgiveness that eternal life had ever been a possibility for him.

For them all.

"You've always tried to keep me down," Eydala said loudly from inside her tent. "You think you know everyone, that you can control everyone. You've always thought so. But you didn't have any control over that blood reader. That girl stood there, right *in front* of your face, and revealed the truth about the vardari to all of Náklav. You call that having control?" She laughed and poked her head out of the tent. "I have allies, too, Nafraím. Now that the whole city is ripe to hunt warow, why should I waste time looking for them?"

Eydala disappeared back behind the curtain again.

"I'm going to spend my time on art, while my new friend finds every single warow in this city. He's quite an impressive orator. You'd like him."

Nafraím smiled at her stupidity. He had seen more than enough orators in his life. Tongues of fire that burn out like a Náklav summer. They disappeared quickly and without a trace.

She emerged from the tent, walked over to a door, and let in a bit more daylight. It spread through the mirrors like a sunrise. From the hallway, he heard a woman's laugh in the distance. Was Eydala sharing this house with someone? Could he pull himself free and get away?

That thought surprised him. The human instinct for survival was impressive. It could not be bridled, no matter how much he had reconciled himself to dying.

"They call him Silver Throat," she said. "People are mesmerized by him. They would follow him to the end of the world. Like they would with you, back when you mattered."

She peeked at him, but he didn't give her the reaction she longed for.

"They love him. So much that he has been given space at Jólshov for his flock."

Nafraím laughed. The movement made it feel as if Yrgen was breathing against his chest.

"Almost two hundred years, and you still need people to follow?"

The twitch at the corner of her mouth warned that she was losing her temper, but she managed to control herself. She rubbed the bridge of her nose between her fingers, as if he were giving her a headache. Then she smiled coolly.

"Now, now, you make it sound so weak. You of all people should remember that words are power, old man. Silver Throat is an artist, like me. He sows fear and reaps action. He can get half the city to hunt the warow if he asks them to. Juva Sannseyr made it easy for him. There's not a soul who hasn't heard about her speech. The fight against the vardari. Against wolf-sickness. It's so simple that it's beautiful."

"So you're going to hunt your own?" Nafraím said, shaking his head. "For what? No one can help you, Eydala. None of them know where the devil is. You're as doomed as I am."

She responded with a wry smile that chilled him, as if she had said something important, something he ought to have understood.

She ducked back into the tent again and came out with a flat box, barely bigger than a book, which she turned over in her hands. Nafraím nearly nodded appreciatively but stopped himself. She had made progress with the process since the last time, even though it had long since deprived her of the ability to immerse herself. Her mood swings had always been there, but now they were pathological.

"It'll be a short-lived friendship," he said. "Just as long as it takes him to realize you're a vardari, too."

"Oh, but my dear, he already knows that." She kept turning over the flat box. He could hear the liquid sloshing from side to side on the inside. The sound reminded him of the sea, the beginning of a storm, and an uneasiness tingled in his chest.

Nafraím gulped.

"Where's he from, this fanatic of yours?"

She snickered.

"Where do most fanatics come from?"

Undst!

Nafraím clenched his fist so the ropes burned around his wrist. He fought to stay calm.

"A priest? Why would a priest from Undst want to hunt warow *with* a warow? That's not a choice a true believer would make. Surely, even *you* see that? Use your head, woman! This has nothing to do with faith. He's not here to help, not to help you and not to help Náklav."

"Of course not. The man thinks he's here to . . ." She looked like she was searching for the words in her memory before she smiled condescendingly. " . . . recreate God's world in his image."

"Like in Undst?" Nafraím let out a mirthless laugh. "The land of a thousand punishments? Where the devil has to be beaten out of children? Spare me that image."

She leaned forward, her lips pursed. Her breath was bad, worse than he had ever smelled on a warow, even the dying.

"Poor Nafraím," she said mockingly. "It's so hard for you to believe that anyone can create anything without you."

He closed his eyes. The cold from the floor crept into his feet and paralyzed them, like poison. It was hopeless. Eydala would never understand what she was contributing to. The only consolation was that she was doomed to fail.

He looked at her, hoping to find a trace of sense to speak to.

"Neither the city council nor the Ring Guard will allow a priest to hunt people at random."

"No," she replied unctuously. "But they will allow *her* to."

He laughed. "You think Juva's going to help you?"

"Oh, now, I'm sure she'd rather fling herself off of Kleft, but she's going to help Silver Throat. Sniff out the warow until you and I are the only ones left."

Don't take the bait. It doesn't matter.

But that thought didn't feel as true anymore. There was a difference between dying out and being eradicated. And if his dawning suspicion was right, far worse things were going on than the death of the warow. The vardari had kept Náklav and the world's seven other henge cities safe and peaceful for centuries. They were the dividing line between order and chaos, and the faithful in Undst knew that better than anyone.

"Good luck," he said caustically. "No one knows all the warow in this city, and few have the teeth that give us away. We've pulled them, filed them, molded new ones . . . And you think you're going to get the city council to hunt powerful people with influence because the girl says so? Because she can *feel* them?" He treated himself to a smile. "Do you really think that's all it takes to convict someone in Náklav, to start a manhunt?"

"Oh, yes," Eydala said, leaning closer. "I think so. Something far more tangible, actually."

She opened the box and lifted up a thin silver plate, hardly bigger than her hand.

"A sign from God," she said, her eyes wide with sensationalism.

She turned the silver plate toward Nafraím, and he stared at a likeness of himself, frozen in time, sitting on the sofa with Yrgen resting against him. A colorless but true copy of reality. Fluid dripped from the edge of the picture.

Nafraím closed his eyes. He felt as exhausted as the image showed. It was the very reason he had made her into a vardari, the images. A marvelous invention she had inherited from her father, and a science he had not felt as free to release to the public. It would make it practically impossible to live forever. You could change names but never your face. The warow council had agreed, despite the immense power of the innovation.

He looked at her. Her fingers trembled with schadenfreude, blackened by the poison she worked with to create the pictures.

She shoved the likeness right up in his face.

"Faith alone cannot move mountains, but evidence from the gods can. And I created likenesses of the whole gang of rats on the council. Every single vardari of significance. Do you remember? My art will finally receive the recognition it has always deserved."

Nafraím didn't respond. Time had caught up with him. Deep down, he had known this knowledge had surfaced, but he had reluctantly suppressed it as best he could. Both in her and in others carrying the same germ of an idea. But of all the people she could have shared this marvel of an invention with, none of the alternatives was worse than fanatics from Undst. Hopefully she would be dead before they understood or learned.

Loud moaning spread out into the hallway. A woman and a man, in flagrante delicto.

"How nice," Nafraím mumbled. "You've made more friends?"

Eydala straightened up, her mouth twitching at the interruption.

"Well, Rugen was *your* friend, so Gaula must know where he got his bad manners from. He is incorrigible, hornier than a cat in heat! He'll fuck anything that's breathing!" Her eyes fell on the corpse in Nafraím's lap. "Even things that aren't breathing. I practically had to beat him away from this guy."

Rugen?!

Nafraím stared at her. That couldn't be true. It wasn't possible!

That miserable boy had wolf-sickness; he should have been dead months ago!

The moaning culminated in a screaming climax before fading away.

"Now then," Eydala said with a sigh. "Where were we?"

Nafraím felt nausea seize him as the truth dawned on him. Yrgen's coldness suddenly became unbearable, chilling his blood like an ice bath.

Rugen, who shouldn't be alive. Eydala's growing madness. The hunt for warow . . . That's why they had bled Yrgen out.

"The Rot . . ." he whispered, paralyzed with disbelief. "You have the Rot. You drink from dead warow . . ."

Eydala shrugged, as if what he was saying was of no import whatsoever.

He tugged at his ropes, pressing his feet against the floor and struggling to stand up with a strength he thought he had lost. Eydala jumped out of the way. Yrgen tipped over and fell on the floor. Nafraím got halfway to his feet before the weight of the sofa pulled him back down. He remained seated, just as he had started, helpless and naked.

He stared at her. How had he ever managed to give *her* such a long life? This beast. What had he been thinking?

Eydala had backed away and lost her mask. She still feared him, and she had let it show. She was clearly aware of it, too.

"You have to drink something while you're hunting for the devil," she said, unable to steady her voice. "Did you think I was going to lie down and die, old man?"

"Blood from the dead!" he cried. "From your own dead? You might as well have been drinking from people with wolf-sickness!"

He was filled with despair. There was nothing more to say. Eydala had the Rot. She would get worse and worse, like someone with wolf-sickness. The only thing she wasn't going to do was die. Not until the vardari were gone; not until there weren't any more people with wolf-sickness to choose from. And she could always make more of them. May all the gods prevent her from figuring out how.

"You pompous prick!" she exclaimed. "You created us, created this, and all the misery that comes with it, and you're judging *me*?!"

Her mood had turned again, and she came closer, stepping over Yrgen's corpse and looking at Nafraím with something resembling genuine wonder.

"I've been torturing you for three months. I've broken your bones, starved you, dehydrated you, kept you from sleeping. But *this* is what breaks you? This is what you can't stand? Why?"

Nafraím tenses his jaw muscles. She knew why. All warow knew why.

She leaned forward again and contemplated him with curiosity.

"You believe that? That it makes us crazy? Well, my dear scientist, then I will imbue you with new knowledge, just the way you like it. Dead blood hasn't made me crazy—it has made me sharper than ever."

She sat down on the other end of the sofa and pulled her feet up like a girl.

"I'm no stranger to admitting that I used to be . . . confused. But now I know what I want. What *other people* want, even. I can look into everyone's minds, and I know what they're thinking. I know what *you're* thinking, Nafraím Sai."

Nafraím knew it wouldn't do any good to say this was proof of madness.

He leaned his head back and stared at the ceiling. A flake of faded paint fluttered to the floor like an autumn leaf. He blinked in response to a burning in his eyes that he had forgotten the feeling of.

SECRETS

Juva finished eating the flounder roll. She had waited so long it had grown cold, and the crispy surface had become soft. Where the Gaula was he?!

She wiped her fingers on the paper cone, leaned out the door niche, and stared at city hall across the street. It was a magnificent building that demanded its own space, one of few buildings in the city that had managed to keep its neighbors at arm's length.

Her gaze followed the staircase. It made a sharp turn, so you had to walk the entire length of the building—twice—to get in. Probably to discourage people enough to leave them alone. The castle-like features gave the impression that they were afraid of being attacked by their own inhabitants, and right now, her nerves made it feel like she could have been a frontline rabble-rouser.

The poor wretch in the guard booth had nearly begged for mercy when he realized that she hadn't gotten the message. They had silenced Dead Man's Horn, without a word, the crowning touch topping off a series of idiotic decisions. Like allowing space for fanatics at Jólshov with the followers of all the other religions, and giving her a deadline to stop wolf-sickness.

What the Drukna are they thinking?!

Anger ate away inside her chest like bad wine, and she had the feeling it was there to stay. When had she last felt anything else? Broddmar would have agreed, at any rate . . .

That thought turned bad to worse, the struggle felt fresh but still surreal. Everything seemed to be tearing apart around her. Juva clenched her fist and crumpled up her paper cone.

Pull it together! Drogg has the answers.

She should have dressed better. The summer had started to cool off, but she hadn't expected the city councilors to work such long days. Judging by how reluctant they were to meet her, they weren't at work at all, and that . . .

There!

Drogg was coming down the stairs, easy to spot, big as he was and wearing purple with a silver-embroidered vest. A couple of carriage pullers waved eagerly to him, but he continued on foot.

Juva slipped though the bookbindery doorway and followed him from a good distance. She stretched her patience so she could confront him at home. He wouldn't have anywhere to go, and she needed answers. More than answers, she needed help stopping the madness and could only hope that Drogg wasn't part of it.

He was nice enough, at any rate, rewarding people he passed with polite nods, even witless kids who stared. He followed Kistestikk the whole way down, out the gate in the old city wall by Brenntorget, and crossed Bodsrabben. Then he turned onto a side street.

Juva ran after him, knowing how easy it was to disappear in Náklav, but she spotted him as soon as she turned the corner. He was let into a stone building that was hardly someone's home. Solid bars blocked the windows, and over the enormous entryway hung what she assumed was a rusted portcullis.

She walked up the steps and knocked using the doorknocker, which seemed newer than the rest of the building, shaped like two intertwined snakes, thick in her grasp.

A young man opened the door, more nicely dressed than anyone needed to be on a weekday. He stared at her with a sharply raised eyebrow.

"I think you must be lost."

Juva put her hand on the door to prevent him from closing it again.

"I'm not lost. I'm meeting a friend here."

The man smiled condescendingly, as if he knew she was lying, but he let her into an antechamber and ducked behind a counter.

"Let me check. What's your friend's name?" he asked, glancing down the piece of paper.

"Drogg Valsvik."

"I'm sorry, there's no Drogg Valsvik here." The man pulled his hand over his brown bangs, which lay as if glued across his forehead. He couldn't have been any more evasive with his eyes if he had wanted to.

Juva yanked the piece of paper from him and read out loud: "Twenty linen napkins, four cases of Ruvian red, three bottles of fortified Martheng wine, candles, brass polish . . ." She looked at him. "Original guest list you've got here. Maybe he's sitting with the fortified Martheng wine?"

His ears reddened, and she handed the piece of paper back to him.

"Drogg Valsvik, big man, wearing silver and purple, impossible not to notice. He's on the city council, and he arrived just ahead of me. I'm Juva Sannseyr, the guild master of the Seida Guild. Does that help?"

The man opened and closed his mouth, as if he wanted to question her claims, before swallowing.

"One moment, Frú Sannseyr." Then he disappeared up the dark staircase that stole the better part of the antechamber.

Juva felt the corner of her mouth twitch into a scornful grimace. If anyone had told her she'd eventually use the name and title she despised, she would have assumed they were high on blood pearls.

She was on the verge of following him when he finally reappeared at the top of the stairs.

"If you would follow me . . ." he said, strained enough that she was sure she had made an enemy for life.

He led her into a sumptuous parlor, heavy with dark bookshelves and deep leather chairs. A whiff of cigar smoke reminded her of her mother, but Lagalune had probably never set foot in here. Everyone Juva saw was a man, and despite their obvious refinement, only a few managed not to follow her with their eyes. She was a fish on land.

They sat in rows of small rooms lining the walls, like alcoves, in deep leather chairs below framed maps and paintings of animals. The lanterns glowed behind cloth screens, spreading a warm but dim light around the tables. Above the entrance to the alcoves, she saw traces of holes, as if there had been bars, and she realized that at one time this had been a prison.

The man with the bangs pointed to an alcove where Drogg sat by himself. Then he gave her worn backpack a reproachful look and disappeared again. Juva took a deep breath and prepared to do battle. She had turned Drogg around before and knew what it was going to take. She needed to be unambiguous and powerful, and right now, that felt so easy.

She walked into the alcove and sat down in the chair next to Drogg. The councilman glanced up from his book and gave a start.

"But in holy Jól's . . ." He glanced nervously around. "Juva, you can't . . . You don't belong here."

Juva scraped some blood from underneath her thumbnail.

"Good luck finding a place where I belong."

A host came over and handed him a shiny copper mug garnished with sourberries. Drogg rubbed his temple, revealing his urge to hide his face.

The host looked at her.

"Anything for the . . . *lady*?" He emphasized *lady* as if he had just learned the word.

"Do you have anything that would go with a dagger in the back?" Juva asked. "Rye liquor, for example?"

He tightened his lips to hide a smile and withdrew. Juva nodded at the mug in front of Drogg.

"I thought you didn't drink?"

"I drink tea with milk," he said, putting away his book. "What are you doing here, Juva?"

She looked around, and a couple of the guys hastily looked away. The others were engrossed with each other. She gave Drogg a crooked smile.

"Not the same thing as you, I'm guessing."

Drogg dabbed a floral handkerchief against his forehead, and she continued before he could compose himself.

"I thought we were friends, Drogg. What the Gaula are you guys up to? The Dead Man's Horn has *never* before been silenced."

"Correct, and it's always incited panic. It's simply not a practical tool for—"

"Not *practical*?" Juva leaned forward over the table. "I'll tell you what's not practical, Drogg. Being alone with someone who has wolf-sickness, without your team, because the horn is silent and none of them were home when the runners came!"

"Oh, but of course more runners can be employed, and the guard booths are being ordered to raise flags, so you'll see it when . . ."

"Flags?" Juva gave a dejected laugh. "Is that supposed to help when the scene of the crime is crawling with people who have no idea what's going on? Who haven't heard or seen any warning? You want to move us into the guard booths, every last one of us, is that what you're thinking?"

Drogg took a sip of his muddy tea.

"You heard them yourself, Juva. You know what they're thinking."

"They?"

His cheeks turned a tad red, and Juva's curiosity tempered her anger. Had he been anyone else, she would have assumed he was just trying to deflect responsibility, but Drogg wasn't the type to do that. That little word revealed a distance he genuinely felt, and that was the opening she needed.

Juva sank back in her chair.

"And here I thought *I* had a tough job, but I just need to bleed the poor things out. I don't need to defend the chaos they create the way you do. And when the month is up, you'll need to look me in the eye and defend the fact that the job you pleaded for me to take is no longer mine."

"What? No!" He cast a stolen glance around and repeated more quietly. "No . . . Where did you get that from? Why would—"

"I didn't take my first waters yesterday, Drogg. You guys gave me a deadline to deal with the sickness, a thing no one can control, and now you're making the job as hard as you can. That won't work, and you all *know* it. You're planning to sacrifice me, as a hunter or a guild master— probably both—to appease fanatics, to convince them you're doing something!"

He opened his mouth to respond but was interrupted by the host, who placed an elegant glass of rye liquor in front of Juva, garnished with a stalk of lavender, which he straightened before leaving again.

Drogg pulled a hand over the top of his head, where his hair was thinnest.

"That's not true at all, Juva. Could we continue this conversation somewhere else, some other time? I'm waiting for a . . . friend."

"Then I'd answer quicker, if I were you."

Drogg sighed, without the wheezing that used to mark his breathing back when he believed every step he took brought him closer to death. When he was trapped in her mother's superstition. He leaned closer.

"No one wants to remove you from office, Juva. But things won't go as well for *me* if you don't keep this to yourself. They . . . We want you to cooperate with Silver Throat."

She looked puzzled.

"The cult leader you just put up in Jólshov?"

"The priest, yes. And what you call a cult is a growing body of followers who fear the warow and expect action, which you have yourself to thank for."

She ignored that dig.

"So the city council wants me to serve as a red hunter with a fanatic and hunt for warow that you guys don't believe in? Did I get that right?"

"Belief has nothing to do with it, Juva. The council has not denied the existence of the warow; it has simply never expressed an opinion on the matter. But as you so aptly pointed out last time: sooner or later, we need to decide whether it's real or not."

"Ah," she laughed briefly, "but you're not the ones who decide. It's the people in the streets who decide *for* you."

"Because you gave a speech that made it necessary to say something. And we can say a lot about the warow. The only thing we can no longer say, thanks to you, is that they don't exist."

His frustration was sincere. His eyes were heavy with challenges she was glad she didn't need to deal with, but she realized that she was making his life more difficult. He was just a pawn in a bigger game—one they would lose if they didn't pull themselves together.

"Drogg, there's rings worth of distance between accepting the cult and giving them a hunter, plus moving them into Jólshov!"

Her words seemed to encourage him.

"Giving them space at Jólshov is nothing new, Juva. The Seida Guild shares space with many believers already, of all kinds, and always has. The Hallowed will just be one of many. You'll hardly notice they're there."

Because I'm rarely there myself.

That was a thought she didn't intend to share, so she let him continue.

"And, yes, I know what they say about Undst, but he's not like you think. He's . . . cooperative, tolerant. They already observe many of our customs and care very little about which God a person believes in. I'm sure you will be pleasantly surprised, if I do say so myself. Jólshov will endure as it always has. The Hallowed mostly have ties to Nákla Henge, and if you think *you're* being harassed, you should have heard Klemens when they received permission to hold a sepulture there."

"A sepulture?" Juva blinked, unsure if she had heard correctly. "At Nákla-ring?!"

He waved his hand to quiet her.

"Jól help me, don't you start, too. It's not what it sounds like. They're going to use the dead stones, of course. It's not as if they were going to sepulture someone dead to Kreknabork." He laughed nervously.

Juva sat up straight in her chair.

"But they're going to throw a corpse between the pair of stones, not knowing where they lead to?"

"We *know* where they go: Nowhere! But the Hallowed believe it is the way to God. Through Drukna, if you understand. And it won't impact sales, of course. Nákla Henge has three days to prepare for this *one* sepulture, and it's going to take place early in the morning, before the shops have opened. It will just be the Ring Guard and goods haulers there."

Juva rubbed her forehead, groping for a reason, something that could explain why someone had gained entry into the only sacred place in the city where nothing was sacred. Drogg continued as if he had read her mind.

"There are practical considerations, Juva. It is . . . expedient to let them use the stones. The priest is from Undst, and the last thing we need is another conflict with them. An official from there died not too long ago, under . . . shall we say, somewhat dubious circumstances. It's business. There are negotiations. We give, we receive. That's how the world works, my dear child."

Juva plucked the garnish from her drink and took a sip. Despite the flourishes, it was the best rye liquor she had ever consumed. The warmth spread through her chest and cleared her mind.

"Sepulture to Drukna," she chuckled. "And here I thought I'd pecled away your superstitions."

"Well . . . Even Juva Sannseyr would struggle to call this superstition. Have you heard about the likenesses? The man has . . . silver likenesses of sinners. Warow. He says they come to him from God, to show us the way to wickedness."

She rolled her eyes. Drogg hid his face behind his hands for a second.

"I know how it sounds, but . . . His followers believe, and he says that as long as God is giving us pictures of the wickedness, it's our duty to fight it. Especially the blood readers. Especially . . ."

Juva leaned her head back in sudden realization.

"Ah . . . Especially the Seida Guild."

Drogg smiled. The twinkle in his eye was back. He was warmed up, and it struck her that he was the only one in the room who had been sitting alone, the friend he claimed he had been waiting for hadn't shown up yet.

He's alone . . .

Juva finished her rye liquor and clunked her empty glass onto the table.

"You know it's a scam, right? These images?"

Drogg stared at his mug, rotating it in his hand as if it might help by giving him a fortune.

"Paintings . . . That's what everyone calls them until they see them."

He looked into her eyes, and she recognized the vulnerability from when she had crushed her mother's lies for him.

"My mother lived off the doubt," she said. "She lived off filling the emptiness in people with words that *could* be true. Silver Throat does exactly the same thing, and you're letting yourselves be controlled by superstition."

As soon as she said it, she realized those words weren't true. It wasn't logical. Náklav didn't believe in any god but money, and the goodwill they were showing this priest exceeded anything she had seen from the city council before. Allowing a sepulture at Nákla Henge, granting space at Jólshov, and cooperating with the Seida Guild. Why?

She snuck a peek at the book he had been reading when she came in. He had set it title-side down, but she could make out the title on the spine.

Undst: A Historical Journey.

What did Undst have, the world's most isolated country, besides fanatics and grotesque punishments?

Juva caught his eye.

"No . . . An inconveniently dead official doesn't make Náklav kneel to a cult leader from Undst. It takes more than that to get permission for a sepulture at Nákla Henge, space at Jólshov, and to hound the vardari. I would believe many things of you, Drogg, but never that you would lie to me."

Drogg wilted in his seat. She might as well have slapped him.

"Eminent blood reader," he whispered. He took another sip of his tea and looked at her. "Could I ask you for a favor, Juva? I'd rather no one find out that I come here. Not everyone . . ."

He's negotiating!

She could get all the answers she needed now that he had pointed out his own weakness. All she needed to do was hold her ground during the bargaining.

The word tasted bitter in her mouth. She and the guys risked their lives dealing with the wolf-sick, and she needed to know what the city council was up to. And now that she had a lead from Ferkja, she needed more time. So why couldn't she make herself pressure him?

Say it! Say that you'll shut up if he tells!

She looked up and studied the painting behind him. Two powerful stags in the act of mating. Both had antlers.

"I think you're underestimating Náklav's tolerance," she said.

He smiled bitterly.

"And I think you're overestimating the city council's."

Juva shrugged.

"I'm not going to talk about where you go, Drogg. And that doesn't depend on what you say. That applies regardless, so I'm not going to barter with you."

He pulled a hand across his face to hide his bright, shining eyes.

"You really aren't your mother, Juva Sannseyr."

She put her hands on the armrests to stand up, but he stopped her with his hand.

"You're right: it's important to us to stay on good terms with the Hallowed. There's a reason they call themselves that. They believe they are protected against wolf-sickness, which would be an absurd thing to claim unless . . . Well, they say no one comes down with wolf-sickness in Undst. So they might have something that . . ."

Juva closed her eyes as the weight of those words settled around her heart.

"There's no cure for wolf-sickness, Drogg. No more than there are pictures from the gods."

He didn't respond, but his eyes mirrored her thoughts. Náklav was struggling. The world's leading henge city was fighting the disease as if it were a plague, and the city council was willing to invest in the chance that there was some relief. No one would have welcomed that more than her, if she had believed a word of it. But she had seen too many people promised long lives by her mother in exchange for coins, and she couldn't be a part of that.

She set a coin next to the glass she had emptied and stood up.

"You're right," she said. "I'm not my mother, and I didn't leave the fanatics I grew up with to hunt with one. Ask someone else."

She turned around to leave.

"I wish we could," Drogg said. "But he asked for *you*."

She turned back toward him, and he shrugged.

"He says you have a gift that can't be wasted."

A gift . . .

Juva felt a chill creep down her spine. A gift for locating the warow? No, there was no possible way he could know that. This wasn't about sensing but rather about the speech she had given. About the will to fight them. She stared at the ceiling and tried to gather her thoughts. All she saw was a row of holes left by the old bars.

She turned and left but looked back at him over her shoulder.

"It may not look like it, Drogg, but you're sitting in a prison."

THE IDOL

The old women in the Seida Guild used to say that thunder was the voice of Jól. That the booms rumbling over the sea were the mother of all the gods sharing secrets only blood readers could understand because they ate the tongues of their dead predecessors. As convenient as it was arrogant. Her mother had always been extra smug after storms, as if she had been elevated and affirmed by the sky itself.

Juva preferred the myth of Hanuk's people, from the icy wasteland of Aure, who said thunder was the wingbeats of Ur, the raven that had created the world.

But it was just weather, and sometimes the weather is bad for no reason. Just like her. Her muscles ached as if she would soon take the waters for the last time. The nights had grown chilly, and the last thing she had time for was lying around sick.

It was the crack of dawn. The morning bells had not rung yet from Jólshov, but she had to get up. Had to see him, find out who he was, this priest who was twisting the city council around his pinky finger with false hope. The man who had said she had a gift and had asked for her. He was just one of the myriad things that had haunted her overnight. The thunderstorm had made everything seem bigger, more fateful.

Worry for the girls. Kefla, who should move to Vinterhagen. The argument with Broddmar. The warow woman who had followed them. What the Gaula did she want wolf-sick people for? What could they help with? They were bestial, sick in the head. Not capable of helping anyone. Or had she lied? Cooked something up in desperation because of the crossbow bolt at her throat?

Then there was the city council's idiocy . . . Still, she was relieved that they weren't going to throw her out as guild master. That emotion went against her nature; she had never wanted the title, although it was reasonably certain that it had kept her alive these last few months. Some tenuous protection from the wrath of the vardari.

Juva stared at the black curtain around the four-poster bed, her mother's room, a mysterious drama like everything else in the house she had never thought she would move back to. If it had been up to her, she would have packed her bags and left it all behind, become one of the old women in Steinnhed who just went out into the woods and stayed there after they had had enough of the world. But she had lost that chance. She couldn't run away anymore. She had the girls to think about and a hometown that was fighting for its life.

Because of me.

Skarr whimpered next to the bed, reminding her there wasn't much time if she hoped to sneak into the sepulture and observe Silver Throat.

Juva got dressed and slipped into the library so as not to wake Kefla. She ate a fistful of seaweed nuts from the bowl on the liquor cabinet, stuck her crossbow in her backpack, and nearly silently snuck out the front door. Skarr squeezed out with her. She would have preferred to leave him behind, but he was nervous when she wasn't there, and his howling up at Florian's . . . That had been unlike him, just like his reaction when she had scolded him. A reminder that he was a wild animal after all.

The rain drummed against her hood as she hurried through the streets. The storm clouds weighed down the sky over Nákla Henge and made the enormous wooden dome sad and colorless. If she had been like all the Sannseyrs before her, she would have said it was mourning what was about to happen in there.

The door in the west gate was open for the last of the haulers who had been transporting cargo through the stone portals all night. They sat on full cartloads and sulked like wet cats as they waited for papers so they could leave. That was how Nákla Henge breathed, in and out, goods at night, people during the day. The breathing that held the city together at the seams. That circadian rhythm must be a disadvantage for other henge cities, but when hadn't the world conformed with Náklav?

Not today.

Today, the morning hour had been sacrificed in the name of diplomacy. A sepulture was being held here, like in the golden age. Juva got chills at the thought. They might as well have sepultured the boy in a teahouse to the sounds of clinking silverware.

The card slot was unmanned, and Juva slipped in out of the weather. The round public square lay deserted under the dome. The emptiness brooded over its own sound, a sort of hollow hum. The rain poured down through the hole in the middle of the roof, making the Witness wet and gloomy. Everything else was covered.

Skarr began to growl, having caught the scent of the blood grating. She pulled him closer to her as he resisted, sniffing at the ornate manhole covers that lay close together around the whole henge. Together they formed an elaborate ring, embedded in the cobblestone square. A beautiful snake that hid Nákla Henge's red sewer: the blood from wolves and people with wolf-sickness that drove the stones.

Juva spotted the man she had bought the music box from. He was there early and seemed to share her sense of discomfort. He certainly took an unreasonably long time letting himself into the curio shop while casting furtive glances at two Ring Guards by the dead pair of stones. They were squatting down and tugging at one of the lids over the blood gutter. It finally budged and creaked upward until it was open halfway. They peered down into the blood gutter for a moment and seemed to be struggling with what they were looking at.

One of them spotted her and came running across the square.

"Hey! You can't have dogs here!"

His mistake dawned on him as he approached, and the panic grew on his face.

"What the . . . ! Aren't you . . . ? Is that . . . ?"

"No, no," Juva hurried to reassure him. "No one here has wolf-sickness. I'm not here in red. I was talking to a city councilman the other day and think it's best to be cautious, just to be on the safe side. You never know with wolf-sickness, and there will be a lot of people here today . . . "

She didn't give him time to consider, just acted as if the matter were settled and nodded toward the stones.

"As if you guys didn't already have enough to do, right?"

"That's what *I* said, too," he replied with a snicker, before his eyes fell on Skarr again. "But we can't have *that* in here while the—"

"We'll be out of sight. So you're really going to hold a sepulture here? Whose idea was that?"

The man pulled a dirty hand over the top of his head and stared at the dead stones.

"Not *ours*, Frú Sannseyr, I'll tell you that much. A sepulture in Nákla Henge? Devil-freeze-me unbelievable, if you'll pardon the expression."

Juva laughed, realizing that she had already won.

"I know. Cargo at night, people during the day, and the dead at dawn?"

"Right?" he nodded companionably. "We're running the world's biggest henge here, not a morgue! And those stones have never been used. They're not even connected to the pumps. We have to pour

101

blood into the gutter from a bucket! It's not fucking pretty, if you'll excuse my language, but what are we to do?"

"Count on this being the first and last time?"

"Damned right, Frú Sannseyr."

Juva pointed to the gallery across the square.

"Well, Skarr and I *won't* be any trouble. We'll stay hidden up there, and it'll go fine. We'll be able to get down quickly if, Jól forbid, the worst should happen."

The Ring Guard crossed the square with her.

"Good, then you'll have company. The historians were getting settled before *I* got here, but that's how they are, that lot. They need to preserve this foolishness for prosperity."

He waved her away and went back to his work. Juva took a few steps up the stairs and overheard two guards talking. She peered down over the wall of the stairs and listened. They were standing nearby below the gallery, each drinking from a dented tin cup while they watched the work going on by the dead stones.

"It's not going to work," one of them said.

"It already did," the younger one said with a shrug, "with the dog."

"That's different. We're not bitches, Arn! The body is going to stay there, lying on the cobblestones with its mouth hanging open. I mean, how embarrassing is that going to be? They'll have to pick him back up and carry him out to Kleft and do a sepulture like normal people. Gaula me, it's gross."

"Yeah. It's not like that dog had done anything wrong . . ."

They tested them . . .

Juva continued upward and tried not to think about when she climbed these same stairs several months ago to give the speech that had shaken the city council and frightened the city into fearing the warow. But it wasn't the speech that had weighed on her. It was knowing that she would never see Gríf again after the Yra Race. That memory stung, not just because she remembered what it was like losing him, but because she had thought he was worth the grief.

Pull yourself together, Juva!

She came out on the gallery and saw the historians deep in conversation. Two women and a man, and they had brought more than she would have believed they could carry: stools, books, paper, and leather folders. The man sat drawing, aided by a board propped at an angle on his lap. He had already made sketches of the stone circle on several sheets of paper. His pencil fell when he spotted Skarr.

Juva picked it up for him and petted Skarr's neck to show that he was harmless.

"Aren't you Juva Sannseyr?" one of the women asked. "Yes, you are Juva Sannseyr! I remember your speech during the Yra Race. It was . . . captivating."

Juva forced herself to smile.

"Yes, I hear that's what they say."

The woman leaned closer.

"Did you intentionally draw inspiration from Dredvin the First? You did, didn't you? And the connection to the fairy tale about the sisters and the wolf, that was—"

The other woman nudged her, and what she thought about the fairy tale was left unsaid.

Juva rested her elbows on the gallery railing next to a well-used box of paints. In the square below, the Ring Guards had taken up their positions, two by each pair of stones and several in the surrounding covered walkways and balconies. A few of them chased out people who were trying to come in by the western gate, a problem they should have foreseen. Náklav ran on wolf blood and gossip, and there were surely plenty of people willing to pay so they could say they had been here. Even the shopkeepers seemed to have brought in extra help today. They lingered outside the doors with lame excuses, wiping each pane in the windows, sweeping and rear-ranging the goods that were meant to entice customers.

There was something surreal about it all, as if they were suddenly strangers in their own workplace.

The guard she had spoken with walked by with a bucket of blood filled to the brim. He poured it down through the grating by the dead stones. He kept to the side, clearly nervous about getting too close and winding up in Drukna. That seemed to amuse the two posted there more than it should have, as if they needed the laughter to relax.

The women from the college started discussing the bucket as an object of historical interest, while the painter captured the guards' likeness on his piece of paper in just a few lines.

Then Juva heard the death drums.

All activity ceased, as if time had stopped. People and guards stared toward the western gate, which let in the death procession. They walked in rows, two by two, with corpse lanterns. The ones in front were carrying the bier with the unmistakable shroud—a pod of starched linen, pointy at the ends, like a boat.

The way through Drukna.

The sketcher's hand raced over the paper to capture the moment, and the historians chatted quietly to each other. They looked up at Juva in anticipation before it dawned on them that she was unfamil-iar with the subject.

"That's a ship's cloth," one of the women whispered. "It's a Slokna custom, the norm for Jól believers, while the Hallowed are led by a priest from Undst! We had expected something else, but then, of course, that's what makes this so unbearably exciting. They don't sep-ulture their own dead in Undst; they bury them. Or use stone coffins, which became customary in the 800s when Liisianity supplanted—"

The other woman nudged her again, and Juva did not learn what Liisianity had supplanted.

The long column of people clustered around the dead stones.

There were more people than she had expected; they filled almost half the square. She spotted Muggen's sister and raised her chin with sudden insight. So this was what *born again* meant . . .

Otherwise, there were all sorts of people, but none of them stood out as the authority figure the whole city was talking about, someone able to make the city council give in.

"Which one is Silver Throat?" one historian whispered to another.

The drumming stopped. All Nákla Henge seemed to hold its breath, and suddenly, she knew for certain where he was.

"He's waiting outside," Juva said with cool assurance.

The three historians looked at her, but she kept her thoughts to herself. Silver Throat knew that time was of the essence, that more people were coming, and he wanted attention. The drama would be worthy of the Seida Guild.

Thunder rumbled above, echoing under the arched dome roof. Juva stared at the west gate, where he came walking in alone. The death procession parted to let him by, like a shoal of herring around a predatory fish. That famous piece of jewelry they all wore glittered around his neck, a thin silver collar necklace, with a nail that sat against the throat.

Nail throats.

That's where their nickname came from.

Silver Throat took his place before them and let his gaze wander along the walkways and his audience, who stood as if frozen in the shadows, watching. The historians whispered about his clothing, which they thought was a break from what was traditional in Undst. She agreed that he was dressed more simply than she had expected, in wide trousers and a thigh-length gray tunic wrapped tightly around his waist. He clutched a book to his chest and raised his eyes toward the stones.

Juva realized she had seen him before.

Who is he?!

She feverishly searched through her memories. A man of about thirty winters with dark hair worn combed back with a distinctive widow's peak, the hairline receding sharply on either side. Almost like small horns on his forehead. There was an intense look in his eyes, with a wry smile at the corner of his lips that made him seem like he took himself very seriously. She knew he would be attractive if he smiled. How?! How did she know that?

Hidehall!

He had once sat at her table in Hidehall. Before she had become a red hunter. Before Grif. Before . . . everything. What was his name again? Lodd! He had been reading a sacred book but hadn't mentioned being a priest. They had talked about the devil, an idea he thought had been stolen from them, from Undst. She had argued. He had set down his book and said she was cute. She had left, to follow Broddmar as he hunted someone with wolf-sickness.

Juva realized her mouth was hanging open. This was the famous Silver Throat? An argumentative guy from Undst who had tried to win her over a glass of rye liquor. He hadn't been particularly pious back then . . .

Her relief was short-lived. She had met him before, but that didn't mean he was harmless. Quite the contrary, he had been the reason she left. There had been something about him, something she couldn't put her finger on.

Silver Throat began to speak, his voice booming shamelessly about the dead, about God's blessing, and the way through Drukna. She snuck a peek at the historians, who were scribbling incessantly in a sort of code that went so fast they seemed to get every word down on the paper.

He didn't open the book a single time but passed it to an assistant when he was finished. Then he walked over and knelt by the bier and revealed the face of the dead. A woman walked over and opened the corpse's mouth and administered the last waters from a drinking horn that resembled the one she herself had used when Solde and the other women had been sepultured.

Drogg was right. He uses our customs.

One of the others from the retinue handed him a glass float like the ones used for fishing nets. Juva squinted to see better. What did a net float have to do with a sepulture? It still had some netting around it and was attached to a long rope. They fiddled with it for a while, and suddenly the glass ball flared up on the inside, flames spluttering in yellow.

Oil of branntang. They're not going to burn the body, then?

Silver Throat placed the glowing glass ball in the body's hands, like a lamp, and secured the rope. It was hard to see from a distance, but it looked like he tied it around the corpse's wrist.

The historians were in ecstasy, judging from their whispering. The guards were bouncing from foot to foot over by the west gate, clearly impatient, so people were probably waiting outside.

A handful of people from the entourage grabbed the bier and lifted it unsteadily onto their shoulders. Nákla Henge was as quiet as the charred forests of Svartna.

They carried the bier to the dead stone pair. And after a bit of embarrassed mumbling, they agreed on how to proceed. The pallbearers in the back lifted the bier as high as they could above them, while those in the front knelt. The body slid off the bier in between the stones and vanished.

Juva felt a shiver run down her spine. She heard someone below the gallery gasp, as if they hadn't actually believed they would to do it, send someone dead to Drukna. Or that the stones would work at all.

The artist looked at her, as if they shared some form of communion now that they had seen the same thing.

"Unbelievable," he said.

"What is?" Juva asked. "That the stones work, or that they're dumping dead bodies somewhere unknown?"

He chuckled as if she were joking.

"Oh, but there's widespread agreement in the schools that these stones don't have any counterpart, so there's no reason to believe that the dead disappear in the distortion."

"The distortion?"

"The void. The big nothing between the stones, Frú Sannseyr. What I meant was that this is an amazing blend. Torches against Gaula, death drums, and yet he still makes the fire sign from Undst with his fists. That's really inclusive!"

"Yes," Juva replied cuttingly. "As if he wanted to attract as many people as possible."

The mourners nodded to each other, giving the tacit support that meant so much after a sepulture. A handshake, a pat on the shoulder, a hug. None of them cried. They didn't even hang their heads, and it occurred to her that that was because of the nail. It sat with the sharp end up toward their chins, forcing them to hold their heads up.

A memory flashed through her thoughts. The corpse of one of the wolf-sick people, up by Florian's. Juva drew in her breath in a silent gasp.

That's where the scar came from!

The strange wound, irritated like an insect bite. She had thought it came from a fingernail, but it had come from an actual nail. He had been one of them, one of the Hallowed.

So why had he taken off the collar necklace before he died? Had he left the group? Been kicked out? A darker thought took shape, and it gave her chills.

People flocked to the Hallowed because Silver Throat said that wolf-sickness only afflicted sinners. One of them had actually contracted wolf-sickness, but they had taken matters into their own hands. Killed him and removed the collar to maintain the myth that none of them got sick.

Mother would have been impressed . . .

Even Drogg had believed they were onto something. That they might even have a cure. Juva felt a strange disappointment, even though she hadn't believed it for a second. The heart began to hope so easily that you didn't even know you were doing it.

One of the guards approached the priest and said something impossible to hear. He seemed impatient, and Juva guessed that they were in a hurry to get back to normal operations. Silver Throat gave him a nod and led his followers toward the west gate, where the doors were opened.

People poured in and spread out along the balconies, but most of them didn't enter the shops. They stood watching Silver Throat, who was leading his flock across the square.

He stopped before he reached the west gate and turned around to his followers again.

"The Hallowed have held their first sepulture in Nákla Henge!" he cried, and Juva realized that he had no intention of stopping at the one. Nor did he intend to leave the area until everyone knew it.

He's intentionally dragging out the time.

"We are the future!" he continued with a natural forcefulness. The guards looked confused. A couple of them spoke to each other, but they were clearly hesitating to intervene. They respected that a sepulture had taken place, and that gave Silver Throat the space he needed.

"We're all that stands between order and chaos. We are the pure, the protected. We have received the word of God, we carry our punishment with us, and the evil cannot touch us. Neither the warow nor the wolf-sickness."

No, not as long as you remove all the traces.

"But I heard that you doubted! You doubted that God would receive the dead. Do you doubt God's word?" He flung out his arms and seemed to be appealing as much to the onlookers as to his followers. "But you need never doubt again! God's word is here. He has

109

sent us his word, his sign. He has given us a new face, a new evil to defeat."

An assistant handed him the book he had been carrying when he came in, and he opened it. A hectic whisper spread around the balconies, and people began gravitating toward him. The Hallowed put the palms of their hands together in what she had understood from the historians was a fire sign. They chanted their approval is if in prayer.

The historians stood up so abruptly that one of the stools tipped over. They leaned over the gallery railing to see better, and Juva realized that what Silver Throat was holding in his hands was no book.

The images! The idols!

Juva rushed down the stairs with Skarr at her heels, running in the shadows under the gallery, past the shops. She had to see them. She had to get closer so she could expose his game.

But she couldn't get close enough, not as long as the Hallowed were standing in the middle of the henge. To do that, she would have to cross the blood grate and stick out like a tree in Náklav. If the guards didn't stop her long before that.

"Look at God's images!" Silver Throat yelled, holding up what wasn't a book but a dark wooden box, hinged like a suitcase with fittings on the corners. It was open toward his followers, revealing two silver plates shiny against the black bottom.

"Look at the devil's offspring! Vardari! Warow in our city! Will we have to fight the evil alone, or will the Seida Guild finally help?"

Juva stopped and looked around, but no one was paying attention to her. Every eye was locked on the pictures, and even regular people were nodding and mumbling in approval. The Hallowed were clearly done mourning because their anger had taken over.

That seemed to amuse him, and he smiled at them, wryly and smugly.

"Now, now . . ." he said. "Anger is also a sin. Let's give them time.

I have no doubt the blood readers want the same thing as us: a city without sin, a safe city, a healthy city."

Juva drew back against the wall and tried to hide Skarr behind her. Silver Throat was showing his power. That was what he was doing. He wanted to show that he could turn people against anyone he wanted to, including the Seida Guild, and she had no doubt that he knew she was there. Or at least knew that someone would tell her what he had said.

He knew a lot of people would come.

Silver Throat has asked for cooperation, and now he was showing his muscles. He wanted to force her.

An iron door squeaked next to her, and Klemens came out of the Ring Guard office. He waved his arms and yelled at two guards, who finally realized the breaking point had been reached. They ran over to Silver Throat and pointed him toward the west gate.

He closed the box again and waved to the onlookers, as if they had come for his sake.

"God's word is God's image," he said. "And it will remain at Jólshov! But you have seen it. You can find the evil. Go, children of Jól! Children of Muune! Children of Fylja, Breg, Frost, and Tina! Blood of Ur! Go, and let the gods who are all one, lead you."

He walked out the west gate with his yelling followers behind him. Juva held her breath as she watched. They left the henge as a united and furious flock. Shaking their fists in a synchronized battle cry that faded away as soon as the last of them was out.

This is a war . . .

That realization left a bad taste in her mouth, and it was even worse to realize that she was the one who had started it. She had talked about the battle against the vardari, about strengthening the blood readers. She had forged the weapons he was using.

Someone grabbed hold of her arm, and she jumped. It was one of the women from the college, one of the historians.

"Did you see that, Frú Sannseyr? Did you see the likeness?"

Juva gulped. Several of the onlookers were staring at her. They had heard her name. She swallowed and shook her head.

No, she hadn't seen the pictures. But she had seen what they led to. The hunt was on, whether she was with them or not.

THE BRIDGE

Juva tiptoed to the door and peeked into the lush conservatory where the girls sat bent over their books. That had to be Náklav's most unique schoolroom, the second floor of a built-in courtyard, converted into a forest of exotic plants. The source of the name for Ester's inn.

My inn.

But it didn't feel like that. The place was just too beautiful, too colorful. Filled with art treasures from all over the world, shiny, embroidered silk fabrics in greens and blues and ornate gilded furniture. She always felt like an intruder, a threat. As if the gap was too big between what she had around her and what she had on the inside. A nagging sense of harboring secrets the girls wouldn't tolerate.

Common sense told her that was bullshit. Kefla was twelve and had spent many years living in the random nooks that Náklav's streets had to offer. Syn was a fourteen-year-old redheaded beauty with eyes devoid of hope, who could never again go back home to her father. Dark Ulie was eleven, had given herself a very short haircut, and had survived the illness that had claimed her parents on a ship from Thervia. Tokalínn was only six but had believed that hiding her mother's bottles would help.

No, Juva knew she had little to teach them about suffering. But she could teach them to trust their own hearts and to steer clear of the warow.

And she could teach them to write.

The girls had each been given their own wrought iron desk inside the cage-like gazebo in the middle of the conservatory, where wealthy guests used to eat breakfast. Where Ester had died. The plants climbed around the pillars and decorative espaliers, framing them like an illustration in a book of fairy tales.

Heimilla walked between the tables and followed along with their work, nicely assisted by Vamm. He was the best read seventeen-year-old she had met, but he came from a family that hadn't been stingy with anything but their love.

Juva remembered the first time she had seen him. It was here at the inn. He had been sitting in a corner, sewing, and she had noticed him because he had a faded bruise and looked like he had been staying for a long time. Her assumption had turned out to be correct. What she hadn't known at the time was that he could sense. He hadn't dared tell the girls that, either. He just helped out, worked here.

He leaned over Syn and pointed down at her book, wanting her to read a word out loud. She frowned and squinted at the text. Her eyes, otherwise so blank, were concentrating intensely. All the bad things seemed to be gone, both fathers and fluttering heartbeats.

Come on, Syn! You can do this.

Syn bit her lip and stammered out the words.

"Words of . . . honor."

Vamm all but jumped and clapped his hand in joy. Syn rolled her eyes as if he were completely hopeless, but a smile snuck over her lips as soon as he moved on.

Juva swallowed. A painful warmth burst in her chest, and she felt dangerously naked, exposed, laid bare. It had started with Kefla, and now she was responsible for more people than she could have ever imagined. The family she had promised never to have. Apart from the guys, but all they demanded was that she perform when hunting. That was harmless. This was something totally different.

What if she ran out of money? What if more blood readers showed up than the beer at Hidehall could keep alive?

She couldn't afford to believe that this would end up well. That *anything* would end up well. She could put a roof over the girls' heads, food on the table, and she could tell them why they had restless hearts. But what kind of hope could she give them? She, who had started a war that was fueling religious fanatics. She, who herself was a target for the warow, and who killed and bled the wolfsick. She wasn't herself anymore, either, sleepless, restless, angry . . . She, who used to be too afraid to help, now she was too angry.

There was hardly anyone in Náklav less suited for taking care of the girls.

So what are you doing here, Juva?

She had come here because she needed to see them. After days of muscle aches and pondering Silver Throat. His likenesses. His followers' wild shouts. It had given her chills and she had dreamt of nails in throats and dead wolves.

The question was what the city council would say when the fake deadline arrived in a few days, and she refused to work with Silver Throat. Presumably they would remove her from office and send newbies and fanatics out to hunt. And when the warow died out on their own, Silver Throat would get the praise for it.

Then there was the runner who had come to the door with the card from Anasolt. Laleika in the Seida Guild had come down with wolf-sickness and thrown herself off the cliffs at Jólshov. She had sepultured herself, and now the family didn't have a body to sepulture.

Wrong. Everything felt wrong.

Like before, when she had thought she was to blame for terrible things happening. Because of her mother who had burned her drawing of the wolf. Because of her father who had lost his life to Gríf, for her sake. To save a child from a monster in an iron cage.

And aside from Laleika, it had been ten days since they had last been called out for a case of wolf-sickness, the one up at Florian's Parlors. She hadn't seen the guys since then, apart from Nolan, who had stopped by to check that everything was all right. She had told him about Silver Throat, and the hair-raising suggestion the city council was going to propose.

But ten days meant that . . .

The sound of the door knocker echoed from the porch downstairs like an evil warning to be careful with her thoughts.

When she opened the door a crack, Juva met Heimilla's gaze and gestured for her to continue her lesson. Then she followed Skarr down the stairs and opened the door.

"Vinterhagen?" the young runner outside asked and handed her a card. He didn't seem worried, and if it was a case of wolf-sickness, they would have knocked at Lok and Hanuk's place next door.

She took the card and let him run off again before she read it. No danger. No wolf-sickness. Just a message that the ointment for Ulie's rash was ready.

Juva closed the door and stood just inside, suddenly aware of the drumming in her chest. Nervous and irregular, like rain hitting her heart.

No! Not warow, not here!

The panic set in before she realized that she had felt this rhythm before. It was Ferkja! The woman who had followed them to Florian's and who was clearly still doing so.

Why?

Her thoughts rushed around like an Yra Race in her head. A river of danger. This girl had claimed she was only after the person with wolf-sickness, because that would help. What the Gaula did that mean? And why were there more and more of them? Had she been there by coincidence, or had she had something to do with that dead body, the corpse with the scar under its chin from a nail? Was there some connection between her and Silver Throat?

This girl had the answers she needed, and if she didn't die soon for lack of blood then surely the Hallowed would finish her off. And worst of all, she knew about Vinterhagen! Or, at any rate, that Juva usually came here. She needed to get her away from here, away from the girls.

Juva stared at the card in her hands. It was completely innocent, but the warow who was waiting outside somewhere didn't know that. And now that they weren't using the Dead Man's Horn anymore . . .

She rushed up the stairs and grabbed her suit out of her backpack. Heimilla came in with heavy understanding in her eyes.

"Another case of wolf-sickness?"

Juva laced up her red jacket and shook her head.

"No, but there's someone who needs to think there is. Lock the door behind me."

She didn't wait for a response but nearly stumbled down the stairs and set off at a run through Myntslaget with Skarr ahead of her. She turned west toward Smalfaret, and her heart told her Ferkja was following at a safe distance. All according to plan. *What plan?!*

She had no idea what to do or where to lure her. But now at least she knew that Ferkja was still looking for people with wolf-sickness, so she would keep up.

People stared and pulled away in fear as she took the stairs over Kong Aug's Gate in a few leaps. They thought this was for real. She couldn't do this; she couldn't terrify half the city. She had to find a place to confront the girl. Corner her or trap her in a dead end. A quiet place to force her to talk.

The bridge!

Juva slowed down through Smalfaret and out onto Villfarsveien until she was sure that Ferkja was still with her. The tower in front of Ulebru rose up in front of her, and she took a detour around the guard booth. Skarr set off through the archway in the tower building and out onto the bridge.

That gave her an idea, which turned into a desperate plan. She set off after him but ducked off to the side as soon as she was through the gate. She rebounded off the edge of the bridge and jumped upward. She got hold of a windowsill and pulled herself up into a niche diagonally over the opening in the tower building. Skarr stopped and circled for a second in confusion before he spotted her.

No! Stay there!

"Stay!" she barked before he could ruin everything. She hadn't counted on him obeying, but he whined and lay down in the middle of the bridge a short distance from a group of kids who were rough-housing near the tower at the other end.

They ran with colorful flags in the wind, some obviously home-made, others more expensive. A raven, with long, black strips to form a tail, and a moth, with painted dots on its wings. They danced against the sky and made her dizzy.

She got her breathing under control and suddenly realized how high she was.

Ulebru hung above the sea at a dizzying height between stiff cliff walls, connecting the two islands together over the narrowest portion of Dragsuget.

She stared down at the ships rounding Skattanger with billowing sails on their way into Nyhavn. There were several at the docks, and they looked far too small . . .

Juva clung to the niche. It was narrower than she had thought, with a carved statue pressing against her back to emphasize that there wasn't room for them both. It took her a moment to regain her balance.

She had never seen the city like this before. The sea surrounded the twin islands as if Náklav was all there was in the world. The sun slowly crept lower, bathing the city in orange and making every stone glow. She leaned forward and saw Náklaborg throne on Kingshill, surrounded by an incomprehensible mass of buildings. It was strikingly beautiful. No wonder there were always power struggles here. Náklav was worth fighting for.

And worth fighting the warow for.

Her heart gave Ferkja away. She was close. Juva cocked her crossbow and got ready. Ferkja came running through the opening right below her. Juva dropped down and landed behind her on the bridge with a thud. Ferkja stopped. She stood with her back to Juva, as if she understood that she had been tricked.

Juva aimed her crossbow at Ferkja's narrow back.

"Hello, again . . ."

Ferkja slowly turned around. Her eyes wandered between her and Skarr, not showing the need to have a go at either of them. Finally, she craned her neck and peered over the side of the bridge.

"Good luck," Juva said in a hoarse voice. "Maybe you'll be the first to survive a fall from Ulebru."

Ferkja appeared to contemplate that for a while. She was far too young for Broddmar. And too young for the vardari. Barely a couple of years older than Juva. What in heaven's name made someone choose to become a warow when they had their whole life ahead of them?

The wind caught her long, black hair, and she looked at Juva without a hounded expression. Then she shrugged.

"It wouldn't be the first time I was the first to survive something."

She stuck her hand in the pocket of her black shirt, which was far too big for her. Juva took a cautionary step closer, in case she needed to pull a knife. But Ferkja took out a thin cigar, the same kind her mother used to smoke. She turned her back to the wind and shielded the cigar as she lit it. Took a deep drag and blew the smoke out with the wind.

Juva took another couple of steps closer and stared at her over the tip of her bolt.

"How is that going to help?"

Ferkja seemed to understand what she meant. The cigar trembled between her fingers.

"There are so many dead," she said. Even her voice seemed young. "I don't know where he is, the one who gave me blood. He's gone. So many are gone, you have no idea . . ."

She took another drag and folded her arms around herself as if she were cold.

"So I'm doing the same thing you would have done. Curbing the thirst. Managing as best I can."

Juva gulped.

"You . . . you drink blood from people who have wolf-sickness?"

Ferkja snorted in exasperation.

"Maybe, if you would have given me the chance."

Juva stepped closer, as close as she dared without sacrificing the upper hand with the crossbow. She pulled it closer to her chest to give her arms support.

"Why? Because it tastes good?" she asked cuttingly.

"No," Ferkja said, averting her gaze, "I suppose you've never needed anything in your life, have you? A Sannseyr. No one has ever refused you anything at all."

Juva couldn't hold back a cold laugh.

"So you've never met a Sannseyr, have you?"

"No, but I lost my father to one."

Juva lowered the crossbow a smidge.

"My mother rarely kept her lovers very long, so I presume you got him back, whoever he was."

Ferkja smiled wryly.

"You really don't know . . ."

Skarr began to circle restlessly between the edges of the bridge, and Juva felt equally impatient. Enough games, she didn't have any time to waste.

"Why wolf-sick people? What the Gaula . . ." she looked down in disgust.

"Ah, there it is!" Ferkja said, flinging up her arms. "That delicious contempt. And from you of all people! You have no shame, and you look at me as if *I* ought to be ashamed of myself? I lived as a Sannseyr, too. Received the blood I needed, but . . ." She gulped. "Everything is ruined now. I don't know where he is, the one I got it from. I don't know where *any* of them are. And that damned speech of yours didn't make it any easier. You have no idea . . ."

Juva felt the girl's heart squeeze nervously around her own, a sorrowful agitation, and she fought it. But she couldn't find the words.

No. You're the one who should have known.

Ferkja had no inkling why the blood she lived off of had stopped flowing. Why the warow were gone. She just blamed Juva for her speech, which had made it harder to live in Náklav with fangs . . .

Ferkja took a hard drag from the thin cigar that had almost gone out before she continued.

"I've heard of warow that have fled to Svartna to hunt wolves. That tells you something."

Juva dropped her crossbow to the side. Wolves, wolf blood, and wolf-sickness. They were drinking anything they could find that might slake their thirst for Gríf's blood. Her disgust grew in her stomach.

Ferkja chuckled.

"You'd think you make your living judging people." She glanced at the crossbow. "But that isn't what you do, is it?" She tossed her cigar butt over the side of the bridge and hugged herself against the wind. "Don't you think I know that?" she asked, discouraged. "People don't drink from people with wolf-sickness. It rots the brain. I know that. I'm not an idiot!"

Juva looked at her, that beautiful, doll-like face.

"So why in Gaula do you drink it then?"

That was an idiotic question, she knew it the instant the words were spoken. Ferkja was like Rugen, hooked on something that took over everything, an addict. Ferkja was what she herself would have been if she hadn't managed to put down the hoggthorn. Or the rye liquor.

Or Grif.

Ferkja shrugged.

"I'm already so rotten in the head it doesn't matter. And if I ever knew anyone who could stop me, they're gone now. I will be, too, if I don't drink it. The alternative is death, not that that's the worst thing . . ."

"Death is . . . the alternative?" Juva brought her crossbow up and clutched it tightly, tasting the word. It was just a word, so why did it seem so menacing, so dark?

The significance was there, like a trap. An abyss she should avoid, but she couldn't stop herself from approaching.

"You're trying to say you want to drink blood from the wolf-sick, not because of the thirst, but to . . ."

Ferkja tucked her hair behind her ear and looked out at the sea.

"They say we can live off it."

Juva lost the strength in her arms. Her crossbow fell against her thigh and her body went cold. She felt dizzy. The sentence grew, exploded, displacing everything else she had heard until it was all there was.

Live off it . . .

Vardari could live off the blood of people with wolf-sickness.

Juva lunged at her and pressed her fist into her chest. Pushed her up against the bridge railing.

"You're lying!"

Ferkja just stood there, as if she were exhausted. Without answering, without protecting herself. Juva fought her nausea.

"That's why there are more of them. It's because you . . . you people are creating more of them! You're creating wolf-sick people for the sake of their blood. To have something to live on."

Nafráim had said that. He was making blood pearls from warow blood because the portals needed the wolf-sick. Had the others started doing the same thing?

She stared at Ferkja and silently begged her to deny it.

"If you want to call it living. You kind of lose something when your brain rots," she replied bitterly. "The person dies, the animal takes over. I'm planning to die before I start behaving like someone with wolf-sickness, so to speak."

Juva realized that she was falling. Ferkja put her hands on Juva's shoulders and held her steady.

"Hey . . . red hunter? Everything okay?"

Her breath smelled like smoke, and Juva stared into those dark eyes, deep, empty, damaged.

Ferkja raised her chin and leaned closer. Inhaled through her nose.

"Fuck . . . You smell good. You smell . . ." She smiled as if they shared a secret. "A hunter who takes blood pearls," she whispered. "Where did you get them from? Please, tell me. We can help each other, Juva."

Her friendliness was as warm and genuine as only desperation could be. Ferkja was so close, and her nervous warow heart snuck its way into Juva's.

"I've never touched blood pearls in my life," Juva said. Her heart hammered warning after warning against her chest, increasing her nausea.

Danger! Danger!

Ferkja put her lips against Juva's cheek. Cool, swollen from pleading.

"You don't need to lie to me. I feel it. You have them in you. If you let me taste you, Juva, then we win. You and I, we can—"

Juva tore herself free and pushed herself away. She wanted to rip Ferkja's heart out of her own body, get rid of that devilry.

"Never!" she screamed. "I've never touched them!"

Ferkja clutched her chest and fell toward the bridge railing. Clung on to it to stay on her feet. Skarr started howling, and the kids ran in panic. One of them lost hold of their kite, and it disappeared in the wind, getting smaller and smaller, a moth against the sky. Ferkja slid toward the ground and sat panting as if she had been running.

Anemia? Is that how they die?

Juva felt her way to Ferkja's heart again. It was still there, quivering nervously against her own. But now there was a division again, a safe distance.

Ferkja looked up at her and calmed her breathing.

"I sense it," she said again. "If it's not blood pearls, then you're . . ." She started laughing. "In Jól's name . . . A sick hunter, that's the craziest thing . . ."

Juva backed away, unsure of her own footing. She felt Skarr nestle up against her. Ferkja's eyes wandered between her and the crossbow.

"If you don't want to help me, you could at least shoot me," she muttered.

Juva snarled at her and took off running.

SILVER THROAT

Juva ran through Glefse, not paying attention to which streets she chose. They were all the same, like the charred trees in Svartna, no beginning, no end. She was caught in a stone labyrinth that was shrinking in around her.

Skarr ran beside her with his mouth open and his tongue hanging out as if he knew that they needed to keep up the pace. The world would stop if she stopped, and everything she had just heard would become true.

The warow weren't dying. They would live forever on blood from dead people who had succumbed to wolf-sickness, and they would go just as crazy as the people they had drunk from. She hadn't saved the world from the vardari, she had given the world vardari with insanity, with rotten brains.

And she was wolf-sick.

She was lying! Ferkja was lying!

Juva raced through Lykteløkka as she clung to that hope. Of course it was a lie! But her tongue felt its way to her teeth, searching for an answer she didn't want, and her mind revolved relentlessly around everything she had been living with for the past several months. The rage. The restlessness. Wakeful nights and aching muscles. Dreams of madness unlike anything she had experienced before.

The Sannseyr home was an unusually welcome sight, a protective castle. She let herself into the front hall, tore off her straps, dropped them on the floor, and went into the bathroom. She opened her mouth wide in front of the mirror and stared into her own mouth. It seemed far too red. Animal-like.

Her fingers were drawn toward her teeth, but she hesitated. What would she do if they were loose?

I'm a red hunter. If I'm sick, I have to die.

Juva wiggled her canine. It wasn't loose, but her gums were tender. The skin was stretched over a barely visible but bone-hard bulge underneath her gums. On both sides.

Her throat tightened. She grabbed hold of the sink and stifled a sob. That wouldn't help her. Nothing could help her now. She had become what she chased.

Skarr whined in the doorway, staring at her. No wonder he had been difficult! All the whining . . . the howling.

This was happening. This was real.

But how? She had never touched blood pearls, so where . . .

Grif . . .

The realization tore at her chest, burning in what she had thought was only a scar. A memory of her own idiocy. But he had given her something far worse than that. He had killed her. Given her the most painful end she could imagine.

Wolf-sickness.

Juva jumped as the front door banged shut. The metallic clang echoed through the hall.

"Juva? Are you here?"

Kefla!

Juva threw her hand over her mouth and stared at her own reflection. Kefla . . . What was she going to do with Kefla? And the girls? Broddmar and the hunting team, they couldn't, they mustn't . . .

Her gums suddenly felt so swollen that they filled her mouth, paralyzing her jaws until she doubted she could speak at all. She squeezed her eyes closed against a burning she hadn't been able to give in to before.

She was sick. Wolf-sick. Deadly.

"Juva?!" Kefla yelled from the library now.

Never let them see a weak blood reader!

Juva pulled her hands over her face, unsuccessful in making herself look presentable. Kefla appeared in the doorway behind Skarr, clearly trying to hide her relief.

"They said you ran off. I thought it was . . ."

Juva swallowed.

"Go and pack your things, Kefla. You need to move in with the others."

Kefla's face wilted for a second before it knotted up in anger.

"You said I could stay here!"

"I said you should always listen to me—that's what I said! Go and pack your things, Kefla. Now! This is not a negotiation."

Kefla clenched her fists. Her black bangs sat like a row of needles over her eyes, which were about to overflow with disappointment. Juva struggled for restraint.

"Kefla, you need to move to Vinterhagen. It's not safe here."

The girl tightened her lips, but they trembled anyway.

"I can help!"

"If you want to help, you'll listen. Now."

Kefla turned on her heel and disappeared into the hall. Juva could hear her stomp up the stairs as if she were trying to break them.

Juva went into the library, supported herself on the lacquer cabinet as she poured a glass of rye liquor. It wasn't long before she heard Kefla come stomping back down. Something sang against the stone floor in the front hall as if she had thrown it down as hard as she could.

Her key.

Then the door slammed shut. Juva flopped down on the sofa with a dark pang in her chest. She exhaled as slowly as she could. Her fingers felt too weak to hold the glass.

Skarr lay on the carpet next to her and pretended to be asleep, but his ears were still pricked. His heart breathed against her. Cautious and at a distance, not like with Ferkja. What had happened?

It was as if she had infected Ferkja with the panic. As if the fear she had lived with her whole life had seized hold of another heart. But Juva knew she couldn't trust herself anymore. She was back where she had started, unable to tell what was real and what wasn't. She wasn't herself; she was wolf-sick.

How long do I have left?

Less time than the warow, who had found a way to survive it. It was grotesque. So incredibly wrong. The vardari should die, and she should live, but now everything was turned on its head. Juva swallowed a far-too-big gulp of rye, which burned its way down her throat. The glass clinked against her teeth.

Get a grip!

It could be completely different than what she thought. Ferkja could have lied about the warow being able to manage. Like a sort of revenge? No . . . Ferkja didn't know that she had anything to avenge aside from the speech. The declaration of war against the warow. And she had told the truth about the chaos and the blood shortage, without suspecting it was due to her. Unless Nafraím was alive and had told them that . . .

No. Eydala would have been at her door ages ago.

Juva fought the urge to reach for her throat, where the rope had cinched. If there was any shred of justice in the world, Eydala was rotting in Drukna now. And maybe Ferkja was wrong, that it was just something she thought, a rumor. That's what she had said, wasn't it?

They say we can live off it.

Even if that were true, it could be that not all the warow knew that.

But *some* knew. Some were still feeding people blood pearls and creating more people with wolf-sickness. Like . . . food. Nourishment. Was she going to end up as a thirst quencher for warow, too, with a half-rotten mind?

Juva drained the last little bit from her glass and stared at the stuffed raven in the cabinet in front of the chimney. It looked right through her.

What did you think? That you were loved?

Down the chimney, down in the rock, in Náklav's bedrock. He had lived there, and before that, he had been held prisoner in other locations and bled for over six hundred years. Six hundred. It was incomprehensible, but she had been stupid enough to believe that it hadn't destroyed him. That he didn't hate everything and everyone. That he was capable of caring. He had been willing to do anything to get free, and she should have understood that. She, who had succeeded in spending her whole life learning to distinguish reality from imagination. Until she found *him* . . .

And he had hated her just as much as he hated *them*. Enough to make her wolf-sick.

The raven's eyes glistened in the semidarkness. Forever trapped in a glass cage and forced to give away prophecies for money. What would it have said now? The future that awaited her was not to be found in any runes.

She glanced out toward the front hall where her crossbow and straps lay strewn on the floor, with the flat bloodskins spread out underneath.

She was going to go mad. Deadly. She could become any one of the people she had killed, a bestial ghost of a person. The red bloodskins might one day swell with *her* blood. Someone would yank out her teeth with pliers. And after her death, the vardari would go on creating and living off the wolf-sick. Forever . . .

No! This is not over!

Juva set down her glass. She had never touched blood pearls, so that should buy her a little more time than usual. Not that anyone knew what was usual. It could be weeks or months. But she still had time to clean up.

She could make the girls secure. And Náklav. She wouldn't die until she had kept the promises she had made to everyone, of a city without wolf-sickness. Even if she had to hunt the vardari until the last fang was pulled. And the rage she had fought against was the only thing that could sustain her until this was over.

Broddmar was going to hate her, but then who didn't? He would have to get in line, behind Gríf, Kefla, and the city council. He was safest away from her, anyway. There wasn't room for anyone in a wolf-sick heart. A butcher's heart.

Skarr came over to her and raised his snout to her face. Studied her with his golden eyes. She rested her forehead against his and dug her fingers into his fur. The smell of wildness aroused a longing that weakened her.

No! There's no room for you, either!

Juva got up and walked over to the raven cabinet. The bird's gaze seemed to follow her, something that had always frightened the wits out of her mother's staff. But there was no staff in the Sannseyr home anymore. It was just her, and she no longer feared fear.

She opened the hatch in the pedestal and plucked a coin from the box. Slid it into the slot and turned the crank.

So, raven of a blood reader, how long do I have left?

The poultry turned from side to side in helpless, mechanical jerks. The bowl in front of it jumped, and the dice rolled through their many runes before they came to rest. Three signs pointed up.

A crime. A wolf. A war.

Juva leaned toward the cabinet and laughed without any trace of happiness.

The door knocker sounded out in the hall. The sound was one

final insult, an impossible demand, but she pulled herself together. She couldn't hesitate any longer. There was no time left to lose.

She went into the front hall and peeked at the front step between the cracks in the planks boarding up the windows.

There he stood, as if sent by Jól and Gaula at the same time. The solution she both needed and feared.

Silver Throat . . .

He stood with his hands behind his back, looking in a different direction. Not quite as simply dressed this time. His rust-colored coat shimmered like silk. The nail flashed in the collar around his neck with the sharp end up, as if he hadn't held his head up high enough before.

What was he doing here?

He was here to ask for her help, she had no doubt about that. Maybe he had already heard what she thought about cooperating from Drogg, but something told her this wasn't a man who gave up easily.

The thought of hunting warow with him gave her the shivers, but she no longer had any choice. The city council would demand it, and if she said no, they would sacrifice her and give him a license anyway. At least as long as they thought Undst could offer a cure. And if he was the bitter type, he would turn people against her. He had already demonstrated that he could, and if that made them refuse to let her hunt for herself . . .

Juva closed her eyes. She had asked for a war, and she had gotten one. She was becoming everything Broddmar loathed: a butcher for a fanatic, someone who hunted warow like rats.

They spread wolf-sickness for the sake of the blood. They're monsters.

But she would do it *her* way. Not his.

Her tongue went to her swollen gums. Her hair hung in tangles on her chest, as if she had just gotten up, and she knew that he would smell liquor on her. But he'd have to take what he got.

She opened the door.

Silver Throat raised his hands to her as if in submission and smiled.

"Don't close the door, Frú Sannseyr. I know what you're thinking, but I'm afraid the city council lacks the necessary insight to present our case in a satisfactory manner. May I come in?"

He spoke quickly but clearly, not waiting for her response.

"I assume that you know why I'm here, but I have reason to believe that we share more interests than you suspect. They have probably asked you to be our red hunter, but the city council hardly has the ability to present what an opportunity this is, and what a difference you could make, Juva Sannseyr, and I must have the opportunity to correct that impression. I know, they have—"

"Yes."

There was a silence, but it didn't last long.

"Yes? Yes, I can come in? Or yes, I can correct that impression?"

"Yes, we will hunt the vardari together." Juva went back inside and left the door open. She heard him follow her in.

"I must say . . ." he continued as he closed the door. "I was prepared to come here and negotiate. I didn't think . . ."

It grew quiet again, and she looked over her shoulder. He was staring at the wrought iron bench that was shaped like a rib cage. His eyes roamed over to the inky black staircase and then the fireplace, that glowing mouth that separated the hall from the library. It ended by the cabinets containing her mother's grotesque collections.

He ran his hand over an engraved skull on a shelf.

"Fascinating . . ." he said and looked as if he meant it. "This is a . . . dark place, isn't it?"

Juva pointed him into the library.

"Yes, you seem overly concerned with sin and evil, so if that's what you're after, you've come to the right house. Here there are bones in jars, dried tentacles, petrified animal penises, and books with words that would make your hair fall out. Please, take a look in the blood reader room. There's an exquisite wall painting of the devil in wolf form."

The corners of his mouth tugged upward into a patronizing smile.

"I think you're prejudiced. I happen to be very fond of curiosities. Actually, I have—" He gave a start to see Skarr, who stood staring at him with his yellow eyes.

"Yes, and I have a wolf. Welcome."

He smiled again, just as arrogantly, but he should have because he managed not to say anything about the fact that he already knew that.

You know less than you think, priest.

He was a liar, like her mother. A swindler who played on fear and tempted people with salvation. The urge to annoy him was almost stronger than the certainty that she needed him. It was hard to choose, and she had never had less patience or less time. She was dying and she had a job to do.

Skarr went over and lay on the sofa, and Silver Throat took a seat in the chair farthest from him. Juva opened the bottle on the lacquer cabinet.

"A drink?" she asked.

He winked at her.

"If you promise not to tell anyone."

She poured two glasses of rye and handed him one. At least he didn't hide the fact that he was a swindler. He accepted the glass, and she noticed a scar on the back of his hand that looked like it was from frostbite. His eyes devoured her red suit with the same intensity as if she had been naked.

She sat down on the sofa.

"I don't remember the nail from the last time," she said, a little more caustically than she had intended. That seemed to please him.

"As I said, I like curiosities. Call it . . . a memory. We both grew up in dark houses." He took off his coat and opened the top button of his shirt, suddenly making himself at home. "I wasn't sure if you'd remember me—"

Juva interrupted him before this deteriorated into unwanted reminiscing.

"Here are my terms."

He rested his chin on his knuckles and seemed to be ready to listen.

"Dead Man's Horn will be up and running again. No hunting without me. No bloodthirsty fanatics in the streets. No amateurs."

His conceited smile reappeared.

"You don't like me very much, do you?"

"And I don't need to."

He nodded, as if that were a reasonable position. The nail didn't seem to trouble him much, but he was a skinny man. He could at least nod his head normally without skewering himself.

"You don't need to worry about amateurs," he said. "The Ring Guard has men available, and I've already picked a few good people myself who will—"

"I choose my hunters myself," she cut him off. "But the hunting team I have now will be kept out of this."

"Of course," he replied. "I can vividly imagine that they have enough to do with the wolf-sick, and naturally, that's work you must continue while you . . . neutralize warow with us."

She studied him. There was no indication that he understood the guys might have refused to hunt warow for him even if they had been unemployed.

"To kill," she said, "that's my decision. If I end up killing them, I kill them, but those who allow themselves to be captured will be imprisoned. I'm not your butcher."

"Of course," he said. "But in all modesty, I think I have a better proposal. No one needs to be killed as long as we place the responsibility into God's hands."

She nearly rolled her eyes.

"And how do you suggest that we do that?"

He leaned forward and folded his hands between his knees.

"We send them to Drukna."

CLOSE YOUR HEART

Third day of Floa. The first month of fall brought dark nights and chilly daylight, but that only meant she was a few days closer to death.

She was wolf-sick.

Juva pulled her sweater around her more tightly and hurried across Slipsteinsveita. Skarr moseyed along ahead of her, loyal, so far. She had no time to lose. The storm of thoughts had already cost her a day. What would happen to her body? Would she know when her mind failed? What would happen to the girls? And in the darkest hour of the night, the most desperate question had occurred to her: What if Undst actually did have a cure?

She hated herself for even thinking the thought. There was no cure. Silver Throat had already proven that by removing the collar necklace from someone who had died of wolf-sickness. Still . . . Not even growing up with blood readers could have prepared her for the appeal of an imagined solution. Its draw was stronger than she would have ever imagined, and suddenly she had a new understanding for why the Hallowed were gaining converts.

But one question overshadowed the others, insistent and unlikely as it was. Would she be able to cleanse the city of warow, or would her legacy be the fall of Náklav?

The buildings loomed in over her as if they were falling down. A glass pane had cracked in one of the beautiful, old windows. The wind had ripped off an ash-wood shingle.

Are these my thoughts, or is it the wolf-sickness?

She wasn't going to tell anyone, that was the only thing she was sure of. But the guys needed to know they had messed up. That *she* had messed up. They had gotten Gríf out of the world, in vain. They had merely gone from bad to worse. The vardari had found a grotesque way to survive without him. They were drinking from the wolf-sick people they themselves had created. Blood from blood in an endless, evil circle that would make them more animal than human.

Juva crossed Ringgata and took the short cut over Glefse. She had to talk to the guys while she still could, because soon she would have to keep herself away from them for good. Never see them again.

But when? Not knowing was its own torment. For all she knew, it would hit her overnight. Maybe they would be out hunting the wolf-sick, and suddenly she herself would . . .

Knock it off, Juva!

She shook off the images. She needed to be clear-headed, make the guys understand what needed to be done. She trusted Nolan; he didn't hesitate to act when it was necessary.

But Broddmar . . . He had not been a man of action in a long time.

Outside Hidehall, a lantern repairman stood wiping his sooty fists on a handkerchief before entering the ale hall. Juva followed him into the usual after-work crowd. It was strange: the worse the world was, the more people drank. If nothing else, the money kept the girls alive and paid the staff at Vinterhagen.

She walked over to the counter and waved at Oda.

"Are the guys here?" she asked, even though she knew they would be at that hour.

"They're sitting in the hunting hall, Frú Sannseyr."

Oda was lifting empty tankards onto the shelf, four at a time. The short woman ran the place like clockwork. Juva didn't regret having let her take over for Rut. Rut had betrayed them, drugging the guys when they had been waiting there to kill Nafraím.

That had not gone as planned. Nothing went as planned.

She had shot Nafraím by the bathtub, and he had sat there with the bolt in his shoulder and told the truth about Gríf. That he had been one of the wolves during the wolf wars and used Slokna as a hunting ground. And that he had made her into a genuine blood reader as a child, a senser, which without any explanation had given her panic attacks.

If she had listened to Nafraím, she would have killed Gríf that night. And she wouldn't be dying now.

Instead, she had tricked Nafraím and sent him into Eydala's arms. *He was a murderer, a vardari. He had himself to thank!*

She took a pitcher of beer, an extra tankard, and a bowl of crackers and went into the innermost section of Hidehall. It had always been reserved for hunters, but there were fewer and fewer of them, and there were more and more beer drinkers, so she had agreed to open the whole place when they had a full house.

But no matter how close together people were standing, they found room to get out of Skarr's way. He led the way between the tables and over to the guys in the back by the fireplace. They had a table to themselves, like a last bastion of hunters backed into a corner.

They sat with their heads bent over a game of bluffers. Juva set the beer and crackers on the table in front of them. They lit up and reached for the crackers without taking their eyes off the game. Except for Muggen, who reached his big fist toward the bowl of crackers, trusting that no one would sneak a peek at his pieces while he did so.

She sat at the end of the table, took a swig of beer, and glanced at Broddmar. He kept staring at his pieces, but he clinked his tankard against hers as if all was forgotten.

Nolan told crude jokes, which Muggen didn't understand. Hanuk was already tipsy—he had no tolerance—and grinned with deep dimples. Lok talked about his kids and said thank you for the hundredth time for letting them stay in Ester's old house at Vinterhagen. Juva forced herself to smile and felt her chest tighten. It was as if her body wanted to tell her that she could never be happy again. The small talk in the room was so unbearably breezy, and she would be forced to ruin it. She dug for courage but only found oppressive loneliness of a completely new sort.

Then the Dead Man's Horn sounded.

Nolan leapt to his feet and grabbed his knife belt, which hung over the back of his chair.

"They've come to their senses, I hear."

Because I said yes to Silver Throat.

The guys dropped their pieces and stood up. The game was over, everyone had lost, and now it was a fight against time. Juva followed them out into the hallway by the back door, where they could change and talk freely. They secured their axes in their belts, strapped their bolts around their waists, and hooked their crossbows to their backs. A ritual that had its own macabre song of sounds.

Then they ran in a pack up to the nearest guard booth by Ulebru Bridge. Two runners came dashing down Villfarsveien, coming to a stop when they saw the hunters. They were gasping for breath.

"Ny . . . Nyhavn! Down at the docks! There's a heart, a . . . living heart!"

"Huh, a heart?" Lok's eyes widened. "What does that mean?" But no answer came because the runners were off again to alert the other guard booths.

Skarr panted, running alongside her over the bridge toward Nyhavn. It wasn't hard to see what was going on. There weren't any people at the docks other than some longshoremen, crewmembers, and a few guards from the nearby booths, who stood in a cluster on the hill leading up from the harbor, ready to make a run for it at any moment.

They pulled back so Juva could pass, pointing at the outermost dock. It was bathed in blood, and Juva felt an icy fear race through her body before she realized it was entrails. Entrails and blood from a whale carcass, towering like a mountain between the dock and the rocky shore.

The stench was obtrusive, mixing with the smell of smoke from the shafts.

Skarr slowed and started pulling toward a piece of meat lying by the edge of the dock. It was as tall as she was. A heart.

The memory came like a tidal wave. The conversation with Grif in the library after she had let him out. She had been thinking about a blue whale's heart that she had seen, and here it lay in front of her, bloody and red, as if it might start beating at any moment.

She pulled Skarr back and gave him to Muggen. Muggen was as big as a mountain, and probably the only one who could hold Skarr. Then she approached the heart. The enormous muscle twitched, and she flinched and drew back.

"What in Gaula . . ." Nolan whispered, raising his ax. He reached a hand out in front of her to stop her from going any closer.

Juva walked all the way around the bloody mountain. Then it moved again with a jerk, a quiver on the surface, and an eerie sound as if . . .

She raised her crossbow, squatted down, and peered into a massive vein that gaped at her like a bloody mouth. She could have crawled in if she had wanted to.

"There's someone in there . . ."

Between the reverberations from the Dead Man's Horn, she could hear sounds coming from inside the heart. Squelching, like footsteps in the mud. She glanced at the longshoremen who had ventured closer, poorly armed with filleting knives and hammers. They stared at the whale heart in open disbelief.

She motioned for them to keep their distance. Broddmar asked if they knew who was in there and received only a shrug in response.

Juva listened to the unsettling sounds.

"Well, whoever it is, they're hungry."

Muggen started muttering a barely audible prayer verse, and Lok was so pale he appeared sick. They turned and looked at Hanuk, who raised his hands defensively, clearly aware that he was the shortest among them.

"No! Not even Ur could get me to go in there!"

"No one's going in there," Broddmar said, drawing his long knife.

Muggen stopped him.

"What if it's a kid or something?" he asked. "Juva?"

She shook her head. Her heart felt cold, but it had a thousand reasons to.

"It could be someone with wolf-sickness," Juva said. "I'm not sure."

"We could drop a shipping crate on it," one of the longshoremen suggested. Muggen flung out his arms as if they hadn't heard what he had just said.

"Do you have a saw?" Juva asked, and they perked up. Two men disappeared behind the mountain of whale and returned with the biggest saw she had ever seen.

Muggen and Broddmar took it between them and raised it over the heart. The sawteeth sank into the flesh, and they began to pull it slowly back and forth.

The heart went silent. The saw sank deeper and deeper until the guys were squatting. They jumped away from the river of blood that spread across the dock planks. Juva held her crossbow in front of her. Her arms trembled. A nascent fear whispered that this was a mistake, that they should leave the heart be and get out of here.

Nolan took a swing with his ax and pulled until one piece of flesh began to tip. The heart ripped in two. Veins and fibers broke off, and half the heart smacked onto the dock. The other half remained standing, a tangle of blood and ligaments.

Skarr started growling.

A woman, or what had once been a woman, sat in a fetal position in one of the heart chambers, eating. Her dress was soaked through with red. She stared at them but continued eating as if that were the only important thing. Her fangs dug into the piece of meat she clutched, and she tore off pieces like a wolf.

Close it! Close the heart!

Juva lost the feeling in her arms. She recoiled. Her shoes stuck to the bloody planks. Her crossbow crashed onto the dock. The woman lurched with a piercing scream and leapt out of the heart, hurling herself at Juva. Nolan came between them. His ax sank into her chest, and the woman stiffened in mid-motion. She was suspended like a phantom before she landed on her back. She lay motionless.

That could have been me.

Skarr was barking now. It got colder, darker. Nolan shook her arm, and she heard her name. She heard Broddmar ask the longshoremen if they knew her.

Who? Me or . . . her?

It didn't matter. What difference did it make? Her tongue found the swelling above her canines, and she stared at the dead woman. This was the wolf-sickness. This was what Gríf had done to her. She would never be older than nineteen.

Is this what I deserve?

All she had done was rid the world of a monster. She had fallen for an all-consuming, immortal beast. In what kind of a world was this a just punishment?

Hanuk handed her the crossbow, and she clutched it between her hands. She closed her eyes and regained her balance, the anger, the rage that kept her alive.

Never let them see a weak blood reader.

She opened her eyes and instantly regretted it. Lok was throwing up over the edge of the dock, and the longshoreman were arguing about how the woman had gotten here. It was hard to say. There were more people at the docks at the moment because they were preparing for the Dragsuget Regatta. The sailing race would take place in just two weeks. Juva looked at the magnificent boats moored along the docks.

"Ship," she mumbled. "She came by ship."

She took a deeper breath and begged her heart to calm down. It was foreboding panic, beating like . . .

Like two! Vardari!

Juva followed the longshoremen with her eyes, the Ring Guards who had arrived, groups of crewmen who stood staring at the dead woman. One of them was a blond man with a crate of food in his arms. Their eyes met, and he dropped the crate and set off at a run.

Juva lunged after him. She slipped in the heart blood but didn't fall. The warow ran as if the devil were on his heels. He leapt onto a small, single-mast boat and started to raise the gangway. Juva jumped up and grabbed hold of it so it banged back onto the dock again. She was up the gangway in two bounds, threw herself over the railing onto the boat, and shot at him. The bolt hit him in the lower leg as he ran. He screamed and fell over sideways.

Someone grabbed her, and she broke free. She brushed Broddmar with her elbow.

"Jufa!"

She pointed her crossbow at the warow, who lay moaning in the bow.

"You knew her! You had her on board, didn't you?"

He clutched his calf with his hands. Blood trickled out around the bolt. Broddmar snatched the crossbow from her.

"Are you out of your mind?! Why in Gaula would he bring

someone with wolf-sickness onto his own boat? What's the damn rush to kill someone who's going to die anyway? Why can't you give them time?"

They're not going to die, and I don't have time!

She looked around for support. For something rock solid to rest her gaze on. Skarr came pulling up the gangway with Muggen in tow. Broddmar and the others were looking at her as if she were crazy. Nothing she said now would get through to them. They wouldn't believe a word of it, so there was no use trying to explain what was going on.

But he can do it . . .

She made the hunting sign for *quiet* and walked over to the warow. She leaned over him and whispered.

"I know you can feel it, smell it. You know that I don't have anything to lose. I can help you. Tell them why, and you can breathe for another day." She backed away again. "Tell them: Why did you have someone with wolf-sickness on board?"

The warow pulled his leg in and winced in pain.

"She wasn't supposed to . . . I have no idea how she got loose. I . . . She wasn't healthy. I took care of her."

Juva gestured with her hands to draw more out of him.

"Tell them that you guys can live off it."

The warow stared at her with something akin to pity. He looked around. The Ring Guard had arrived and stood waiting on the dock. He had nowhere to go, not even if he could have.

"Yes," he said. "Yes, it's possible to live off it."

"Off what?" Broddmar asked.

The man tried to make himself more comfortable without touching the bolt in his calf.

"People with wolf-sickness, the wolf-sick, you can live off their blood, but it's destructive. I haven't . . ."

"You live off . . ." there was a touch of revulsion to Nolan's lips.

"And you create them!" Juva said. "You churn out blood pearls so you'll have enough wolf-sick people around to live forever!"

The warow shook his head.

"I swear, I don't know if blood pearls are being made anymore, and I have no idea where the sick people are coming from. I've heard that, too, but I would never . . . You've got to believe me!"

Juva believed him. The guys' sallow faces told her that they believed him as well.

Muggen gaped at him.

"You guys can live forever this way?"

The warow averted his gaze, as if that were a repugnant accusation, but it was true.

"And it does something to you, right?" Juva caught his gaze again. "It's not exactly good for your health, is it? How much do you know about it?"

"About the Rot? Fylja flay me, I'm barely two hundred years old. I've never seen it! I have no idea what it looks like or what it does."

"I guess the more appropriate question is: How did *you* know that?" Broddmar said, eyeing her.

Juva wiped the sweat on her sleeve and realized she had whale blood on her face.

"I was planning to tell you," she mumbled. "Today, but . . . I found out from Ferkja. She's been following us to locate people with wolf-sickness, so I . . ."

"Pressed her?" Broddmar's eyes glowed a cold, steely blue.

"No! I asked her. I let her follow me, and . . . She said so, said they're going to live forever. That it was all for nothing, that we . . . we failed."

The word tasted poisonous. It felt truer now that she was saying it out loud.

Broddmar walked in a circle and pulled his hand over his close-cropped hair. Hanuk took Juva's crossbow from him and handed it to her, as if to give her something to hold on to. Broddmar pointed to her.

"Don't give her a weapon! She's going to kill him. That's her answer to everything! Jól forbid that there be anything or anyone she can't control."

Juva felt his words harden her. He made it so much easier than she had feared.

"No," she said. "I'm not going to kill anyone. We're going to leave him to the Ring Guard."

"The Ring Guard?" Broddmar cut off his laughter. "What's the difference? They're going to leave him to Silver Throat, and *he's* going to kill him or let him rot in jail."

Juva looked into his eyes, without blinking.

"No, he's going to leave him to the gods."

Broddmar stopped his restless pacing. He looked at her as if she had just driven spikes into him.

"You said yes to him . . ."

She cast a glance at Nolan.

You blabbed.

"Juva . . ." Nolan said, reaching for her.

She pulled away, folded up her crossbow, and hooked it to her back. It was over. Her gaze fell to the ship's deck. There were six planks between her and Broddmar. It might as well have been six thousand. A chasm she would never be able to cross again. But it was exactly what she needed. Distance. Before she became . . . Before the end.

Broddmar clenched his fists.

"Why?! Why in Jól's holy name would you . . . *You* of all people, Jufa! He's a believer from Undst, a cult leader for the nail throats. When were you going to tell me *that*, hmm?"

"Innocent people are dying!" Juva yelled. She pointed to the body on the dock and the split whale heart that had pumped out the last of its blood. "That's why. Because we failed, because it was all in vain!"

"In vain? We saved a life from an eternity in captivity. Isn't that good enough for you?"

Juva clenched her jaws and swallowed the lump in her throat. No, it wasn't good enough for her. If the warow survived, everything she had been through would just be for *him*. For Gríf. A savage from another world who had used her, marked her, and given her wolf-sickness. It was unbearable.

The scar he had given her burned on her chest. She leaned on the gunwale. For a second, she thought she was going to throw up, but she got a grip on herself. She looked down at the Ring Guards on the dock.

She pointed at the wounded man.

"Take him away! Give him to Klemens and Silver Throat."

She stepped onto the gangway and turned to Broddmar again.

"And take Skarr back. I can't have that animal anymore."

Then she left as the guardsmen ran past her up the gangway to board the ship.

LAST RESORT

Eyrir pushed the will toward her, across the polished desk.

"And you're quite sure of this, Frú Sannseyr? There are considerable real estate assets . . ."

The skinny banker clearly didn't take things lightly. This was the third time he had asked.

Juva responded by signing the papers. With her signature, one of the stones around her heart evaporated. One less worry. Stamped with blue and sealed here inside Náklabank. No one would be left wanting after she was gone, not the girls, not her hunting team, not the staff at Vinterhagen.

Unless I fail.

Because what would money matter if the city was drowning in wolf-sick people and warow?

She got up, and Eyrir was quick to do the same. He reached out his hand and smiled warmly.

"And, of course, you must come back and amend it, Frú Sannseyr, when you have children of your own."

The words caught her somewhat off guard. Children? She had chased Kefla off, given Skarr away, and the guys would never forgive her for or understand her saying yes to Silver Throat—especially not Broddmar. She didn't have anyone left. It was just her.

And a fanatic from Undst.

Juva forced herself to smile and thanked him. Her hand felt numb.

She left Náklabank and rounded the hill with the colleges for her most depressing errand: finding a way to die.

The herbalist's shop was characteristically busy. She had hoped to speak to Dr. Eitur one-on-one, but there were three people working and a lot of people waiting. People browsed, gaping at the shelves that filled the rooms from floor to ceiling. Rumor had it there were over six hundred drawers. Customers fiddled with boxes, jars, and bottles, despite the brass signs that clearly said *Do not touch* in multiple languages. But the only thing she could say in Ruvian was *beer*.

A girl was working there, scarcely older than her but with the mark of the herbal guild inked on her arm: a plant growing out of a heart. It sounded like she was explaining to a customer that they were out of something, things they couldn't get anymore.

If you can't find it in Náklav, it's not to be found.

Juva went into the poisons room. It was a popular place with the clientele, more exhibit than shop, filled with the most dangerous substances on Jól's earth. Hundreds of bottles, locked in cabinets, behind glass doors set in wooden frames, carved like grapevines. An elaborate lie that gave the impression they were live-saving elixirs, which seemed like a mockery under the circumstances. Nothing could save her.

Her eyes wandered over the neatly written labels, looking for a way to die as quickly as possible when it became necessary. Preferably something that could mitigate the effect of the wolf-sickness, but if that had existed, it wouldn't be a secret. So she needed something that could kill her instantly.

The vials of poison looked deceptively harmless. Shiny liquids, black seeds, golden salves that could have been honey. She leaned close to the glass and read the descriptions on the cards. What should she choose? Suffocation? Cardiac arrest? Paralysis? She couldn't choose passing away peacefully; that would take too much time, which could cost lives.

Will I even realize it when it's time?

Nothing she had seen as a hunter suggested that. Only Ester. Ester had never had time to lose control. On the contrary, she had planned her own death, chased the guests and staff out of Vinterhagen, sucked the blood of the songbirds that lived there, and sat down to wait for the red hunters.

But that was a luxury Juva didn't have, being able to trust that someone else would help. Even Nolan wouldn't be able to kill her and far less Broddmar.

Laleika had flung herself off the cliff, but people had survived that in the past. And Rugen . . . The gods only knew how he had died. She had almost expected to come upon him, have to pull his teeth in the end, but he must have kicked the bucket somewhere else. Probably in a whorehouse in Kreknabork, full of blood pearls.

No . . . Based on everything she'd seen, only one thing was certain about wolf-sickness. No one died with dignity.

"That bad?"

Juva jumped at the voice. She hadn't noticed anyone come in. Dr. Eitur set a stack of small wooden boxes on the counter.

"So, Frú Sannseyr, bolt poison or hoggthorn?" he asked, taking off his glasses. He patted his hand over the pocket of his buttoned vest without finding what he was looking for. He was charming, Broddmar's age, but far more handsome. Bald and with a goatee, he attracted many people, but his profession made him blind to that.

She felt a pang of uneasiness penetrate her numbness. What if this experienced man could see what was wrong with her? Maybe he could somehow read it off her body, like a blood reader, or smell it, like Skarr.

Get a grip, Juva.

"I've given up hoggthorn," she replied and felt like the esteem she saw in his gaze grew. "But I need stronger bolt poison."

He polished his glasses on his shirt sleeve.

"Strong as in bigger wolves, or . . . ?"

"Or."

He put his glasses on his nose and studied her.

"Hmm. Yes, I heard people got a shock on the docks yesterday. You have your permit with you, yes?"

Juva showed him the newly stamped card. He glanced at it and waved for her to follow him into a back room. She had expected it to be less tidy than the shop, but it was quite the opposite.

The walls were covered with square drawers made of dark wood with brass knobs that showed which were opened most. Some had a shiny luster whereas the others were dull, revealing their pattern of use over time. Small labels hung from each one.

He opened a drawer and peered into it.

"Anesthetic?"

Juva shook her head.

"Give me the strongest you've got. I need to kill someone with wolf-sickness, an adult male, before he has a chance to kill other people."

"Hmm, that's what I was afraid of." He climbed up onto a wooden stepping stool, pulled out a drawer, and held up a sealed bottle the size of a thumb. "I must say, I'm glad, Frú Sannseyr, that I'm on this side of the business and not yours."

Juva looked down and gulped. He was right. She could have done so many other things with her life than this, and now it was too late.

"Does this . . . hurt?" she asked.

He eyed her with one eyebrow raised.

"I doubt they'll have time to feel anything at all before their heart stops, but with wolf-sickness, it probably doesn't matter very much, right? They say wolf-sickness makes a person blind to pain, but you know that better than I, Frú Sannseyr."

Dr. Eitur climbed back down.

"It's expensive, seven runes thirty. We need to handle the payment in the other room." He let her out and then locked the door behind them.

She followed him through the poisons room and into the hectic part of the shop. He opened a thick book and pushed it toward her.

"Sign there, please."

Juva signed, gave him ten runes, and looked around. There was a large basket on the counter full of small linen sacks labeled *wolfsbane*. A little snort escaped her.

"Right?" Dr. Eitur rolled his eyes. "It's essentially sneezing powder, and wolves don't like that, so people believe it protects against wolf-sickness."

"No animal likes sneezing powder."

"That's exactly what I used to tell people, but the more I said it, the more people wanted to buy it! Customers came all the way from Ruv to buy something they thought I was trying to keep secret, and let me tell you, Frú Sannseyr, I don't have time to argue with people. If nothing else, it pays for the cost of producing more important things."

He handed her the small bottle while he emphasized the importance of storing it away from children and making sure it was well labeled.

It's never going to leave my pocket.

She took her change and spotted a stack of drawings by his cash register. A city map for visitors. Náklav was full of them.

A thought struck her, taking shape like a shimmering point of light in her sadness.

"Can I buy some of these?" she asked.

Dr. Eitur gave her almost half the stack.

"Take what you need, the trade guild positively throws them at us." His eyes lingered on her for a moment, then he gave her a green paper cone. "Try this tea, Frú Sannseyr, on the house. It helps many people sleep. That can be difficult during these bright nights and the midnight sun."

Juva took it and turned to go. But her feet wouldn't carry her out of the shop. This might be the last time she was here. She turned back around to face him again.

"You are a beautiful man, Dr. Eitur. I think half of your customers are here more for your sake than for your wares. And that's saying something about such a skilled man. You've been an invaluable help, for many years. Thank you so much, doctor."

Dr. Eitur's cheeks burst into flames, and he adjusted his glasses.

"That was an . . . exceptionally nice thing to say, Frú Sannseyr."

The young woman with the herbal guild mark on her arm suppressed a smile and pretended she hadn't heard. Juva slipped through the customers and out onto the street.

A feeling of urgency chased her toward Myntslaget. She had to talk to the girls while she still had the chance—and the courage. They could be the key to success. How else would she manage to weed out every single vardari in Náklav?

She ran her tongue over the swelling in her gums, checking that she wasn't a danger yet before entering Vinterhagen.

The girls sat in the parlor folding clean laundry. Kefla made a point of not looking at her, whereas little Tokalínn came running, doing her Juva dance.

Juva pushed aside the piles of laundry.

"Girls, you have more important things to do than laundry!"

They peered at her as if she were about to give them even more work. Kefla crossed her arms in front of her chest and leaned back on the sofa in defiance.

Juva tossed the maps onto the table in front of her.

"You want to help? Here you go!"

She looked at each girl in turn.

"You know what I've said: Steer clear of warow. Let your hearts guide you and tell each other where it's safe and where it isn't. But you need to show *me* that, too, and it's our secret."

The girls stared, wide eyed and excited. Juva handed the maps out around the table.

"Spread out all over Náklav and go over the city with a fine-toothed comb! Never go alone, never let them see you, and hide what you're doing. But everywhere you sense them, mark it on the maps. You're hunters now, too. Do you understand?"

Their joyful howls left no doubt that they understood. They threw the piles of laundry up in the air. The clothes rained down and filled the parlor with the scent of freshly washed linen.

Juva leaned over the table to Kefla.

"And you're in charge. The others listen to *you*. But be careful, you understand?"

Kefla rubbed her nose where her freckles almost resembled a scrape, but she couldn't hide her smile. Heimilla rushed in, holding up her skirts, alarmed by the noise. She looked at the clothes strewn across the floor.

"What in the holy name of Jól . . ."

TO DRUKNA

Glasses clinked, shoes clacked, and the hall was filled with small talk and feigned laughter.

Juva drew back, not getting far; she was already standing against the wall. Her dress was damp and tight around her shoulders, but it was the only one in Solde's considerable collection that could be called plain. A simple, gray silk dress, but she thought it was possibly too shiny, a concern that had obviously been completely wasted. Náklav's most influential figures were not here to vanish into the crowd.

Stiff skirts in vivid colors swept across the floor, and countless pieces of jewelry glittered beneath the chandeliers. It was so lavish that at first she thought she was in the wrong place. She had been envisioning a low-key celebration at Nákla Henge with a handful of people, which she had reluctantly said yes to.

But this was no sepulture. This was a party, a grand celebration of sending a man to Drukna. Warow or not, it was eerily tactless.

City council chairman Skattanger gave a pompous speech, mentioning that the room was called King Aug's waiting room. Her mother must have dragged her here as a child because the place tugged at the back of her memory. There was barely a surface that wasn't filled with paintings in gilded frames, and the floor was laid in such a complicated pattern that she suspected it was once meant to entertain the long-since deceased king's guests while they waited.

Juva crept along the wall, which ran in a gentle arc, the only thing that gave away the fact that they were inside the walls of Nákla Henge.

A host with a forced smile held out a tray with stemmed glasses. "Wine from Undst?"

She took one and hoped it would be strong.

The city council chairman intoned about reciprocity and respect, about the friendship between Slokna and Undst, represented by the cooperation between the Seida Guild and the Hallowed. Juva took a sip from the glass and was disappointed at the cheap, sweet wine. She pulled her tongue over her teeth in a grimace and located the tender swelling. She could feel it on the inside and outside of her canines, and it seemed bigger with each day.

She looked around for Drogg. As soon as he had seen she was there, she could leave.

He stood in the front of the hall by the city council chairman who was now ceding the lectern to an official from Undst. Drogg took the opportunity to approach her. His sheepish smile suggested he knew what awaited him.

"Good, good!" he said disarmingly. "You have something to drink."

He did, too, she saw, but something different than she had. It was the first time she had envied someone for drinking milk.

"Is this what you call a few people?" she asked, unwilling to spend time on platitudes.

"As few as it may be, it could hardly have been fewer, and more of the guilds should have been represented, but . . ."

"It's a sepulture, Drogg! You're holding a ball to kill a man!"

A woman who was in danger of being strangled by her own pearls scowled at them and pointedly took a step away so that she could hear the speech better. Drogg pressed his handkerchief to his forehead and pretended he was listening, but he kept talking, quietly out of the corner of his mouth.

"We're holding this sepulture specifically to get *out* of killing a man. My dear, don't forget the benefits. The city council demonstrates productivity. Silver Throat can boast about having the confidence of the Seida Guild. Undst is satisfied and has already indicated they want to help. Everyone wins."

Juva looked at him. He seemed to believe every word he said.

What if it's true?

"Of course you're right," he continued. "This isn't how we do things here, nor will it continue like this. This is just a celebration, this one time."

She raised her glass but remembered the taste and caught herself.

"This one time? Like the previous sepulture he held here? Like when he borrowed a room at Jólshov? Every time you people say *one* time, we can be sure of a new tradition in Náklav."

Drogg hid his smile behind his handkerchief.

"Ah, Juva . . . You're a freshly opened window in a dusty attic. You cause me enough worries, but your honest lack of understanding gives me more joy than I can put into words."

"Honesty isn't a lack of understanding, Drogg. Unless you're a politician."

He let out a belly laugh.

"I'd have liked to see you on the city council. It wouldn't have been boring."

"Boring? You're making theater out of a sepulture. You're falling in line with a priest who's turning the city's residents into fanatics with promises he can't keep. It doesn't seem like you're having a hard time finding things to do."

The official from Undst droned on, thanking Náklav for its benevolence and highlighting opportunities for future cooperation. Promises of help were baked into his pompous sentences.

Drogg nodded to people he knew in the room as he responded quietly to her.

"It will work out. Now that they have the Seida Guild on their team. Now they know we're taking them seriously. That's often all it takes to calm things down."

"You're a councilman," Juva said, stifling a snort. "I'd have expected you to know not everyone calms down when you give in. Many people will take the hand once they get the little finger. How long are you guys going to humor them? Until they're sitting in the royal court in Náklaborg?"

Drogg chuckled as if she had said something clever.

She stared at him with budding concern.

"What?" she said.

Drogg took a sip of white milk from his decorative wine glass.

"Funny you should say that. Silver Throat asked that the queen attend. So, you see, there are limits to our diplomatic obligations."

Until you're desperate enough.

He put his hand on her shoulder.

"Have you not been sleeping well, Juva? You look a little . . . You'll see. It will get better once the nights are dark again."

Juva took a sip from her glass and immediately regretted it. This was no way to spend her final days. She had to get out of here. She nodded toward the speaker.

"Is he going to hold forth for a long time?"

"Hard to say. I've rarely heard a speaker from Undst. Be glad you don't have to give a speech yourself."

As if you would ever let me speak again.

An elderly man with someone who Juva hoped was his daughter came over and laid claim to Drogg without any humility. Juva tried to withdraw, but Drogg put his hand on her shoulder.

"Wait, it's Silver Throat's turn now."

"You're letting the priest speak? To the politicians?"

Drogg looked around, scanning the hall.

"Yes, but I haven't seen him here, so . . . I wonder if . . ."

"No worries," she said dryly. "I dare say he's standing just outside the door."

Juva set her still-full glass on a shelf that ran along the walls. Her dress limited the mobility of her arms, and she felt constrained. Strangled by an article of clothing that would have cost her her life if she were hunting wolf-sick people, impossible to run or defend herself in. Not that she could, anyway; her crossbow and suit were in a cupboard on the floor below. All she had was the knife she had strapped to her inner thigh. And a bottle of poison wedged under her corset in case the sickness caught up to her.

The doors swung open and Silver Throat walked in wearing the spartan linen shirt he had worn at the previous sepulture. He walked toward the lectern and looked around in surprise, as if he hadn't realized everyone would be waiting for him. As if they were honoring him unnecessarily with their silence.

The assembly suddenly seemed as stunned as she was. The most privileged people in the city were visibly uncomfortable at the contrast, to meet a man of God. He put on that strange, impassive smile that she felt anything but sure about. It was secretive, smug, and threatened to turn at any moment. He raised his chin as if to draw attention to the nail in his silver collar.

"There you have it," Silver Throat said. "Send the priest up and watch the room collapse."

It took a second before people realized he was joking. A timid laugh spread cautiously through the room, and he winked, as if to all of them.

"I know what people are saying about us," he continued, pointing with both hands to his own chest. "Fanatics from Undst. They call us bestial killjoys, judges. They say we want to deny people everything that gives life meaning." He smiled broadly, full of flirtation. "Beer, money, women, men . . ."

Each word elicited laughter, gradually getting louder.

"The truth is that we're not so different. I thought I wanted to be a politician once, too, but then God found me. And now . . ." His gaze wandered from face to face. "Now I don't get a moment's peace!"

Laughter exploded in the room. Drogg nudged her in the side, as if to say, *There, you see? He's not so bad.*

Juva realized her mouth was hanging open. She had thought Lagalune was good at reading people, but Silver Throat would have made even her mother sweat.

He waved his hand in false modesty and silenced the hall again.

"Yes, I talk to God. Don't ask me which one; they're all one. But to tell the truth, I don't make a big deal out of it, not at all. Nor am I here to recruit for the Hallowed, so you can relax." He squeezed his thin silver collar necklace between his fingers. "But if you should be tempted, we have these without nails, too. Also in mother of pearl, the latest from Thervia."

His eyes swept over the room and stopped on hers. He held the eye contact as he allowed the laughter to die down in the room. None of what he had said was terribly funny, but Juva knew what he was playing at. No one would have expected this from a fanatic from Undst. There wasn't a soul left in the room who remembered that this was actually a sepulture.

Enough was enough. Juva headed for the doors and heard him yell her name.

"Juva Sannseyr!"

She stopped, painfully aware that everyone was looking at her. She turned toward him and forced herself to smile.

"Juva Sannseyr," he repeated. "I want to direct a big thank you to the Seida Guild's youngest guild master ever. The heir of Lagalune Sannseyr is a hunter of rank, fearless in the face of evil, and she has an unrivalled gift for catching its scent. No fang escapes her."

Juva clenched her teeth to maintain her smile, but his words made that difficult. He spoke as if he knew.

He means it figuratively. He doesn't know anything.

"I'm proud," he continued. "Proud to be working with her. And even if her abilities as a hunter far exceed anything I could hope for, we share the belief that a city without warow is a city without sin. Vardari are the source of the plague that ravages the world's henge cities, Náklav more than any of them. This truth was an infected boil no one wanted to touch until Juva Sannseyr lanced it right here in Nákla Henge in that speech none of us will forget. Together, we will take Slokna and the world into the future. No foaming wolf-sickness, no more executions in the streets, cash for teeth, or blood offering for the stones." He closed his eyes to the hall again. "And you call *us* barbarians?"

More laughter. He had talked his way into a free pass, and she could see that he knew it. He accepted a glass and raised it as he looked at her.

"The world will never be free as long as the devil walks the streets. But God is nothing if not perfect, so as of today, we will entrust the judgment of the fangs to him. Without killing, without bleeding. We send them to Drukna, because even fangs should be treated with dignity, the true mark of Náklav and civilization. And God shows us the way!"

He turned to one of his helpers, the ones he flattered by calling "initiates," and accepted a box, which Juva recognized right away.

The images! He's brought the silver images!

An excited whisper ran through the hall as he opened the hinged box and set it on the shelf behind him. Three small silver plates gleamed against the dark lining.

What a fool she had been to come here! The city council was wrong. This man had not come to calm anything at all. He had brought the likenesses he claimed to have gotten from God—and why shouldn't he? Náklav was widely known for its love of curiosities.

Juva stared at Drogg.

"How could . . . Who let him do this?"

Drogg was sporting a rare frown.

"No one, as far as I know."

The most curious crowded forward for a glimpse of the increasingly famous idols, while others made do with congratulating each other, as if gathering in the same room were an achievement. Someone held out a hand to her, and she got goosebumps when she realized she had just officially become part of the team.

Silver Throat pushed his way between her and the outstretched hands, like a savior. He asked the others to excuse them for a second. Then he put his arm around her shoulder and led her past the curtains with the decorative beaded hem and out onto the gallery outside.

He leaned against the wall in one of the archways and looked out at the circle of stones as he lit a cigar.

His eyes wandered over her body.

"Very becoming," he said, without any sign of an ulterior motive. But she had thought that the first time she met him, too. He had just sat down and started reading, as if he hadn't given her a thought. Maybe that hadn't been a chance encounter at all?

Juva got goosebumps. She had the unpleasant feeling that she was the seasoning on a much larger meal.

"You call that performance low-key?" she asked. "And I thought we agreed to mention the Seida Guild but not me."

He averted his gaze as he smiled a tad disdainfully, as if he had heard something so unbearably silly that he couldn't be bothered to look at her.

"Well, I've heard that you also surprise people with your speeches."

She crossed her arms in front of her chest and looked down at the henge below. Menhirs, giants towering in a ring, practically the same height as where they were standing. The Witness glowed with the intense bluish-green of verdigris copper, catching the light from the many corpsewood lanterns around the square.

He blew smoke out of his mouth and laughed briefly.

"You take things too hard, Juva. We have the same goal, and this will help us. Smile, girl! Tonight we sepulture our first vardari."

"The same goal? My goal is not that the whole city should become red hunters, but the way you're carrying on . . ."

"Ah, yes . . . the likenesses? You would prefer to hide them? If he chose you, of all the people in the world, you would deny God's word?"

The words suited him, a delicate balancing act between self-aggrandizement and self-deprecation.

"Which god?" she asked. "You use so many of them that it's hard to keep track."

His smile faded with frightening abruptness.

"Derision? Is that all you have to offer? The images are genuine. They show real evil, real vardari. If you're in doubt, then go look at them rather than fear his word."

Juva took the invitation to go, but he grabbed her elbow and held her back.

"You're lucky that I am who I am, Juva Sannseyr. I know you have a gift, but who else would interpret it that way?" He nodded to the doors to the hall, which stood open. "These people would see something entirely different in such a gift. A nose for the devil; isn't that the devil himself? Few would understand the way I do."

He knows!

Her thoughts ran to the dagger resting against her thigh, as if the threat were immediate and lethal. But this was only a game. So far.

She pulled her arm back with forced calm.

"Where do you get these ideas from?"

He stared at her with a look worthy of a fanatic.

"You forget that I talk to God."

Juva left him and went back into the hall. She stopped reluctantly in front of the images, hesitating as if it would validate them to be seen, but she couldn't help herself. Three unfamiliar faces looked back at her in warm shades of gray. But one of them . . .

I know him!

It was the warow they were about to sepulture. The man she had shot in the calf. His hair was different and his facial features softer, but it was him. It wasn't possible . . .

Juva squinted at the image. It was lifelike, like a disgusting dream. Smooth as the silver plate it sat on, not like any painting she had seen. Yes, they had had him in custody for a few days, and he had time to make it, but . . . She fought the urge to touch it, to feel for the brushstrokes even though she had an unsettling feeling that she wasn't going to find any.

How does he do that?!

She knew he was watching her. Following her from outside, gleefully anticipating her reaction. He forgot that she was a blood reader. She didn't need to know how he swindled people to know that he did.

Still . . .

Juva hurried out of the hall and down the stairs. She went to the closet to retrieve her jacket and backpack, but she stopped with her hand on the handle. Her heart had been joined by what she knew was the evening's guest of honor, the warow, the man who was to be sepultured.

They were keeping him in the room next to her. It was unguarded. The door was ajar, and she heard two Ring Guards talking outside.

Juva felt an intense urge to see him. As if that would disprove the picture. She cautiously opened the door and went in.

He was sitting on a bench, his arms crossed as if hugging himself. A touch of anger in the dull look showed that he remembered her from the docks. She had hoped he would look different, that he wouldn't resemble the picture, but it was him. Pale, as if he were already dead, and with a dark bruise on his jaw.

"Did you come to say goodbye?" he asked sourly.

She didn't have a good response.

This room was colder than the hall, and she rubbed her arms, which was challenging in Solde's dress. It occurred to her how out of place she must look in what was clearly a storeroom.

He watched her with disgust.

"I know you're going to send me to Drukna. Because Jól wants that. Do you believe in Jól? Do you believe in any god?" Talking seemed to take a toll on him; he did not look well.

"I doubt it." Juva forced herself to smile. "But I've seen the devil."

"Haven't we all, in one way or another?" the warow said, chuckling.

Juva felt like she ought to say something, but the words remained a heavy fog in her mind. Shadows of apologies she didn't owe him, explanations he didn't need, and contempt for things he might not be responsible for. But he was a warow. She couldn't go to her death knowing they would continue their eternal, messed up lives. At the expense of ordinary people who came down with wolf-sickness and attacked each other. That was too horrible of a reality, to live with or to die with. Blood readers would never be safe.

The girls would never be safe.

Juva moved closer with new courage. An unexpected touch of fear crossed his face.

"It's you guys or us," she said. "You get eternal life. We pay the price. We've always paid the price. We're the ones who come down with wolf-sickness and attack our own like wild animals. And every time that happens, I'm the one who has to clean up the streets. Find them. Stop them. I've bled women and men, young and old. I once bled a pregnant woman, so forgive me, vardari, if I don't indulge you with another eternity."

She caressed her budding fangs with her tongue, and the thought came again: Was this her or was it the sickness talking?

"Take comfort in the fact that you will have a respectable death," she said. "He wants that, Silver Throat. He just said that: even fangs deserve dignity."

"Dignity?" The warow let out an exhausted laugh. "Him? He doesn't know the meaning of the word! Do you know what they do with people where he comes from? Ask him! Ask him about the nail. In Undst, you are born sinful, and they need to get the devil out of you before you . . ."

He slumped on the bench as if he gave up.

Juva fought against a compassion she could not afford. But she lost nothing by making it easier for him. She gulped.

"I have poison. It's painless."

"No, thank you. I'd rather take my chances with Gaula."

Juva stepped over to him. He sat motionless, his head bent forward. She pulled up the skirt of her dress and put her foot on the bench next to him. Her thigh touched his cheek and he turned toward it. Grazed his nose over her skin and inhaled the scent.

"This isn't poison," he whispered and looked up at her.

Juva drew the knife and placed the tip against her thigh until the blood trickled out.

"You're on your way to Drukna. It can't hurt anyone. And I said I could help."

He leaned his forehead against her thigh. Cool, but sweaty. He opened his mouth and brought his lips over the cut, lapping up the blood like a suckling piglet. She could feel his tongue and teeth working against her skin, and suddenly Gríf was there, in her thoughts. So strong and real that she backed away and let her skirt fall again.

The warow closed his eyes and bit his bloody lip. He let his head loll backward and laughed quietly. He looked at her again with tears in his eyes, but a stronger man all the same.

"You hunt and kill your own?"

The two Ring Guards came in and jumped when they saw her.

Juva flung out her arms.

"I cannot find my things," she said in a frustrated voice that said it hadn't even occurred to her that she had no business here.

"A leather backpack, I'm sure that I . . ."

"Everything is in the closet out here, Frú Sannseyr. Come, it's not safe for you to be . . ."

The guard swallowed his final words when he remembered who she was.

The sound of jovial guests spread into the stairwell, and she left them with a smile. The civil servants had grown tipsy, but they were able to make their way down and out into the square in a disorderly line. Drogg came over to her eagerly, clearly excited. He leaned toward her and whispered.

"Juva, they've already sent the ships! I never thought I'd get to see—"

"The ships? With a cure?"

"Just between us! I wouldn't have dared to reveal it to you if it weren't extremely important that you understand the significance of what you're doing, of your being here. They hope to make it here for the Dragsuget Regatta. That will be a wonderful celebration of the cure. Or . . . it's not a cure, I've realized, but something that prevents people from getting sick. I was almost moved to tears, I must admit."

His words were a mockery. A disgusting weight in her chest. It wasn't true, not a word of it, she was sure of that. But even if it had been true, it would still have been too late for her, anyway.

"It's something in their diet, I understand," Drogg continued, blind to her pain. "And apparently they've been working with it for generations!"

Working for generations with a disease they don't have there?

Silver Throat gathered all the guests around the dead pair of stones. Then the Ring Guard walked over with the warow between them. The many arches surrounding Nákla Henge seemed to stare like coal-back eyes.

She wasn't sure what she had been expecting, but Silver Throat treated the warow as if he were one of his own dead. He lit branntang in a yarn lantern and put it in the man's lap as if the lantern could ever protect a man in Drukna. He tied the rope around the warow's waist. Then he said a few words that Juva was glad she was standing too far away to hear.

The warow turned around and looked into her eyes. She thought he was smiling. Then he walked between the stones and vanished with the echo in her heart.

THE ARTIST

The Floa wind swept through the streets, stronger every day. If it continued to pick up, it would be the wildest Dragsuget Regatta in living memory. There was a significant risk of capsizing when circumnavigating Náklav, not that that stopped anyone from taking part in the regatta. To the contrary. The desire to show heroism was impressive, as if being the first one through Dragsuget—named for its dangerous undertow conditions—was worth more than life itself.

This might be the last time she watched the boats foam their way through the waves under Ulebru Bridge. Or maybe it would all be over before then.

No!

There wasn't a lot of hard-and-fast knowledge about the course of wolf-sickness, but she had half a month. She needed that if she was going to fit everything in . . .

Juva stared at the drawing and couldn't help but smile. The girls had exceeded all her expectations. They had been scouring the city for several days and had combined their maps into one for Juva. A complete picture of Náklav's beating hearts.

Tokalínn had decorated it with a drawing of a fanged monster, which was considerably less scary than the warow. They had thrown themselves into the task as if it were a matter of life and death—without suspecting that it actually was.

Every instance of sensing was labeled with a small triangle, representing a fang. Orange where the anxiety seemed stationary, and red where it was moving, like when a vardari walked by or was otherwise in motion. The girls were most strongly opposed to the red ones, and she understood how they felt. She had lived with the panic, which could arise and then vanish just as suddenly, with no inkling of where it came from. Helplessly ignorant. It elicited a paralyzing fear that the girls would never need to experience.

She had hoped that *no one* would need to experience it. That the warow would kick the bucket, and that she herself would have all the time in the world to teach each fresh blood reader what ailed their heart, but nothing had turned out the way she'd expected.

She was going to die. And if the warow were going to die, too, then she had to kill them herself.

The wind tugged at the map so its corners flapped. Juva folded it up and hid it in the inside pocket of her red hunting jacket. She knew which mark she was going to cross off that night. It had been carefully chosen to create the minimum number of challenges for a new hunting team.

She looked around for Skarr before she remembered that she had handed him over to Broddmar. She felt naked without him. It was like going hunting but leaving one arm at home.

She neared Nákla Henge, relieved to see that they had stopped checking people's teeth for the day. Not that she had a travel card, and they wouldn't have bothered checking her anyway, but all the same . . . The feeling of being dangerous felt hard to conceal.

The cargo haulers inside had started stacking up their wares. Pallets of crates grouped and labeled with codes. Parts of something bigger that couldn't be carried through the stones without first being disassembled. If the burden was too heavy, it might be lost on the journey. They said the same was true of people, too, if they refused to let go.

Would that be better than poison? To just walk through the stones and disappear into an eternal, dark undertow?

Outside the teahouses, the hosts cleared the tables, and the guardsmen chatted their way through the shift change. The only unusual thing was the group hanging around outside the Ring Guard office.

There were about twenty of them: a mixture of guards, watchmen, and civilians. Two of them sat on the ground but got to their feet when they saw her. Juva realized they were there for her sake.

This was the team they expected her to work with to hunt the warow. She stared at them in disbelief. A clearly inexperienced slacker with his hands in his pockets. A woman who had lost one of the clasps off her leather armor and was fiddling around trying to tie it. Two men who were play fighting with swords, hardly better than children. She counted five members of the Hallowed wearing silver collars, including one guy with a spear. A spear! What in Jól's name did they think was going to happen?!

No amateurs, she had said . . .

Juva walked past them and pretended not to notice their furtive glances. The iron door was open, and she entered the small office. There was no one to see behind the stacks of cards, maps, scrolls, and stamps, but she followed the sound of cursing into the back room.

Klemens and a guy she didn't know were squatting down, tinkering with the blood tap. The device looked like a complicated water pump. Gleaming copper piping ran along the walls and down into a rusty drain that was spitting blood up onto the floor. Klemens tightened a nut, but his hold slipped, and he swore again. Juva cleared her throat.

Klemens glanced at her.

"They're waiting outside, all of them," he said and kept tinkering with the metallic monster that provided liquid nourishment to the stones.

"I saw," she replied. "And that's not going to work. My impression was that I had been invited to choose from an established and experienced group."

Klemens stood and wiped the blood off his hands with a rag.

"We have too much to do as it is and have lost people to Krekabork and Skippalun. Many people prefer to work in henge cities that have fewer cases of wolf-sickness, so what you see is what we have to spare. You can't have any more, Sannseyr."

"I don't want more. I want fewer. We're hunting for a person in the middle of Náklav! We can't just spread out in a big line and walk through the city trying to flush out the warow."

"Well," Klemens sighed, "at least that's a problem that can be solved."

Juva peeked at the blood still regurgitating up onto the floor.

"Unlike that one there?"

Klemens limped over to a shelf and grabbed a new tool.

"Dry clots clogging up the pipes. It's the same everywhere, from here to Au-Gok."

"Can't you use red clover? It stinks, but it works in the bloodskins."

"We've always used the same mixture as the other henges, but the guy who usually delivers it decided to disappear without a trace from Slokna, so we're scraping by on leftovers." He waved her out. "I'll be right there. Pick out the guys you need, Sannseyr, but make sure that you choose *someone* who—"

"Has a nail on his neck—got it. Jól forbid we think about survival instead of politics."

Juva headed back out and stopped in the doorway, scrutinizing the group for people she thought she could trust. And who could trust each other. If anyone lost their life, it would be her fault. Should she call off the whole hunt? With a little training, they would improve. They just needed a little time to . . .

What time? There was no time left.

No. She needed to take a chance and pick. Who here could replace Broddmar? The man was sixty and had lost his desire to do the work, but still, no one here could measure up to him. Who could think like Nolan and work in a team like Muggen? Was anyone here as caring as Lok? Could they run or laugh like Hanuk?

Juva gulped. The guys would never support her in this hunt; she had already known that before she said yes to Silver Throat. Sadness was a waste of energy. If she was going to compare, there was only one thing that mattered: some hunters were here, others weren't. It was as simple as that.

Klemens appeared beside her and nodded to one of the Hallowed, a robust man in his thirties who stood waiting, chin up, thumbs hooked into his belt.

"Tord. He needs to go. He's the leader of the nail throats to the extent that they have one. Besides, it's always possible they're better than you think." He rubbed his face and got a trace of blood on his forehead.

"Maybe," she replied, not believing it. She pointed to the ones sitting on the ground. "I'll take those two. They understand that you've got to rest when you can. And her, the one who tied her broken strap. She can improvise. Him, the one who's double-checking how his shoelaces are tied, and . . . Tord. No more."

Klemens eyed her with what she would have interpreted as appreciation on a better day, but it had been a while since she'd had any of those. Her muscles ached. Irritation and a sore jaw reminded her that she had no time to lose.

Juva took a couple of steps toward the herd.

"Listen, I appreciate your being here, but there are too many of you. This is not a search party for a missing person. We need to be cunning and avoid making noise. I wouldn't even be wearing red if it weren't necessary, but when all Drukna breaks loose, people need to be able to see who we are. To know that we have the right to be doing what we're doing."

Her words elicited nervous looks, giving away the most inexperienced. She allowed them to silently tell her who they were as she continued.

"That means no long scabbards, no clubs, no spears. We need crossbows that can be hidden on our backs, nothing bigger. And no armor."

The woman unstrapped her leather armor. Juva pointed to her and the others she had chosen, one by one. They took a couple of steps forward without gloating, which made her feel more confident about her choices.

Klemens armed them with crossbows, considerably less discreet than her own and probably nowhere near as effective. They didn't fold up, either, but at least everyone seemed to have used one before.

Then they followed her out the west gate while Tord drowned her in questions about strategy and how they were going to find and catch warow when there were so few of them. Juva assured him that she knew where they needed to go and explained that the information came from a rumor. If nothing else, that meant Silver Throat had kept her ability to sense to himself.

Juva had memorized the map and led them northeast down Murgata and out toward Tunga, the point at the tip of the island, while she explained the most basic of the hand signals. *Wait, come, split up, shoot.* The wind got worse the farther out they got, as if it wanted to shame them for their voyage. It howled through the narrow passageways, and she could hear the sea boiling against the rocks.

The old city walls gradually came into view on either side as space became more limited. They crept closer and closer until they met at the old lighthouse, Náklav's outermost tip. The massive tower had served its time but hadn't been used since they moved the docks to Nyhavn.

Juva slowed down and raised her hand to slow the others. She studied their surroundings. The tower was part of a larger building complex, and like everything else, it had melted into the rest of the city. It was densely built up and hard to get an overview of, but this should still be a simple arrest. The plan was to minimize the risk of injury. There was nowhere to flee when you were squeezed into a corner.

The stone buildings were some of the oldest in the city, crooked and leaning, but the doors were unusually elaborate. Painted in intense colors and decorated with figures. A woman stood in a backyard, taking dyed yarn down from a clothesline curving in the wind.

She spotted them and hurried indoors, leaving the rest of the yarn hanging. Dead Man's Horn or not, a red hunter was bad news.

Juva approached the door to the lighthouse and felt from the tingling in her heart that she was on the right path. She shushed the others who came tramping along behind her. Then she unhooked the crossbow from her back and unfolded it with a snap. The few souls out vanished in a flash.

The door was decorated with a white clay figure, a falling bird. The motif seemed as fragile as the material.

She gestured to the others to spread out and hoped they had the sense to do it as soon as they got inside. Tord nodded and waved the others closer. Juva braced the crossbow against her chest and put a hand on the doorknob. The door was unlocked. It creaked open, but the only heartbeat that sped up was her own.

Maybe the warow was asleep? Or hard of hearing?

Juva stepped inside and stood face-to-face with a ghost. She jumped before she realized it was a statue, a naked man made of stone with his hands outstretched as if he were waiting for her to give him something. She clenched her crossbow tightly and slowly exhaled.

The front porch opened into a large workshop. Two blocks of stone towered by the door, and vast canvases stood stacked in groups. Some white, some with motifs she couldn't interpret in the semi-darkness. A multitude of clay masks and sketches covered the walls, and sculptures threw long shadows across the scarred wooden floor toward her.

A thin man stood with his back to them, painting a canvas. Juva held her breath. He used tiny, intense motions, as if he were racing against the dying light from the mullioned window that covered most of the wall. It looked centuries old. The panes of glass were warped in their frames.

Half the ceiling had been removed to make room for an enormous statue of a wolf. Unfinished. It looked as if the animal were still fighting its way out of the stone. A crooked spiral staircase wound its way to the floor above, and she could hear the wind whistling through a window up there.

The sketches rustled in the draft, as if they were breathing.

Moving shadows revealed that the others had entered. They walked past her, spread out, and flanked the warow. He had no idea they were there. Juva could feel his heart, both close and distant at the same time. He stood a few paces ahead of her but might as well have been in another world.

Juva stared at his canvas and the all too familiar face that stared back. Her stomach tensed in anguish.

Nafraím . . .

Tord stared at her questioningly, and for a second, she felt exposed, naked. But then it dawned on her that he was waiting for confirmation. Juva nodded and instantly regretted it.

"Turn around, vardari!" Tord's voice shattered the silence and interrupted the artist's battle with the shadows under Nafraím's eyes.

The warow stood with his back to them, frozen, as if he knew what awaited him. Then he turned and stared at Juva with an out-of-place smile on his lips.

He was younger than she had thought—under forty—although she had no idea why she had expected an elderly man. He raised his hands as if to surrender, but she knew that was a lie. The look in his eyes was that of someone who would never give up. No fear, no surprise.

Would he come willingly?

Juva doubted it, but she opened her mouth to explain. Tord threw the rope to one of the guys, who walked right over to the warow.

"No!" Juva reached for him, but it was too late. The artist grabbed the rope, and in a flash, he had wrapped it around the young man's neck. The Hallowed man gurgled and fought against the superior force, who forced him to his knees. The warow stared obstinately at her, with a tight hold on the rope. The tip of a dagger glimmered in his other hand.

Tord rushed toward them. Juva fired. The bolt sliced the warow's neck and vanished through the canvas. It rained red over Nafraím's face. The warow fumbled for something to hold on to and crashed into a shelf of boxes. A myriad of paintbrushes drummed onto the floor. Then he keeled over.

Tord unwound the rope from the young guy, who gasped for air.

Two hearts pounded in a race inside her, and one was losing. She could feel him dying, bleeding out on the floor. The sight awakened her instincts, and she yanked the bloodskins off her back. The blood would go to the stones. Maybe that would help Klemens with the clotting.

She barked out orders to the wide-eyed hunters, who had obviously realized why they were there. One of them managed to help her by lifting the warow. That didn't last long. He threw up when she drove the spout into the dead man's neck. The bloodskin swelled between her hands. She shivered, not understanding why. She could do this! She had done this many times before.

Not like this. Not like now.

The young guy was kneeling next to her, as if in a trance. He was rubbing his neck where the rope had tightened. He seemed shocked to still be alive.

"The nail," he mumbled. "Silver Throat saved me. God saved me."

She clenched her teeth and struggled to keep from hitting him. She didn't know him. She didn't know any of them. They stood around her, bewildered and staring.

"What are you guys waiting for?!" she yelled. "Fetch the Ring Guard and the corpse carriage!"

Two of them disappeared from the room, too willingly. Tord hesitated.

"But—" he began.

"Now! Get out of here!"

Her outburst sent them heading for the door. She sank onto the floor and sat against the wall with a bloodskin in her lap. The dead artist lay on his belly in front of her. In his hand, he held what she had thought was a dagger. It was a painting knife. Blunt. Harmless.

Her chest tightened, and she felt like she might break.

Nafraím stared at her from the canvas. The bolt had made a tear by his ear, but he had escaped unharmed. A couple of nearly burned down candles on a workbench made his inscrutable eyes seem eerily alive. He rested his chin on his knuckles with his thumb pushing up against his lower lip as if he were studying her in deep concentration. A picture of a learned man. Only the drops of blood from the painter revealed the beast behind the noble shell, the murderer, the warow. The man who had captured Grif and changed the world forever, changed *her* forever.

"Why won't you die?" she whispered. "Why do none of you want to die? You're like . . . like *him*."

Grif.

Only a few weeks of her life, and it was as if nothing else had ever existed, not before him and not after him.

She closed her eyes, squeezing the bloodskin warm with warow blood. Eternal blood because it had traces of him, created and re-created by him. Her unquenchable desire. Her murderer. Grief would continue to chop away at her as long as there were warow. Her mind would continue to darken until they were dead—or until *she* was.

Hundreds of vacant eyes watched her from the walls, from masks and paintings. Waiting for an explanation, as if she were before the council. As if she hadn't already been sentenced to death.

I can't take it anymore.

Her scar itched, as if it were screaming for something, demanding something. She touched it, but her fingers were sticky with blood. She stared at them, and they seemed to come closer to her lips on their own until they touched her tongue. It tasted like sweaty steel.

It's over. The sickness has taken me.

Her eyes stung, and she squeezed them shut. She fumbled for the bottle of poison but abruptly stopped. Had she heard something? The wind made the windowpanes rattle. The candles flickered. Her heart was joined by company, squeezed between two others.

Juva grabbed her crossbow and got to her feet. Pulled out a new bolt and placed it in the groove. Carefully. Where were they?

The rhythms felt familiar. She had sensed them before. One of them was standing right outside, but the other one . . . Juva looked up. A shadow swept by, and a woman dropped down by the spiral staircase.

I'm surrounded!

She was caught in her own trap, cornered without anything but

179

the rocky coastline and the sea around her. Two warow, one bolt. Would she have time to load a new one if she shot right away?

A man appeared in the doorway as if to confirm the thought. The woman approached her slowly, like a predator. Power in every step. Her clothes were so tight that they could have been painted on her strong body. She was dark with rust-colored curls, a rain of pale freckles on her face, as Ruvian as could be.

Juva held her in her sights and realized that she had seen her before, seen them both.

The pictures!

The woman stared at the dead man, and her eyes hardened.

"Where is he?" she asked in a deep voice that trembled with self-restraint. The woman's heart smoldered like embers against her own. The man's was softer, although he looked like a wild man, muscular, with long hair that resembled tree roots. He must have crocheted his sweater himself.

His eyes seemed laden with grief. He was probably the only one of the two who had realized they would never find the devil.

"Don't be scared," he said so gently she almost believed him. "We just need to know where he is. That's all."

Juva chuckled coolly.

"He's gone forever."

The woman pulled a curved knife and lunged toward Juva with a roar. Juva gave a start and shot her crossbow. She heard the bolt hit the wall. The door banged open. A man's yell echoed through the room, and it sounded like another bolt hit the wall. The woman whipped around and strode up the spiral stairs in a couple of leaps, with her partner on her heels. Juva heard them pull open a window. They left it open, banging in the wind.

Silver Throat came walking in from the front porch. He pulled a knife out of the wall and sheathed it in his jacket.

"Did you see them?" he asked. "Do you know who they were?"

Juva shook her head, unwilling to say a word about his likenesses. That would be a confirmation. That would be agreeing that he was right.

She let her crossbow drop. The fear seeped out of her body, taking the last of her energy with it. She dropped down onto the floor again.

Silver Throat pointed to the dead man.

"You call this arresting? Did you at least question him about where more of them might be hiding?"

His question revealed that he had not met very many warow. Juva hadn't met that many herself, but she couldn't imagine they would betray each other.

"You followed me?" She scowled up at him.

He stepped over the dead man and sat down beside her. His gruff expression softened into indulgence, a shift that happened more quickly than in a child. There was something creepy about it, as if he wasn't actually feeling anything at all, just imitating.

"I was worried. It was your first hunt with the new team, and I was afraid someone would take advantage of the opportunity. And I was right."

Congratulations.

"It seemed prudent," he continued. "Just this once."

"Yes," Juva said, looking at him. "That's your method for everything, isn't it?"

He smiled and looked away.

"You're right," he said. "We'll obviously have to do this several times so you don't kill everyone before I get to talk to them."

She folded up her crossbow.

"Mm, I noticed that you had *talked* to the guy you sepultured, too." Her words seemed to make no impression on him. She glanced at the wall where his knife had been.

"What kind of priest are you, actually?"

181

"A prepared one." He looked around the workshop. "It's a shame. He had some beautiful paintings."

"Yes, you would think they came from God."

Irritation flitted across his face for a second, but it ended in laughter.

"Juva, I was joking! When I said that God had told me about your gift, your ability to sense this scum . . . When you actually get images from God, you don't need to pretend anymore." He leaned his head against the wall and looked at her. "That warow we sepultured said that. During the interrogation."

Juva felt sick to her stomach. She got up and gathered the bloodskins.

"I don't hunt for warow because it gives me pleasure," she said. "I don't enjoy it. I do it because I have to. But if you lay a hand on anyone during questioning, warow or not, then I've hunted for you for the last time. We're not animals. Do you hear what I'm saying?"

His laughter rang out in the room.

"You shot him in the leg!" He appeared to realize that she wasn't going to laugh it off and averted his gaze. "If you had any idea what it's cost me to be here, you would view me with less contempt. Undst has . . . traditions. Customs that no one here would tolerate; they're not wrong when they say that. It's a fact. The most bestial things always happen behind closed doors, and Undst *has* no doors. Our collaboration with Náklav will give us the freedom that was stolen from us. And we will show the way to enlightenment, you and I, Juva."

His nail caught the light, gleaming against his throat. It didn't look like the others'. This one was either silver-plated or forged from pure silver. It had a faint curvature, as if it had been used, and she remembered that he had called it a keepsake.

She walked over to the wall and pulled the bolt out. It had splintered at the tip. Useless.

"Okay, okay!" Silver Throat stood up. "You have my word, Juva.

It's easy to give; we don't torture anyone unnecessarily. I just want to be rid of them, all of them, so we can avoid all this."

Juva looked at him, realizing that this was probably the only thing they agreed on.

THE PARTY

"Has something spoiled your appetite?"

Eydala broke the oppressive silence with forced cheerfulness. Nafraím didn't answer. The table was covered with food, and he couldn't see or smell anything obviously wrong with it. Had he not been bound at both hand and feet, he would hardly have been able to control himself, but the only thing that was placed in front of him was a wineglass. He could reach it if he wanted to.

The shirt she had dressed him in itched and smelled of old perfume. Unused for centuries, like everything else in this abandoned palace. The silverware was tarnished, and the heavy draperies were faded. Dust-free patches of brighter red revealed where Eydala had touched them when she had closed them. He could just make out the sky through a crack at the top. Dark with heavy clouds.

He should say thank you and get home before the rain came.

The thought caught him off guard, a reflex after countless dinner parties over the centuries. Absurd for someone who would never again leave a party. That certainty was merciless, a fresh and unexpected pain.

He lowered his gaze to his hands to hide that he was struggling, and it hit him that they seemed alien, old and anemic. If it hadn't been for the scar that buried itself under his shirt sleeve, he would hardly have believed it was his own. The rope forced him to keep his hands folded in prayer. He didn't think he had ever prayed in his life.

His joints ached. He must have consumed enough sickle flower to drown a whale. A dose here, a dose there, every time she needed to knock him out to set up a new performance.

This time she had gone for a seemingly ordinary dinner, as if they were a family. She sat at the end of the table across from him, and Rugen sat in the middle of the long side, shoveling in food as if there wasn't much time.

Eydala cast an irritable glance at the boy. Her silence appeared to require significant self-control. She rubbed a discolored finger against her temple, something she did with increasing frequency. Frequent headaches, tremors, madness . . . Terribly visible evidence of the rottenness she was incubating, but she would never admit that she had been poisoned. It was tempting to hope the sea silver she used to develop the images would kill her before the Rot took over, but Nafraím feared he had run out of luck.

"Oh, yeah! Mikkel is dead," Eydala said suddenly with renewed schadenfreude. "Did I mention that? Was it Mikkel, the painter?"

Mikkje . . .

Nafraím pursed his lips to suppress the twitch at the corner of his mouth, but her smile indicated that she had seen it. He had imagined the worst, many times, over and over again. Steeled himself to the unavoidable news of more dead friends, but what he never got over was the flippancy with which she broke the news. As if she had never felt grief and wanted to inflict it to observe how it turned out.

She skewered a boiled beet with her fork.

"I'd forgotten his name. He used so many names when he signed his schlocky paintings. An overrated artist, I've always said that. Tell me, what's the point to making art when it bears no resemblance to reality?"

Nafraím closed his eyes. Nothing he said could remedy her non-sense. Mikkje's paintings appeared in his memory by turns, as if he were falling past them. Bold and vivid, with multi-colored brush strokes, imitated all over the world. As a warow, he had never been able to enjoy fame, just used a series of different names. He was probably the only painter who had ever been accused of copying himself.

"He died as he lived. Uselessly." Her words made Rugen laugh scornfully with food in his mouth, and she cast him another icy look before she continued. "She's a wonder with the crossbow, the blood reader. And you said she would never hunt us. Do you remember that, hmm? Now Juva Sannseyr is eating out of Silver Throat's hand like a dog!"

Eydala tossed her head and laughed, silently as usual.

Rugen soaked up the last of the sauce from his plate.

"Juva . . . Damn, she's fine . . ." Rugen muttered and licked his fingers. "I'll soon fill that clam of hers until she tears."

Eydala looked at the boy with obvious disgust.

"Rugen, why would I grant eternal life to someone who cannot behave himself? Hmm?"

Rugen swallowed a mouthful and met Nafraím's gaze, as if Nafraím's presence should somehow spare him from criticism. Eydala leaned back in her chair.

"I said we'd have a nice time, didn't I? Can't you see you're embarrassing our guest? No wonder he's not drinking. You talk and eat like a pig. Are you in a hurry?"

Rugen glanced at the door, a reflex that was impossible not to notice. Eydala dropped her silverware so that it sang against the table.

"You dragged someone home with you!"

"No! Or . . . No one important."

"Ask me first, I said! And you bring people as if—"

"She's not people! It's a whore from the Rafts. They never talk!"

"*Everyone* talks, you gaula-gut!"

Rugen wiped his pouty mouth on his sleeve.

"You know I need it. I can't fucking sleep in this house!"

Eydala rubbed her temples.

"So I'm forced to murder women because you're afraid of the dark?!"

Nafraím interrupted, hoping to change the topic.

"The boy eats off dead people's plates, sleeps in dead people's beds, and drinks dead people's blood. Can you blame him for realizing the ghosts in this house might be getting irritable?"

Rugen paled. His gaze wandered between the empty chairs. The candles on the table started flickering, and he pulled back.

Nafraím hid a smile. Where the draft had come from, he didn't know, but the timing was impeccable. He heard footsteps, and the door creaked open. A young woman came in wearing a worn dress that pressed her breasts unnaturally upward. She ran her hand through her tangled hair.

No!

Nafraím struggled against the ropes under the table, but it was futile. He was helpless. Completely unable to assist this woman, who had no idea who she was dealing with.

"I got hungry," she said, dropping onto the chair across from Rugen. She reached over the table and pulled his plate toward her. "Wow, meat! Rugen, is it okay if I ...?" She didn't wait for his answer, greedily helping herself to the stew.

Eydala stared at Rugen.

"And she knows your name."

"Wyldbloom," the woman replied, having obviously misheard. She took a mouthful of food and looked around. "Nice place, if you ... fix it up a little. But it's not yours, is it?" She glanced at Rugen.

"Ours!" He laughed a little too loudly. "I said it was *ours*. Or rather ... We're borrowing it."

"Got it," Wyldbloom said, winking at him. "I've borrowed a couple of houses myself. But this is crazy big! And right in the middle of Náklav, where even a piss pot can't sit empty. What's up with that?"

Eydala squeezed the butter knife so hard her hand shook.

"World peace," Nafraím said. "The house belonged to a wealthy family from Undst. The heirs have been arguing about it for generations, and the city council doesn't dare touch it since officials from Undst can be . . . sensitive."

Wyldbloom rolled her eyes.

"I've never understood politics." She looked at Eydala and stopped chewing for a second, as if she realized something was off. The silence revealed that it had started to rain.

Nafraím noted a nascent concern in Wyldbloom's eyes. She stole a sip of wine from Rugen's glass without putting it back.

"So, um . . . What were you guys talking about?"

"Ghosts," Nafraím replied, trying to make eye contact with her to warn her somehow.

Eydala gave an artificial laugh.

"Don't scare the guests! Or Rugen, for that matter. There's no such thing as ghosts."

Wyldbloom pointed to her with her fork.

"The Gaula, they exist! The wailing at Kleft, the Ulebru Bridge Death Diver . . . and that guy at the Yra Race! I have a client who saw him."

Wyldbloom downed the last sip and cast a longing glance at the wineglass in front of Nafraím. He shook his head slowly and clearly enough that she decided against it.

Eydala smiled condescendingly.

"That doesn't surprise me. I'd imagine your clients have seen all kinds of—"

"I'm not kidding! I know someone who was there when that guy disappeared during the Yra Race. It's true. A lot of people saw it, right in the middle of Nákla Henge!"

Nafraím stiffened. A cold uneasiness settled around his heart as he understood.

Grif. She's talking about Grif.

His thoughts were jumbled, and he was unsure how to prevent the coming disaster. Should he stand up? No. If the woman saw that he was tied up, it would be a death sentence for her. And if he stopped her from talking, it increased the chance that Eydala would understand the significance of what was being said.

The woman kept enlightening them, unaware of what she was doing.

"Do you think so many people would just make it up? Some people said his eyes were black, like the devil. And that he attacked that Seida Guild lady. Attacked her before he disappeared. And I know at least three people who have seen the Ulebru Bridge Death Diver."

Nafraím could hardly hear her anymore, his pulse was pounding in his ears, drowning out her words. He watched Eydala, who was staring into space as the realization dawned on her. Then she turned to him, ever so slowly.

She knows.

Rugen disputed something Wyldbloom had said, and they talked over each other, equally blind to the damage that had been done. Eydala slammed the knife handle into the table, instantaneously silencing the conversation.

Wyldbloom cautiously rose.

"So . . . I'll just wait in the room." She took a step, turned around again, and brought the plate with her. Then she disappeared out the door with Rugen in tow.

Eydala stood up, leaning on her hands on the edge of the table.

"The Yra Race . . . He disappeared during the Yra Race. You've known that this whole time . . . The devil isn't in this world anymore. The blood is gone. Forever."

She stared at him, her eyes unruly, as if she were still putting the pieces together. Then she threw her wine glass at him. It slammed into the wall behind him and rained down in shards. She straightened up again with renewed force.

"She tricked me. Rugen's old minx lied to me! Juva Sannseyr *had* the devil, and she sent him back where he came from. That's why you never said where the letter was. There wasn't any letter, was there?"

Nafraím closed his eyes. They felt swollen, and he would have cried if he could. A months-long battle was over. He had hoped that his last deed would be a good one. To spare her from whom he had taken so much, whom he had caused so much pain. But nothing could save Juva from Eydala's wrath. *No one* could be saved. Eydala's last hope was dead. Her final reason to think like a human being.

He smelled the stinging whiff of sea silver and opened his eyes again, looked at the monster he had created. Eydala raised his chin by force and let out a laugh saturated with madness.

"And you would rather die . . . Rather be tortured to death than admit that you were tricked by a child. Oh, my dear Nafraím! There you see the price of your arrogance."

Nafraím pulled his head away. There was a fragile hope in her misunderstanding. She had no idea that Juva meant something to him, and if he found the right words, it would stay that way. But what could he say that had the power to save Juva? What could soothe Eydala's rage at having been betrayed?

That Juva was also betrayed. Forced to help.

"Well," he said. "If nothing else, we can take comfort knowing she got what she deserved when the devil attacked her."

Eydala cackled.

"Nowhere near enough! Juva Sannseyr declared a war, and she's going to get one. Náklav is a powder keg of branntang just waiting to go off. You'll see, Nafraím. Silver Throat is controlling the city council like puppets. They're dancing, dancing to his flute."

She spun around so that her thin dress fluttered. Nafraím knew he was looking at what he feared most in this world: decay. The Rot had finally caught up with her. Nothing she said made sense. This was the unavoidable collapse of her mind. And she had nothing more to lose. The devil was lost, and Eydala knew she would die sooner or later. In the meantime, she could milk the warow for blood and do irreparable damage.

She clapped her hands together.

"I know what you're thinking, you pathetic figure. But I won't let the fact that he's gone break me. I have enough time to find him. Or I can make a *new* devil! What if we use a wolf to get a female warow pregnant? Will we get a new source of eternal life? You didn't think of that, did you? It's a disgrace that you call yourself open-minded! And now we have Juva to sense for us until we've cleansed Náklav. Until there isn't a single free vardari to share the devil's blood with. Just you and me, old man. And when I'm done with Juva, Rugen can have her."

Nafraím searched her eyes for any hint of humanity without finding any.

"And afterward, Eydala? What will you drink when you fail and it's just us left?"

She looked at him as if she had pulled one over on him.

"The cycle keeps me alive. He creates the wolf-sick from me, and I live off of them. Nature's wondrous cycle!"

Nafraím stared at her. Her babble took on meaning, the meaning became certainty, and it crept down his spine like an ice-worm.

"*He* gives people wolf-sickness? The priest?"

She nodded, eager like a child.

"The city is drowning in them! And the more there are, the more followers he gets. All he needs to do is promise them a cure! It's so wonderfully simple. And when all of Náklav is groveling before God, I'll give them one! I will. The woman behind the likenesses."

Eydala cocked her head.

"But poor Nafraím, was that something you didn't know, hmm? Is there knowledge that you are not the sole possessor of? Can someone other than *you* spread wolf-sickness? Use fear and power to shape Náklav? Can the world really be so inconsiderate as to keep you from being an autocrat?" She chuckled at her own derision.

She was so infinitely wrong. He had never spread the wolf-sickness to sow fear but rather to keep the gates alive. They had needed it before the Might had re-emerged. The illness had been an absolute necessity, not a barbaric quest for power.

Nafraím opened his mouth to explain, but what good would it do? She was right: the priest from Undst had found his weapon, his control. What Eydala didn't understand was that she, too, danced to his flute just as much as all the others.

Nafraím stared at her. He had opened his eyes when this day began knowing that all hope was lost. It hadn't seemed possible that it could get worse.

"I've learned what breaks you, Nafraím Sai," Eydala said with a smile. "You fear nothing but madness, the Rot. The warow will die like flies because they believe in the same myth, even if all the blood they could wish for ravages the city. They will deny themselves survival. Like you're doing."

She took a long drink from his glass.

"Do you know which wine this is?"

Nafraím didn't answer. It was dead blood; he knew that. Blood from someone with wolf-sickness or from a dead vardari. And now that she no longer needed him to tell her where the devil was, she would find a way to get it into him. Destroy his mind.

She grabbed his shirt collar and yanked him toward her. His chair tipped, and he fell. His knees hit the floor with a sharp pain, and he remained on his knees.

She leaned closer to him.

"It's Mikkje," she whispered.

Nafraím collapsed forward, bracing his hands against the floor. The rope forced his wrists together so his fingers splayed out on the stone tiles like a pale, bloodless raven.

"Ah, you see?" she said contentedly. "I can control you already."

He pressed his palm to the floor and felt the outline of a shard of glass. He formed a fist and clenched it.

GOD'S TEARS

The old blood reader room in Jólshov was unlike anything else the Seida Guild had left its mark on. Atypically sparse, completely devoid of ornamentation. Hardly bigger than a closet, its stone walls had preserved the room for centuries.

All that was in there was a bench with a sheepskin fleece and Muune herself, carved out of an ancient beam.

Juva sat on the bench and looked at the goddess. She had three faces: one for all that was, one for all that is, and one for all that is to come. Her hair curled over her shoulders and spread out between her fingers as threads of fate, so masterfully woven, it was a wonder that only one of them had broken.

I had no choice.

The painter had been a warow. A grave desecrator, one who drank from the wolf-sick. Even monsters could create beauty, be beautiful. Her mother had never been Jól's best child, but always beautiful. And Gríf...

The thought came to her too suddenly to ward off the pain.

Why me?

She leaned her head against the wall. Every damned day she told herself that the knot in her chest was a false emotion. It was neither grief nor love. It was anger. And shame at having let herself be used. Why should it be anything else? A treacherous figure, a monster who had fed the warow, and whom she had hardly shared any time with. She had known Rugen longer than that and never shed a tear at his death. Should she waste her energy grieving for the beast who had given her wolf-sickness?

She had even defended him in her thoughts! Maybe she had consumed blood pearls by accident? Or maybe people with wolf-sickness were contagious? Things could get out of hand. It wasn't inconceivable that blood had somehow gotten into her one way or another.

Wishful thinking. Foolishness.

He had taken more than her life from her. He had robbed her of her chance to rescue the rest of the city—that felt more impossible every day. Her pulse pounded in her tender gums as if agreeing with her.

Anasolt appeared in the doorway with a tray full of tankards.

"They couldn't find their way to the kitchen, and now they want beer," she said dryly and disappeared again.

Juva took a deep breath, which felt insufficient. She couldn't hide now. Anasolt and the others must have seen that she was there, that she was witness to everything going well.

She got up and reluctantly walked out into Muune's Hall. It had been the Seida Guild's Hall from time immemorial. She had run between the benches as a child, finding hiding places when the fear came. She had listened to countless speeches, watched children take the waters for the first time, and seen grown-ups take it for the second time when they got married. She had drunk sepulture beer here for her mother and Solde and for Ester. And for her father before that, although she had been far too young for beer then.

Now she was a stranger.

Anasolt planted the tankards on the long table unnecessarily roughly one by one, while thirsty believers flocked around her. It was an uncomfortable sight, a leader of the Seida Guild serving the Hallowed in Jólshov.

The phases of the moon on the back wall were hidden behind a curtain, and on the dais where the Seida Guild used to sit, the box with the images sat open on a table, flanked by two members of the Hallowed. So Gods could make images but not protect them, apparently.

Juva had a feeling of having lost something she had never valued, of watching Náklav itself erode.

Anasolt tucked the tray under her arm and disappeared past her. Juva avoided making eye contact with the accusations in Anasolt's eyes. She had not hidden how she felt about lending out the hall, but the Hallowed had grown too numerous, and the city council was pragmatic when it suited them. And Anasolt had conceded that Silver Throat had won over many of the fiercest opponents in the Seida Guild with gifts and wine.

He looked too smug, standing there at the front of the hall, shaking hands with his thronging followers. The only light came from the blood reader lamps that bathed him in red, concealing the corners of the room in a bloody darkness.

If he had only known what people used to call this hall. The curved walls with grooves that met in a pointed ceiling. The fanatic from Undst was going to be worshiping inside an enormous female sex organ, and that gave her a certain foolish joy.

He stepped onto the platform, and the room quieted in anticipation. Silver glinted off several hundred collar necklaces, as if they were dogs, the lot of them.

"Death!" he yelled, so his voice resounded through the hall. "Death is God's punishment for sin. And we've heard his will. We, as humble servants of the one who is the almighty of all, have conferred the punishment on *two* sinners who must answer to Him right now."

The followers broke into cheers that gave her chills. Juva retreated toward the door, uncertain of how much she could bear to listen to.

He pointed to the silver likenesses. His eyes swept over the hall, as if he were trying to capture them all.

"But what about *your* sin?" His question silenced them all. "No, your sin is so much smaller, isn't it?"

He wandered from one side of the room to the other, gesticulating like an actor.

"*You* have never been a warow, never mocked your gods by cheating death. *You* have never taken a life or inflicted bodily harm. You have only . . ."

He looked at them again.

"Lied? Stolen? Cheated? Drank too much? Ingested sinful blood. Spilled a secret?"

He gave an oppressive pause, and Juva could hear them gulping.

"You're not safe. In his eyes, a sin is a sin, big or small, and the penalty is death. Also for you! Look around in Náklav and what do you see? Wolf-sickness! Dying sinners! There is no safe haven except God!"

He put his hand on the nail at his throat.

"And we carry our punishment with us!"

People inched forward slightly in the hall, as if they would be safer the closer they moved. Juva spotted Muggen in the crowd, along with his sister. She had probably dragged him here, the tradeoff for his getting to keep hunting with the guys. She felt a pang of disappointment, even though she knew she had no right to. After all, she was here herself and far closer to the priest than Muggen and the other innocent believers.

Silver Throat continued to intone about how near the evil might be and how blessed were they who were Hallowed, who had chosen life rather than death.

Juva clenched her fists and ran her tongue over her canines. If there was a single god or goddess who could hear her now, may they let the sickness take her while she was near him, so she could take him to Drukna with her. The man was extremely dangerous.

She could stop the warow and the wolf-sick, but who would stop Silver Throat when she was dead?

A whisper ran through the room and tore her from her thoughts. Silver Throat stood motionless up there in the front with his hand on his forehead as if he had forgotten what he was going to say or suddenly felt unwell. He mumbled something and held up a hand to silence the flock.

"God!" he yelled. "God is speaking! Give me silence!"

Juva craned her neck to see what this delusion was about, but he did nothing. He just stood with his eyes closed. Then he ran toward the initiate and began to yell.

"Lock the doors! Silver, give me silver! Blessed water! Quickly! I must catch God's tears!"

The closest initiates exploded into action. They set a stool in front of him and a sort of trough that they filled with water from drinking horns.

He is going to get a likeness!

Juva tried to suppress her smile but doubted she would succeed. She had him now. She finally had the chance to reveal his scam.

She jogged along the wall to the dais, but she wasn't the only one. People were crowding together to be a part of the miracle, and she pushed her way through them to get to the front.

Silver Throat squeezed his head between his hands, and it was a convincing performance. She had to give him that. One of the initiates brought a black box and opened it. The initiate raised her hand to take out the shiny plate that lay inside, but Silver Throat brushed her hand away.

"Don't touch it, woman! It must be pure. Free of sin and untouched."

He accepted a leather glove that he put on. Then he lifted the silver plate with the utmost caution, touching only its edges. He turned it over in front of him and it shone like a mirror.

Juva pushed her way between two men who were yelling, until they recognized her and let her through to the front row. It was hard to see in the flickering, red darkness, but there was no doubt the plate was clean. Maybe the likeness was hidden between two thin plates?

She locked her eyes on him while her thoughts raced through all the tricks her mother used to use. Whatever he was doing, she would catch it. A bad smell prickled in her nose, as if she had thought something sinful. It sent an inexplicable wave of fear through her body.

Silver Throat made a sign over his chest with one hand and mumbled to himself in what she realized must be the language of Undst. Then he lowered the silver plate into the trough of water. It glittered under the ripples.

Juva could hear someone behind her swallow. She would never have believed that a room so full of people could be so quiet. She kept her eyes trained on the plate, waiting for Silver Throat to try to distract them, maybe a quick motion, an outcry . . .

Nothing happened.

Then it came. Dark splotches grew forth on the plate, drawing a picture. Slowly, like watching someone approach through the fog.

That's impossible!

Juva felt shivers on the back of her neck. It was an unfamiliar face. A young man with his eyes closed. Someone behind her was pushing, but she stood her ground. What was this? Where did it come from? How . . . ?

She stared at the man appearing before her eyes, in terrifying detail, out of nothing. The woman next to her folded her hands together and began to pray. More people followed her lead and did the same.

"God has wept!" Silver Throat yelled. Liquid, what the Hallowed would call God's tears dripped from the likeness, and Silver Throat held it up so everyone could see it. The woman next to Juva knelt down and reached forward to touch Silver Throat's feet.

Juva heard someone gasp. She tore her eyes off the image and looked around. The Hallowed were rocking back and forth in a sort of eerie trance as they mumbled unintelligibly. One woman had covered her mouth with her hands as if she actually couldn't believe it. Some people were crying. One man was pulling on the doors to get out, but some of the other people calmed him down. In the red light, all the faces looked the same. A nightmare.

An initiate took charge of the image, washed it, and put it in the box with the others, leaning against the open lid so everyone could see. Had it been covered with a coating of some sort that dissolved in water?

Silver Throat asked for silence, and he got it. He requested an orderly line, and he got it. He asked everyone to look at the image, one by one, and they did. He asked them to remember the face of evil, and Juva knew they would never forget it.

The initiate passed out drawings of the three other likenesses, and Silver Throat asked people to go out and disseminate them to the whole city, to the whole world. Juva knew they would, too.

The doors were opened, and people left the room as if intoxicated. Juva was left standing there, staring at the likenesses. Two of them were the warow from the lighthouse, but the third one had been swapped out. The man they had sepultured at Nákla Henge had been replaced by a familiar face.

Ferkja . . .

But it was the newest image that intrigued her. Juva stepped closer. The man in the picture looked like he was asleep. She didn't recognize him, but there was some memory she couldn't place . . . He was sitting in front of a painting in a frame she had seen before. No, it wasn't a painting, it was a mirror.

A mirror.

And she *had* seen it before.

Juva went weak in the knees, dizzy. She sank down and sat on the edge of the dais. Her hand went to her neck, and she felt the pain as if it had just happened.

Eydala. The man in the picture was sitting in Eydala's room in the hall of mirrors where she herself had sat with a steel wire around her neck, fearing death. And that prickling smell . . . That was also Eydala.

Juva felt a hand on her shoulder and jumped. Silver Throat sat down next to her.

"I know, Juva," he said. "Don't be afraid. I did the same thing the first time I saw God's will. It's a natural reaction. You get . . . over-whelmed." His smile was sincere but with the usual trace of smugness. His hand snuck downward, caressing her back. "It's exhausting doing God's work, but you do it well, Juva. And I know you didn't believe, but now you do. That's the most important thing."

Juva looked at him. At those intense, dark eyes. His widow's peak, which looked like horns. He was so . . . ordinary. There was no obvious reason that gods would choose him.

But he wasn't lying. The images were authentic and they showed true evil.

He slapped his thighs, as if he had done a respectable day's work. "So . . . a new hunt on Votansdag?"

The pale scar on his hand was more evident in the red light, and it struck her that it could have come from a nail.

We carry our punishment with us.

Juva gave him a quick nod and left. She made it out without running, an instinct that was hard to curb. The streets seemed narrower, the alleyways tighter, because there was evil out there, and it was hunting her. The wind blew her hood off every time she pulled it up, as if it wanted to expose her.

Her thoughts were all over the place, as if caught in the same gusts of wind. Disconnected statements, questions she was afraid to dwell on, because if she found an answer, it would come crashing down onto the ground like a wedge and open a chasm. What had she just seen? Why Silver Throat? Who were the warow in the images, the ones who had threatened her at the painter's place? And scariest of all: Had this even happened or was it her imagination? A dream, while she had actually been sitting in a whale's heart, eating, overripe with wolf-sickness?

She wanted to visit the girls, wanted to curl up on a silk sofa surrounded by laughter and fresh, clean laundry raining down from above. She wanted to see Kefla try to hide her joy at seeing her, hear them humming to the music box, and swearing at letters and math problems. But she couldn't. Never again.

She put her hand under her breasts and found the outline of the bottle of poison. The last resort. What she had just seen was madness.

Get a grip, Juva! You know what you saw.

She felt a familiar breath against her heart and looked up. She was home. And Skarr sat on the front steps waiting for her.

The sight seemed so genuine, so down to Earth that she could have wept. She squatted and wrapped her arms around his neck.

"Damned furball," she mumbled. "Did you run away again?"

Someone cleared their throat behind her, and she jumped back up. An elderly man stood in the street with his hands behind his back. He had gray hair and was well dressed. Harmless.

"Juva Sannseyr? Pardon me, I would have waited by the steps, but . . ." He glanced at the wolf.

She put her key in the door.

"I don't do blood readings. You'll have to go to someone who has a lantern out."

"Frú Sannseyr, I'm not inclined to believe in that sort of thing. I'm here about an entirely different matter."

She looked at him and waited until he realized that he needed to elaborate. He cast a discreet glance around and took a couple of steps closer.

"My name is Ofre Durne. I was the estate master for a warow, and I can help."

An informant.

Juva opened her door and let Skarr in. The elderly man hesitated, so she waved for him to follow. He came up the steps with a hand on his knee to steady it. Juva glanced around at what her visitor might see. Dust motes danced in the light that filtered in between the planks in the boarded-up windows, and the floor was dirty. Hopefully he understood that she had other things to do.

"Frú Sannseyr, could I trouble you for a little water. I've been waiting a while."

Juva nodded. She set down her backpack and crossbow and went down to the kitchen. She washed a cup and filled it with water. She went back upstairs and felt her heart squeezed between two others.

She had been tricked.

OLD FRIENDS

Juva dropped the cup and pulled her knife. It seemed far too small compared to the security of being behind her crossbow, but that was up in the entryway with the two warow.

I'm not going to survive this.

What an idiot she'd been. Preoccupied with the silver image at Jólshov. Distracted. Reckless. Groggy with wolf-sickness. They had tricked her, and they were here. Now.

The heart pounded loudly in her chest, a strangely sluggish but strong pulse that rushed in her ears. Vigilance took over, like when she was hunting. Details stood out sharply, as if she hadn't seen the kitchen in years. The handle on the oven door, the ash on the chimney. Under the counter was a shard of glass from the time she had thrown a mug at the wall where Rugen had been sitting.

Everything around her changed character. The room became a fortress, the utensils weapons. What should she do? What could she use? It was the same feeling as when Nafraím had been here, hunting for Gríf. But this time, they would not settle for searching.

Juva tugged open the bottom drawer by the oven and grabbed the meat cleaver. It was bigger than the knives at any rate. She had never used a cleaver against anyone, but she had seen Nolan throw weapons like this. How hard could it be?

She held it in her fist and swung it a few times, as if to convince herself that she could. Should she wait down here? No, better to let them think she had no idea they were here.

She took a couple of steps up the stairs before it hit her that they might know she could sense them. Otherwise, why would they have used the old man? Someone who could send her to get some water while he let them in. And what about Skarr? Had they set him free from Broddmar, too? To distract her from them?

Broddmar! Had they hurt Broddmar?!

Juva quashed her anxiety before it had time to take hold. Skarr was a coincidence. He had to be. Unless they had been watching her for so long that they had known he would run away . . .

She crept up the stairs and recognized the heartbeats, the two from the lighthouse on Tunga. But Skarr was there, too, so at least they hadn't done anything to him.

The staircase felt infinitely long before it opened out next to the hallway alongside the library. She stopped, searching in her heart to try to place the enemy. A challenging exercise, but she had improved. Her instincts told her that one was in the front hall, which she could just barely see from where she stood, along with Skarr. The other was in the library, nearby. Possibly just inside the wall ahead of her.

Surrounded.

She would have done the same. *Had done* the same, all the time with the hunting team, but she didn't have a hunting team anymore. It was just her against two armed warow in ridiculously good shape and a gray-haired old man with bad knees, but that could have been an act.

If she could just make it to the front door unseen, she could get out.

Juva clutched the meat cleaver against her chest and stealthily crept along the wall. She could see more and more of the entryway. Freedom was only a few steps away.

No . . .

The warow was squatting in front of the door. He had such broad shoulders that she doubted the meat cleaver would be effective. He was scratching Skarr behind his ear, as if he had any right!

Eat him, you furball!

Maybe she could back her way into the old living room and get out the window? If only she . . .

The man stood up and stared right at her. Juva jumped back and heard a click behind her. A sound she was eerily familiar with.

She turned around and stared at the dark woman behind her crossbow. It occurred to her that she had never seen it from this angle before. The bow unfolded like thin silver wings on either side of the straight arm pointed right at her. The bolt was nothing but a dot glinting in the semi-darkness.

So this is what it feels like . . .

The woman came closer, slowly, sizing her up.

"Expensive toy for such a little girl," she said.

Juva pressed the cleaver against her thigh and hoped the woman hadn't seen it, while allowing her other hand to slide toward the dagger in her belt. The woman smiled. She had already seen it.

"Tell me what you did with him or die now with a bolt in the throat."

Her voice was deep and hoarse with anger.

Juva slowly backed away, into the entryway.

"I haven't touched him. He left of his own free will, and no one can reach him anymore. It's over. The devil is gone. There's nothing you can do."

"I'm not talking about the devil. I'm talking about Naf! Nafraím Sai!"

Nafraím?

The name sent a wave of shame through her body, which she knew she wouldn't be able to conceal.

"Ah," the woman said with a chilly smile. "You remember him . . ."

"Hard to forget," Juva replied through clenched teeth. "He killed five women in this house."

The woman took a couple of quick steps toward her.

"What did you do with him?!"

Skarr began to growl.

"Seire . . ." came from the nearby man. The voice was surprisingly gentle, like his heartbeats, but he was unable to calm the woman.

"Answer me?! Is he alive?"

Probably not.

The thought sapped her strength, but she didn't know why. Filled her with a dawning suspicion that nothing was the way she thought. Juva looked down and dropped the cleaver. It clanged against the floor. The woman roared like an animal and lunged at her. Juva staggered backward and pulled the knife. Barely out of the sheath before the woman grasped her. An intense pain in her wrist. The knife slipped. Juva fought against a strangling arm suddenly around her neck. Kicked frantically behind her, hampered by the woman's hold on her.

The man started yelling. Skarr bounded forward. Juva was drowning in a mountain of fur, and she heard him snap near her ear. Felt his breath as his jaw locked on to the woman's arm. Juva wriggled free. Her feet gave way, and she fell to the floor. She crawled backward, feeling around for the knife, but it was nowhere to be found. It . . . She looked up. The knife gleamed in the woman's hand.

Skarr!

His jaws were locked around the woman's arm as she screamed and raised the knife to strike.

"Seire!" the man snapped, without any trace of gentleness. She hesitated. The woman flipped the knife in her hand as if she hadn't been about to use it. She whacked Skarr in the jaw with the handle, and he let go with a whimper. The man grabbed him and held him in an iron grip. He embraced the animal and stroked him until he was calm.

Juva stared in disbelief. His heart was soft as a pillow against her own.

The woman who was apparently named Seire showed him the bleeding bite on her forearm, as if he hadn't noticed.

"Pet this, you nitwit!"

Her outburst was followed by what were presumably a few choice lines in a foreign language.

The elderly man showed up in the arcade to the library, completing the absurdly chaotic tableau.

"Oh dear . . ." he mumbled.

Juva suspected that this was as afraid as Ofre could be. She seized the opportunity, trying to crawl to the front door without being noticed, but Seire was alert and pointed her index finger at Juva.

"Stay put, you beast! If you've killed Naf, then you've just taken your last breath."

I'm going to die anyway.

Juva swallowed and shook her head.

"I haven't killed him. I have no idea if he's alive."

"No, I suppose maybe it's hard to recall who you've killed when that's what you do for a living. Is that it? How many more besides Mikkje?"

Mikkje . . . the painter.

Seire took a menacing step toward her. Blood poured down her forearm. Gríf had stood in that same spot, bleeding the same way, but his wounds had knit as she watched. A gift the warow didn't appear to have.

The woman's heart flared up within her own, an unbearable heat, like white corpsewood coals. Juva was not able to nor did she want to extinguish it.

Yes . . . Burn me. Burn me like the wolf.

Seire took an unsteady step backward and looked around, suddenly at a loss, anxious, like Ferkja had been on the bridge.

A heart you can sense, you can control.

That thought was as ludicrous as it was false. That's what Gríf had said, a lie he had rattled off as he stressed her heart to the breaking point. The warow were anemic, all of them, and the gods only knew what it did to them when they drank the blood of someone with wolf-sickness. Seire was also badly injured. Skarr had left bite marks that she would bear as long as she lived, which hopefully wouldn't be long.

Juva realized that everyone there was dying. Her from wolf-sickness, the warow from a lack of blood. The elderly man would probably outlive them all.

Seire leaned against the stair railing. Her partner unhooked and removed his backpack, which looked every bit as homemade as his sweater. He dug out a small jar, which he tossed to the woman.

"You need ringborre," he said without making a move to assist. He just continued scratching Skarr.

Seire caught the jar with her uninjured hand.

"I mean, by all means, you don't need to overreact," she muttered.

The elderly man approached Juva.

"Frú Sannseyr, if you would permit me. Where can I find the medical items?" Juva stared at him. He continued as if this were the most natural thing in the world. "Bandages? Wound dressings? That sort of thing?"

"Bandages?!" Juva got to her feet. "Did you think I was planning to *help* her?!"

Seire flopped down on the stairs and rested her elbows on her knees.

"No, that would be downright unnatural," she replied sarcastically.

"I have some," the man said and shoved the bag toward him. The elderly man found what he needed and began to tend Seire's wound. He wiped it clean, applied ringborre, and started bandaging her arm with no response from her.

Juva looked into her eyes, just as fiery as her heart. Pure, infuriated contempt.

"So you fight for Undst now, girl? Or are you so stupid that you don't understand what that young guy with the silver at his throat is up to? Are you just tagging along to kill on his command? Slaughtering innocents like Mikkje?"

Juva searched for her anger so she could respond just as hatefully, but all she found was pain. The memory of the painter forced itself to the forefront, lying there surrounded by paintings, and it felt like his blood diluted the rage until she no longer recognized it. This was a battle she needed to win, but victory shouldn't look like this.

I didn't have any choice. He wasn't supposed to die, he was . . .

He was supposed to sit in captivity until Silver Throat saw fit to send him to Drukna. Was that any better? Would he have been any less dead if she hadn't been there when it happened?

Remember what they're doing.

She looked at Seire again.

"You thought we would give up without a fight? That we would lie down and die, all of us, while you guys give us wolf-sickness so that you can have blood to live off of? You won't make *me* feel ashamed because I know what you're doing."

Seire swept the old man's hand away as if she was tired of being tended and stood up. She pointed to Juva and looked questioningly at her partner.

"Faun, explain to me what he sees in her."

"Himself?" The man shrugged.

Juva took note of the names in case she made it out of this alive. The front door was close.

Faun, Seire, old man Ofre.

Seire came toward her.

"Juva damned Sannseyr . . . We neither create nor drink from the wolf-sick, you *sekla* pelt! I'd rather drown in sand; it's poison to us. We don't know who creates them. That's why we're *here*! And I'm not known for my patience, so tell me: Where is Naf? Don't you realize that our whole damned world will fall apart without him?!"

The world or you?

Juva let out her breath.

"I don't know where he is. All I know is that I told one of you that he had the devil. Since then, I haven't seen him."

"You told . . . *who?* Which one of us did you tell?"

Juva hesitated. The name would not pass through her lips. It should be forgotten, vanish forever.

She looked around, groping for solid ground. She saw a man with a gentle heart, who was still scratching Skarr. She saw Ofre, an old estate master with pleading eyes. And Seire, who claimed that she would rather die than drink from the wolf-sick, and who called Nafraím by a nickname. And the strangest thing of all . . .

I'm still alive.

Juva closed her eyes for a second.

"Eydala. I told Eydala."

"Eydala?!" Seire yelled, making Juva jump. The warow woman turned her back and squeezed her head between her elbows as if she couldn't bear the thought.

"Eydala? You sicced *her* on him?! The worst one he's created in seven hundred years?! His only regret?!"

Seire's heart flared up in her chest, like a shriek of grief.

Juva stared at her hands. She was trembling. These thoughts brought up the picture at Jólshov, the warow in Eydala's room, and she felt like she was falling.

THE TEMPTATION

Nafraím could hear himself breathing. The cool darkness in the crypt had reflected his emotions for many months. A silent, resigned man, he had accepted his punishment with as much dignity as he could muster and accepted that he was going to die. That they were all going to die.

But that was before he knew what was at stake.

He was hungry enough to no longer recognize it as hunger—debilitated, battered, his hands tied behind his back. But his chest smoldered with a power he hadn't felt in a long time. Maybe as long as half a millennium. Life force. Pure, raw will. A red-hot need to fight.

No injustice could be remedied by dying, but he hoped he could save everything that was worth saving by living.

He adjusted so he was sitting in a more comfortable position, as best he could with his hands strapped behind his back. He picked up the shard of glass between two fingers and then dropped it. His patience would no longer allow itself to be summoned; he was at the mercy of instincts he thought he had forgotten.

He tried again. His fingers were numb and wet with blood, but he rubbed the glass shard in place until he could just barely file it against the rope. If he made it out of there, he would bleed to death overnight. Unless Eydala suspected trouble and saved him with ringborre.

His eyes fell on Yrgen. Still beautiful, but he had been dead long enough not to look asleep. And there was no mistaking the smell anymore. Senseless death. The unfathomable cruelty of a warped mind. The Rot.

Enough. That's enough now.

Nafraím stopped filing. Had he heard something? The door . . . A flickering light approached the round opening in the ceiling. A bottle broke and someone swore. Rugen came into view at the edge above. He wasn't wearing anything but a shirt, stained with wine, and not long enough to hide his genitals.

Nafraím leaned against the wall as if he had been sleeping.

Rugen rocked on unsteady feet, and for a moment, it looked like he was going to fall, but he recovered.

"Have you seen her?" he asked thickly.

"Who, Eydala?"

"No! She's at some guy's place . . . priest. The floozy from the Rafts—she ran off. I was getting more wine, and . . ." He looked around, as if the poor woman had just gotten lost.

For her sake, Nafraím hoped she had gotten out and would never come back. He kept filing. Carefully, carefully. Intensely aware that this opportunity would hardly come again. He might be able to get Rugen to fall, but what use would he be with a broken neck? It would buy time, but nothing in this crypt would help him up. He knew that all too well.

No, he had to get Rugen to open the massive wooden door, had to lure him in. *Who are you, Rugen? What do you want?*

Nafraím knew the answer. It made him sick, but then so many answers had over the ages.

"So she left you here without any company?" he asked. "I hope she gave you the ground rules first?"

"The ground rules?" Rugen took an unsteady step to the side. "No one makes rules for *me*."

Nafraím felt a hair-thin thread snap in the rope and laughed.

"Oh, she owns you, man. She won't let you bring people home, won't let you speak, won't let you touch me . . ."

Rugen's face darkened, and his eyes roamed with new thoughts. Nafraím clenched the shard of glass until he no longer knew what was glass and what was his fingers. It was all one cold, painful knot.

"But at least your hands are free," he moaned. "Look at me! Hands tied behind my back and helpless. Hard as a rock, but I can't even reach my own dick."

Nafraím looked up at him and knew he had won. Rugen hardened where he stood, so maybe he wasn't as drunk as Nafraím had thought. Maybe it was just the mess of wolf-sickness and dead blood that was eating him up inside.

Rugen's eyes grew greedy, and his face contorted into a bleak sneer Nafraím hoped no lover had had to see.

Then he pulled away from the edge and disappeared.

He's coming! He won't be able to help himself.

Nafraím pressed himself against the wall and sawed his fingers against the rope, unsure if he was filing or just shaking. But little by little, it yielded.

Come on, Rugen . . . Come on . . .

Any minute now . . .

He heard the heavy squeak of the bolt, the most beautiful sound he had heard in ages, the sound of freedom, of victory. The door creaked open, and Rugen walked stiffly in. He set the oil lamp on the floor, and the flame lit up his erection from below. He hesitated a moment, then he came closer with a sheepish smile.

Nafraím filed, with the smallest motions he could.

Easy.

He had to get free, then wait until Rugen was on top of him. Only then could he . . .

Rugen shuffled closer, fiddling with his shirt. Uncertain, as if his ravaged body remembered what the boy no longer could, that he ought to be afraid.

Come to me, you beast . . .

Rugen stopped next to Yrgen. His eyes roamed over the dead body.

"No . . ." Nafraím tugged at the ropes without coming free. He felt suddenly withered, numbed by a disgusting realization. Dead men were easier prey.

Rugen squatted down next to Yrgen. Poked him, as if to check if he was really dead. Then he tipped the body over onto its stomach and snorted out a laugh.

Nafraím gritted his teeth and pulled his wrists apart. His skin burned, but he received the blessed reward. The rope came loose, and he was able to stealthily slip his hands free. The relief was short lived. His shoulders had stiffened, and his arms refused to obey. He fought the paralysis while Rugen knelt between Yrgen's bloodless thighs, groping in blind ardor.

Nafraím crawled toward him on trembling arms and managed to get to his feet. The exertion hunted his heart, and he had an eerie feeling that it was on the outside of his chest, beating. He was heartless.

He grabbed hold of Rugen's brown curls and dug the shard of glass into his throat. Warm blood burned against his frozen fingers. Rugen stared up at him with a contorted look. His fist held his grotesquely ready penis, ready for an act of debauchery he would never complete. His blood dripped onto the flame-patterned tiles. The fire from Undst. God's warning to sinners. The boy made a wheezing sound.

Nafraím wheezed back, in a whisper he could scarcely hear himself.

"I may have saved you from God's wrath, but nothing can save you from mine."

He pressed on the glass shard. Felt it sink in deeper, both into Rugen's neck and his own fist. Then he let go and left Rugen lying in the ring of fire, bleeding out.

Nafraím stared at his hands, unable to tell if the blood was Rugen's or his own. He limped to the door, painfully aware that he was operating purely on willpower. There was every indication that this was his last night in this world, and he needed to make it count.

BACK FROM DRUKNA

Skarr walked over to the sofa and laid his head in the lap of Faun, the warow wild man, and sniffed his rootlike braids.

Juva stared at them, and before long, he snuck back to her. Trapped in a circular motion of alternating attraction.

Faithless furball.

But what right did she have to expect loyalty from wolves?

The man's eyes were far too gentle to be a vardari, intensely blue and childlike. There was an innocence that didn't belong to someone with fangs.

Or anyone here in this house.

The old man, Ofre, had lit a fire and warmed up the library. Then he made himself comfortable as if he had always worked in this house. There was nothing to fear from either him or Faun. They seemed strangers to violence. The woman, on the other hand . . .

Seire sat backward on the chair, her arms resting on the chair back. She wouldn't stay seated for long. She had to be the most restless person Juva had ever met.

"So you sent the devil home. Is that what you're saying?"

Juva leaned forward in the chair. If she tried to stand up, she would again face the choice between sitting back down or being shot with her own crossbow. She pulled her hands over her face and repeated, "Yes, during the Yra Race. Nafraím was there. He saw it. Ask him if you don't believe me. If he—"

Seire's eyes killed her sentence with their unconcealed scorn.

"And you haven't seen him or Eydala since, and you also have no idea where she's staying? Is there anything you *do* know, red hunter?"

Juva felt the corner of her mouth twitch with disgust.

"Well, I know that it won't kill you, since you create wolf-sick people and then drink from them."

"Did you hear that?" Seire glanced at Faun. "Bloodthirsty *and* slow."

She hopped to her feet again and came closer.

"I put a coin on it being *you*, Sannseyr. Young woman, charms a warow, gains access to his blood and can spread it until the city is drowning in wolf-sickness. Nice way to hold on to your job, right?"

She's crazy . . .

What could you say in response to such nonsense? Juva rubbed her forehead with her fingertips.

"You've never hunted the wolf-sick, have you? It's not a job anyone wants."

Seire looked around.

"I've hunted more than you, but I can see that you don't need the money. So you hunt for fun? Even though you knew we were dying without the blood. The thirst for blood was so strong that you couldn't even take time to wait, could you?"

"I have no time to waste!" Juva stared at her, and for the first time, she saw the woman's eyes wander.

If they realize you're sick, you're dead!

Juva kept going so the words wouldn't give her away.

"If you really need somewhere to lay the blame, vardari, then try the guy you're looking for, who told me flat out he's been spreading blood pearls to give people wolf-sickness."

Seire tapped her chest with her index finger.

"Don't talk as if you know him! Do you know who we are? We are the first ones, Juva Sannseyr. I've known Nafraím for more than six hundred years, and he doesn't do anything without a reason. He made as many as he needed to dilute the wolf blood and never more than the gateways required. This isn't his doing. This is *sick*!"

"There, you see?" Juva leaned back in the chair. "That's *one* thing we agree on."

That response seemed to annoy her. She turned her back and stood by the raven cabinet. She studied the taxidermy bird. Leaning forward, she tapped on the glass with a knuckle and seemed disappointed when nothing happened.

Juva glanced at Faun.

"She'll relax, eventually," he said. "Give her time."

"How much time? Six hundred years?"

Seire either hadn't heard or pretended not to.

"I need a drink," Seire said. "It doesn't look like you're short on those."

Juva seized the opportunity and was about to get up, but Ofre beat her to it.

"Right away, Frú Seire."

His words seemed to amuse Seire. She grinned at Faun with her eyebrows raised, as if to check that he had caught that.

Ofre filled and served the glasses. Water for Faun from a pitcher he had prepared earlier, and wine for Seire. Juva accepted the glass of rye liquor and wondered how he knew what they all wanted. Did you develop a special sense for that sort of thing when you were an estate master?

She took a big swig and felt the blessed heat spread through her chest. It calmed her nerves and muted the intrusive heartbeats from the others. And the pulse around her canines.

Think, Juva!

What were the facts? She was trapped with two warow who were poisoning her with words she didn't want to hear. Her job was clear—she had to find them, catch them, and send them to Drukna, and the longer she sat there, the more credible their claims became. They didn't create the wolf-sick, and they didn't drink from them.

They had only one obsession, and it was to find Nafraím. The man she had betrayed and sacrificed to Eydala. She had no reason to trust any of what they said, but Seire's concern for Nafraím was painfully genuine.

And I'm still alive.

They would not have been if she had the upper hand.

The corpsewood crackled in the fireplace, a hoarse laughter, as if the gods were enjoying the realization that was taking hold. Juva watched the warow and realized she wasn't the only one. The silence was oppressive, as if everyone had been forced inside themselves. Maybe she would survive the night after all . . .

Ofre cleared his throat.

"Shall I make some sandwi—"

The door knocker rapped from the front hall. Juva jumped. A wave of hope washed over her—until Seire leapt to her feet and grabbed the crossbow again.

"Are you expecting someone? This late?"

Juva struggled to clear her mind. To find something to say that could become a way out of here.

"It could be runners, about people with wolf-sickness, but . . ."

"But?"

"We would have heard the Dead Man's Horn, so it could be . . ." She swallowed Broddmar's name, unwilling to share it with them. "It could be the man who owns Skarr."

Seire's forehead creased, tugging the freckles toward the bridge of her nose.

"That's not your wolf?"

The question was so sincere and such a relief that Juva suddenly felt how high she'd been holding her shoulders. They hadn't set Skarr free, and they didn't know anything about Broddmar. He was safe!

But not anymore.

Juva swallowed.

"He's only here to get the wolf. He doesn't have anything to do with this."

The door knocker sounded again, and Seire waved her out of her chair.

"One word, and I swear . . . Get rid of him."

Seire followed her to the front hall and stood against the wall, the crossbow clutched to her chest.

Juva put her hand on the door handle. If it was Broddmar, she needed to warn him, a hunting signal for *danger*. Would he even see it or care?

She glanced at Seire.

"I . . . It might be difficult. We're not—"

"A lover?" Seire grinned broadly, revealing her fangs.

"No, no! We just haven't talked in a while. He . . ."

He hates that I'm hunting you guys.

Seire squinted between the planks boarding up the window.

"You don't need to explain to me that you have a hard time holding on to friends, bleeder. Just get rid of him!"

The door knocker banged again, and Juva jumped. For a second, she thought something had touched her heart, but it was just Seire and Faun.

"Sannseyr?" an unfamiliar voice called from outside.

Juva took a breath and opened the door a crack. A young man stared at her with obvious relief.

"Thank goodness, I thought I was going to have to . . ." He glanced behind him at the cart he had pulled there, judging by his sweaty hair. "He needs help. I wanted to take him to the infirmary at Kviskre, but he said he was coming here and was very . . ."

A trap?

"Who? What happened?"

"I have no idea, Frú Sannseyr, but I don't think . . . Please, I don't want any trouble!"

Juva put her hand on her chest, searching for the weakened pulse that quivered against her heart. It was not a stranger's.

It's him!

The cart-puller rubbed his hands as if he feared touching something.

"He can't walk on his own. I think . . . I don't want any money. I just want to go home. Please, this has nothing to do with me." He trotted down the steps toward the cart.

Juva gulped and stared at Seire.

"It's Nafraím . . ."

Seire's eyes widened, and she ran outside. The cart-puller opened the door of the cart and tried to lift the man lying on the seat. He was bloody. Skinny. Almost unrecognizable. Seire went over and helped the runner get him onto his feet. She stuck her arm through the crossbow so it dangled from the crook of her elbow by its bow then grabbed a better hold of Nafraím.

This is my chance . . .

Juva knew she should run. Now. As soon as she was past the cart, the streets would save her. Even so, she stood there as if spellbound, watching her moment of escape fade away. Seire dug around in her pocket for money, but the runner frantically shook his head. He backed toward his cart, grabbed the pull-bar, and vanished as fast as his feet could carry him.

Faun pushed past Juva and helped Seire through the door with Nafraím half hanging between them.

Run. Run now.

The warow tried to bring Nafraím farther into the front hall, but he resisted, looking around as if he had no idea where he was, disoriented, pale as a corpse.

"Juva?"

He was struggling to keep his eyes open but saw her and took a step forward.

"Juva . . ."

His feet couldn't hold him up. Seire and Faun caught him and broke his fall. He ended up kneeling and looking at her. His eyes contained inconceivable things, more than anyone could bear.

Juva backed away, without escaping the pain that penetrated her chest. She searched his haggard face for something to cling to—hatred, rage, scorn—without finding any trace of it. All she found was pleading.

He reached out his hand to her.

"Juva . . . She knows."

Then he slumped. Seire allowed herself to be pulled down with him and sat holding his torso in her arms. Faun rummaged in his sack, found the jar, and began to rub Nafraím's bloody wrists with ringborre.

Seire pulled the crossbow off her arm. The bolt fell out of the track and rolled across the floor. She didn't notice and patted Nafraím on the cheek to keep him awake.

"Naf? Naf! What does she know? Who knows?"

Nafraím opened his mouth without responding. Seire scowled up at her.

"What is he talking about? She knows what?"

"That I lied to her." Juva felt cold to the bone.

She knows. Eydala knows.

Eydala knew that she had been tricked, that the devil was gone.

"What the nag's ass is he doing here then?!" Seire hissed. "Of all places! Why did he come here?!"

"To warn me . . ." The truth of those words turned her stomach. A distasteful certainty grew in her stomach.

Seire laughed despairingly.

"Why would he risk what little life he has left to warn you? A damned human-hunter, someone who wanted to kill him?"

Someone who tried.

She could hear Ofre coming up from the kitchen. He came into the front hall with a wooden serving board heaping with food and looked around, puzzled, before he realized what was happening.

"Master?" He practically tossed the food aside, setting it on a stair-step, and hurried over to the others. They lifted Nafraím onto the bench. The ribcage-shaped wrought iron received him like a bad omen. Skarr whimpered beside Faun.

The old estate master fetched his jacket.

"Master, I'll go get the doctor!"

"No!" Seire stopped him with a hand. "We don't know who we can trust. Even the doctor may have become one of the Hallowed for all we know."

"She's right," Faun said. "We need to get him away from here."

"And go where?!" Seire flung up her arms. "Mikkje is dead. Domnik is dead or has run off to the end of the world. Storm probably killed himself, and the gods only know where those who are still alive are. We have nowhere to go, Faun! And *if* we go, they'll come after us."

They. She means me.

Faun put an arm around Seire.

"We can get to Fimle again, and . . ." he hesitated.

"Fimle?!" Seire pulled away. "How are you going to get him through the gateways, Faun? He's in no condition to travel anywhere, and we've run out of places to hide."

Juva walked over to the front door. No one noticed her, so why didn't she leave? She put her hands on the cold wrought iron and locked the door. The click shut everyone up, and she could feel them staring at her.

"I know a place."

She turned around and looked at them. Seire's boundless contempt faded into overt desperation.

"They'll search . . ." she mumbled.

Juva tugged her sleeves down over her fingers in hopes of finding some warmth.

"Trust me," she said. "I have a place that takes centuries to find."

THE GIFT

The shaft was narrower and darker than she remembered, the cold more biting. She glanced up at the opening and the warm light from the library, but there was no way out anymore. The depths already had a hold of her, like in the dream. If she tried to climb back up, the whole house would turn over and send her farther down. Everything would be turned on its head.

Two warow are up there trying to save the life of a third. Everything is already turned on its head.

Juva hooked the storm lantern over her arm and clung to the thin iron rings that could hardly be called rungs. The walls seemed to close in around her, creeping closer in a promise to never let her out again.

She hadn't set foot down here since he'd left. The urge had been there—far too often—and it was harder to defeat than hoggthorn, but she had always won because she feared the longing. Now she feared finding herself.

What if she was no longer who she'd always been? She was a red hunter, a bleeder, someone with wolf-sickness descending into madness. Would she be able to peer through the bars in the iron door and see the true Juva Sannseyr in captivity?

A girl who had never killed anyone, never sent anyone to be tortured by Eydala, and never seen the devil.

Get a grip, Juva!

She wasn't there to dig, not into herself and not into the scar from Grif. She was there to make room for Nafraím and the others. She, who was hunting them for Silver Throat, would become a safe harbor for the vardari.

Why?

The question was dangerous to dwell on. It would open her up to a sea of pain. No answer would lead to anything good.

Her feet felt around for the next rung, but there weren't any more. She had reached the bottom, and all she could hear was the rush of the sea. The others' hearts had quieted. She was alone. Squeezed into the rock below the house, under Náklav, in the old whaling shafts. It sent her thoughts to Mikkje, the dead artist.

No one but Sannseyr women had seen these shafts since her great-grandmother, Síla, had forced the city council to move the docks. And with the docks, they had also shut down the lighthouse where the artist had lived.

Where I killed him.

Her body felt uncomfortably heavy. Muune had been spinning her threads of fate for generations, and only now were the loops beginning to close like nooses. Like the one that had been around her neck at Eydala's place.

She knows.

Juva followed the tunnel to the end and raised the lantern up to the iron door that had kept Grif in. Or had it kept her out? The memories pressed in on her, challenging the shell she had spent months building.

Never had she felt more than she had down here. Not of any emotion—not fear, rage, or desire. She had thought she knew her limits, but her heart had been stretched to the breaking point. As if everything before him had been small tastes.

Both the iron doors were ajar.

Juva squeezed her way in, and their hinges screamed. The room was empty, barer than she remembered. It had been full of him before.

The wooden floor creaked underfoot. She walked toward the wide bed bench, and it seemed untouched. The long-haired hides lay neatly, as if he had tidied up after himself. Cleansed after centuries of captivity. A ridiculous thought.

Had she imagined it all?

Juva set the storm lantern on the floor and sat down on the bed. There was plenty of room, enough for three warow.

You are going to house the vardari . . .

She could almost hear his voice. Deep and husky, with that sharp dialect. Sharp on the edges, like Old Norran. His eyes would have blackened like ink if he had known. What would he have said, if he had seen her hiding Nafraím, the man who had captured him.

He can burn!

Why should she care what he would have said? That bastard had hurt her, used her, and given her wolf-sickness. He had killed her before running off for good and leaving her in a city full of desperate warow. Why in Gaula should she give him a single thought?

She pulled her feet up to keep warm and heard a sound. A clink under one of the hides. Juva picked it up and felt around until her hand found cool glass. She pulled the storm lantern closer and stared down at three red vials, strung on a chain. They were all the same. Barely bigger than a finger and curved like fangs. They lay arranged on a thin linen pillow, like crown jewels.

Blood. He left blood.

Her body broke down. Juva leaned forward and put her face in her hands, hearing her own laughter, devoid of joy.

That damned, rotten, Gaula's bastard . . .

It hadn't been enough of a punishment to give her wolf-sickness; he had made provisions for an even worse fate. He had given her a minute, painful chance to survive, to become a warow. The thing they hated most. It was the final humiliation.

Her pulse throbbed in her canines, rushing in her ears. She didn't have long, and this was what he had wanted. How long could she hold out before she chose to drink from him? Before she chose to take the chance and become one of them? It was a test that was beyond cruel.

Gríf . . . Why?

What had she done to him to deserve this? What kind of creature could wish so much suffering on others?

She grabbed hold of the vials, and the urge to throw them at the stone wall made her shoulders twitch.

Smash them! Smash them now!

But she doubted they would break, no matter how hard she threw them. They were made to last. The curved glass was thick and protected by a delicate web of tarnished silver. The pattern was exquisitely detailed, as if they were meant for perfume and not the rottenness that had caused the world to break.

How old were they? Were these the ones they had always used to bleed him? She pulled the rough chain through her fingers. Had her mother ever worn this around her neck? Had her grandmother, Agla, or her great-grandmother, Síla?

Juva picked them up by the chain. The light from the storm lantern made the deep red contents come alive, like lava. She ran her tongue over her teeth. The rushing in her ears grew, and she could no longer hear the sea churning against the rocks. Her body suddenly seemed alien, impossible to control. It was begging her to drink. Her tongue swelled in her throat. Her teeth burned.

Was it the power from the wolf-sickness or was it the urge to live?

Smash them!

But her arm wouldn't obey. It fell, as if she were powerless, and the vials lay in her lap. The city was full of warow who would have torn her to shreds for these vials, and that allure had been completely incomprehensible. Until now.

Juva sank down on the bed and lay with her head on the pillow. A faint whiff of woodfire and leather cut through her heart. Forcing out the memories she had worked so intently to forget. The bottomless black gaze, the claws he flicked, the muscular cracking as he stretched his neck. This body she had felt against her own. The voice with the dark wit. The merciless smile.

The kiss on the roof. Tongue against teeth.

She buried her face in the pillow and let out a long scream. It ripped at her throat, and she thought she was going to choke. The first words he had said to her came like an echo.

Breathe in.

She had been scared out of her wits and thought she was going to die, that her heart would explode. She had backed away, up against the wall.

Breathe out.

She had listened to him, back then, and she listened to him now, forced herself to breathe calmly.

It's not your heart you're feeling. It's mine.

He knew that because it was his fault. He had guaranteed that she would become a genuine blood reader, a senser, from when she had seen him as a child. Condemned her to a life of fear, and now . . . Now she could sense everything and everyone that bore a trace of his blood within them. That was her sentence, for the rest of her life.

Which he had made sure would be short and painful.

THE REALIZATION

They had put Nafraím in her bed.

Juva stood in the doorway, watching the others tend to him. He was fighting against time the way her mother had, in the same four-poster bed, framed by the same black curtains. It was unreal, like a nightmare.

He looked like he had been through Drukna. Low on blood and hollow-cheeked. What had that insane woman done to him to learn where the devil was?

His heart was beating just as fast as hers. Like a human, without the slow heaviness she had learned to recognize him by. This man had shaped her life with evil deeds and ruined everything it could have become, so why couldn't she look at him and think that he had gotten what he deserved?

The blood that could save him felt heavy around her neck. A cool, hidden weight between her breasts.

You are not the vardaris' salvation. You are the vardaris' demise.

Seire paced in circles and rubbed her knuckles as if she needed someone to punch.

"He's lost too much blood. He's not going to make it."

Faun wrapped the bandage around his wrist with a slow serenity. "He has always made it."

"He's sweating without a fever, Faun!"

The wild man didn't respond. Seire growled at him and kept

pacing in front of the fireplace. The flames pulled toward her every time she walked by. The windows were growing dark, and the modest light faded from the floor, melted into the shadows, and disappeared.

Ofre snuck by her in the doorway and set a tray on the nightstand. Water and a plate of flatbread and liverwort. He lit the candles in her mother's candlesticks, which were almost as tall as him and weighed down with old, melted wax. The old estate master looked at the ghost in the bed, opened his mouth to say something, but appeared to change his mind. He bowed, even though Nafraím didn't see him, then he left the room without a word.

Juva tensed to shield her heart. She was surrounded by warow, and it was impossible to think clearly.

I'm a blood reader. They can't fool me.

That didn't feel true anymore. It hadn't since Gríf, the biggest misjudgment of them all. The one that had cost her her life. Her heart could lie, and she couldn't afford to be deceived, so she needed to use her head.

What is real?

The blood on the chain around her neck was real, Gríf's heartless gift. The teeth pressing their way into her mouth. Eydala. And the fact that no one in this room had created wolf-sick people to survive.

That certainty grew but was impossible to grasp. It was stalking around her like a wolf, a predator waiting until she was vulnerable enough to attack. She couldn't give it that chance.

Fine, maybe these three, the first ones, weren't the sinners behind the wolf-sickness, but plenty of others could be. And if it hadn't been for Nafraím, it would never have existed. No Gríf, no warow, no blood pearls.

And why should she trust the murderer who lay dying in her own bed? She had betrayed him! The price he'd paid was painfully obvious, and yet she was supposed to believe that he had used the last of his strength to *warn* her?

No—Nafraím was here for a reason, and she needed to know what it was. He couldn't be allowed to die with all the answers. If she saved him, there was no other reason than that.

Nafraím groaned and opened his eyes a little.

"It's . . . the Rot. She's . . ."

Seire leaned in closer to him.

"Naf, you need to gather your strength. We need to move on."

Nafraím strove to lift his head. His lips were dry and cracked.

"Dead blood, Seire. They're drinking . . . dead blood. Mikkje . . ."

Seire turned his face toward hers.

"Listen to me, Naf! You're not thinking well. You don't have enough blood in your carcass. They'll find us here. Eydala will come straight here with the devil knows how many others!"

"No . . ." Nafraím said, shaking his head. "This is the last place . . ."

Seire pointed to Juva without taking her eyes off Nafraím.

"We're at Juva Sannseyr's house. A cursed murderer!"

Nafraím made a sound that was maybe meant as a laugh.

"Then she's in . . . fitting company."

Seire put her hands on her hips and paced in another dejected circle in front of the fireplace. Nafraím continued in a hoarse voice.

"Seire . . . Who would seek shelter with . . . with the woman who betrayed him? What . . . warow would go to the one who is hunting them?"

He knows . . .

Juva approached the bed. Seire moved the crossbow to the windowsill, demonstratively farther away. Juva acted as if she did not see it. She forced herself to look at Nafraím.

"A warow who wants revenge," she said. "A warow who wants to draw Eydala here. Wasn't that why you blabbed?"

Nafraím groaned again. "You can call me a lot of things, but . . .

no. The blabbing came from what you despise even more than me: superstition. She heard a . . . rumor. And the ghost in Nákla Henge, the man who . . ."

The man who disappeared.

His mouth twitched, a weak smile.

"We'll stay here," he finished.

Seire turned her back and banged her fists on the windowsill. The window seemed to bow out more than usual over the frothing sea, as if it were trying to get away from her. She glanced at Juva over her shoulder.

"Someone might have seen him come here, and the cart-puller might gossip. This house needs to become a fortress. We need to seal the windows facing the street and all the doors that can—"

"I did that many months ago," Juva replied. "And we have Skarr."

Seire nodded with something resembling acceptance.

"Four months . . ." Nafraím mumbled. "More. I have no idea of the extent of . . . the damage. What she's done. We don't know who's a friend . . . an enemy. Who's alive. We have . . . nowhere else to go."

Faun raised the water glass for him, but Nafraím turned his face away.

"Juva . . . you descended on me like . . . the wrath of the gods. Without mercy. Without . . . understanding. A furious child became . . . the end of an era. And now you have found God yourself . . . I hear . . ."

"Seire is right," Juva said with a quick laugh. "You have too little blood between your ears."

He fumbled for her hand, and she let him grasp it, let those cold, dry fingers close around hers.

"Do you understand . . . absolution now? You are my punishment, Juva."

Seire let out a snort.

"Don't listen to him!" she said. "He's been a masochist for almost seven hundred years—not because he believes he deserves it, but because he enjoys it!"

"Good," Nafraim muttered. "Hold on to your will to fight. You will . . . need it. Listen. You need to listen . . . Eydala . . . it will get worse. She . . ."

"It doesn't matter," Juva said. "Let her come. I can protect myself, and I have plenty of people to help."

Nafraím tried to reply, but it ended in dry heaves. Faun supported his head and put the water glass to his lips, but Nafraím pushed the glass away with renewed force and spilled on the pillow.

"Listen! That's what I'm trying to say. You think you have people, but he . . . The priest you're hunting for . . . He's working for her."

Juva pulled her hand back. The words were a threat. That eerie certainty, the wolf stalking around her heart was coming closer. Smelled blood. Smelled weakness. She knew what was coming, but she shook her head and searched for words to keep the predator at bay.

"No," she replied. Her mouth felt dry. "Silver Throat wants to annihilate you all in God's name. That fanatic wouldn't work for a warow. Why would he?"

Nafraím tried to raise himself up in the bed without success.

"Because he's no fanatic, Juva! Not at all . . . Listen. You need to understand . . . This has nothing to do with God or . . . fear or contempt, it's . . . politics. That's why he is spreading wolf-sickness."

Juva backed away. His words filled the room until there was no space for anything else.

Seire stared at Juva.

"What did I tell you?" she said through clenched teeth.

"He's no priest. He's working for Undst. Don't you see? We are vardari! We created Náklav! Nafraím more than anyone. Do you think the world builds itself or something? How old are you, girl? Twenty? What the fuck do you understand about those you are hunting? We hold the world together at the seams. You can thank

Nafraím for the fact that you have never witnessed war. He has given Náklav the peace and freedom you take for granted. Domnik created prosperity with Náklabank. Mikkje created art. And you . . ."

Seire's eyes narrowed. Her lips quivered.

"And you . . . What have *you* created? You who don't know how to do anything but ruin things. All you do is destroy, without an idea of what you're going to build!"

"Seire . . ." Nafraím began coughing but fought his way through it. "Seire, we did the same thing . . . once."

Juva sought support in Faun's gentle eyes. He shrugged his broad shoulders.

"The Vardari are the city's best defense," he said as if it pained him. "Without us—"

"Ha! Let them try," Seire scoffed and sat down on the windowsill. "Not even Undst is so dumb. No one can invade Náklav."

Without weakening it first.

"Ships," Juva said, clutching her chest. "They've sent ships."

"Undst?" Faun asked.

The warow stared at her. What should she say? How should she begin? She was up to her neck in things she needed to say.

"They say they have a cure for wolf-sickness. They have . . ."

The city will welcome them with open arms . . .

Her heart chilled and pumped the cold through her body. Her heart beat heavier and heavier, pushing out the others until the only thing she could sense was the predator. The knowledge of what she had done.

I have been fighting for the enemy. I've been killing warow, for Eydala, for Silver Throat, paving the way for a foreign power.

The warow had always controlled Náklav, and she had always hated them for it. She hadn't known that . . . And now they were fair game. Because Silver Throat had spread the wolf-sickness, feeding on the fear, the chaos.

She grabbed the bedpost. The room darkened and stiffened into a painting, as if it were something she was staring at from the outside. Like his images. The idol she had seen Silver Throat create, showing Eydala's hall of mirrors. They knew each other. Nafraím was right.

"The images . . ." she mumbled.

Seire leapt to her feet again.

"You fool!" she said to Juva, pointing to Nafraím. "*Look* at him! These are the monsters you work with, and you're blaming the images?! They're made of light and sea silver. They don't come from the gods!"

"I know that," Juva said and looked at Nafraím. "He gets them from *her*."

Nafraím let out a deep sigh. He closed his eyes and let his head sink into the pillow, as if those words had given him peace. Seire grabbed his hands.

"Naf? Nafraím?" she said.

Faun stood and put his fingers on Nafraím's neck, as if to check he was still alive. Seire walked over to the window and squeezed her head between her arms, as if she wanted to shut everything and everyone out.

Juva turned her back to them and slipped her hand under her shirt. She opened the clasp for one vial and took it off the chain. Then she walked to the window and held it out to Seire.

"Take it," she said, not recognizing her own voice.

Seire stared in disbelief at the curved vial in her palm. A fang. A work of art made of glass and tarnished silver. Full of the invaluable, crimson blood. Seire's face fell, as if she had lost the strength to maintain her constant mask of scorn.

Then she snatched the vial and was next to Nafraím in one bound.

Juva turned her back to them and left the room. She could hear them struggling to get him to drink, and she hoped he did. She went into the library. Skarr lay on the carpet sleeping. His body rose and fell along with his calm breathing. The opening to the shaft gaped in the chimney.

Gríf.

She had just used Gríf's blood to save his worst enemy, and that was the closest she would ever come to revenge.

She filled a glass with rye liquor. The wolf-sickness pushed at her teeth, and it felt like her brain was dying. Fragments of everything that had ever meant anything swirled like ash above the embers, and it wouldn't be long before there was only darkness.

THE FORGOTTEN DOOR

Juva slipped past the iron doors and peered in. The corpsewood glowed in the fire pit, a scant light that flickered up toward the slit in the stone wall, as if the sea were trying to absorb it every time it roared against the rocks outside.

In what had been Gríf's bed, three warow lay sleeping. The first ones. The trinity that had found and captured him and changed the world forever. Even so, they slept like innocents judging from their heartbeats. Tightly entwined.

Nafraím lay in the middle with his arms pressed to his sides, straight as if he were to be sepultured. He hadn't been far from that, either, but he had more color in his thin face now. Faun clung to him, with one arm and a knee over Nafraím's body. Faun's rootlike braids bent around his strong arms. Seire lay sprawled with one foot over the edge, as if the bed couldn't contain her, one arm over her eyes. Shielding herself from the dawn, which must surely be much brighter where she came from. Not in Náklav.

They were an unlikely trio: a pale nobleman, a golden child of nature, a dark warrior. What would Gríf have said if he had seen them here? If he had seen her save Nafraím's life?

What would Silver Throat have said?

The cold ate through her wool socks and crawled up her legs. It wasn't too late; she could inform on them now, tonight. Everything Nafraím had said could be lies. She had seen a warow keep someone with wolf-sickness prisoner with her own eyes, and Ferkja had followed her, for blood's sake, and . . .

They wouldn't have done that if they could make them wolf-sick.

She knew Nafraím was right. Every aching bone in her body knew that. Still, her mind groped for some way out, an explanation that was easier to swallow than the sickening truth. She had killed innocent people, without any sentence other than having fangs. She had hunted for *her* and Silver Throat. Hacking away at the mainstays of the city he wanted to conquer. The city he had already had in his grasp, with promises of a cure that didn't exist, for the wolf-sickness he himself was spreading.

Who am I?

Juva pulled her shawl more tightly around herself. She let the warow sleep and climbed back up again. Skarr stuck his head in the chimney opening and received her with his wet nose. She crawled into the library and stayed there, on her knees in front of him. The wolf sniffed her chest as if he understood the weight of what she carried around her neck. Or could he smell the blood? She buried her fingers in his fur and felt her strength ebb.

She had believed she was saving Náklav. Keeping the city and the girls safe from the warow and the wolf-sick. What an idiot she had been. Blinded by wolf-sickness, righteous because she was dying. As the gods gave people unerring understanding when their time was up.

But there were no gods. Silver Throat's likenesses were manmade. And she was going to die knowing that she had killed for him and sentenced Slokna to chaos.

Broddmar was right: she was a murderer. And she had dragged the girls into it with the maps, effectively used them as a weapon. Exactly what she had wanted to protect them from.

The Vardari aren't the enemy. I am.

Skarr whimpered. Juva stifled a sob against his fur, knowing that a single tear would give way to ten thousand. She couldn't start crying.

Her heart started murmuring, and she realized she was no longer alone. Nafraím was coming up the shaft. She got to her feet and pressed the palms of her hands to her eyes as she tried to maintain her composure.

Breathe in.

Nafraím appeared, a pale head in the dark opening, as if he had been decapitated. He was uncharacteristically winded, and she could feel from his heart that the climb had taxed his strength. He reached his hand out to her. Juva grabbed it and helped him up the last bit. Her thumb sank into his bandaged wrist, and she remembered an ancient injury Gríf had given him when they had caught him. The devil had marked them both.

Nafraím nodded in thanks and brushed the dust off the old-fashioned shirt, which was too big for him.

"I dreamt that the wolves came," he said, his voice dry. "In hordes, on a blue field, like a tapestry I have hanging in the hall. It was the strangest thing . . ."

He looked at her and lost his fragile smile. A sort of realization seemed to hit him, an expression she recognized from the time he had accidentally expressed admiration for an herb, the same one that had taken the life of Solde and the other blood readers.

He seemed embarrassed but appeared to shake it off quickly.

"I don't want to trouble you, but I would really like something to eat. Could we . . . ?"

"Eat?" Juva stared at him. "You want to eat?"

"Very fervently."

She shrugged and nodded for him to follow her to the stairs. He followed her down to the kitchen, and she felt a touch of the same fear as the last time he was here. The cold paralysis in her body. The panic that he would find Gríf.

She could never have imagined that she would sacrifice anything at all to save this man's life.

"There's not much here," she said, not understanding why she was apologizing. "My mother's staff doesn't work here anymore. It's just me."

Nafraím walked over to a wooden bowl she couldn't remember having set on the counter. He lifted the linen cloth to reveal bread dough, inhaling the scent with his eyes closed.

"Ofre, blessed man! Is he asleep?"

"He left after you . . . once you got better. He had work to do but is coming to check on you later and bring . . . tea."

The words were so innocuous and ordinary that they were an insult to her feelings. She followed Nafraím with her eyes while he nosed around the pantry, smelling things.

"Wonderful!" he said. "Have you ever had haeyna rolls?"

Juva shook her head, although he didn't see her do it. The kitchen wasn't hers anymore. Nafraím seemed more comfortable here than she had ever been.

He came back out of the pantry, set down an armload of earthenware and glass jars, and lifted a corpsewood log into the smoldering oven. Then he patted out two flat rounds of dough on the counter and covered them with seemingly random ingredients: mushrooms, goat cheese, pickled onions, and cured ham.

Juva dropped down onto a step and sat there, unable to wrap her head around what she was witnessing. This was lunacy. The source of all the misery in the world stood in her kitchen making haeyna rolls while he spoke as if she understood how yeast mushrooms were used for burns, the differences in leavening agents here versus Slokna and Grimse, how King Margen, who was so sure it made hair grow, had slept with dough on his head for several months.

He laughed, softly but heartily, as he shaped the dough into two large rolls, which he placed on the baking stone over the fire. A hectic flush blazed in his cheeks, and he had flour on his pants legs. It was disturbingly mundane; he should have been talking about having been tortured for months and cheating death. Or lashed out at her for having killed his kind.

She should have let him have it, too. For the threats, the fear, all those lost lives . . . His mistakes were neck and neck with her own, two snarling wolves he couldn't see but who nonetheless filled the room.

"So who is he, this Silver Throat?" Nafraím asked, disappearing into the wine cellar.

Here it comes.

Juva stared at the dough, which was sweating over the fire.

"I thought you knew better than I did. Isn't that why you're here?"

She heard clinking, as if he were restacking the bottles.

"I know what he *isn't,* and that's a spiritual man. Otherwise I'm afraid the information I have is . . . unreliable."

Juva's jaw tightened, painfully aware of who his source was. She focused on the bread that was darkening in the oven so they wouldn't burn.

"He could have been a blood reader," she replied. "What my mother could do with one person, he can do with a full hall. He was no one. Then he was a priest. Then he had enough followers to fill Jólshov. Then he had the favor of the city council, and they wanted me to . . ."

The sentence withered in her mouth, and she started over.

"He was just a guy who sat by me at Hidehall ages ago. Before . . . everything. He said his name was Lodd. He was reading a holy book from Undst and talking about how we had stolen the idea of the devil from them."

She heard him sigh.

"He's right in a sense, but he probably didn't acknowledge that they did the same thing. There's no saga, no gods, no customs that

243

any person can lay claim to. We're all thieves. But then that is the eternal problem with Undst: the sacred robbery."

"The sacred robbery?"

"Yes, that's what it's called, in derision. Not by Undst, of course, but by men and women who have negotiated with them officially. You understand . . ." He emerged from the wine cellar with a bottle in his hand. "They have this delusion that they've been robbed of something. That the country is being excluded from good society, to put it simply."

"Because they don't have a henge city . . ."

Nafraím looked at her with irritating respect, as if she should care what he thought of her.

"Precisely! You understand, Juva. The stones mean far more than you thought the night you shot me."

His words came abruptly, and she searched for a response but couldn't find one. He rubbed the shoulder where her bolt had dug its way in.

"You would have let me bleed out for the blood pearls I made," he said. "For the wolf-sickness they left in their wake, which kept the gateways alive, and you thought it was about money. Of course, the gates lift the world out of poverty, and prosperity has built bridges we could only have dreamed of otherwise, but the stone henges give us something far more valuable."

"What could be more valuable in Náklav than money?" Juva said, stifling a snort.

Nafraím smiled.

"Proximity." He leaned on the counter, visibly fatigued from talking. "The countries of the world are talking to each other. We know each other, which has bought us peace and freedom. Triumphs that are impossible to appreciate when you've never seen anything else, and you haven't, young Sannseyr."

Have you?

The mocking reaction did not cross her lips. The man in front of her was as old as Gríf. He had seen everything since the wolf wars.

"I doubt that Undst wants to conquer Náklav for the sake of peace," she mumbled.

"No," he chuckled. "Undst wants to conquer it because that's what they've always wanted. Because Náklav has gates to all the henge cities in the world. If you own Náklav, you own the world."

"So all Silver Throat wants is power?"

Nafraím smiled again.

"Did you know that milfeyr water is the only thing we know of that cures kolm fever? It's difficult to produce, an art few have mastered, but what's worse is that it deteriorates incredibly quickly. We can make it in Kviskre and have it in Thervia or Au-Gok in an instant."

"What's your point?"

"That it has never survived on a ship to Undst."

Juva felt an embarrassed heat in her cheeks. She didn't need shame. She needed anger to survive this night, but every time it flared up, he drowned it. She felt like branntang at a sepulture. Sparks struggling in vain against the far mightier sea.

"What about Eydala?" she asked. "Are you going to tell me she's from Undst and can be excused for churning out wolf-sickness and forcing Náklav to its knees?"

Nafraím opened a drawer and started looking for something.

"Now . . . Pointing out connections is no absolution. Undst has itself to thank for being excluded; they maintain customs that seem bestial to the rest of the world. As far as Eydala's concerned, that's the appeal. But it also blinds her to who he is, the priest. She is isolated enough to believe all he wants is admiration and young enough not to see the conquest coming."

Juva felt the cold creeping in from the stone step.

"No matter what their motivation, no one would be foolish

enough to try to conquer Náklav by force. What are they going to do, surround us with ships and starve us out? Climb up the cliffs? Half the men who try end up as food for Gaula."

Nafraím pulled the cork tongs from the drawer and held the tool up in triumph.

"And it takes a lot to starve out a city that gets everything it needs through Nákla Henge. Unless you first ally yourself with Kreknabork, Skippalun, Steinherad, Haeyna ..."

Juva stared at him. A nauseating disbelief grew in her stomach. Nafraím's eyes met her gaze in a way that was possibly meant to be reassuring.

"But you're right, Juva. No one has taken Náklav from the sea, and the henge cities have loyalty treaties older than lust. Breaking them would be self-destruction."

He wiped the dust off the wine bottle and set it on the counter.

"This was a gift from me to your mother. It's touching that she's looked after it."

Juva couldn't help chuckling.

"Forgotten it, you mean? It was probably drowning in the multitude of bottles in there."

Or she was afraid that you would poison her.

Nafraím chuckled, as if he were glad that she had kept that last thought to herself.

"You open it. I need to rescue the rolls!"

He took a linen cloth in each hand, grabbed hold of the rolls, and in a practiced motion, he wrapped each one to go.

"I've missed the wind," he said. "Let's enjoy them out on the balcony."

Juva gulped. Gríf had also missed the wind and weather after an eternity in captivity. Now Nafraím had gotten a taste for the same thing. Yet another thought she couldn't bring herself to share.

"I don't have a balcony, but we can go up to the roof."

"Of course you have a balcony!" He looked around. "But do you have glasses?"

He's confused.

It would probably take a while before he was himself again, but she caught herself hoping that he never would be. She took two water glasses from the cupboard, and he looked at her with a disappointment that there was no mistaking.

"I'll see what I can find," she mumbled and went up the stairs. He followed her, and she caught a faint whiff of sick sweat mixed with the tantalizing aroma of freshly baked bread. She went into the storeroom and got out what she assumed to be her mother's best wine glasses, with pretentious silver stems and large rounded bowls.

Good. Gaula knows I need it.

The glasses clinked in her hands, and she made an effort not to shake. She set them in a basket along with two wool blankets in case he wanted to go to the roof.

She peeked into the library, where Skarr lay sleeping. He pricked up his ears but didn't get up. Nafraím was waiting in the front hall, like a ghost of the last time he had stood there, pale and motionless in the gloomy space. He added the haeyna rolls to the basket and took it from her with an old-fashioned matter-of-factness, as if it were unthinkable to let her carry it. He followed her up the stairs but lagged behind before they reached the roof. He opened the door to one of the cluttered attic rooms and walked in.

"Ah, I see," she heard.

"Nafraím?" Juva followed him into the chaos. He started pushing things away from the back wall. A couple of chairs with silk cushions, a chandelier under a dust cover, a rolled-up carpet, an old door. His heart beat faster against her own, and he wiped his sweat away with the back of his hand.

What is he doing? He's not well.

"Nafraím?"

"There, look!" he replied, pushing aside an enormous painting of the old docks. A round window came into view, and it immediately jogged her memory. It was big, taller than her, cased in copper turned completely green. The frame curved around faded glass doors. Nafraím opened them wide and stepped out onto the balcony.

Juva followed him, and the Floa wind hit her. She gaped out at the night-black sea.

"I remember, but . . . I didn't think this was *here*. Just a glimpse, a memory from somewhere else."

He smiled as if he understood precisely. Then he ducked back inside and fetched the two old chairs. Juva sat down. She felt completely exposed, naked. This was her house, her home, and the man she had spent a lifetime hating was able to show her things she had had no idea were there. Things she had long since forgotten.

She wrapped one blanket around herself and watched while he laid out their meal on an old wooden crate as if it were a banquet table. She accepted one of the rolls. The linen cloth was warm against her hands as if it was the only thing that was real this night.

The aroma of burned bread made her eyes sting, and she squeezed them shut to stop her tears.

Everything was so infinitely wrong. The world was coming apart at the seams, and it was her fault, Nafraím's fault. She couldn't just sit and eat as if nothing had happened.

"Don't you like it?" he asked with a warmth that revealed he knew what she was holding back. He had no right to be here! No right to care, after having turned everything she was upside down.

She wiped her nose on her sleeve.

"How can you live with it?! If you hadn't captured Gríf, we wouldn't be here. You created Náklav to match what you envisioned, without thinking about what would happen if you disappeared. You say you made everything better, but what's better about this? You've made us more vulnerable than we would have been without you."

He handed her a glass of wine.

"That may be true."

"It *is* true! And you created *her*! Gave eternal life to that . . . monster."

"Yes. And I did that to prevent her from showing the world the images. I tried to put a lid on the progress I myself claim to love, because that would have made it difficult to live forever. I relegated her to a life in the shadows. It's my fault that she now seeks the fame I robbed her of, so you understand . . . my sins are both greater and more numerous than you think."

"Like spreading wolf-sickness? And killing Solde and the others? And you sent Rugen to spy on me."

"Rugen is dead."

"What do you want me to do?" Juva said, clenching her wineglass. "Grieve?"

"No," he smiled wryly. "I didn't think you would."

"I've lived in fear my whole life, and it's *your* fault!"

"So you're going to live the rest of your life angry?"

"I'm going to *die* angry."

Juva felt stabbed by her own words. They had been waiting in her jaw to be yanked out, like fangs. All that was left was a bleeding crater. She felt her wineglass slip. Nafraím caught it and set it on the crate.

"Not anytime soon," he said, and she clenched her fists to keep from telling him exactly how wrong he was.

"What have I done?" she sobbed.

Nafraím put a hand on her back.

"Fought, Juva; you have always fought. We are the same sort, you and me. No limits. When other people say it's impossible, that nothing can be done . . . Then we do it. This city is drowning in wolf-sick people, and folks are getting used to it—but not you. You have to do something. And when you think the vardari are the problem, and other people just whisper about it, then you declare war on us. And when you find the devil in captivity, then you set him free. You're learning that everything has a price."

"I didn't know," she sobbed. "I didn't know what she would do to you, that you would be . . ." She gulped again. "And now we're just sitting here as if . . . We don't have *time*. We need to do something that means something!"

"We're eating, Juva. There's little more important than that. Trust me when I say that."

His words squeezed her heart, and she felt like she was breaking. Her tears made the food grow in her mouth, and she struggled to swallow it.

"Why didn't you say anything? Why didn't you tell her what I had done?"

Nafraím smelled the wine in the glass and closed his eyes.

"I wanted to die doing a good deed."

So did I . . .

She looked out at the sea.

"I hate you," she said.

He smiled.

"I know that. Enough to save my life."

TOOTHLESS

The conversation faded again, leaving an oppressive silence in the library. It was intensified by rhythmic grating from Seire, who sat on the sofa sliding a whetstone along the curved knife blade.

After several rounds of intently searching for a solution, the pauses were the only assured outcome. There were too many problems, and they were too big. The answers too risky.

Juva put her hand on her shirt to feel the vials under her fingers, the worst option of all. The one she would never take. She would rather take the poison still wedged into a seam pocket in her corset. Blood and poison. That's what she was now. A roving choice between instantaneous death and eternal life.

Although there was no guarantee someone with wolf-sickness would survive taking the blood, and even *if* she did survive, she would need to take more in a year. Even *eternal* had lost its meaning.

Nafraím was an ailing testament to that, sitting hunched over and writing.

Faun paused his wandering along the bookshelves in front of a diorama of shimmering beetles. He ran his fingers over the glass and frowned sadly. Juva understood him well. What could be more tragic than crossing all the world's seas and countries only to end up mounted on pins for display in the Sannseyr home?

Ending up with wolf-sickness.

She had been much too close to revealing it to Nafraím. Maybe she should have, but where would she start? She was so over-ripe with secrets that she felt rotten. Way too much that should have been said, including the fact that Silver Throat was expecting her tomorrow for another hunt.

It was a grotesque and unsolvable problem that she had had many opportunities to tell them about. They had talked about him and how he was spreading wolf-sickness. Nafraím didn't think it had to do with blood pearls. It was a demanding art, and the rapid increase suggested a far more careless approach.

The three warow had talked about not knowing where their friends were or even if they were alive at all. Some had probably sought refuge in other countries with safe contacts. Some would have assumed new names and lines of work, while others were maybe still working behind the scenes to make sure the henge cities functioned, that the world functioned. The world, as she had always known it, without thinking about what or who separated order from chaos.

She had believed wolf-sickness was the worst thing that could happen to her, but these three were discussing far bigger things. Who could secure Náklabank, the city council, the Ring Guard, and the water supply. Whether they still knew anyone who could warn the Queen's Guard about the ships from Undst. It was too much to bear.

"I still vote to kill her," Seire said abruptly. "You know where she hangs out. This can be over before nightfall."

Nafraím set down his pen and looked up from his letter. "What will that give us, other than losing the upper hand? If we kill Eydala, the priest will smell that something is wrong. And unlike Undst, she poses no danger. My guess is that she's prioritizing little else besides looking for *me*."

Seire tested the knife edge against her thumb.

"You're right. The ships from Undst will be here for the Dragsuget Regatta. The fanatic is spreading wolf-sickness and killing our own, but by all means, the most important thing we can do now is write letters . . . Remember to talk about the weather, Naf."

Nafraím smiled and kept writing.

"I refuse to be a prisoner here," Seire said, standing up. "I don't care how many likenesses he has. We need to warn someone!"

"Who?" Nafraím asked without any hint of irritation. "We don't know who we can trust or where they are."

"Domnik wouldn't sell us out! Nor would Vippa or Hemvil."

"I don't think so, either, but we can't be sure."

Seire dropped back down onto the sofa and picked at the brads on the armrest.

"We need to warn the henge cities no matter what. The gods know how many other places they've finagled their way into."

Nafraím turned his paper over and continued writing.

"What do you think I'm doing?"

Juva got up and went into the front hall while they continued the strangely one-sided argument. Seire was right; they had to do something. And of all the distressing alternatives, only one offered any hope. For everyone but her.

The red suit hung from the peg like a bloody carcass. She reached into the pocket with trembling fingers and found the map. It felt heavy in her hand, as if it were begging to be lost, hidden and forgotten. But the warow needed to know, even if Seire would chew her head off.

She ripped off the corner with Tokalínn's drawing. The girls needed to remain a secret. Then she returned to the library and set the map on the table in front of Nafraím.

"I know where they are, every single vardari in Náklav."

Seire jumped to her feet and grabbed the map, flattened it out with her hands. Her eyes wandered between the little red and yellow marks until she appeared to understand what she was looking at. Her face contorted in disgust.

"So, a hunting map, huh?" she spat. "I see you have been quite busy."

Faun leaned over the table with childlike wonder.

"So it's true? You can really sense us?"

Nafraím looked at her.

"She's the first one in centuries."

But not the only one.

"I don't know who they are," she said. "But I know where. Some are in the same place every time. Others move around, or just . . . pass by."

Seire stared at her in disbelief.

"And this you share with *him*, with Silver Throat?"

"No—no one has seen this. It's my own."

"But you've used this to find warow!?"

"Seire . . ." Nafraím glanced up at her.

Seire snarled and paced in a circle.

"The map is useless if we don't know who we can trust."

Juva looked at her and steeled herself against the fury doomed to follow.

"We do know *some people* we can trust. His victims."

Seire flung up her arms.

"So we can trust the people Silver Throat has killed? Great, that really helps—"

Nafraím held up his hand and silenced her. Understanding dawned in his eyes.

"She's right. They're not hunting their allies."

"So . . ." Seire said, her eyes wandering. "We can rely on . . ." She stared at Juva and smiled. "Everyone he shares an image of."

"Exactly!" Juva smiled back. "And in addition to you and Faun, he has a picture of someone named Ferkja. She was the one who followed me and told me that you guys can live off the blood of people with wolf-sickness."

"Who's Ferkja?" Seire glanced at Nafraím. "Do we know . . . Oh, wait! It's Storm! She uses that name. Storm's alive!"

The warow gathered around the table as if it were a life raft.

"There was one more; someone I don't know," Juva said. "He was attractive. Blond and maybe your age, Faun. He was asleep, and I recognized Eydala's room. It was . . ."

"Yrgen." Nafraím looked down. "He wasn't asleep. He was dead."

Seire shook her head.

"Why would he share an image of someone they had already killed?"

Juva got a bitter taste in her mouth.

"Because he needed to show that the image had been created. He wanted everyone to see that."

"The man is a monster," Seire said, staring at the ceiling in disgust.

"Is that all?" Nafraím asked.

"No, I saw another one . . ." Juva gulped. "He hid his image because . . ."

"You killed him," Seire growled.

"No! No, but . . ."

I was just there.

The words were too pathetic for her to get out. She searched for another way to put it but only came up with miserable excuses. The memory made her sick. She had seen a man go to his death in Drukna, disappear between the stones, while the sophisticated people had toasted to her and Silver Throat's honor.

"He was dead," she whispered. "But I don't know who he was."

Nafraím looked at her with pleading eyes.

"Domnik? Young? Reddish-blond hair combed back into a ponytail? He's incredibly important. Don't tell me that—"

"No, No. He was blond and had short hair. Strong guy . . . He had a wolf-sick woman on a boat down in Nyhavn, and she—"

"Reiko." Seire clenched her fists and stared at the table.

"Who was he?" Juva forced the words out. Nafraím smiled sadly at her.

"He was one of the foremost in his field, mental illnesses. He dedicated his life to alleviating madness and the impacts of a difficult life. You would have liked him."

Juva stared at her hands. Reiko had been telling the truth. He hadn't caught the wolf-sick woman to drink from her. He had been taking care of her.

Skarr crawled under the table and lay down on top of her feet. She could feel him breathing. Broddmar should have come to get him ages ago, but that hadn't happened. The chasm was too deep, the one that had formed the instant she had shot Reiko in the calf and handed him over to the Ring Guard.

Seire sat down on the sofa.

"You've been hunting innocent people for a damned fanatic from Undst—"

"Yes, and I need to keep doing it."

"Keep doing it?!" Seire's eyes widened. "You're going to keep working for him?!"

"No," Nafraím smiled and looked Juva in the eye. "She's going to let him think she's doing that. She will do what blood readers do best—mislead."

Juva nodded, and it felt as if she were confirming her own death.

"I have no other choice. If I refuse to cooperate, I'm not useful anymore. The city council will fall, and Eydala will come. And just by being close to Silver Throat, we can know who he wants dead, who his friends and his enemies are. Just tell me who I should look for. Who are most important to warn? And time is of the essence. He's expecting me tomorrow evening."

Seire chuckled.

"So you're going to warn the warow rather than murdering them? Do you think you have God-given gifts, girl? He'll never fall for it."

"*I* did," Nafraím said, hiding a smile.

"That's because you're an idiot, Naf. That man is going to figure it out fast. It can't possibly last long."

"It doesn't need to last long," Juva said. "Just long enough. We only have until the Dragsuget Regatta, anyway. If we don't have a solution before the ships arrive, we've lost."

Seire looked at her with an inscrutable gaze. Juva realized that she had rarely seen anything but pure contempt in her face.

Skarr suddenly got up and slinked out from under the table. After a brief moment, Juva heard the same thing he did. The distant echoes of the Dead Man's Horn.

No!

Juva braced herself on the table and closed her eyes for a second. Her body felt heavy and steadfast, like a mountain.

"That sound . . ." Faun said. "Does that mean . . . ?"

Juva ran to the front hall and left it to the others to explain what was going on. He obviously hadn't spent most of his centuries in Náklav. She pulled on her suit and looked around in confusion without locating the crossbow. Seire came running and tossed it to her. The warow woman looked like she wanted to say something but made do with a nod.

"You all stay here and don't answer if anyone knocks," Juva said and set off running through Lykteløkka. She saw a runner coming toward her, so focused on his goal that he didn't notice her. Juva grabbed him before he could dart past.

"Where?!"

"Hidehall!" the boy gasped, breathing hard.

Juva raced down the streets, and Skarr could barely keep up with her. Hidehall was her responsibility. Someone could be in danger, the guys or someone who worked there, or . . .

She rounded the corner around Blodrenna and ran into the square by Hidehall. It was teeming with people who had hurried outside, leaving their coats behind but not their beers. She clenched her teeth to protect herself from what awaited her inside, even though that had never done any good.

The customers got out of her way and let her enter with Skarr at her heels.

A chair came flying toward her, and she only barely managed to duck before it crashed into the door. Juva stared at what didn't look like anything but a huge melee. She spotted Broddmar. He smashed his fist into the jaw of one of the Hallowed men, who grabbed his chin and wailed. His head had grazed the nail in his silver collar necklace, and blood ran between his fingers. More members of the Hallowed arrived, and Muggen looked like he was desperately trying to mediate. Nolan and Lok held Broddmar back, and Hanuk poured a pitcher of water over the angriest of the Hallowed brawlers.

Juva held on to Skarr firmly and yelled, "Don't force me to shoot!"

That calmed things down somewhat, and she kept going before they had time to change their minds. "Who triggered the Dead Man's Horn?"

The Hallowed men all pulled back, looking at each other. Apart from one, a tall guy she recognized from Jólshov, who remained where he was, chin up and steely eyed.

"He's the devil!" he said, as if that would explain anything at all.

"Who is?"

The man pointed at Broddmar.

"He looks like the image, and he's had his teeth removed!"

The image?

She looked around. There was a row of paper on the wall, right by the beer barrels. Drawings of Silver Throat's idols.

Juva stepped over to the Hallowed man and stared up at him.

"He's missing teeth because my father knocked them out years ago. Do you want to keep your own?"

The man chewed his lip.

"He could be a vardari," he muttered.

The Hallowed guy who was bleeding from his chin came over and thumped him on the back.

"That's her. She's God's hunter."

That was not news to the man in front of her. He was clearly fighting a battle against himself.

"We could at least let the Ring Guard check," he tried. "So we know what we're dealing with."

Juva unhooked the bloodskins from her backpack and held them up in front of him.

"I know what I'm dealing with. The Dead Man's Horn means someone with wolf-sickness, and I have two empty skins to fill. You look a little sweaty . . . Are you sure you're healthy?"

He raised his hands and backed away. Juva hooked the skins back into place and pointed to the door.

"Get out, all of you! I don't want to *see* you laying a hand on people again. And send runners to call off the Ring Guard, otherwise I can promise that you're going to pay for the party."

The members of the Hallowed disappeared out the door and the remaining customers relaxed. Hanuk handed Broddmar a bundle, which he put on his jaw. Broddmar made eye contact with her.

"Do you expect me to thank you?" he said, his voice rough as if his tongue had swollen.

Nolan nudged him.

"Shut up, Broddmar."

Broddmar drained a glass of liquor that she doubted had been his before the fight broke out.

"They used to respect me," he said. "Red hunter. I did something good for this city. That doesn't seem to be enough anymore. Now you have to be on the side of the gods."

Juva felt paralyzed. The knowledge that he was right burned like fire in her chest, and she longed to say so, longed to explain. But how could she? Muggen had been at Jólshov with his sister. He was one of the Hallowed now. And Broddmar . . . He never could keep his mouth shut. He always dragged the other guys into it. Was she going to let five guys know she was sheltering warow?

Juva looked at them all, and they seemed like strangers. Broddmar bore a grudge. Muggen looked like he felt he'd been tricked. Only Lock was on the verge of tears, as he so often was. He stepped toward her.

"Juva . . ." She felt the lump grow in her throat and hurried to interrupt him. "Take care of the girls. Tell them I'll stop by soon."

He caught her gaze.

"And will you?"

Juva didn't reply. She walked over to the beer barrels and ripped the drawings down from the wall.

"People will be safe in Hidehall," she told Oda, who stood wide-eyed behind the bar. "We don't hang up drawings here, no matter who brings them. Do you understand?"

Odda nodded.

Juva went out. She could hear Skarr padding after her and Broddmar yelling from inside, "keep him!"

She crumpled up the drawings and threw them in the gutter.

GRACE

Nafraím's hand slid over the paper as he pointed.

"So, you see, the light is captured through the glass and imprints on the silver plate."

Juva rubbed her eyes. The drawing was clear enough. It was the result she struggled to comprehend.

"But . . . how can the silver know what people look like?!"

"No, no. The silver plate doesn't *know* anything," he said, eager as a teacher. "It reacts to the substances that make it sensitive to light. The motif remains invisible until you bathe it in sea silver."

Seire folded her arms across her chest.

"And, voila, you have likenesses of every single warow in Náklav", she said.

"Wait . . ." Juva raised her hand to stop Seire. Every time the warow opened their mouths, something came out that made bad things even worse. "They have pictures of all of you?"

"She's exaggerating," Nafraím said. "Eydala has pictures of several members of what we call the council, but fewer than fifteen, I'm guessing."

He curled his index finger around his chin and looked like his thoughtful self again, the way she had seen him in the painting at Mikkje's place.

"Maybe she was sick in the head even back then and held on to them specifically to bring us down? Difficult to say."

"Difficult?" Seire spat. "That sounds exactly like something that bitch would have done!"

The door knocker banged on the front door and silenced the conversation. The warow exchanged looks before they jumped to their feet and gathered their things. Seire drew the knives.

Juva ran to the front hall and peeked between the gaps in the boarded-up window. It was a runner. She gestured to Seire, who darted against the wall and then opened the door a crack. The boy on the front step gave her a card and ran off. Juva closed the door and stared at the card. The severe handwriting awakened a sudden horror.

"What is it?" Seire leaned over her shoulder to see.

Juva looked at her.

"It's *him*. He wants to see me at Jólshov as soon as possible, ready to fight."

Seire snatched the card and turned it over as if she couldn't read.

"Silver Throat? Why?"

"I guess I'll find out."

Juva took her suit off the peg and put it on. Seire cocked her head and squinted as if she feared trickery.

"I didn't think you were going out until tonight."

Me either . . .

Skarr padded in from the library with Nafraím and Faun in tow. They started talking over each other, wanting to know what was going on, but she didn't have any answers. It could be anything. At worst, Eydala had grown weary of the cat-and-mouse game and was ready to finish her off.

No—at worst, they knew she was sheltering warow. And that she had wolf-sickness.

She strapped on her harness and looked at the warow. They grew quiet, as if they suddenly realized what the order might mean.

Nafraím opened his mouth to say something but didn't appear to find the words. Juva nodded and walked out. There was no indication that this was related to wolf-sickness, so she left Skarr. Or was it because deep down she feared she wouldn't be coming back?

Get a grip, Juva!

She locked the door herself, in case anyone was watching the house, then she set off at a run through Lykteløkka.

What should she do? What should she say?

These were pointless questions to ponder until she knew what he wanted. Other than to summon her as if she were his servant . . .

The wind howled along the old city walls down toward Jólshov, and the square was deserted. Her body felt strangely weightless, like one of the children's kites by Ulebru Bridge. She was nothing but a fragile piece of fabric, helpless in the gusts of wind. Her feet threatened to fail her, and she had to force them into the Halloweds' hall, aware that every step she took could be her last.

She, who was supposed to hunt the warow, was their secret salvation. Trapped working for—and trusted by—the man spreading the wolf-sickness. A priest. A scout. A spearhead. For a country whose only aim was to conquer Náklav. What could she do against such forces?

I started this war. I can end it.

The new hunting team sat in the hall, eating. Juva recognized only three of the men she had selected. The rest were new. At one of the long tables, a couple of initiates were packing up boxes of food for the poor. Was that how he was spreading the blood?

No—if so, wolf-sickness would only be around the Rafts, and that was far from the truth.

Juva had the unsettling feeling that someone was approaching, and she turned around. Silver Throat indulged himself in a slow smile, as if to show that he had been anything but happy before she saw him. She lifted her chin and reminded herself who she was. If she was suddenly meek in dealing with him, he would have every reason to be suspicious.

"I'm working *with* you, not *for* you," she said as bitingly as she could. That appeared to make his smile a notch more genuine, and he put a hand on her back.

"We work for each other, Juva, for a better world. Forgive the haste. Naturally, I wouldn't have bothered you if it weren't important, but God waits for no one. When he speaks, we are compelled to listen."

He led her through the hall and unlocked the back room. A storeroom that had been converted into a plain workroom. Not what she would have expected of a popular faith leader. This was a space for a practical man with a job to do. How many clues like this had she overlooked?

"God has shown us his will again, Juva; the person in the likeness has been recognized by someone who believes they know where the evil one is staying. We don't have a lot of time."

He unlocked a chest, took out the dark box, and set it on the desk. His hands lingered on the lid.

"I hear you had a . . . confrontation with some of our people? At a tavern?"

Juva took a deep breath to buy herself time to come up with a good response.

"They obviously weren't aware of the terms of our agreement."

"Which terms are you referring to?" he asked, raising one eyebrow.

"No fanatics hunting in the streets."

"Fanatics? They were our own people!"

"Well, *our own people* need to get out of their blood fog, their thirst for revenge," she replied without breaking the eye contact. "Enemies of the people? Huge bar brawls? How does that look for your cause?"

"*Our* cause, you mean?" Silver Throat put the key in the box. "And if I understood correctly, someone was missing teeth?"

Juva looked around with a look of feigned indifference.

"Drukna will get full if you send everyone there who's missing teeth."

He gave a clipped laugh.

"You are . . . amusing, Juva, although I do wonder what sort of people you're associating with. Did you know them well, the men you stood up for?"

"I thought you said we didn't have a lot of time?"

An irritated look crossed his face before he recovered his patronizing smile.

"Of course."

He opened the box, lifted out the silver plate with both hands, and turned it toward her.

Juva stared at Nafraím's colorless face. Elegant, inquisitive, awake . . . The way he used to be, not tortured half to death. Was this a test? Her mouth suddenly felt dry, and she was at a loss for words. What was it that Nafraím had said?

My guess is that she's prioritizing little else besides looking for me.

He was right. Of course they were looking for him now. But if Eydala had shared everything, then the priest knew that she knew the man in the picture. She couldn't lie. She would have to resort to a half-truth, the thing that had always saved her.

Silver Throat scrutinized her, seemingly unaware that he held the final evidence of his own treason in his hands.

"You know him?" he asked.

Juva drew upon a contempt that came from everything but the likeness.

"He's the reason I hunt warow."

"As I said," he replied. "I'm surprised by the people you associate with."

"That bastard has haunted my family for generations. *Associate* with is far from the word you need there."

Silver Throat set the likeness down again and closed the box.

"So you know where we're headed, where he lives?"

Juva clenched her jaw. Her pulse throbbed faster in her canines.

"If I knew that, he'd have been dead a long time ago."

Silver Throat chuckled. He threw on a jacket and showed her out into the hall again. The hunting team spotted them and emptied their bowls. The new guys were strong, some with marks from rough treatment on their arms and jaws. Where had he found these bruisers? Not in the Ring Guard . . .

It doesn't matter. No warow will die today.

Silver Throat stuck close to her as they walked, spinning a tale about where the tip had come from, which was far too detailed to be true. Juva clung to his lie. It was a good sign. It hadn't occurred to them that Nafraím might be at her place.

Even so, she felt her relief liberate her breathing once Silver Throat led them past Lykteløkka and on up Bodsrabben. He questioned her about Nafraím, and she replied as harmlessly as she could. They walked in a group across Ringmark, all the way to Dauvrák, the outermost street along the cliffs. Silver Throat stopped in front of the gate of the first of a row of hanging houses.

Juva had seen them before. The Sannseyr home was also the farthest out, facing the sea, but still . . . It must be quite unique to live beyond the cliffs, with nothing between you and the sea but the wind.

The house was a dark stone estate with a crooked pine tree in the front courtyard. The guys swaggered their way through the gate. None of them seemed to notice the coat of arms forged into the wrought iron railings—a dead wolf on a spear with the name *Sai* underneath.

Nafraím Sai.

Silver Throat looked at her, and she realized she needed some excuse for hesitating. She raised her index finger and cocked her head to the side, as if she needed a second to sense. Then she shook her head.

"There's no one here," she announced.

That appeared to disappoint Silver Throat, but he waved for her to follow him through the gate. One of the guys kicked in the front door and grinned at them.

"He didn't even lock it!"

He never got the chance.

Or someone had broken in before them, if she were to judge by the marks in the wooden door frame.

She followed them inside and stood in the entryway as they spread out around the house like animals. They broke open doors and tipped over shelves as if destruction were the goal. The space deserved better. There was something venerable about it; like an old royal hall with a gallery, a sort of interior balcony supported by columns, all made of wood set against the rough stone walls. Two tapestries hung on one wall, old enough that the colors seemed faded, but they didn't show any wear. A blue field with wolves chasing across one tapestry.

From his dream.

The other was harder to recognize. A slaughtered animal? No . . . The subject grew clearer to more she stared at it. Hearts, a heap of them, red and bleeding.

One of the guys hooted from the basement, and Juva ran down a spiral wooden staircase wound tightly next to the wall. Small openings set back in deep niches made it dizzyingly clear she was in the part of the house that was hanging off the cliff, nothing below but the sea. The stairs opened into a room like none she had seen before.

The man she was guessing had yelled stood with his nose to a liquor glass with a heart on the bottom.

"This is the sickest thing I've ever seen!" he said.

But it was far from the strangest. The room was filled to the brim with books, instruments, models, drawings, skeletons . . . Someone had been here before them and yanked the books off of the shelves and emptied the drawers onto the floor.

Eydala searching for the last of the blood.

The youngest of the guys sniffed a jar and dropped it on the floor with a grimace. The liquid flowed out and remained in the grooves between the stones.

"Be careful!" Silver Throat snapped. "There are dangerous substances here!"

Juva glanced at him quickly. That was more than a clever guess. It was a revelation. He knew more about Nafraím than if all he had to go on was a sign from God.

"Is that . . . ?" One of the new men, a guy with crumbs in his beard, pointed wide-eyed to a dried whale penis. That triggered a chorus of jokes and more broken glass.

Juva gritted her teeth. If she opened her mouth, she would reveal the disgust that sat like a lump in her stomach. This group had no idea where they were or what they were dealing with. They were blind to the passion that surrounded them. This was what Nafraím burned for, what he had always loved. Science. An almost seven-hundred-year-old quest that had ended in Eydala's brutality. And here was the legacy of his long life, a playpen for a gang of reprehensible bullies.

Juva couldn't watch anymore. She turned to go and spotted a bundle under the stairs, an open sack and several books that lay strewn across the floor. She recognized one of them.

His diary . . .

Her memory cleared as she stared at the brown leather binding. Nafraím had shown it to her in Florian's Parlors. Set it on the table between the silverware, fish roe, and butter biscuits, when she had tricked him into believing the letter. If she had only known back then . . .

Thin cords were wrapped around the book, but the leather was pulling up in the corner, as if to lure her into reading about his projects, everything he had been so childishly eager to tell her. The first book press. The ice rink under Kingshill. A formula for anesthesia.

It had all seemed so insignificant to her then, despite the hope he had expressed.

Perhaps it causes us to understand each other better.

But she hadn't understood.

She couldn't leave it to be sacrificed to vandals, booze, and broken wine bottles.

Wine bottles . . .

She looked around. There was a door ajar at the other end of the room, which looked like it led straight into the rocky cliff itself. A storeroom, if she was lucky.

"Hey, is that a wine cellar?" she asked, pointing. The guys immediately lost interest in the workroom and fought to be the first one into the storeroom. Juva grabbed the book and ran back up the stairs, slipping the book into her backpack. She came out into the front hall and heard some of the guys banging cupboard doors upstairs. They were tearing apart the nearby kitchen, too, judging by the sound of breaking glass.

She clenched her fists and tried to swallow the upsetting mix of anger and grief but to no avail. Her chest was pounding like . . .

A heart!

Juva froze. She hadn't noticed anyone there, so whoever it was had just come in.

Or was trying to get out . . .

She followed the wall below the gallery to a simple wooden door. The heart beat anxiously in time to her own. Possibly the most human vardari heart she had sensed.

What do I do?

She had to act fast. She cast around furtive glances while her mind shuffled through the hopelessly small number of options. If she went in, she risked an attack. If she did nothing, the guys would find the warow. And it could be anyone, even an ally of Eydala's, placed to test her.

That thought chased her heart up higher in her chest. This seemed like an incredibly risky chance to take, but she couldn't not do it, couldn't go home and say she had saved her own skin and watched yet another warow be sent to Drukna.

Juva put her hand on the door handle and opened the door agonizingly slowly, to give the warow time to hide. She squeezed her crossbow and peered into a closet, a long, narrow darkness. Coats, suits, and shirts hung, impeccably sorted along the wall above a row of shoes. Hats stood out on the shelves, filling the room with faceless shadows.

The extra rhythm began to race faster than her own. The warow was in there and knew it was over. She squinted toward the contours. The closest hat shelf was full of coats in an untidy heap that revealed the unmistakable shape of a person. Juva took a step into the room and banged on the shelf. Reddish-blond hair came into view, hanging over the edge.

The color jogged her memory. Someone Nafraím had said was important.

Juva glanced into the front hall, and then closed the door almost fully behind her again. The coats on the shelf were trembling almost imperceptibly.

"Domnik?" she whispered. "You need to get out of here before they find you!"

The coats moved, and a face came into view. The man stared at her in disbelief. Tired but handsome with a short, sharply clipped full beard, and his hair in a ponytail.

"I'm Juva Sannseyr," she said, worried that he wouldn't understand how serious the situation was. He pushed the coats out of the way and dropped onto the floor, eyes narrowed.

"I know who you are . . ."

The shame boiled in her body, but she didn't have time to play the repentant sinner. What in Drukna could she say? What could explain all that was going on and at the same time, chase the man out of here?

"Nafraím is alive!" she whispered frantically. "And Undst has people in Náklav. They're spreading wolf-sickness and planning a war. The ships are coming for the Dragsuget Regatta! Warn those you trust and *only* them." She fumbled around to get the right key from her hip bag and gave it to him. "That opens the back door to Hidehall. We'll find you there when we can."

Domnik came closer and peered into the front hall, obviously having doubts, which she couldn't blame him for.

"Think, man! I wouldn't have known who you were if I were lying."

He put his hand on the door, ready to run.

"The images . . . Have they shared mine?"

Juva shook her head.

"They've shared Nafraím, Faun, Seire, and Ferkja. Go now!"

His shoulders seemed to drop a little with relief. He pulled a hand over his chin as if he were looking for words neither of them had time for.

"Tell him . . . Say that the money knows, and that the law will know."

His words were a simple riddle. He trusted her but not enough to give her names.

Then he set off at a run through the front hall and disappeared outside. The front door banged shut behind him, and she felt his heart fade in her chest.

Juva stepped out and saw Silver Throat coming up the stairs. Fear tore through her, cold and paralyzing. What had he seen? He must have heard the door. She couldn't risk taking a chance on anything else.

"A drunk from the Rafts," she said, rolling her eyes. Silver Throat studied her without responding.

"He didn't know anything," she continued. "Had just found a roof over his head. Houses like this don't sit empty long." She hooked her crossbow on to her back again. "Are the dogs done tearing the place apart? You're wasting my time."

Silver Throat treated her to a smile that did not reach his eyes. She turned her back to him and walked out onto the front step. She closed her eyes and took a deep breath, but her heart would not settle down. It was something about the way Domnik had asked.

The images . . . Have they shared mine?

There were more. Nafraím had said the same thing, that Eydala had long ago captured them on silver plates, which meant they weren't difficult to make . . .

Juva felt an uncomfortable certainty thicken in her throat. Her breath whitened in front of her, as if the world had suddenly grown colder. Her teeth screamed for blood.

Silver Throat came out onto the front step and stood beside her.

"I almost forgot," he said in a way that revealed he hadn't forgotten at all. "Something . . . remarkable happened, which will necessitate us holding a sepulture tomorrow. At Nákla Henge. And I need you there." He looked at her. "If you can," he added with a supercilious smile.

Juva shrugged as if it were all the same to her, but she had a sickening feeling that this sepulture might be her own.

LIFE'S WORK

The Sannseyr library was a rare treasure. Even in Náklav there were very few places one could find a handwritten edition of Unna Mirger's *Official Positions of the World* from 1284, but it was said he had given it to Síla Sannseyr himself.

Nafraím leafed through it, pulling his finger down the pages. The succession of the nobility, generals, and bureaucrats—many he could still remember—competed with his nagging concern for Juva and Seire's restless pacing.

"She should be back by now," she said, mirroring his own thoughts. He didn't respond, and a brief spell went by before she broke the silence again. "I can't believe they held him *here*! For multiple generations. Right under our noses! And they knew it, all of them?"

Nafraím used his notes as a bookmark, inexorably drawn into the conversation.

"Well, the three initiates in the Seida Guild and the three heirs knew."

"The ones you killed?" Seire picked up one of his books, turned it over, and then threw it down again. "What did you do, exactly?"

"The inevitable," he said. The words weighed on him more heavily than he had expected. He was seized by an unfamiliar need to justify, which drove him to elaborate. "Lagalune was killed by her daughter, Solde, but the girl had taken enough blood pearls to drown Gaula, so she wouldn't have had much time left before the wolf-sickness got her. I allowed her to . . . pass on, along with the others. Here in this very room, actually."

Seire cast a curious glance around, as if this information had altered the room.

"Juva found them," he added.

Seire started at him, discouraged.

"And you think she's forgiven you?"

"No."

"So why is it inconceivable to you that she could have betrayed us? That this house could soon be surrounded by fanatics? That blood-thirsty seed has failed you before!"

Nafraím looked at her, searching for the right words, but all he had to go on was instinct.

"Juva is young. We can't trust her judgment of what's right, but we can trust that she will do what she *believes* is right. That the price is unpayable does not seem to stop her, and after seven hundred years, I can count on one hand the number of people I could say the same thing about. So yes, it's unthinkable that she could have betrayed us, even though she herself does not expect anything but deception. Think about it. She could have killed Gríf, too, and achieved what she wanted. That would have been easier than risking life and limb to free him."

"You praise her, even though she did the opposite of what *you* would have done?"

"That's correct. I was willing to correct an old mistake by making new ones."

Seire let out a snort.

"You have become weak."

"That is also correct," Nafraím smiled, "and that is my strength. A broader view."

Seire pulled her hand across her freckled face.

"If your view got any broader now, your eyes would roll out of

274

your head, Naf! She's softened you by saving your old, wrinkly hide, and you've forgotten that she's still a blood reader."

"Oh, she's much more than a blood reader." Nafraím opened the book again and continued skimming the list of official positions in Skaug.

The windows creaked with a wind gust, and Faun got up from the windowsill.

"What's her judgment worth?" Faun asked quietly. "When it depends on your own? The girl is a hunter. She knows the dead forests in Svartna better than anyone, but you still haven't told her the truth about the stones."

"The truth, he says . . ." Seire rolled her eyes. "None of us *knows* what the truth is, Faun, and it's not our problem, anyway. We have to act on behalf of humans, not wolves. On what's real, not on thousand-year-old, feverish hallucinations."

"We know all too well what we're doing." Faun turned around to stare at the sea again. Nafraím knew he was right, but so was Seire. There were riddles with more power than the world could bear, and they had to be permitted to rest in peace.

Seire juggled the curved knife.

"Three days, and all we've done is wait! Sent letters with Ofre and hidden in the shadows without having accomplished shit!"

"To the contrary." Nafraím was browsing again. "Now I know who keeps watch over the Ring Guard in Skippalun."

"Brilliant . . ." she replied dryly. "Now all we need is to get you back on your feet so we can warn them."

Skarr started whining out in the front hall.

Juva!

Nafraím's shoulders relaxed, more relieved that he liked to admit. He set down his pen and listened. The metallic clang of the door was followed by a peculiar silence. Something was wrong.

Juva came into the library with Skarr padding behind her. She tossed her backpack and crossbow onto the sofa, opened the black lacquer cabinet, and poured herself a generous glass of liquor, which she downed in one gulp. Her hands were shaking. Nafraím was dying to ask but gave her time to collect herself.

"Well . . ." she said, pouring herself another glass. She pointed to Nafraím with the glass. "God has seen fit to release a likeness of you."

Seire gasped. Nafraím raised a finger in warning before the rage seized her. They had known this would come.

Juva sank onto the sofa.

"We went to your house to look. Nice house you've got there, especially all the dubious decorations on your liquor. Almost as upbeat as this place. Don't ask what shape it's in. There has been . . . someone there. People. I don't know."

The pause was short, but it clearly tried Seire's patience.

"So what happened?" Seire asked. "What did he say?"

"Who?" Juva asked, looking up at her. "Silver Throat or Domnik?"

Nafraím stood so quickly that it made him dizzy. He braced himself on the desk.

"Domnik? They have Domnik?!"

Juva's lips took on a caustic look resembling a snarl.

"No, I chased him out of there. What do you think?" She took another sip from her glass. Nafraím felt an urge he could not give in to. A need to help. To ease the fear and anger she was obviously struggling with, but that was bound to make a bad situation worse. And he had no right. All he could do was listen and let her find the words.

"He was hiding, badly, in a clothes closet. They would have found him as soon as they . . ." She swallowed and continued. "Maybe he's been staying there for a while or was just there looking for you. . . I have no idea. But we surprised him. His heart was easy to find, but I didn't know who he was, not for sure. But I saw the reddish-blond hair, the ponytail. He seemed . . . sharp. Like you."

"Juva," Nafraím sat down on the sofa next to her. "Juva, what did he say?"

Skarr pushed his way between them and rested his head in her lap. The girl dug her fingers into his fur.

"Nothing at first. I told him you were alive, that Undst was planning an invasion. I took a chance, told him not to talk to anyone except those he trusts. Then I gave him the key to Hidehall and said we would meet him there when we could. He said I should tell you that . . . the money knows, and that the law will know. Then he ran off."

Seire squealed with joy and caught the crook of Faun's arm.

Nafraím felt weightless, gripped by a hope he hadn't dared put into words. But there was no joy. He knew he hadn't heard the whole story. Juva's eyes met his, tearful and hopeless.

"Juva," he said, "the banks and the state council will be warned. This means we have a chance."

Her smile was strained. She opened her backpack and handed him a book. Nafraím took it and recognized it right away. The leather under his fingers, the weight in his hands. His projects. His diary.

"That was all I was able to take with me," Juva said. "There were a lot of people there. I didn't exactly have a chance to wander around alone."

Nafraím felt an unfamiliar stinging in his eyes. A compelling urge to cry. He rested his hand on the book he had thought was lost. Like everything else. Like immortality, like Náklav, and like himself. Everything he feared he would lose, and here she sat, giving him hope.

Her blond hair hung over her shoulders in tangles. She had dark circles under her eyes, and she was clutching her glass so that her knuckles turned white. Nineteen years old. Grew up with blood readers. In a house with the devil who killed her father and doubled her heartbeats. She had lost her sister in this room, been forced into the role of leader of the Seida Guild, a job no one wanted because his murders had made the job into a certain death.

How would her life have looked without me?

The weight of everything he was and everything he had done seemed to crush him. *Had* crushed him, literally. But this exhausted girl had saved his life, had risked her own to help him.

"Why?" he asked, his voice husky.

Juva shrugged.

"You showed it to me, at Florian's, and said it might help us understand each other better."

He swallowed and let out a hoarse laugh.

"We didn't."

"No," she said, looking at him. "But we understand each other *now.*"

The room went quiet. Seire picked at the dagger, clearly uncomfortable. The Sannseyr library seemed to sense them all with a curiosity amassed over the centuries.

"So what is it you're not telling me?" Nafraím sought out Juva's condescending eyes.

There was a tug at the corner of her mouth.

"Domnik asked about the likeness."

"That's understandable. He knows there are more."

Juva took another sip of her liquor, and he could hear her teeth clink against the edge of the glass.

"You said they were created from time and light."

"That's right," Nafraím said, stroking the diary with his hand. "Everything you see, you see because the light hits it in different ways. There are substances that cause surfaces to be sensitive enough to capture it, just as it is. But that has a price. It's toxic, and that's why—"

"That's why Eydala smells like vinegar and has black fingers?" Juva interrupted.

"Yes. And that's why she doesn't think straight anymore. The Rot makes it worse, but she would still be . . ."

Nafraím ate his own words. He looked into Juva's eyes and realized what she had said, what it meant.

"You've been there," he whispered. "At her place. There's a picture of you, too?"

Juva didn't respond, and that was more than enough of a response. Faun, who was ordinarily sensitive to the mood, pulled Seire out of the room with him and left Nafraím alone with Juva. Nafraím weighed his words but feared it wouldn't make any difference.

"If they have one, it's not a given they'll share it. You are still useful to him."

"Not anymore," she laughed coldly. "When Domnik ran off, I explained that it was some drunk from the Rafts. I don't know how much the priest saw or believed. But he asked me to attend a sepulture tomorrow. My own, I'm guessing."

"Then you shouldn't go. That's not a risk we can take. We still have time to—"

"We have no time," Juva said, staring at him with dead eyes. "I have wolf-sickness."

Her voice was rough. The term he had been hearing for centuries suddenly seemed new, eerily real, as if it had taken on a whole new meaning.

She's wrong. She must be wrong.

"Juva, you're the last person in Náklav who would have taken blood pearls or drunk from a warow. It can't affect you. And Silver Throat wouldn't . . . It's your conscience lying to you. You—"

She dropped her glass on the table and stood up.

"Spare me. I'm not imagining this. I'm getting teeth, Nafraím! Do you understand? And they're not coming from Silver Throat or blood pearls. It's coming from *him*. The last thing he did before he left was kill me. I was wrong, and you were right. He was a beast."

"We all are."

His words did not seem to comfort her. Nafraím set down his diary and got up.

"Juva . . . I was there when Eydala realized she had lost him, that Gríf and his blood were lost, when she realized you had lied to her. She was furious but not enough come after you. Do you know what stopped her?"

"That she needed me."

"No, Juva. Eydala is not a practical woman. She's a slave to her impulses. But when she heard about the ghost in Nákla Henge who had injured you, she assumed you had also been tricked. Or were forced to cooperate with him. That mollified her. Did it never occur to you that Gríf might have done what he did for your sake? Not out of revenge, but to give the impression that you never had any choice. Maybe he wanted to save you from us, from people like her."

Her eyes wavered as she alternated between tenderness and rage, and he knew that she could not afford to hope. Maybe he had made a bad situation even worse, yet again.

Nafraím approached her.

"Do you have a fever?" he asked. "Pain? Sweating?"

"No," Juva said, shaking her head. "But you can smell it yourself if you're in doubt. Both Ferkja and Reiko could tell."

He raised his hand and searched in her eyes for consent before he placed it on her jaw. He squeezed cautiously, ran his thumb over a warm swelling, just above her canine. He leaned closer and put his nose to her throat. Inhaled and had a feeling that this was the first time in a long time. Her smell was alluring, almost intoxicatingly saturated with promises of life.

"Yes . . ." he whispered. "Yes, I can smell it. That's not the problem."

"What's the problem?"

He tore himself away and took a step away from her.

"In all my seven hundred years, I've never heard of a warow who can smell wolf-sickness."

THE THREAT

Nafraím sat down on the skeletal bench, and it hit her how infinitely healthier he looked than the last time when he had lain there with only seconds left in his far-too-long life.

"I want you to stay," he said.

Juva checked her crossbow one more time before folding it up and putting it in her backpack with her suit. She sheathed the daggers in her belt and slid the skinning knife inside her boot. It did not help with her feeling of being naked, unprepared.

Skarr paced back and forth in front of the door, expecting to go with Juva, but she could not bring a wolf to the sepulture.

Especially not if it's my own.

"It doesn't matter what you want, Naf."

She emphasized his nickname in the hope of gaining the authority Seire appeared to enjoy, and that coaxed a tentative smile from him. She swung her backpack onto her back, and a jolt of pain shot down her neck. Her body begged for a mercy she could not provide—not yet. Everything hinged on whether Silver Throat knew that she had been working against him. And if he knew that, she could witness the creation of her own image.

Let him try.

If this ended up becoming him against her, he was a dead man. And if he overpowered her with henchmen, then she had already won. They had thwarted his plans by warning the warow, and

Nafraím had sent letters to allies in the henge cities. Now he had ambitions of reaching Queen Dröfn directly. Regardless of what Silver Throat was planning, it would come as no surprise.

"He might have seen you with Domnik . . ."

He had said it so many times that he no longer expected a response from her. She had to go, and he knew it. If she didn't, it was over.

"Yes," she said. "Silver Throat might have seen Domnik or found out that I'm housing warow. Or even simpler, maybe Oda at Hidehall doubted her instructions to close the hunting hall to guests again. So for all we know, they have already gotten Domnik. But maybe not. I'm not tipping over the pieces until this game is over. We can't afford to do that. We have warow to find, commanders to warn, and we still have no idea how he's spreading the wolf-sickness. Fight this war with words if you must. That's not my forte. I prefer steel and bolts."

"The best war is the one you avoid."

Juva looked at him. He was quick to continue, as if he didn't personally subscribe to what he had said.

"And I'd rather you wait until we know what's wrong with you, Juva."

She had almost laughed. Here he sat, the man she had spent a lifetime fearing, his voice filled with worry on her behalf.

"We know what's wrong with me. You just won't admit it." Juva showed him the fresh wound on her thumb, as if to remind him of what he had just done. "Drip blood in water? Read the movements? I thought you were a learned man. Do you really think that blood water is a reliable method for finding the wolf-sick? That's what Kefla did for money!"

"Kefla?"

Juva bit her lip. The slip of her tongue sent a new jolt through her neck, a useful reminder that she had allowed him to get too close, closer than she could afford to let anyone get.

"She was a guildless blood reader my mother told me about," she muttered. "Doesn't matter. It's a cheap street trick, not science!"

"*Imprecise* is not the same as *useless*."

"And exactly how many wolf-sick people created by Gríf have you tested?"

Nafraím looked at her, and she felt the doubt return. What if he was right? What if she was something else, and Gríf had never meant to . . .

No!

She had devoted too much to shielding herself against a betrayal Nafraím was suggesting had never happened. The hope felt too painful, too dangerous to dwell on.

"If I come back, then you know where to find Domnik," Juva said, putting her hand on the door handle. "And if the Hallowed break in here, then be ready. Go down and close the shaft. You're safe down there."

"We can take care of ourselves," he replied. "Just make sure you do the same. And remain vigilant in the boat on your way out to Kleft. That's the easiest place to catch you by surprise."

"We're not going to Kleft. It's up at Nákla Henge."

His eyes revealed a confusion that she didn't have time to clear up.

"I'll explain when I come back."

If I come back.

"You stay here," she said, pointing to Skarr.

Nafraím petted Skarr's back to soothe his rejection. Juva opened the door and found herself staring straight at Silver Throat. He was walking up her front steps, dressed in gray like the sky. His intense gaze was trained right at her.

Her heart sent a panicked jolt through her chest. She made an effort to close and lock the door slowly behind her, as if she had all the time in the world and nothing to hide.

You're not scared; you're furious!

Juva took a breath and regained the balance she needed to be the person he knew. If he smelled fear or docility . . .

"I was born and grew up here," she said, walking past him down the steps. "I know where Nákla Henge is."

He followed and walked alongside her at a rapid pace. His face softened into the false sanctimoniousness she had come to know.

"Of course, but I was worried something would happen to you. This city is full of people with wolf-sickness and outlaws who have never walked with God. Náklav is no longer safe."

Juva looked at him but nothing gave away any indication that this was his fault. He had a stubborn look in his eye. Dangerous. Explosive, like branntang.

"Whose sepulture is it?" she asked. "Have the Hallowed been stampeding each other to death to get near you?"

He laughed, and for a change, it sounded genuine.

"And here I thought your goal was to make sure I remained grounded in reality. No, Juva, I'm afraid you overestimate my appeal." His eyes roamed over her, hungry for a protest she refused to give him.

"It's good to see you in something other than red," he said. "A young woman can go far without blood-splattered leather, they say."

Juva thought she managed to hide her distaste.

"What does it matter how far you go if you're going the wrong direction?"

He assumed a mask of self-important seriousness.

"It is never wrong to walk with God, but it is demanding. Can I confide in you, Juva?"

I doubt it.

He didn't wait for her to answer.

"Perhaps you think it's a blessing to be God's voice, and of course, it's an honorable job I bear with the utmost humility, but imagine being me, Juva . . . Imagine knowing that your own hands are doomed to call forth evil. That it will always find you, even if you travel to the end of the world. Nothing can stop the pictures, and you are forced to see them or lose your mind trying not to."

He wore the lies as naturally as his own skin, savoring those pompous words with a visible relish that undermined his message.

"It's so much larger than most people can comprehend," he chanted. "Frightening, of course. I fear that one day something will come that pains me more to see. Someone I know. Someone I care about."

His flat smile chilled her to the bone, and she struggled to hide it. He knew. Maybe he had seen the picture of her a long time ago. What he *didn't* know was whether she realized he had.

"Or yourself," she said with a shrug. The silence that followed tasted so good that she ran her tongue over her budding canines. They were more tender than before.

The narrow alleyways seemed to be listening as she walked by. The Floa wind had chased away the fog, and the city was silhouetted with a glass-like clarity in the chilly dawn. Ornate lanterns hung like jewelry from the buildings, muted by ash. Mullioned windows bulged outward from all the shops, filled with everything a person could desire, from books to rune stones. Models of magnificent ships and games with pieces of pure gold. The teahouses hadn't opened yet, but it still smelled of spices and cured meats, and in one of the windows, a black cat had curled up in a crate of wine bottles. A small city map danced in the wind under a wrought iron bench. Náklav, her Náklav. More beautiful than she had ever realized until she was dying.

Nákla Henge lay still. The songbirds that had been fluttering in and out of the cracks in the wall all summer were gone.

Juva followed Silver Throat in the West Gate. The square lay deserted, aside from a group of Hallowed waiting by the Witness. Worry writhed like a worm in her belly, and she looked around for escape routes in case everything went wrong. She saw only two Ring

Guards. One was busy manning the card slot, the other was coming from the dead stones with an empty blood bucket. The haulers had already cleared out. The daggers felt weightless in her belt. Useless.

There were no death drums to be heard. No dead body to be seen.

In a worst-case scenario, she would have to run between the stones to another city . . . That thought came with an eerie recognition. It was too late. She was ripe with fangs and would never be able to use the stone gateways. Here in Náklav, no one bothered to check her jaw anymore, but the Ring Guard in Kreknabork, Skippalun, Haeyna . . .

She was trapped.

Silver Throat gathered his flock in front of the dead stones. They were fewer than she had expected, and there was no indication that they had been bereaved or were grieving. They were a chosen group of initiates, the most dedicated. The only thing reminiscent of a sepulture was the yarn lantern in one of their hands.

Juva remained behind them all so she had a clear path to run.

Two of the Hallowed men crossed the square and disappeared in the door where the posh people had celebrated during the first sepulture. Two men to fetch the deceased?

Silver Throat cleared his throat as if that were necessary for a man constantly using his voice.

"It's good to see you here," he said. "This is an unusual event. And one that pains me because it shows evil can reach anyone. But the good news is that the person in question has taken the nail and is one of us now, one of the Hallowed, determined to do what's right."

The flock rewarded him by drumming their knuckles against their chests. It sounded like a heavy rain. They turned around, and for a second, she thought they were looking at her, but their eyes were tracking someone else. The two Hallowed individuals came back across the square with a woman between them.

Haane!

It was her. It was Haane, one of the Seida Guild's own! As stooped and cowed as always, but she seemed to be coming willingly. No one was forcing her. To the contrary, her head hung less than usual because of the nail on the silver collar necklace that gleamed around her neck.

This was a game. He had manipulated her. It wouldn't be the first time. She had been exploited before, by a warow who had hidden to eavesdrop on a Seida Guild meeting.

The one I killed.

Still . . . To get a member of the Seida Guild to give in to the Hallowed? How in Drukna had he done that?

Juva tried to catch her eyes without success. Haane stepped forward and knelt before Silver Throat. He smiled, pretending to be embarrassed, and he helped her to her feet.

"Woman, do you denounce the devil?" he asked.

Haane nodded as if her life depended on it. He put his hands on her shoulders.

"And do you acknowledge that you have lived in sin?"

Haane nodded, more hesitantly now.

"You have consorted with warow, have you not? And now you seek protection and forgiveness?"

Haane's lips formed a silent yes.

"Because you feel your teeth giving way, don't you? You carry the devil within you, pregnant with the dog, with the wolf, with the beast!"

Fraud!

What had he paid her to lie about being wolf-sick? And why? So he could demonstrate her healing while everyone watched?

"Have you consumed the devil's blood?" he asked.

"No!" Haane shook her head. "No, I have never touched blood pearls!"

He closed his eyes for a second, as if her words weighed on him.

"Blood pearls . . . How does a woman like you know these words? Where does that come from?"

Haane looked around in confusion. If they had agreed to an act, he had clearly changed the rules now.

"That's . . . that's what they're called," she stammered. "Everyone says that."

Silver Throat swept his head in a semicircle toward the flock.

"So everyone here would have taken such words into their mouths, is that what you're saying?"

"No! No . . . I . . ."

He raised a finger in warning, and Haane became quiet.

"The words create the person. You speak with the devil's tongue, so what are you but his spawn? Do you acknowledge your sin? Do you acknowledge having pained God with your dark speech? Do you understand that you have opened your soul to the wolf-sickness and have yourself to thank?"

Juva gritted her teeth. This disgusting show had gone too far.

"Yes!" Haane nodded despairingly. "Yes, I need forgiveness. I need protection. I have wolf-sickness."

It's true . . .

Juva stared at her, at the hair sticking to her sweaty forehead, the tired look in her eyes. Yet another wolf-sick member of the Seida Guild, and one he could exploit. This was far too convenient . . .

The realization drove her heart faster, awakening the throbbing pulse in her ear. He wasn't spreading wolf-sickness at random. He was choosing carefully! He was going after his opponents: leaders, the Seida Guild, the city council . . .

Anasolt has said as much at Jólshov.

He had won over many of the fiercest opponents in the Seida Guild with gifts and wine.

The memory of the state councilman's wine cellar at Kingshill forced its way into her mind. Hjarn Gisting. What if he had been targeted as well? A gift of wine from Undst, which had wound up in his cook's hands . . . And that warow they had sepultured here the last time . . . pale, anemic.

He's spreading warow blood in wine.

Juva felt dizzy. Her thoughts seemed clearer than they had in months, and yet she couldn't pin them down. There was too much that needed to be done, too many people to warn, and she had so painfully little time . . .

"And protection shall you have, child," Silver Throat said. He put his hand on Haane's head and pulled her to him in a half-hearted embrace. "God has seen the evil, and in his infallible care he has given us his vision! We bear our punishment with us. We forge our own death. You shall have final peace. We are the Hallowed."

Haane sobbed with relief as he snuck his hand up to her chin and pulled the nail out of her necklace.

Juva froze. An eerie certainty came over her. This was no sepulture. This was an execution!

Silver Throat ran his hand over Haane's hair and drove the nail into her throat with a clenched fist.

It's too late!

Haane jerked, but he held her tight as the blood trickled out between his fingers. Her body wilted in his embrace. An initiate wrapped the rope of the yarn lantern around her hand and lit it. The branntang flared up. The glowing orb dangled from her limp arm.

Silver Throat turned her body toward the flock, supporting it against his own so they could see her face. Haane stared blankly ahead, already dead. Then he pushed her between the stones.

Juva watched her fall and disappear.

Silver Throat started chanting again, but Juva couldn't hear his words. The pulse in her ears was deafening. Her body felt paralyzed, heavy, impossible to move.

He killed Haane.

He had given her wolf-sickness and then killed her. And she wasn't the only one. He was purging the city of opposition with promises of a cure for a disease he himself was spreading, and Juva knew full well that as soon as she protested, her likeness would appear. A death sentence.

No! He can't do this!

Why hadn't the Ring Guard stopped him?! Juva looked around and couldn't see more than three guards in the whole square: two talking to each other and one cleaning lanterns. They hadn't even seen what just happened; they were blind to the murder that had taken place in the midst of their everyday lives.

I need to talk to Klemens! Drogg! The city council!

And tell them what? That she had seen someone with wolf-sickness be murdered? Everyone had heard her say it: they were doomed to die anyway. They didn't even have a body to inspect because the man had dumped the evidence into Drukna! Silver Throat would say Haane had attacked him, and the flock would back him up. At best, he would be disciplined for his barbarism, but who would feel that someone with wolf-sickness was worth irritating him over, when the man had promised them a cure?

And the wine . . . She had to tell, share, explain to the city that . . .

Juva heard her name and jumped.

"Thank you, Juva," Silver Throat said, gesturing to her with his whole hand. "You never know with the wolf-sick, so I'm especially glad for your support today. You prove that there are still people willing to do God's work, even in the Seida Guild."

The Hallowed flock looked at her and drummed their knuckles against their chests. God's work . . . What a shameless, brazen joke! She turned her back on them and left. Her heart pounded as if she were drowning in warow, hammering in her chest, in her ear, in her mouth . . . Her canine tooth yielded to pressure from her tongue. She could wiggle it.

It's over.

She got out the West Gate and hurried across Brenntorget. The city was coming to life, and she felt exposed. Naked to the bone. Surely, they could see it in her, all of them?

A blood reader lantern was lit some distance down Lykteløkka, and she ducked into a narrow passageway. Running into someone she knew now would be unthinkable. Any attempt to carry a conversation would be doomed to fail.

Get a grip, Juva!

She stopped by an archway, leaning against the wall to find her balance again.

She looked up and was staring at a red dress. The wide skirt filled half the shop window. The windowpanes reflected her and made it look like she was wearing it. She was staring at an illusion. A hoax image of herself and the life she could have lived if she had stayed home and followed in her mother's footsteps, without anything to worry about besides whether her skirts were wide enough and her corsets tight enough.

Muune had clipped that thread of fate. Instead, she had wolf-sickness and was at the mercy of the temperament of a fanatic from Undst who was spreading wolf-sickness to everyone who might stand in his way. And who dumped those he had killed into Drukna, where no one could find them.

He murdered her.

Juva forced herself to picture it again, to remember whether she had sensed anything that could resemble wolf-sickness, but maybe Haane had not progressed far enough in the course of the disease. Rage ate through her chest. She wiggled her teeth with her tongue. Her heart pounded so the vials trembled under her shirt, warm against her skin. She placed her hand over them and knew that she had already lost her battle against the thirst. This wasn't like hoggthorn or rye liquor. This wasn't an urge she could suppress.

Was this what Gríf had wanted the whole time? That she should sink so low that she would drink from it and become what they had both despised the most, a warow?

Nafraím had weakened this conviction. What if she had believed it because she hadn't dared to hope otherwise? In that case, maybe it wouldn't make much difference if she tried . . .

She could make do with far less than it required to become a warow. All she needed was a taste, to know why the allure was so intense, to get it out of her mind . . .

She reached inside her shirt and pulled out the vials. She opened the lock over the one stopper and dripped a few drops into her hand, no more.

The small pool of blood trembled and flowed along her lifeline. Gríf's blood. The source of all misery. Warow, wolf-sick, blood reader, so many dead . . . Just for this.

Juva ran her tongue over the palm of her hand.

Her body quivered with sensual pleasure. The yearning for more was so demanding that she closed the vial and clenched her fists so as not to give in. The rage changed form, from a bonfire of garden prunings to a smoldering glow she could control. As if someone had arrived to carry it with her.

Gríf . . .

Her heart calmed and the rushing in her ears went away. Her body was waiting, as if time were standing still. Her fingers found the scar on her chest, and she could almost smell him. As if he were standing there, right up against her. It felt so solid, so sure.

Blood sure.

That's what she had called it when her mother took blood pearls: a charisma, a radiance of invincibility. And that hadn't even been Gríf's blood. Was that the secret behind the blood, that it gave you what you most craved? Was she going to stand there and smell him, feel him, as Náklav was destroyed around her?

No!

Juva ripped herself out of her trance. She had no time to lose. She set off running, down toward the Sannseyr home, and heard Skarr whine as she unlocked the front door. The wolf wasn't the only one who welcomed her. His whining had alerted the others, who were waiting in the front hall.

Nafraím closed his eyes as she came in, visibly relieved. Seire sheathed her knives and let out a breath that she seemed to have been holding for a while. Juva realized that Faun was the only one who had expected her to survive.

They started talking over each other. Juva could feel their three hearts, closer than ever, like a wild, rhythmless song within her own. Like the music box at Vinterhagen. They needed to relax and let her think. Juva took a breath and it felt nourishing.

Calm.

The warow fell silent again, as if the thought had rubbed off on them.

"I know," she said. "I know how he spreads the wolf-sickness. It's not random at all. He mixes warow blood into wine and then presents it to the people on the city council, the state council, the guilds . . . his most difficult opponents. I can't stay here. I need to warn people."

"We don't know who we can trust," Seire said, looking disgusted.

Juva rubbed her face.

"The people we can trust are already dead."

THE CHANCE

The blood reader light was off, and a couple of holes in the red door showed where the sign had hung. Had Anasolt moved? Had something happened to her?

Juva felt a new worry creeping in. Everything had been about the chance she had taken in trusting her, so she had barely had time to consider that Anasolt was also a target for Silver Throat. The woman was dutiful but unfriendly toward the Hallowed, and wolf-sickness had already taken Laleika and Haane . . .

Juva knocked, still unsure how to warn of the danger without giving away too much. She could blame gossip, say that she had heard that blood pearls were being spread intentionally in food and drink. Even just a rumor would make people cautious.

Anasolt opened the door, wearing colorful clothes that suited her red braids. She made no attempt to hide her surprise.

Juva struggled to find the right words.

"There's been . . . a lot going on," she said, hoping her regret would shine through.

Anasolt nodded and waved for Juva to follow her up a narrow staircase that ended in a simple attic with rough stone walls and cracked beams. Herbs hung drying below the slanted roof and filled the room with protective scents. A workbench by the window was overflowing with tools, clips, and needles that were so small they looked like they were made for children.

An unfinished silver brooch of Muune's three moons sat clamped in a vise. Juva ran her fingers over the details and smiled.

"You make jewelry?"

Anasolt shrugged as if it were easy.

"Hairpins. It's an old activity I used to do when I was your age. Twelve years ago now, but I picked it up again when . . . I just needed to see beauty again. Blood reading hasn't been the same since . . . everything."

"That's why I'm here." Juva set her backpack on the floor, sat down in a chair with a sheepskin fleece, and felt her body relax, as if she had already said everything she had come to say.

Anasolt smiled, visibly relieved.

"I'm glad to see you," she said and planted two wineglasses on the table. She folded her feet under her in the chair, her movements lithe, like a cat. She reached for a wine bottle and opened it. Juva bit her lip to keep herself from asking for something stronger. She squinted at the label and realized she had seen it before. It was the wine from Undst, the one they had boasted about at the first sepulture.

The wine . . .

Juva felt her fingers stiffen around the armrests. The danger she had come to warn her about sloshed into the glass, a deep red, almost brown, and Anasolt handed it to her with a cautious smile. Was that a traitor's smile? The gentle mask of someone trying to poison her?

The scents from the ceiling suddenly felt heavy and cloyingly sweet. Juva glanced at the stairs to make sure she still had a clear path, but leaving wasn't an option. She needed to know.

She took the glass and swirled the wine.

"From Undst? I didn't think they were good at winemaking?"

"Terrible, as far as I've heard," Anasolt replied. "It was a gift from Silver Throat—it's the least he could do! As if there were enough wine in the world to make up for the damage he's done. I hope that's what you want to discuss?"

"Yes . . ." Juva leaned back in the chair with a strained calm. What should she do? Pretend she was drinking or corner her? Should she actually drink? She was already wolf-sick, so what harm could it do? Was it worth it to see if Anasolt drank from the same wine?

She turned her glass and imagined that she could detect the smell of dead warow.

"You don't like him?" she tried.

Anasolt chuckled.

"Even reptiles have a place in the world, but you don't need to work with them, do you?"

Juva looked at her. If Anasolt wasn't his ally, she was brave, willing to speak openly with the red hunter working with him, the leader of her own guild.

"No," Juva replied, "you don't."

Anasolt nodded, as if they had agreed on something important. Then she raised her glass and took a generous sip of the wine.

Juva lunged forward and knocked the glass out of her hands.

"Spit it out!" she yelled and heard the glass shatter against the floor. She grabbed Anasolt by the throat as the woman sprayed red across the table and coughed as if she were being strangled.

Anasolt tore herself free and flung her arm over her face to protect herself. Juva swept the glass shards away with her foot and squatted down in front of her.

"Anasolt, have you drunk this before?"

She lowered her arm hesitantly and shook her head. She coughed again.

Juva took her face in her hands and gazed into her eyes. Those infinitely beautiful, loyal eyes, which had never looked more confused.

"Listen to me, Anasolt. Silver Throat is intentionally spreading wolf-sickness. Not in blood pearls but in wine. That's why so many people have come down with it, and that's why it's also infecting people who have never touched blood pearls. You mustn't accept food or wine from *anyone*, especially not from the Hallowed. Do you understand?"

Anasolt's eyes took on a distant look. The words appeared to sink in.

"Laleika . . ." she whispered. "Laleika got some, before she . . ." She clutched her chest. "Haane! Haane also got some, and . . ."

"Haane's dead. I'm coming straight from her sepulture. I was there. I saw it happen. He said she had wolf-sickness and sent her to Drukna."

"Haane? Who would . . . ? Why would . . . ?" Anasolt brought her hand up to cover her mouth.

"He's wiping out the resistance, Anasolt. These are enemies of Náklav, and it's much bigger than I can say, and there's nowhere near enough time. But I need your help. I doubt that he poisons every single bottle. Some are random and some are targeted, but we can never know the difference, so you need to spread the rumor. Don't name him because he would figure out that it's coming from me. Just say it's being spread through the wine. Can you do that for me?"

Anasolt pressed her hands over her eyes, but her tears kept flowing.

"Tell who? The Seida Guild? Who are they trying to—"

"Everyone! Make sure the whole damned Náklav is talking about it. That no one consumes it ever again."

Anasolt's face darkened, and Juva could see that she was getting a grip on what had been said. The realization robbed her of an innocence that she would never get back.

"Why?" she asked. "Why would anyone . . . ?"

"For Náklav," Juva said, standing up. "For everything this city has to give."

Anasolt stared at the bottle with disgust. Juva slung her backpack on.

"I have people in the city council to warn. Spread the rumor about the wine, blame it on gossip you heard from someone you trust—but stay safe! Don't share more than that, not with anyone. Can I count on you?"

Anasolt nodded weakly. Juva knew Anasolt needed time to process everything, but she couldn't stay. She had no time to console her. She patted the back of Anasolt's head, like Broddmar would have done, and ran down the steps.

She took all the shortcuts across Ringmark, through Kistestikk, and up toward the city hall. She ran up the long staircase and in the front door. Calmed down and caught her breath as she mulled over what to say.

People were walking back and forth between elegant looking desks. Mumbling together over paperwork, as if they had all the time in the world. As if the city were not about to fall.

Where's Drogg?

Juva hurried up the stairs and heard his booming laugh nearby. She stopped and peered down a carpeted colonnade. There he stood with his arm around the shoulder of a man she recognized. One of the emissaries from Undst. They seemed to enjoy each other's company.

Disappointment settled heavily in her stomach. Drogg . . .

No . . . It could be innocent. It was politics, and Drogg was friendly with everyone. But he hadn't come down with wolf-sickness the way so many others had . . .

Drogg patted the man's back, and they continued on their separate ways. Juva took a couple of steps backward, but it was too late. Drogg spotted her and flung out his arms.

"Juva!" he cried, and practically running over to meet her. "I have tremendously good news! But . . . what brings you here?"

A simple lie begged to be told. She could say it was a real estate matter or something else mundane. But if Drogg was a traitor, he would check . . .

A half-truth.

"I'm here because I saw Haane from the Seida Guild murdered this morning! By Silver Throat, Drogg!"

Drogg's face wilted.

"Yes, I heard about that. She was wolf-sick, and he warned us that something like that might happen. You know, there are many who feel drawn to the Hallowed when they get sick."

Juva felt paralyzed. Silver Throat had beaten her to it, probably weeks ago. How long had he been planning this? And the city council had been prepared. It had been smoothed over so the incident would seem unavoidable.

"It's barbaric!" she said without concealing her anger.

"It really is," Drogg replied. Then his smile returned. "But it will be over soon, Juva. The delegation is en route, and Undst will be here for the Dragsuget Regatta." He put his hands on her shoulders. "Never again, Juva. Can you imagine a city without wolf-sickness? It's more than we ever dared to hope for."

Does he believe that or is he one of them?

Drogg led her down the stairs as he chatted about the preparations, the reception at the docks and the marking of a new era. Juva weighed each empty word, all infinitely light. She couldn't trust him, couldn't trust anyone in this city. Trust had already cost her her life.

We don't know who we can trust until they're dead.

Drogg could be a traitor or a useful idiot. What he couldn't be permitted to be was an obstacle. This battle had to be fought with or without him.

And without the guys . . .

A word to Broddmar was a word to all of them, and if Muggen found out, then it had reached the Hallowed. Juva left City Hall.

The streets were hectic, but she was utterly alone. All she had was a house full of warow and even them she couldn't really let in.

She unlocked the front door and went into the library, where they sat crowded around a table.

"What did she say?" Seire asked, standing up.

Juva poured a glass of rye liquor and began to explain. She had barely gotten going before the door knocker echoed in the front hall. Their conversation died.

Anasolt? Silver Throat? Did she betray me?

Juva stepped into the front hall. The door knocker banged again, more desperately. She peeked out the gaps in the boarded-up window. Out on the front step stood Kefla, frantically banging the knocker. Behind her, Tokalínn lay motionless, face down on the cobblestones.

AN ARMY

Juva rushed past Kefla down the front steps. She squatted down beside the small body, which lay eerily still, arms out to the sides.

"Tokalínn!" Juva took hold of her and propped up her upper body, feeling for a pulse. The girl's head lolled backward and her blond hair swept the cobblestones.

"Now!" Kefla screamed.

Juva heard the front door bang shut so the wrought iron reverberated. Tokalínn opened her eyes and leapt to her feet, fit as a foal. Noora, Ulie, and Syn came running around the corner of the house and grabbed hold of Juva.

What is going on?!

The girls struggled to pull her with them. Kefla backed away from the front steps, holding her arm out straight, pointing at the house with her knife.

Juva pulled free and raised her hands.

"Wait! What are you girls doing *here* and *what* are you doing?!"

Tokalínn stared up at her wide-eyed, as if it should be obvious.

"We're saving you!" she cried.

Ulie grabbed her arm with one hand. In the other, she held a piece of old wooden molding as if it were a sword.

"We need to run, Juva!" she cried.

The girls started talking over each other while they continued pulling her along. Juva stared questioningly at Syn, the eldest of the group of five, and the only one who wasn't armed with a dagger, piece of wooden molding, or a brick.

Syn rolled her eyes and crossed her arms in front of her chest.

"This is completely ridiculous. I *told you* it was the wolf."

Kefla stepped over with her head down, ready to fight.

"It's not Skarr!" she hissed, and the other girls backed her up.

"There are more," Tokalínn said as she inhaled. "So many!"

Warow! They're sensing the warow!

Juva closed her eyes to pull herself together, not knowing whether to laugh or cry. She was awash in problems; they had grown deeper every day, and they were closing in around her like mud. Silver Throat spreading wolf-sickness, the terrifyingly vague threat against Náklav, and the cursed battle against time, against death. She had been living behind a stone mask, with poison and blood between her breasts, and in the middle of it all, it hadn't occurred to her that there'd be consequences to sending the girls to map warow when she had a group of them in her house.

Despair welled up inside her. Of course they had sensed them, but the girls ought to know better than to come here. They knew they weren't safe here, that they should avoid vardari, the Hallowed.

And me . . .

But here they were. An army of blood readers, ranging from age six to fourteen, and they were willing to confront what they feared most in the world to rescue her.

Juva rubbed her face and pleaded with them to calm down.

"I'm not in danger," she said. That was a truth with far too many caveats, so she hurried to add. "Not *here*." The girls stared at her. Their panicked looks faded into confusion, concern.

People ambling by glanced at the girls. They must have thought she was being robbed by a mob, armed with rocks and sticks.

"Listen, I'll explain," she said quietly. "But we need to go inside. We can't—"

"No stinking way. Absolutely not!" Kefla said and tossed her black bangs.

Tokalínn made do with feverishly shaking her head. Juva realized that she had done her job deplorably well, well enough that she would never get them in the door as long as they sensed warow. The list of things the girls didn't know was growing bigger than she had time to deal with.

"Then I'll come with you. But I need to get my backpack and crossbow first. It'll just take a second."

Kefla crossed her arms but didn't protest. Juva went inside and left the door ajar so they could see her. Seire stood hidden behind the door, squinting out the window.

"What the fuck is going on?" she whispered. "Who are those kids?!"

Juva grabbed her crossbow and threw on her backpack.

"They're . . . I'll explain when I get back. Keep Skarr here," she said and darted out again. She locked the door while the girls stood by, ready to run. They stared at the house as if it were going to eat them, and she knew she had been doing the very same thing, her whole life.

She told them to follow her at a distance so no one would see them together, but every time she looked over her shoulder, they were only a few paces away. Juva caught herself smiling but felt it fade immediately. She couldn't bear the thought of explaining Eydala and all the terrible things that could befall them. Or what she herself had turned them into, a part of the hunt for warow.

An unfamiliar pain settled like a lump in her throat, one she had fought vehemently to avoid. She had drawn innocent children into the life of the red hunter, even though she had known better. Even though she had known she couldn't afford to feel more, not for anything or anyone, and now it was too late.

She led the way through Fettveita, between alehouses and busy food stands. The crooked buildings leaned out over the street as if they were trying to inhale the scents. Fragrant dumplings over steam, small fish dripping on skewers over glowing coals, and a crowd of pans sizzling over open flames.

At the end of the street, she could see the top of Kingshill, shining in the last of the daylight. Gudebro Bridge arced over the city on stilts, like a silver snake from Náklaborg, and she felt weakened by the sight, by the smells. As if Náklav were trying to say there was more here than she suspected, much more than the darkness.

She looked over her shoulder. The girls were following, apart from Kefla, who had stopped a way back. She stood staring straight ahead, as if lost in her thoughts. Juva waved discretely, but the girl just stood there.

Something is wrong...

Juva gestured that the others should wait and walked back toward Kefla.

"Aren't you coming?"

The girl clenched her fists and stared at her, her eyes dark, without answering.

She senses someone!

Juva looked around, without detecting danger. A man in a stained apron smiled at them as he turned thick whale steaks over the fire. The flames sizzled, and the scent of roasting fish wafted behind Kefla.

"Kefla, what is it?"

"I still feel it," Kefla said. Her boyish voice broke. "I sense vardari, but we're far from your house..."

Juva listened to her heart without finding any trace of danger. Either she was mistaken, or Kefla had become a stronger senser than her.

"There's no one here, Kefla."

Kefla grimaced, crinkling up the freckles on her nose. She backed away, an accusatory look filling her eyes. Juva felt the certainty awaken, a realization that pierced her like a sword.

It's me!

Juva clutched her chest. It was purely reflexive, a meaningless attempt to muffle or hide the heartbeats Kefla was sensing. The smell of burned fish became oppressive, nauseating.

She knows I'm wolf-sick!

Or was it the blood she had just tasted? Could such a small temptation make her into a warow?! Her thoughts betrayed her. Juva could feel the fragments tearing free and forcing themselves forward, without context. A porridge of possibilities.

Was she wolf-sick or something else? Nafraím was convinced she wasn't wolf-sick. He said the scent wasn't there. And that warow they had sepultured, he had smelled of *something* and said she hunted her own. But she couldn't be a warow without having . . . No, she was neither wolf-sick nor a warow, or maybe she was both? Either way, Kefla could sense her.

What did he do to me?!

"Juva?"

She jumped at Syn's voice. The girls had joined them. Juva held her hand out to Kefla, who backed away a step.

"Kefla . . . It's not what you think. I'm . . . I don't know what I am. I thought I was wolf-sick, but that's not it."

"No," Kefla said. "You're one of them. You're one of them, and that's why they're at your house!"

Tokalínn put her hands over her mouth, wide-eyed. The girls looked at each other, as if they hoped someone had the right words. Juva felt powerless, robbed of something she never would have used anyway: the chance to explain it all herself. In the right place, which didn't exist, and at the right time, which would never have come. And now she had to ask for trust from a twelve-year-old she had thrown out and avoided spending time with. She would never understand . . .

Juva sat down on the end of a cracked bench.

"Kefla, I'm not . . ." She wanted to say dangerous, but that was a lie. "I'm not evil. You don't need to be scared."

Kefla shoved Juva's shoulders, and she nearly lost her balance.

"You're an idiot, Juva. I'm not scared, I'm mad! You should have told us! I don't give a damn if you're wolf-sick, or . . . one of them, or . . . You should have told us. I thought . . ." Her face tensed. "I thought you didn't like us anymore."

Juva took hold of her hands and pulled her closer.

"*Like* you?" She looked at the girls, who were staring at the ground. "Kefla, I've done . . . terrible things. They follow me like a shadow, and I've taken part in things that haunt me in my dreams. But you girls . . . Helping you is the only thing I've done in my life that I'm proud of. You're . . . There's not a thing in the world I wouldn't have done for you."

"I told you so, Kefla," Syn said and pulled her shawl tighter around her shoulders. "Some people know they're dangerous, and the best of them stay away. It's the worst ones who stick around."

Kefla kicked an empty paper wrapper.

"I could have measured your blood in water to see if you were sick! You should have told me. And you should have told us that you were living with . . . with *them*. Do you think we're stupid? That we wouldn't have understood good and bad people are among them, too? Does a person need to be Juva Sannseyr to be smart enough to understand that kind of thing?"

Juva pulled her close and put her hand on Kefla's cheek. She studied the girl's bone-hard face as she fought to keep from crying.

"You're right, Kefla. You're not the ones struggling to see the difference between good and evil. I am. To understand such things, you need to be a far better person than me."

Kefla half suppressed a smile that was so beautiful it hurt.

Tokalínn climbed up onto the bench and sat down next to her.

"We know the ones you're living with are nice, Juva."

Juva looked at the girl, who was so maturely trying to comfort her. Her conviction was so genuine that she couldn't help asking.

"How can you know that?"

"Because you know it," Tokalínn said with a shrug.

Juva let out a laugh that sounded more like a sob. She knew nothing. Everything she thought she knew was wrong. She had hunted for the worst of them all. She had believed she was saving the city from the wolf-sick, and maybe . . . maybe she had been wrong about Gríf. Nafraím's words in her mind felt devastating.

"Has it never occurred to you that Gríf may have done what he did for your sake?"

A group of tipsy guests stumbled out of an alehouse, arguing with the man in the apron about the price of mussels flambé. The streets were far too busy. It wasn't safe to stay.

With that thought came another, one that was more frightening.

"Girls, have you told anyone? About what you noticed at my place?"

Kefla tossed her black bangs off her face.

"You mean, have we gossiped? Have we told anyone the thing that you've been nagging us for months never to say?"

"I didn't say anything!" Tokalínn exclaimed.

The girls looked at each other. Syn bit her lip and looked down.

Kefla gaped at her.

"You blabbed?!"

"No!" Syn rolled her eyes. "But I *did tell you* this was crazy. What would you have done if there were dangerous people there? We could be dead now. So I . . . I left a note for Heimilla about where we had gone. I didn't say a word about why." Syn looked at Juva, and a shy pride warmed her cheeks. "I wrote it myself . . ."

Juva broke down. The tears she had struggled to prevent flowed, faster than she could wipe them away. The girls became infinitely silent, and she realized how much she had hardened herself to spare them.

Tokalínn took her hand. She opened and closed her mouth a couple of times without saying anything before suddenly remembering something.

"We have more butter cookies at home!"

IN GOD'S IMAGE

Juva reached across the table and helped herself to another slice of Floa bread. Heimilla had decorated it with the sharp petals of the blossa flower, which always bloomed during Floa, and she remembered the taste from when she was a girl. The feeling of being lucky, of having waited a long time for something that took time to grow.

It was a good memory, which gave her the sudden idea that it must be false. Like when Nafraím had shown her the balcony. It was as if good things had been so unthinkable at home that she hadn't believed them. Forgotten them. Packed them away in a vault until it was safe to open.

But it would never be safe. If she'd learned anything, it was that nothing good ever came out of hidden vaults.

The vials suddenly felt warm against her skin, as if they knew she was thinking of him. Thirst thickened her tongue, but she couldn't bring herself to ask for the key to the liquor cabinet. It wouldn't help anyway. Not against this thirst.

Out in the living room, she heard the music box plinking. The girls struggled to turn the cranks at the same speed, so the melody was strangely hesitant. The notes were never quite in time, but it was still beautiful. There could hardly have been a more suitable place for it than right here in Vinterhagen. The elegant inn, now a home for ailing blood readers.

One set of notes quickly pulled away from the others. The girls laughed and started again. Juva met Heimilla's smile across the table and felt less alone than ever. It felt like time was standing still.

But it moved unrelentingly on, and Undst had come another night closer. Five days until the Dragsuget Regatta. Every second she wasted was lost preparation. And lost lives.

She needed to get to Hidehall and check that Domnik was safe. The guys needed to know how the wolf-sickness was being spread. She had no idea how to tell them without revealing too much, but that was a headache she would have to tackle later. Right now, she needed all the help she could get to spread the rumor.

Then there was Drogg . . . Could she trust the man enough to tell him what was going on? Or should she let the news break on its own, like with the girls?

They know I have warow at home . . .

The threat smoldered in her chest. Sooner or later, one of them would slip up, even though they had all agreed that no one would know, not even Heimilla. The woman began clearing the table, as if she had heard her thoughts.

"So everything is not as it should be with you?"

Juva stopped chewing. "Why do you ask?"

Heimilla ran her hands over her apron.

"Because Tokalínn insisted there absolutely, positively wasn't anything wrong with you."

Juva smiled cautiously to hide her relief.

"I know everything is as it should be right now, right here."

"I can see that," Heimilla replied. "They said you told them you were proud of them. That means more than you think, you see. That you dare to show them you care. Don't let them grow up doubting it the way you did."

Juva swallowed her last bite. Those words hurt so much more than she could show. She would never be able to control whether the girls doubted or not. Not because she didn't care, but because she wouldn't get to see them grow up.

She opened her backpack and handed the letter from Náklabank to Heimilla.

"If anything should happen to me, they're provided for. You, too. Vinterhagen will live on, no matter what, and you will never want for anything."

Heimilla accepted the letter without looking at it.

"If you think we can lose you and never want for anything, then you're missing the most important thing there is in this life, Juva Sannseyr."

Juva closed her backpack and turned to hide her face. Everything had become so fragile. So easy to break.

Heimilla continued, as if to spare her from having to answer.

"It has always bothered me, Juva . . . That I wasn't able to stop him, that bastard of a boy you were seeing, when he came for the key to the Sannseyr house last spring. I tried. I realized he could hurt you, but he was so strong . . . and sick! But I still wish I had—"

"Rugen is dead," Juva said, standing up. "And you would be, too, if you had tried to stop him. If anything should weigh on your shoulders, let it be everything you've managed to accomplish because you're alive: Vinterhagen, the girls, me . . ."

Those words seemed to make her a smidge taller.

"I have to go," Juva said. "I need to warn others about the wolf-sickness. Just remember—"

"Don't accept gifts, no food or drink, not from anyone," Heimilla interrupted. "As if we don't make our own food here in the house!"

Juva smiled and walked into the living room. The girls tried to hold her back but reluctantly gave in when promised that they would see her again soon. She closed the door and stepped out into Myntslaget. Reality returned with the Floa wind. It blew through the streets as if nourished by memories of Haane's sweaty face, Silver Throat's sneering smile, Eydala and the rotten apple . . .

People didn't seem to care that it was chilly. According to Heimilla, the rumor about a cure coming on the ships from Undst had spread through Náklav faster than money; she could tell by people's light footsteps and in the wave of errand runners at the businesses. They believed. They hoped. They were awaiting a cure that would never come. Even the lamplighters looked down from their ladders and greeted her as she walked by. The city was looking forward to its own demise.

Juva followed Nattlyslokket down toward Hidehall and glanced at the handbills. In a couple of places, news about the ships had been glued over the drawings of Silver Throat's sinners. That was something. Her smile faded as the Dead Man's Horn sounded. The upper stories hanging over the street funneled the reverberating tones toward her, like a trumpet. Doors banged shut, businesses locked up, and windows were closed. Juva set off running back toward the guard booth on Kong Aug's Street, which was suddenly deserted, now that everyone had been reminded that it wasn't over yet.

She raced into the booth, dropped her backpack, and pulled out her suit and crossbow.

"Where?" she asked, pulling on her leather pants. The pants had been stiff and new just six months earlier. Now they were worn and stained with dark blood. She laced up her jacket and looked at the young Ring Guardsman, who stood staring at her in confusion.

"Where?!"

He jumped.

"We . . . We don't know yet," he stammered. "I haven't . . . This is the first time I've been on duty when the Dead Man's Horn went off."

Juva slung the crossbow onto her back. She wanted to tell him he would get used to it, but that would be a lie. She strapped on her harness and hooked the bloodskins onto her back. The door opened, and a runner, hardly ten years old, raced in.

"It's at Kaupa!" He braced his hands on his knees and gasped for breath. "At the top of the street. I was alerted by another runner. She didn't have a map."

Juva slipped past him and set off running. Her mind swept through potential victims, but it could be anyone: someone on the city council, the state council, the guilds . . . or an ordinary person. Silver Throat had gone after the townsfolk, too, spreading the disease at random to keep fears high.

The thought was devastating and hounded her heart to a hastiness she couldn't subdue. She spotted Nolan, visibly stressed, the first one out since he lived nearby. He started running as soon as she drew near, so he must have gotten details from the guard booth at Ulebru Bridge.

She caught up to him.

"Where? Anyone dead?"

"No one dead," he replied without stopping as he continued along Muunsvei.

"Where are we going?" Juva asked, looking back. "The runner said it was at the top of Kong Aug's Street?"

Nolan didn't answer. He stopped by a shop she recognized, and her chest tensed with anxiety when she realized where she was. This was Nolan's childhood home, his father's workshop. A stuffed raven hung in the window, its wings spread in a flight it would never feel.

No . . . not his family!

Nolan walked in to the jingle of a little bell over the door. Juva followed him and stood face-to-face with Broddmar. And Hanuk, Muggen, and Lok. They were all there. How had they gotten the message faster than her?

There was no one else in sight other than the blank stares from the dead animals on the walls. An owl without eyes stood on a workbench next to her. Broddmar peered out the window and nodded to Hanuk, who ran out and closed and locked the door behind him. Juva felt trapped. Why were they just standing there waiting? Her eyes went to the silver collar necklace around Muggen's neck.

Have they betrayed me?

"Where is Hanuk going?" she asked unemotionally and checked the bolt in her crossbow with forced calm. Broddmar glanced out the window again, as if he feared that someone might be waiting outside.

"He'll find a runner and say it was a false alarm so the streets aren't drowning in Ring Guards."

Juva looked at them, searching for some explanation, but all she found was stress. Muggen rubbed his huge knuckles and stared at the floor, although the nail prevented him from hanging his head the way he usually did. Lok tightened the knot holding his red braids in place, and she spotted the names on his arms. His kids. Nolan raised his hand as if he were going to put it on her arm, but he didn't.

"I'll put the tea on," he said and vanished upstairs.

Her fear of betrayal died away. These were the guys, her hunting team! This was Broddmar, Muggen, Hanuk, Nolan, and Lok. They would never do anything to harm her. So what was she doing there? Why had they sounded the alarm about someone with wolf-sickness?

They want to confront me!

Juva rubbed her forehead. They had good reason to confront her, but the timing couldn't be worse. She didn't have time right now, and there was way too much to say.

"I put the water on," Nolan said from the top of the stairs, and the guys looked at her. She glanced at the door, but they had considered that way out and remained on their feet. Broddmar pushed her up the stairs ahead of him, and she felt her courage waning with every step. She emerged into a room that seemed like an extension of the workshop. In the middle of the crowd of dead animals was a group of deep chairs, the only indication it was a living room.

The guys sat down but on the edge of their seats, as if they knew they would not be able to relax.

Or that I'm going to run away . . .

The bell jingled downstairs, and they stiffened until they heard Hanuk lock up again and come upstairs. He didn't say anything, just nodded to Broddmar and handed the key to Nolan. Then he sat down and let out a deep sigh.

That reminded her to breathe, although it felt difficult. She could handle disloyalty, the gods knew she had learned that, but this was something else, something worse. A fear she wasn't used to.

Nolan put a handful of mugs on the table. A strange assortment of various shapes and colors. Juva leaned the crossbow against the table leg and sank down onto a chair.

"You guys are wrong about me," she said, although that didn't feel true. "But I can only say I don't have time to stay here. You have no idea what's at stake, but it's not like you think."

Nolan poured tea into her cup.

"So Náklav won't be besieged by ships from Undst, and you're not working with the Vardari?"

They know?!

Juva felt paralyzed. She looked at Broddmar for an explanation and he looked into her eyes. He was steadier than she had seen him in a long time. He looked like himself, the way he used to be. Before Gríf.

"A new guy showed up at Hidehall the other day," he said. "He probably hadn't hunted more than a crab in his life, but the key to the hunting hall, that he had. Then another one showed up, whom he called a friend. And then one I am quite familiar with."

Juva closed her eyes.

"Ferkja . . ."

Domnik had gathered the other warow there, without knowing Broddmar and Ferkja knew each other.

"That's right," Broddmar replied. "And Ferkja trusted me enough to share what was going on. Unlike someone else in this room . . ."

Juva clutched the armrests with no idea what to tackle first. The anger or the hurt?

"She doesn't *care*, unlike certain other people in this room! You don't know Silver Throat. You don't know what he's capable of. I couldn't say anything without putting you in danger." She looked at Muggen pleadingly. "Say it, Muggen! You know I'm right. The man is dangerous."

"More dangerous than you think," Broddmar said. "Muggen just saw one of his likenesses."

"I know, he has likenesses of warow who—"

"It was of *you*."

Juva felt cold. Dead animals stared at her from all sides, and it seemed as if they were closing in, surrounding her, a dead forest like in Svartna. She could hear Broddmar explaining, but his voice was muffled as if he were talking through layers of wool. About how that was why they had sounded a false alarm, to get her out of her house as quickly as possible, before the Hallowed arrived.

Juva stared at Muggen. He was one of them, so what was he doing here? Why had he warned the guys?

"You believe him, don't you?" she said. "You believe the likenesses."

Muggen fiddled with his silver necklace, as if it had become uncomfortable. He undid it and threw it on the table.

"That was before I saw *your* image there," he mumbled. "You don't have an evil bone in your body."

Juva inhaled, hearing how she trembled doing so. She took a sip from her cup to hide what the words did to her. They were so touchingly beautiful. Ripe with new chances. Forgiveness. And hope of surviving. If Muggen turned his back on them, other people could, too.

"Why is he doing this?" asked Nolan, as if he had been thinking the same thing. "It's pointless. No one wants to send the head of the Seida Guild to Drukna!"

"Unless she has fangs . . ." Broddmar said, looking at her.

Juva pressed her hands to her face. Ferkja had blabbed about *everything*. He knew. The guys knew that she was wolf-sick, and they were there anyway. She could smell the scent of Floa bread from her palms. The timelessness was over. Overtaken by the taste of blood from her canines, which she could wiggle with her tongue.

"Ferkja said she smelled it in you," Broddmar said. "She says you're wolf-sick."

Juva felt Nolan pat her back. She straightened up again, forcing herself to look at them.

"I thought I was." Her voice threatened to fail her. "I'm getting . . . teeth, but . . . I don't have a fever. No sweating fits or headache, and Nafraím says no one can smell wolf-sickness, so I don't know—"

"Nafraím?" Broddmar said, standing up. "So it's true that he's alive?"

Juva felt the weight of everything she hadn't told them pressing her down onto the chair. It felt like she would remain there until death came and took her.

Broddmar started pacing restlessly in front of the forest of dead animals.

"So Nafraím is alive. You're working with the Vardari, even though you were convinced they were purposely spreading wolf-sickness. We're awaiting a battle fleet of fanatics from Undst while you're growing new teeth, and you didn't think any of this worth sharing with us?"

"Sit down, Broddmar!" Nolan said with a sigh. "You'll have to mend your darned wounded pride somewhere else. Did it never occur to you that she was staying away for *your* sake? She might be wolf-sick, man! Don't you realize what she's been going through? She's been working for Silver Throat in secret, risking everything! She kept her mouth shut for *our* sake."

"Nolan is right," Hanuk said.

Broddmar sat down and scowled at him, and Hanuk hurried to continue.

"Right in that it doesn't make any sense to release a likeness of Juva." He looked at her. "So does that mean he knows you're getting teeth?"

"No," Juva shook her head. "He doesn't know. But he might know I've betrayed him."

"Either way, he has no idea how the city council will react," Lok said.

"No," Broddmar said, nodding at Muggen. "He doesn't even know how his own followers will react."

Juva pulled her sleeves down over her fingers. The cold seemed to follow her no matter where she went.

"He doesn't need to know that," she said. "He only needs enough people to want to get rid of me."

The truth silenced their conversation. It was over. The animals stared at her, as if they were expecting her to become one of them. A lifeless body, frozen in the same position forever.

"Regardless of what happens, they've won," she muttered. "Him and Eydala."

"Eydala?" Broddmar's question opened yet another floodgate. A torrent of all she had been bearing alone. Juva stood up.

"He's working with Eydala," she said. "She's the one who gives him the images, and they're . . . They can be made with light and sea silver. Nafraím explained it . . . I didn't know that until he . . ."

There were too many thoughts. She had no idea where to start. Her words rearranged themselves as they tumbled out.

"Eydala tortured him for several months, because I . . . It's my fault, and now they want to eradicate the warow. And everyone who stands in their way. That's why he . . . Wolf-sickness, Silver Throat is the one spreading wolf-sickness. He has amassed followers by promising them a cure that doesn't exist, and now they're weakening us, weakening Náklav's defenses."

"That was Domnik's theory, too," Broddmar said. "That the blood pearls are still in circulation."

"Yes, but it's not pearls. He has it in wine—bottles of wine that he gives away as gifts. He's given them to people on the city council and in the guilds! Haane, Laleika . . . Anasolt almost drank some yesterday, but I . . ."

The guys looked at each other. Lok started to look ill, and she was afraid he would throw up again. Nolan's eyes darkened.

"He's the one who made you sick?" Nolan said. "Silver Throat gave you wine?"

"No! No . . . the disease or . . . the teeth, they came from Gríf. Call it a kind of parting gift." She heard the bitterness in her own voice, but it sounded weakened.

"No," Broddmar chucked. "That man would never hurt you, Juva. I *saw* you two together."

Juva opened her jacket and pulled down the collar of her shirt, revealing the scar his claws had left in the middle of her chest. Two thick grooves, curved like fangs.

"So what do you call this? This is the last thing he gave me before he left. You saw what he did. You were *there*!"

Their gentle looks turned her stomach. They were oozing the

compassion she had been trying to avoid. She let go of her shirt and pulled out the vials.

"And here's the antidote! So, yeah, he poisoned me. He gave me teeth, gave me the bloodthirst, and he gave me his own blood because he knew that when I got sick and thirsty enough, I would drink it. He wanted to turn me into a Vardari, the only thing he knew we both despised."

Her words sounded false. She had said them so many times to herself that they had lost their force. She looked at the guys and suddenly knew why she had told them everything. She was beginning to hope. She wanted them to disprove every word, to find reasons for Gríf's actions that she herself had been unable to find.

The guys exchanged glances. Muggen paled and stared at the vials.

"Can you guys imagine what a warow would give for those . . . They're going to . . . They would have killed you just for *that*!"

"Oh, really?" she replied bitterly. "That hadn't occurred to me."

"Fuck off, Muggen." Nolan said effortlessly, but his clenched fists revealed that his voice was lying. "The most important thing is what we do *now*. She cannot leave the house. Silver Throat knows she's betrayed him, and her likeness is out there."

Juva dropped the vials under her shirt again.

"He, or Eydala. He's working for her, and she knows I tricked her. That I lied about the devil."

"Probably not," Hanuk said, leaning back in his chair. "That woman is nuts, so she would have retaliated on you in person. The likenesses are Silver Throat's thing."

Juva closed her jacket back up. Her fingers lingered on her chest as his words sank in. He was right. Sending her to Drukna would never be enough for Eydala. And Silver Throat wouldn't have done it as long as she was useful. Unless he had other help . . .

An unbearable dread suddenly grew in her chest.

The girls!

"Relax, Juva." Broddmar was looking at her. "He's not going to come after you."

"No, he's going to go after them!"

Juva snatched up her backpack and crossbow and raced down the stairs. The guys came tumbling after, and she heard them yelling as she ran outside. It didn't matter. Nothing mattered beside the girls. And she had put them in danger like a complete idiot! They had come to rescue her, and she had followed them back, led Silver Throat right to them. No wonder he had spread her likeness. What did he need *her* for when he had an army of blood readers to choose from, who had already thoroughly scoured the city for warow?

Juva ran so hard she tasted blood, through Muunsvei and down toward Myntslaget. The street narrowed to a single point. Vinterhagen.

She tore open the door and took the stairs in a few bounds.

"Kefla! Girls?!" She ran into the living room and stepped on something. The gameboard for Last Warrior. The wooden game pieces lay strewn across the floor. Juva's body began to tremble. Her heart pounded in her chest as if it were trying to hammer its way out, and she remembered Ester. A broken cup. Dead birds.

She flung open the doors that led into the garden room. A piece of paper was caught in the draft from the door and sailed down onto the floor in front of her. One of the girls' maps. Next to an up-ended table, in the middle of the cage-like well house, sat Heimilla. Her head hung limply forward, and she wasn't moving.

Juva supported herself against the door frame. She felt dizzy and the room became hazy, but she groped her way forward to Heimilla. Lifted her head. Heimilla stared at her with dead eyes, like the animals at Nolan's place. A nail head was bleeding from her neck. And they had pulled her canines, so no one would care that she was dead.

Juva heard a half-choked sound come out of her own throat and sank to her knees.

GRÍF

The bloodstain drew a curve on the floor, as if it had congealed around Heimilla's foot. The guys had moved the body to a bedroom, and she could hear them talking in the living room with Vamm, Gomm the cook, and the staff girl, Ive. They had been locked in when Silver Throat arrived with his men, so Heimilla had attempted to stop them, alone.

Juva fiddled with the key. Her hands shook, but she got the cabinet open. Poured some liquor that had been there since Ester. A small splash first, which she drained. Then she poured a generous glass and felt the unbearable despair quiet down into an undercurrent in her chest. A maelstrom of everything she had lost, chances she had wasted.

Her teeth ached.

She sat down on the chair and pushed her foot closer to the blood. Placed her boot next to the red moon sickle, but it didn't fit. Heimilla wore smaller shoes than she did.

Unfamiliar plants climbed around pillars and elaborate trellises, like a beautiful cage around her. Denser and greener than she remembered. Ester must have pruned them aggressively, but now they grew wilder, as if they wanted to devour the whole gazebo. The roses hung their heads, grieving for her, for Heimilla and the girls. Maybe the gods didn't allow anyone to live in so much beauty, so they had cursed the place?

No, they cursed me.

There was an overturned wrought iron table in front of her and an open book with Syn's tidy letters. The girls had learned so fast, even though they had hardly been taught anything before. Neglected by their parents, if they even had any. The city had failed them.

I failed them.

Juva struggled to hold it together even though she was alone in the room. She couldn't fall apart. Not yet.

In the living room, she saw Muggen strolling around the music box, at arm's length, as if he felt unsure of what the device might do. He hesitantly reached out his hand and turned one of the cranks. It disappeared completely inside his enormous fist. The box plinked, and his underbite pulled back into a childish grin. He looked around as if he had discovered something utterly marvelous before frowning again, unable to locate a melody in the notes.

Vamm came over and took pity on the bald giant.

"It's no good on your own," he explained and turned the other two crank handles. The melancholy melody spread through the room and silenced them both. Vamm suddenly looked older than his seventeen years. He let go of the crank handles and spotted her through the door, which was ajar. He came in. His face was swollen, puffy from crying. His ponytail was coming undone.

"They don't know what to do," he said under his breath. "They say they can't alert the Ring Guard."

Juva remained seated, spreading her fingers on her things to stop them from shaking. She smiled bitterly.

"No. It turns out they may believe I'm the devil."

Vamm came closer.

"They say we can't trust anyone, and that your life is in danger."

"My life has always been in danger."

Vamm's eyes wandered, and she realized that wasn't what he needed to hear.

"We'll find them, Vamm. The girls would be dead, too, if that's what they wanted. But they need them. They need blood readers to find warow."

Feeling cold, he wrapped his arms around himself and didn't respond.

"They didn't take you," she said, but it didn't sound as encouraging as she had intended it to.

"They couldn't tell that I can sense." He stared at the floor. "They locked us in because we . . . We hid. We didn't do anything . . ." His eyes caught the blood by her shoes. He started to cry.

Juva got up and wrapped her arms around him. His sobs were warm on her shoulder.

"If you had done anything, you would be sitting here, too, with a nail in your throat," she said, realizing it was almost the same thing she'd said to Heimilla only a few hours ago. Was that why she was dead now, because of Rugen? Because she hadn't stopped him from taking a measly housekey to the Sannseyr house? It was an unbearable thought.

Juva took a step back and forced him to look at her.

"If you were dead, I'd be worse off. Do you understand?"

Vamm wiped his eyes with his fist.

"Then you're going to be worse off next time," he said, "because I'm never going to hide again."

Juva gathered his hair and twisted the ribbon back around his ponytail. A thin section of his bangs remained plastered to his cheek. She looked up at the round skylight. It had already grown dark outside. The sky was full of stars that drew her to them.

"Vamm, tell the guys to alert the Ring Guard. And if asked, you guys should say they haven't seen me. I'm going to hide on the roof until they've taken Heimilla away. They'll see that she's missing teeth and say she was wolf-sick and needs to be bled. It's not true. Tell them that."

Vamm straightened up, touchingly relieved to have something concrete to do. He walked out and closed the doors behind him. Juva downed the last splash from the glass and hooked the crossbow to her back. She walked to the trellis and tugged on it. Solid wrought iron. The roses shook, but it would hold her weight. She climbed between the plants, up onto the curved top of the gazebo, until she stood just below the skylight. She had seen correctly, the round window in the middle was a hatch. It probably hadn't been touched for decades.

Juva opened the hasp and used force until it creaked open, a gap into the night sky. She pulled herself up and closed it again. The glass squeaked against the framing bars beneath her. She felt like she was floating, staring down at the conservatory as if it were a kelp forest in the water. It brought up a childhood memory. She was sitting in a boat, looking down into the sea until the bottom disappeared into darkness. She was young. The boat had a yellow keel, so it must have been the longship to Kleft. A sepulture.

Father . . .

Juva crawled over the windows until she reached solid footing, ash wood shingles against her knees. Her father was the first person she had lost, the first in a long line: her mother, Solde, Ester, Gríf, Heimilla, and the girls . . .

Myself . . .

She had tried to hide the girls, protect them by keeping them at a distance with an iron shield around her heart, which had never done anything but choke it. Futile. Corrosive. The rage hadn't helped her, only made it less worth fighting. Left her burned out and the girls in greater danger. The guys, too. Broddmar had said it many times: within the hunting team, they shared to survive. But she had grown up with blood readers; all she had learned were secrets. *Never let them see a weak blood reader. Never tell anyone what you saw.*

Burn the wolf.

But it was the wolf who had burned her. Soon she would be ashes in the Floa wind, strewn across the roofs that rearranged themselves before her, very close together, the sea to the north and Náklaborg towering up in the south.

That was where Silver Throat wanted to go. He wanted the power of Náklav, over the city and the realm, over the henge, and over the blood readers. And now he had the girls and the maps. He would get out of them that she was housing the warow, too. It was only a question of time.

Time . . . That was what she lacked most of all.

Juva unhooked the crossbow and the bloodskins, setting them in a bundle against a chimney. Then she lifted the jewelry over her head and set the two vials in front of her. Small works of art, curved like fangs. The glass was encased in an ornate silver overlay, which protected the precious contents. Blood. Eternal life, if you had regular access to it.

The vials seemed out of place on the worn shingles, between dead leaves and the seaweed the storms had blown up.

Silver Throat had released the image of her. She was a fugitive in her own city. And if they caught her, her fangs would prove she was what he claimed: evil. That was all he needed. It would justify anything they might do to her.

It was over. Nothing was would be the way she had thought. Her plans had vanished with the girls. All she could do now was follow her heart.

If he said she was the devil, then that's what she would have to become.

Juva opened the clasp on one of the vials and put it to her lips. She closed her eyes for a second, far too aware that nothing would ever be the same again. Whether it was the wolf-sickness or something else, Gríf had given her this thirst for a reason. She would become a warow if she survived this night.

Later, new torments awaited and probably death once she had exhausted her supply, a fate she had condemned all the warow to. She had just never imagined she would share it.

But it didn't matter because there was no *later*. There was only now. Silver Throat and Eydala. They were not going to get the girls, and they were not going to get Náklav. That was a promise she would keep. She would save everything she loved, even if it meant she had to become what she had feared and despised.

Juva tossed her head back and gulped it down. A salty, raw blood taste spread through her mouth. She steeled herself against a nausea that didn't come, only pleasure. A heavy calm, a feeling of having given her body what it needed, stronger than she had ever experienced from hoggthorn or rye liquor.

Then came the cramps—sudden, painful contractions as if someone were twisting her stomach. She was going to throw up! Juva stifled a scream and curled up on the roof. She remembered how her mother had thrown something up before she died.

What have I done?!

The pains ceased just as suddenly as they had begun, leaving behind fragile relief, tender like a wound. And she wasn't alone anymore.

Grif!

She looked around but there was no one to see. She rolled over onto her back. The leather of her suit creaked, and she breathed cautiously to avoid bringing on the pains again. The stars sparkled against an ink-black sky, and she remembered Hanuk had said that many people from Aure believed every single point of light was another world. Was she dead? Had she taken her own life?

No . . . She could feel her heart hammering in her chest, her own and his. His pounded around hers as if he had swallowed it— heavily, slowly, expectantly. He was here, just as surely as she was herself.

Juva closed her eyes.

"I can smell you," she whispered.

Her words were lame, and they weren't anything like she had imagined they'd be if she ever encountered him again. But that had been her imagination, and this was real. He was with her, *in* her. Or had the wolf-sickness finally claimed her and done what it always did, given her what she desired?

"You made me wolf-sick," she said. "And now you've made me into one of them."

No. I've made you into one of us.

Juva opened her eyes. His voice . . . silent but resounding. A husky echo through her head. The wound in her heart tore, and her longing for him bled into her arteries, so fresh and painful that she heard herself gasp. The wind chilled the tears than ran over her temple and collected in her ear.

"Why?"

It was an unbearable question. She had never feared an answer more than the one she expected now. Her body felt stretched to the breaking point. Something was going to snap.

Her heart was racing, chased by the madness of what was happening. She groaned and tried to get up to no avail.

Breathe in . . .

She collapsed back onto the roof. Breathe in . . . that was the first thing he had said to her when she had found him in the shaft. Real words from a real, living man, who had helped her understand that she hadn't lost her mind. She had listened then and she listened now, inhaling the leathery smell of him deep into her lungs. She could almost feel the heat from his lips and felt that the answer was on its way.

You wouldn't have survived without it. I knew they would come after you.

His words struck her like a chisel, and she felt herself splintering. All the reasons she had given herself . . . all the explanations, each worse than the last, like a stone building cracking at the seams. Nafraím was right.

Grif hadn't hated her, hadn't killed her. He had known the vardari would come, and he had done the only thing he thought could save her.

Her fingers curled around the roofing shingles as if she were going to pull them off. She fumbled to find words, and she could feel him waiting. Something was wrong. He was here grudgingly, as if he were protecting himself.

"This isn't happening," she mumbled. "I'm crazy. This isn't possible . . ."

It is the only thing possible. We are wolves. Blood strengthens bonds no distance can tear apart.

Bonds . . . The word quenched her thirst more than his blood had. Her missing him, the longing she had worked so determinedly to smother grew in her chest. Pressed upward and forward until she opened her mouth to tell him so, but the words failed her. Nothing she could say would be enough.

It made you stronger.

He said it hesitantly, as if only now realizing what it had cost her. But he was wrong. As ludicrously wrong as only Grif could be.

Juva laughed despondently.

"Stronger . . ." she sobbed. "You let me believe that you hated me, despised me, that you had killed me. Stronger? You made me weaker than I have ever been."

You should have known better than that. And better than to turn to them!

"Them?"

I heard you with them.

The warow . . . He knew she had been cooperating with Nafraím, with the man who had imprisoned him. How?

Juva squeezed her eyes closed. Remembered the thirst she had quenched with her tongue, a tiny drop of blood in the palm of her hand. She had sensed him nearby then, without suspecting it was real, and he had heard her with the enemy.

His heart grew heavy and hard in her chest, an impossible weight to lift. How should she begin? There was too much to say, too much to explain.

"Nothing is the way you think," she said meekly because she knew it wouldn't help. "They're defending Náklav! Running the city, running . . . the world!"

At my expense.

"Yours? No! No, they . . . they're all that stands between us and Undst. And . . . they have the girls!" Despair welled up within her when she realized he had no idea about the girls. Or Undst.

"It's too late. I can't . . ."

You should have taken the blood right away. No one should be able to resist as long as you have. I was waiting.

Another blow. She had protected his room, refused to let herself go down there because she was sure of his betrayal.

"I thought you had betrayed me!"

He gave a brief laugh. A fragment of the laughter she remembered.

You speak of treachery? I gave you the power to stop every warow heart, and you took them in. You look for nothing but lies, so lies are all you find.

"You don't understand. Gríf . . . There's going to be a war!"

Yes, Juva. There's going to be a war.

His heart receded from her chest, and she could feel him disappearing. She wanted to cling to the delightful sound of her own name from his lips. Hear him say it over and over again, but nothing she could say or do would make him stay. He had given her something she didn't understand and probably never would, because he had wanted to prepare her, arm her to withstand the vardaris' rage. Instead she had allied herself with them.

Juva sat up and pulled her hands over her face. Her heart was beating alone again. Her body felt alien, like it didn't really belong to her. She felt infinitely strong yet still shattered.

It was over. She loved a man she had doubted and betrayed, and she would never get the chance to tell him. But she could tell herself, feeling the loss condense in her throat, knowing it was real.

She was done hiding what she was fighting for. War was war, and she was going to win it because she loved.

She had to find the girls, but first she had to get the warow out of the Sannseyr home. Before the Hallowed came. If they hadn't been there already. No . . . they would wait for her, for her to come home, which meant that there was no way to reach Nafraím. Unless . . .

Juva looked up and gazed out at Náklav's roofs. The way home.

She felt a jolt of pain and touched her jaw. She tasted blood and nearly swallowed her own teeth. She spat them out into her hand in a pink puddle. They were eerily common. Flat. Not like any she had pulled before.

Her tongue found her fangs, which had grown in. Short but sharp. She was an animal. She was the wolves she had always hunted. An enduring abyss of grief and anger.

She was the devil.

AN OLD HEART

Nafraím followed the sentence with his finger, but the words seemed to bleed into each other. The silence in the library felt oppressive, malevolent. He closed his eyes, letting them rest for a moment before he continued reading. The merciless wear and tear of old age was a burden he had never been inconvenienced by until these last few months.

It was not a flesh and blood problem. His body had recovered, supported by the precious drops Juva had sacrificed. No, this was a weakness of his soul. His eyes had seen centuries, watched sovereigns come and go. He had seen them groping around in the dark and had helped them fight their way toward a fragile liberty, an understanding of life's inherent value. He had seen the birth of Náklaborg, the liberation of Ohrad, the founding of the Council of Jórd . . . But now, in the year 1447 after Esja, he had seen enough.

The wolves chased him in his dreams, closer every night. He was at the end of the road. All he could do was point the other warow in the right direction, even if they couldn't make a difference in the long run.

He heard Seire approaching with hurried footsteps, probably to tell him they were out of time. She stopped beside him.

"Someone just threw an egg at the window."

Nafraím found the neatly handwritten name in the book and picked up the pen. Seire took a step closer.

"Naf, did you hear me?"

"I heard you," he replied and added his name to the list.

"Are you going to sit there writing? The street is full of lunatics! They're going to break in!"

"That's likely." He continued writing.

Seire flung up her arms in annoyance.

"Well, there you have it. As long as you acknowledge that it's *likely*."

Silence settled over the room, simmering with the commotion coming in from the street.

"Seire's right," Faun said. "We can't stay here. She may not even be alive any longer."

Nafraím added the last name to the list.

"She's alive."

"You heard the Dead Man's Horn," Seire said. "We haven't seen her since. Either she's dead or she's betrayed us."

Nafraím stood up with a strange feeling of having borrowed his body.

"If she were dead, would they be waiting for her outside? If she had betrayed us, would they have thrown eggs at the windows?"

Faun and Seire exchanged looks in a silent tug-of-war.

"It's getting late," Faun said, resigned. "And it's going to rain. They'll go home."

Skarr suddenly leapt to his feet and ran past Seire. His claws clicked against the floor, followed by an uncharacteristic whine as he disappeared up the staircase in the front hall. Seire pulled her knife.

"They're inside!"

Nafraím raised his hand to tell her to stay put. He cocked his head and listened. The wolf was coming back down, but he could hear that it had company.

He folded up his notes and stuck them in his breast pocket.

"Like I said, she's not dead and she hasn't betrayed us. The noise outside means something else entirely."

Juva walked in, dressed in red like a bloodskin and pulled down her mask.

"It means they have released my likeness."

Seire exhaled and sheathed the knives.

"How in Drukna did you get in? I thought you had boarded up all the openings?"

"Not the balcony," Juva replied.

"On the sea side?!" Seire glanced at the window with obvious skepticism.

"Yes, and we need to go out the same way. Now."

Juva's voice bore traces of fake calm. A dead-calm sea that hid powerful currents of rage, and Nafraím sensed he was seeing her for the first time. The red leather had faded over her knees and bore scratches he had no idea from where. Teeth. Knives. Nails. Dried blood lay in the cracks between her fingers.

Nafraím walked toward her, drawn by necessity, a feeling of being half frozen to death, a few steps from the fire. A blue vein throbbed below her ear. It was a strange thing to notice, but he couldn't help but stare.

What has happened?

She seemed to sense his attraction and pulled away, not allowing him to get close.

"He has the girls," she said, her voice hoarse.

"What girls?" Seire asked. "The ones who came to pick you up?"

Juva nodded.

"They're blood readers. They can sense, all of them. They're the ones who drew the maps."

Seire let out a dispirited moan.

"He doesn't need you anymore. Why didn't you *say* so . . . And now he has . . . They will lead *him* here, too, and they can . . ."

Faun shot her a look and everything that Silver Throat might do was left unsaid.

336

"It doesn't matter," Juva said. "We're not going to be here. Come on. We need to get up to the roof."

Nafraím leaned on the table for support. He felt drained, like a tree in Svartna. Lifeless but standing out of habit because he couldn't remember anything else. He would never fire another shot. War, violence, and anger were no longer his burdens to bear. Even escaping from the roof was an insurmountable obstacle. It would be pointless to try. The end would catch up with them all anyway.

He took a barely restorative breath and nodded toward the opening in the chimney.

"Clean up our things. Juva and I will be waiting upstairs."

Seire and Faun exchanged glances, a silent worry, but they did as he asked.

"Close up the shaft when you're done," Juva said and left the library with Skarr at her heels.

Nafraím followed her up the stairs, his legs heavy.

"What's the plan? Where will you all go?"

Juva glanced back over her shoulder at him.

"*We* are going to Hidehall. To Domnik and those he has gathered there. That's the safest place we have right now, but it won't last."

He followed her into the attic storeroom. She had lit a lantern by the balcony door, which was exquisitely framed in the circle of verdigris copper. Time had stood still there, since Síla Sannseyr was at his strongest.

A rope swayed in the wind outside, thin and inadequate, like a straw against the eternal, black sky.

Skarr slipped past him and sniffed around the room but ended up next to Juva again, unwilling to realize that this was not a way out for him.

Nafraím sat down on a chest and watched her while she flipped through a rack of old clothes. She shook out a wadmal coat and tossed it onto his lap.

"It was my father's. It's on the big side, but it's gotten chilly out there."

A storm of dust danced before her face, where he saw all his mistakes woefully reflected. The coat weighed on his lap, as if to hold him in place. He realized he could have loved her as a daughter if he had had the time and the energy, but now it was too late. He was no longer man enough to wear her father's clothes, nor did he have any right.

He smiled.

"I've grown too old to escape over the rooftops, Juva."

"You were *born* too old," she replied, opening the balcony door. The wind gusted in off the sea. Her blond hair whipped like white tongues of flame, and he sensed that that was the only thing the gods could play with. She was unwavering. Shaped by everything he had let her suffer; wrongs there were hardly words for had sharpened her like a knife's edge. He would have been proud. Before.

He took the notes out of his pocket.

"These are people who can help, both in the short and long term, and you must remind the Queen's guard that there are catapults in the caves at Kviskre. I hope and believe we can count on Klemens, but we need to be cautious because—"

"Spare me." She handed him a shirt and a pair of gloves. "Here, take these, too. And we can rely on Klemens."

"What makes you so sure?"

"When I hunted warow with Silver Throat, Klemens gave me the most inept group of hunters you can imagine. Not exactly the choice of a man who wanted us to succeed."

He smiled at the far-fetched but strangely precise conclusion.

"That may be. But regardless, this is a road you will have to travel without me."

She started to laugh, but her eyes darkened.

"Yes, you'd like that, to be allowed to sit down and die? After centuries based on injustice, on a crack in Náklav's bedrock, just as your own edifice is being overthrown? Then you'll call it a day? Don't you dare. I won't die without fixing my mistakes, and neither will you, Nafraím Sai."

He set the clothes aside.

"So you're going to Hidehall," he said, hearing the powerlessness in his own voice. "Where the last warow will receive you like a savior, even though you have hunted and killed so many of them that they are the last of their kind. Is that what you're envisioning? Do you think they're going to fight for you?"

"No. But I think they'll fight for *you*."

Nafraím stared at her mouth, at the sharp fangs she had just revealed, and suddenly, he realized what he was seeing.

She is Vitnir . . .

His certainty was absolute, but the reason was an unparalleled riddle. She wasn't wolf-sick or a warow. Gríf had given her the strength of his people's blood. Why?

She came toward him with a fearlessness he finally understood the source of.

"You're so old that you've forgotten what it's like to be afraid," she said. "You think it means something's wrong with you, but that's a lie. It's true that it steals from you, the fear. You might not remember it, but I do, and I know what it actually wants to tell you. It's not telling you to stop; it's saying that what you're doing means something, that you care. You try not to listen because it feels perilous, but the day you're not scared, you have nothing left to fight for."

He smiled and lowered his gaze. Nothing he could say would convince her how wrong she was. Yes, he feared seeing the destruction he himself had caused devour the city, and he cared more than she could understand, something he couldn't blame her for. But he did not fear the outcome. He already knew what the outcome would be; he knew her courage was wasted. The world would end anyway.

She stood before him.

"No," she said, squinting as if with sudden insight. "Your heart is too heavy for fear. You're not afraid. You think you've already lost." Her eyes lingered on him for a moment before she continued. "Believe what you will but keep it to yourself. You have people to lead, Nafraím. Maybe only two, maybe twenty, but lead them you shall, even if I have to carry you there."

Nafraím stared at her wrist, at the strength he could sense in those blue veins. He felt a heavy beat in his chest and clutched his heart. The deep jolt was followed by several others, and he felt like he was waking up. His fingers started tingling, suddenly warm. The will grew within him like a tender sprout, and a sudden memory came to him. The green shoot from the forests in Svartna. He had received it from a monk, held it in his hands, sure he was beholding the end of all things. The sprouting sign that the doors between worlds was open again.

So why had Grif made her into what she was?

He could have killed her or just left her alone. That would have been simpler, and more like the wolves. He had done this with the deepest of intentionality. Why?

Could it be a helping hand, a reluctant forgiveness, a peace gesture, or . . .

Understanding dawned on him, an impossible thought so saturated with hope that he caught himself with his mouth hanging open like a child.

"He loved you." Nafraím looked up at her, gazing in wonder.

She smiled, and it caused him great pain.

"Yes, and in return, I'm saving the skin of his worst enemy. Now, change!"

Nafraím stood without having time to think about it. As if his body were listening to her. He pulled on the shirt she had given him and heard Faun and Seire coming up the stairs. His thoughts began revolving around problems that suddenly felt smaller, solvable. Like how she could meet the warow with veins full of the blood they all longed for.

They can never find out.

A faint drumming on the window revealed that it had begun to rain. Skarr let out a resigned sigh and lay on the floor, almost as if he knew he would be left behind. Náklav's roofs were no place for wolves.

Juva squatted down and pet him.

"I'll come back and get you," she said.

Nafraím believed her. Then she put out the lantern.

THE SURVIVORS

Juva reached down to Nafraím, who dangled dangerously from the rope. His coat whipped in the wind, and he stared up at her, pale as if he were about to take the waters for the last time. The balcony stuck out well below him, far too meager to catch him should he fall. He would smash into the railing before he plummeted into the sea. The waves crashed against the rocky coast in a far slower rhythm than his heart. She could feel it laboring in her own chest.

The feeling was the same as it had always been, but it couldn't control her anymore. Couldn't pull her down into an undertow of panic. She knew better now.

Warow hearts had no power over her. They were just there. She had her own heart, and it was strong enough to bear what she sensed, but not to bear the guessing she had always done, the stories she had told herself about what she knew, the judgements she had made.

To sense was to see, not to interpret.

Nafraím glanced down at the sea, and she waved to stop him. The rain lashing her face had already made the roofing tiles slipperier. She wriggled farther over the edge, caught his eye, and nodded. He grabbed hold of her hand with a strength she hadn't thought he still had. She braced her heels against the edge and helped him onto the roof. He crawled over to the broken flowerpot and lay on his back, breathing. She let him rest while the other two climbed up.

The noise from the street increased. Something was happening. Juva snuck along the edge of the wall, peeked down at Lykteløkka, and felt her stomach clench. There were more of them. Náklav had come out in force to smoke the devil out of the Sannseyr house.

Some seemed to be there out of sheer curiosity while others slowly strolled by. The worst ones had the nail around their necks. They were shaking their fists and gearing up for a fight Juva had no plans to give them. The dense crowd parted to let someone through. There was no mistaking the large figure.

Drogg!

The city councilman pushed his way through the last of the crowd and stood on Juva's front steps. His words barely reached her through the rain. He spoke about disrupting people's ability to move freely, and he threatened to call in the Ring Guard. That appeared to thin the crowd a little, but a stubborn core of Hallowed followers remained.

Juva cocked her head and listened.

"The devil has taken this house!" an unfamiliar male voice yelled. "She is an enemy of God!"

Drogg waved his handkerchief as if to shoo him away.

"Go home, man," he thundered. "Otherwise, I'll show you a real enemy of God! There must be some moderation to this nonsense!"

Juva suppressed a smile. The stranger looked around for support, but no one was willing to oppose a councilman.

Drogg banged the door knocker.

"Juva?" He banged it again, and the wrought iron clanged. "Juva Sannseyr!"

Seire came up next to her.

"What's going on? Who is that?"

Juva raised a finger to shush her.

"Someone I think we can trust."

But not now.

She coiled up the rope and threw it over her shoulder. Then she got a running start and jumped across to the house next door. She glanced back and saw three shadows follow in the darkness.

Náklav's rooftops were close together. The height differences were a bigger challenge than the distances, but the skybridges helped them to Skjepnasnaret before they had to descend. From there, she followed the quietest alleyways, even though the weather had chased most people indoors.

She stopped in Blodrenna to wait for the others. The rain drummed on her leather hood in irregular gusts with the wind. She couldn't see Hidehall, just the glow of the lanterns in the courtyard. A lopsided arc of light glistened on the wet cobblestones.

The other three appeared behind her.

"What if no one is here?" Seire asked. "It could be a trap. They might have found them. They could be dead, all of them."

The warow woman looked at her and shrugged, as if she realized that her discouragement was uncharacteristic.

"They're here," Juva replied. Then she slipped around the corner and into Hidehall. The shadows in the windows revealed that the beer hall was full. A good sign, implying Oda had closed off the hunting hall as instructed.

Juva snuck along the exterior wall, stopped by the back door, and listened. She couldn't hear anything, but she didn't need to. Every heartbeat had a swarm of echoes, more than she had ever felt. It was as if her heart lay exposed to the rain.

She knocked on the door with cold knuckles, the signal that she had prearranged with Broddmar. He opened the door a crack and let her into the hallway. She heard conversations from out in the hunting lodge. Many voices, but they were muted.

Seire followed and stopped abruptly. She seemed to listen to the voices. The hard glint in her eyes misted over with joy, and she turned to Faun and Nafraím.

"Jút!" she exclaimed.

She vanished into the hunting lodge with the others behind her. Juva hesitated, painfully aware of who she was to the vardari and the reactions her suit would elicit. She walked toward the opening and stopped.

The hunting lodge was barely recognizable. It had rarely housed more than a couple of solitary hunters. She had lived here for three years but had usually been alone. Now it was full, and for a second, she thought she had been mistaken, that Oda had opened the place up to the tavern guests after all, but her heart was never wrong. They were warow.

They sat around the tables and on the benches along the wall. They stood chatting in the gallery, and Juva heard someone pumping water in the kitchen. She recognized Ferkja, who sat with her knees pulled up in a chair before the fire—exactly the way she used to do.

Nafraím walked in among them, and the conversations died. The silence slowly spread through the room until it was as quiet as Drukna. She could see disbelief in hundreds of eyes. Then came the exclamations of unconcealed joy. She could feel it, practically taste it. Hope.

Seire beamed and threw her arms around a pale man, her exact opposite, until she nearly lifted him off the floor.

"Jút! I can't believe you're still alive!"

"Of course I am," he laughed. "I knew it would annoy you."

More people joined in, setting off a flurry of hugging. Juva withdrew into the shadows. A fresh feeling of loneliness pressed on her chest. The joy of reunion stood in stark contrast to the pain she felt for Heimilla and the girls. They were not mentioned in all the questions raining down.

"I heard you were dead?"

"Are there likenesses of all of us?"

"Where have you been?"

"Where's Reiko?"

It grew quiet. Hearing his name spoken aloud sucked the life out of the room. Seire's smile faded, and she shook her head. Jút slumped as if he had suddenly been given something heavy to carry. A woman she had heard them call Vippa turned her back as if to conceal her grief. An elderly man they had called Hemvil made no attempt to hide his fear.

Ferkja lit a thin cigar with trembling hands while Broddmar caressed her back with fatherly care. The gesture brought a memory of something Ferkja had said to her on the bridge, that she had lost her father to a Sannseyr.

Broddmar...

Juva had assumed she'd meant her mother had taken Ferkja's father as a lover. That would hardly have been surprising. But it had been about Broddmar. Was that why he had been a warow for a while? He hadn't fallen for a young woman; he had been there as a father figure. As a rock. Until he had chosen Valjar Sannseyr instead ... Her own father. And over the years, he had become *her* rock, maybe at Ferkja's expense.

Juva felt something akin to shame, but the feeling was too pitiful to last, a drop in the sea of grief and anger. They had all lost people—she because of them, they because of her. All that tied them together was the devil. And the threat to Náklav.

She saw it in the tired looks that lingered on Nafraím; the anticipation, the uncertainty, the hope had become a demanding call for more effort.

"So you swam back from the dead to say Náklav will fall to Undst?" Domnik said.

"Is it true that the blood is gone for good?" another asked before Nafraím had had a chance to answer.

Let him speak!

Nafraím climbed onto a table and held up his hands to silence them.

"I know you're . . ." His voice broke. He cleared his throat and started again. "I know you're thirsty, of course you are. And I understand the exhaustion that brings, but we all knew this day would come."

A woman Juva didn't know crossed her arms in front of her chest.

"*You* knew it would come! It's hard for us to know what to think, Nafraím. A few months ago, Eydala said you had gotten rid of the source on purpose. That you wanted to end your own life and take us all with you. Now they say that she's behind Silver Throat and his warow hunting ways."

Juva closed her eyes and listened to Nafraím try to explain the grotesque: Eydala's lack of judgment, how she had drunk blood from dead warow, about the Rot that was eating her from within, about the pictures she had supplied Silver Throat with in a futile quest for recognition.

We don't have time for this!

Juva looked around and spotted the guys by the far wall, but she couldn't just collect them and leave. There was too much at stake if Nafraím wasn't able to rally the warow. He had finally gotten to wolf-sickness and how Undst had been spreading it to get rid of opposition and create the fear he needed, but there were many objections.

"Let them try it," Hemvil said. "No one can take Náklav from the sea."

"And while all this was going on," Vippa asked, "where were *you*, Nafraím?"

"Being tortured, Vippa!" Ferkja hissed in response. "He was tortured since the spring race, held captive by that monster, and the last thing he needs is your doubt!"

Nafraím raised his hands to silence them, but that wasn't so easy anymore. Juva could feel his heart weakening beneath the others. The arguing spread through the room like poison.

She looked down at her own hands, still bloody from pulling the nail out of Heimilla's throat—all this blood . . . from Ester, Solde, her mother, and her father; from wolf-sickness and wolves; and from warow.

That was more than enough. She was done losing.

"And where is the blood?" a bearded man asked. "We're in this mess because of you! You can't demand that we risk anything until we know if we're going to survive this!"

Juva pushed her way through the crowd to Nafraím. Silence fell. Their eyes brimmed with contempt and disbelief, and she felt the drumming growing denser against her heart. She leapt onto the table beside Nafraím.

"I can help you all with this uncertainty. You are not going to survive this."

No one responded. The rain kept drumming on her heart, and she realized the mutiny she had been expecting wouldn't come. Broddmar and the others must have paved the way for her, explained how things fit together, and promised explanations. But she had none.

She had hunted them, killed some of them, seen one of them sent to Drukna. It seemed pointless to explain or defend. They were here anyway, bound together by mistakes.

"I am Juva Sannseyr," she said, all too aware of how unnecessary that was. "I am the daughter of Lagalune Sannseyr, and I inherited the devil from her. I wish I had inherited some knowledge about him as well, known who he was and what he meant, but I didn't. I found a man in captivity. A man who had kept you alive for far too long, and I set him free. He has left us for good and taken with him the blood you were living off of. There's nothing more you can do. So, no, you're not in this mess because of Nafraím. You're in it because of me."

Juva looked at them all in turn. The vial of blood felt frighteningly heavy inside her shirt, and she tried not to think about what would happen if they knew.

"You've killed us," Vippa broke the silence.

"Yes, and I would do it again. You built eternity on violence, on injustice. You created wolf-sickness, which I've spent my life cleaning up, so spare me." Juva bared her teeth. "Besides, I'm one of you now. That was the last thing he did, so I will meet the same fate as you."

Her words made an impression. Their surprise quickly abated, leaving behind an eerie satisfaction that they didn't have the shame to hide.

"What are you doing here, blood hunter?" Hemvil asked. "If I hadn't known better, I'd have thought you were here to lock us in and burn the place down. So if you think we should trust you—"

"I don't give a damn if you trust me! Whether you live or die doesn't matter in the least to me. I'm here because we have a common enemy. I've helped you get here because I don't want to kneel to fanatics from Undst. Because right now, all of Náklav is waiting for the ships from Undst to dock with a cure that doesn't exist. The only thing coming on those ships is doom."

Hemvil approached with a caustic smile.

"How old are you?"

"I'm not old," Juva said, looking into his eyes. "I'm young. You've moved slowly for centuries, but the Vardari method can't save us anymore. We need to act *now*. But if you feel too old to fight, then by all means, please lie down and die, Hemvil. I'm not here to stop you."

Ferkja chuckled, and a couple of delicate smiles appeared.

349

Juva nodded to Nafraím.

"Rage at me as much as you want. I'm not asking anyone to follow me. I'm asking you to follow *him*. You've been here for days, aware of what's going on, without making yourselves useful, while he . . . Tell them where we stand, Nafraím."

Nafraím looked at her with a wonder she couldn't interpret. Then he pulled out his notes.

"The best battle is the one you avoid," he said. "I have notified many people anonymously to spread word of what might be coming. I've notified people in the state council and contacts abroad who will prepare their governments for the fact that the henge may be a target for Undst. If any of you have contacts in the ocean fleet, we need to remind them that there are catapults in the caves at Kviskre. They're hundreds of years old, but they will be useful if needed. We also need to make sure they protect Naar. It's possible that they will come ashore there to demolish the bridge, believing that that will make a difference."

"They must know that that's impossible," Hemvil began, but Nafraím didn't let him seize the room's attention.

"Yes, they should know that it's impossible, but there are three ways they can defeat us. They could have an unknown weapon; I doubt that. They could have allied themselves with other henge cities, which I also doubt. After all, we haven't had any major diplomatic crises in our time, aside from when King Margen called Náklaborg the world's ugliest castle."

The laughter was a relief and infectious, but Juva was glad she had the sense not to let go.

"The final way is what they've already done: do away with the opposition and infiltrate our institutions. We won't be able to see the extent of it until it becomes obvious."

Juva climbed off the table and let him do what he always had, lead the Vardari. She reluctantly admitted that he had mastered the art. There were no objections, and what she heard was a far more fruitful discussion about who should do what and how.

"I'm going to Jólshov!" cried a voice she knew. Juva turned and saw Muggen. He stared at the floor, as if suddenly realizing he had gotten carried away. "To steal the images . . ." he mumbled. "They can't . . . If they're allowed to keep . . ."

"He's right," Nafraím said. "As long as the images are out there, more of us are doomed to live in the shadows."

Muggen smiled, his cheeks red.

"And I have a queen I need to speak to," Nafraím said, sticking his notes back in his pocket.

"How about you?" Hemvil asked, staring at Juva. "What will you do?"

"I have five young girls to save. Silver Throat has taken them, and I intend to get them back."

"Girls?" Hemvil snickered. "We're awaiting a possible invasion, a hostile fleet. Haven't you been paying attention? There are more important things going on than young girls. We're running out of time. Some of us are near death already!"

Juva stepped closer and captured his heart in her own. The myriad of rhythms paled into a distant vibration while she embraced the worry he had for his own life. It felt so small. So pathetic that it drowned in her own. She had a violent urge to show him what fear could be, and with that thought came the beats, faster, heavier, in pace with her own. But she was used to fear. He wasn't. Her body grew hot, the sweat beading. Gríf's words rushed like an echo through her head.

I gave you the power to stop every single warow heart.

Hemvil took a wobbly step backward, sweaty, panicked, confused about his own body, his own feelings. She could see the realization dawning and he looked at her as if she were the devil himself.

She could control his heart, and now she knew for certain why.

Because she was willing to sacrifice her own. The feeling was intoxicating, even though the knowledge was useless. She could never do to others anything that she didn't simultaneously do to herself.

If it became a question of life and death, in the end, it would come down to who had the strongest heart.

"Stop her," he whispered, pressing his hands to his chest. He stumbled backward, but Seire caught him before he fell.

Juva let go, leaving his heart alone.

"I know what I need to do," she said, maintaining control of her breathing. "You don't need to help me, Hemvil, but you can never stop me. You fight for what you care about, and I will do the same."

She turned her back and strode toward the door.

"So you're going to kill Silver Throat?" Seire called after her.

"I'm going to do more than that. I'm going to kill all the illusions people might have about him. Everything he has made them believe."

THE WINE

Juva took the road through Nattlyslokket. The overhang from the buildings protected her from the rain, but it didn't last long. She would be soaked before she reached Ringmark. Her suit would have helped, but it had to stay in her backpack if she had any hope of getting to Drogg's house unseen.

Can I trust him?

Many who had opposed Silver Throat were already dead, and generous bribes had clearly found their way to Náklav's power brokers, but that didn't mean everyone left was a traitor. It just meant she couldn't know for sure. And Drogg dispersing the mob outside the Sannseyr home could have been an act to get her to open the door, but her instincts said otherwise. Either way, it was a chance she had to take. She needed his help.

It was late, and few people had ventured out into the rain, but his building could still be under surveillance. She had to find another way.

Juva felt like an outlaw. A hunted animal. But if the wolves had taught her anything, it was that they fought as long as their hearts were beating, and hers was pounding like never before.

She crossed Haergata by Náklabank and spotted a poster on a closed shop door that claimed they sold only safe food. The rumor about the wolf-sickness had spread, and that was something. She followed the alley and stopped at the mouth, right by Drogg's building. Ringmark was old and expensive. The neighborhood was home to the oldest money in town, but this building was shared by multiple families. Drogg didn't have any family, as far as she knew.

A man hurried by with his back arched against the weather. There was no one else to be seen, but she couldn't risk anything.

Juva walked on with her head down, past the front door. She squinted at the brass plaque without stopping and saw his name. Top floor, left wing. She continued around the corner behind the building, where the street turned into a staircase. She jumped onto the railing and got onto a window ledge, slick from the rain. She felt around above the window for the carving she had seen.

There!

She got hold of a stag's head and pulled herself up. The proud animal stared at her with its vacant, stony gaze. Its humiliation wasn't over. She had to crawl on top of it to proceed. She climbed upward, finally pulling herself onto the windowsill on the top floor, where she hoped to find Drogg.

It was dark, but a smoldering lantern between the buildings revealed she was right. She stared into a workroom and recognized the purple jacket hanging over the back of a chair.

He had probably already gone to bed; if so, she would have to wake him.

Juva drew her dagger and coaxed it between the windows, bringing it upward until she flipped the hasp. Then she opened the window with a slow creak and climbed into the dark room. It was nice enough that she found herself wiping her shoes on her pant legs. The heavy bookshelves were labeled by year, and the desk was hidden beneath neat stacks of paper folders and books. Several of them were about Undst, and she recognized the one she had read in the men's club. *Undst: A Historical Journey.*

He had made notes on a stack of loose paper.

Juva bit her lip. The urge to find a sign of his loyalty took over, and she skimmed through the notes. They were messier than she had expected, as if he had been lost in thought as he wrote. He had circled names and years and underlined one of his own sentences, which seemed to have been written in haste.

They have done it before.

Done what before?

Juva turned the paper over and continued reading until she realized what he had noticed. Undst had promised a cure before. Generations ago, for a completely different ailment, but to Drogg it had obviously indicated a pattern.

Juva smiled in the dark. Blessed Drogg! He knew! He had understood, and it wasn't too late. She needed to find him.

She crossed the room and avoided stepping on the carpet. The tip of her shoe bumped into a basket by the door, and something in it clinked. It was full of goodies from a bakery she had never heard of. Two wine bottles stuck up in the middle, one with a card around its neck. Juva squatted down and turned it over, even though she knew what she would find. It was a gift for Drogg from Silver Throat on behalf of Undst.

He doesn't drink!

Juva stood and felt a lump grow in her throat. Drogg was a target, and if he had been a drinker, he might be dead now, wolf-sick. Shame and relief washed through her, and she realized just how much she had been hoping he was a trustworthy friend. Drogg hadn't let her down, but Juva's hesitation had risked his life.

Juva yanked open the door and found herself staring straight at Drogg. He was wearing a shiny red nightshirt, and he was swinging a hammer at her. Juva screamed and jumped out of the way as he caught himself and stared at her.

"Juva?! What in the name of everything holy are you doing here?! I thought . . ." He looked around in confusion. "How . . .? Are you aware of what's going on? I've been searching for you like a crazy man, and you won't believe what—"

Juva threw herself forward and hugged him with arms that felt far too short. She pressed her head to his prodigious belly.

"You don't drink!" she said tearfully.

"What? No, of course not. What does that have to do with anything? But, my dear, you can't be here. Silver Throat has . . . There's a risk of . . . Well, I don't know where to start, Juva."

She looked up without letting go of him.

"Drogg Valsvik, you are the biggest man in Náklav, in every sense!"

He looked at her. Then he gently patted her hair, as if she had completely lost her mind.

FOREVER YOUNG

Juva woke up feeling like she was falling. It took her a second to remember she was in the storeroom at Hidehall, in the bed that had been hers during the years she had lived there.

She heard Broddmar and Muggen snoring in the next room. Otherwise, everything was as it always had been, as if she had never left. She had fallen backward in time.

If she got up and went down to the common room, it would be winter. Dark. Maybe someone had lit a fire in the fireplace, and it would smell like blood and pelts from the hunters. The salt containers would be full, and Ester would bring money. Then, suddenly, Solde would come sailing in in a red dress and say that Mother was sick.

The memories tormented her with everything she hadn't known back then, when blood readers were the worst thing there was, and the Vardari were scarcely more than a rumor. The time before Gríf.

I heard you with them.

His words cut like a rip through her chest, and they would do so over and over again. She could forget them for brief periods, but they came back, sharper every time.

Nothing she could ever say to him would give her forgiveness or even understanding. She was cooperating with warow. She had saved the life of the man who had held him captive for over six hundred years. The reason would never matter. It was over.

Juva sat up in bed. Her tongue ran over her sharp fangs, an unfamiliar and yet familiar feeling. She had done it so often in fearful fantasies that now it seemed unavoidable. As if she had always known they would one day be there. Whatever she was, she didn't fear it. She wasn't wolf-sick and she wasn't vardari. She was something else.

One of us, he had said.

She loved him. The certainty of that had dawned on her abruptly and mercilessly the instant she had heard his husky voice again, the iron wolf, her lifelong nightmare, and everything her life had revolved around.

Juva got up and put on her clothes. Tugged at them, impatient, because she knew there would be nothing but pain if she dawdled. She had the girls to think about. And Náklav. The last thing she had time to do was cry over a broken heart like a child.

She opened the door, stepped into the gallery, and looked down into the hall below. It seemed more familiar now, still quiet for the night with almost everyone gone. Each off to do their own task, hoping that Náklav would be prepared when the sea no longer brought food but enemies.

Hanuk and Nolan lay sleeping on separate benches while Seire struggled to fold a map of the city someone had procured. Faun was packing his bag, and Nafraím was coming up the stairs, probably to try to stop Juva yet again. But even he would have to learn to live with uncertainty. They needed to go their separate ways.

Juva met him halfway down the stairs. She shook her head before he had time to say anything.

"Forget it. Eydala has the girls, and we're going to find them."

He smiled, oddly frail for an immortal man of fifty.

"Eydala's not the type to surround herself with children."

"Neither is Silver Throat. And he can't have them at Jólshov. As far as we know, he still thinks Eydala is a secret we don't know about. You yourself are proof that it's a good place to keep prisoners. Besides, she has something I need."

"No," he said, looking down. "I didn't think I could stop you. I just wanted to urge you to be careful. You're fighting someone who doesn't think like regular people."

"I've been doing that for a long time," Juva said with a shrug.

Nafraím put his hands on either side of her head and leaned forward until his forehead rested against hers. His heart beat warmly and heavily against her own. Her thoughts went to her father, which seemed infinitely right and wrong at the same time.

"I don't deserve you, Juva Sannseyr," he mumbled.

Juva smiled.

"Don't be afraid. I'll never forgive you, Nafraím Sai."

Out of the corner of her eye, she saw Seire grin and nudge Faun with her elbow. Nafraím let go of her and walked back downstairs. The three warow looked at each other and at her. Their eyes were filled with the weight of everything that could happen, everything that could have been different. Then they left the hunting hall.

Juva went down to the kitchen and pumped water into the kettle. Broddmar came in and sat down at the crooked little table. He didn't say anything, as if he knew she had something to ask. But how should she ask for help after everything that had been said and done?

After the hunt for warow, after she wanted to shoot Ferkja, after their argument on the docks . . . She felt like she was brimming with mistakes, but he had made mistakes, too. Still, she needed to ask the guys to go with her. She couldn't retrieve the girls alone.

There was a pot of lukewarm sour porridge on the counter, and she dished up a bowl for each of them. Then she sat down across from him and ate. The taste was a memory from their days in Svartna, of frozen feet and tracks in the snow, of wolves howling their grief.

The kettle began to whistle, and she got up again. She poured water over the tea and put it on the table. She took a sip and looked at him. His stubble was grayer than she remembered. His cheeks had sunken in a notch, but he was the same.

He scraped the last of the sour porridge from the bowl and got up. Rinsed the bowl in the basin. For a second, she thought he was going to leave again, but he stopped beside her. Patted the back of her head, as if everything was as it always had been.

"Let's go find the girls, Juva."

She pulled her hands over her face and fought a sudden urge to cry. She nodded. There was nothing more to say. He had said it all. If only she could feel his heart now, feel everyone's: Hanuk, Muggen, Nolan, and Lok. The girls.

Gríf had called it a gift, but what sort of gift hid those you were closest to? She could sense only Silver Throat's sinners. People who would have been dead eons ago without Gríf's blood. Ghosts. She was haunted by shadows who didn't belong to this world, and now she was one of them.

It was no gift; it was a curse.

Muggen yawned in the doorway.

"We're ready," Broddmar said.

"Good," Muggen replied. "What for?"

Hanuk and Nolan woke up and came into the kitchen. They had barely finished their food when Lok knocked. Juva fought the feeling that this would be their last hunt together, that nothing would ever be the same again.

They left Hidehall through the backdoor and followed the alleyways up toward Tunga. The rain was lighter and would probably be over before dawn.

They walked along Kistestikk until they reached the old city walls and could climb up. The walls were far from secure, but it was the best way to get there unseen. They went straight toward their goal.

Juva looked for the house Nafraím had described: a secluded old mansion, the subject of a generations-long property dispute. It was not Eydala's house, but it's where she had done whatever she liked.

The mansion came into view, ghostly in the light from the lanterns around the neighboring houses. Statues in faded colors stood in the niches between the closed windows. The repugnance hit Juva like nausea, as if her body knew that she had been there before without knowing where she was. At the time, she had been sent home in a carriage, blindfolded.

The thought of the girls drove her through the rain. The walls surrounding the mansion ran close, making it easy to get onto the low wings of the roof. From there, they could climb onto a ledge and reach the nearest window.

Juva paused just before the window to avoid being seen through the glass. She gestured to the guys to wait while she sensed in her heart. It beat by itself. No pinprick from Eydala. If the woman was in the house, she was somewhere other than here.

Juva peered into the dark room. It was impossible to see anything. A couple of the windowpanes were cracked, and she broke them with her dagger. She felt around for the hasps and got the window open. She hopped into a bedroom, seemingly unused for centuries. The top of the four-poster bed had collapsed and a picture hung on the wall. Juva jumped as she recognized herself, but it wasn't a picture. It was a mirror, faded with dust.

She lifted the crossbow off her back and unfolded it. Pulled a bolt from her thigh belt and placed it in the track. She heard the guys coming behind her. Heavy Muggen first, then the others.

Juva opened the door carefully and peered into a stairwell. Several of the steps were broken, and the paint had flaked off. Sand and dirt had collected in the corners, dried seaweed, bird feathers.

Where are the girls?

She walked down the stairs with the crossbow in front of her and reached a room with less dust on the floor. There were footprints in front of a double door. It was so familiar that her heart climbed higher in her chest. A phantom burn spread around her neck with the memory of the last time she had seen it, alone, helpless in a chair. Juva clung to the fact that she had won that time, and she had won this time, too. Because no matter what Eydala was planning with Undst, it was futile. Náklav was ready and waiting for the ships. All that remained was to find the girls.

Her heart sensed no sign of Eydala, no warow. The guys retreated to either side of the doors, and she flung them open. The hall of mirrors sat empty and dilapidated before her. A place few had seen in centuries. Hundreds of candles seemingly flickered in the mirrors, but the source was only a few candles burning in a high candle holder in the middle of the room, next to the chair she had sat in. Someone else was sitting there now.

She approached. The figure sat slumped in the chair, surrounded by bottles. A man, wearing nothing but a sweater.

Rugen . . .

A smell of death filled the room. She heard the guys spread out behind her to check the room, but there was only Rugen. Or what was left of him. His neck was a half-rotten wound, green and malignant, but he was still alive.

He rolled his eyes, shiny, as if feverish. His brown curls stuck to his face. He breathed with an eerie wheezing sound. His fangs gleamed in the flickering light: wolf-sickness, Rot. He had thought he would live forever, but this was all he had gotten.

She spotted a pale bundle on the floor behind him. A dead body. As dead as a man could be. He lay on his stomach with his arms and feet spread out as if he had tried to fly.

The guys had done the rounds and approached the chair. They spotted the same thing she had and turned away in disgust. Lok backed away, and she heard him retch.

Juva stopped in front of Rugen and recognition darted over his face.

"Juva . . ." He touched his hair the way he used to, to pull his fingers through his curls, but his strength failed him.

"She said . . . She said you would come," he wheezed. "With the blood you promised. Eternal youth."

Juva swallowed her nausea. How long had he been sitting there? What had he done? She stared at his wound and couldn't comprehend how he was still breathing.

"Where are the girls?" she asked.

"The girls . . ." he chuckled. "So many girls. I've had . . . all of them."

"The girls!" Juva hissed. "The blood readers—where are they, Rugen?!"

His eyes roamed. If he had any idea what she was talking about, he hid it well. She doubted he was capable of that now.

They're not here . . .

Broddmar and the guys stood behind his chair as if stunned. Lok had turned his back, and she assumed he was going to throw up again.

Rugen's breathing was shallow and rapid.

"We drank beer, Juva. Do you remember?"

Juva nodded.

"Beer, Juva, at the food stall in Jólshov. Do you remember? And in Hidehall. You kiss like no one else, Juva."

"Where is she, Rugen? Where's Eydala?"

Rugen jerked into a spasm.

"That bitch ran away, rushed off like Gaula was after her."

Juva curbed her impatience. Being furious wouldn't help. Rugen was beyond reason.

"Is she with Silver Throat?"

Rugen shook his head, barely perceptibly.

"She's a monster. Who the fuck wants to be with her? She said you would come. Do you have it, Juva? The blood?"

Juva stared at him, the beast calling someone else a monster.

It's not him. Rugen died a long time ago.

"Yes, Rugen. I have the blood."

He sobbed, but she couldn't tell if he was laughing or crying.

Juva handed her crossbow to Nolan, and he stared at her in disbelief as she stuck her hand under her shirt and found Dr. Eitur's vial wedged into a seam pocket in her corset. She opened it and walked over to Rugen. He opened his mouth and gave her a weak smile. Something in his eyes told her that he knew, deep down.

She emptied the little vial into his mouth. He started shaking. He twitched and bumped his head against the back of the chair. It lolled forward, his chin resting on his chest. He sat there as if he had fallen asleep while drunk.

Nolan reached out an arm to comfort Juva, but she had neither the time nor the inclination to accept it. She walked over to the black curtain she remembered far too well and pulled it aside. Rugen was right. Eydala had left in a hurry. Toppled wooden vats lay on the floor, and the smell prickled her nose. Shiny silver plates lay strewn on the bench, but only one finished likeness. It lay alone, so clearly left behind on purpose.

Juva picked up the silver plate and stared at the familiar face, the conceited smile, the dark hair with the pronounced widow's peak, the exposed forehead like little horns.

The guys crept up behind her. Muggen gasped.

"That's him!"

"How did you know?" Broddmar asked.

Juva weighed the shiny plate in her hand. The weight was appropriate for an idol.

"Something Nafraím said," she replied. "That she might have kept the likenesses of the warow to have control. I figured she wanted to have control over Silver Throat, too." She stuck the picture in her hip bag, carefully. "But I thought we would have to look for—"

"So what does it mean?" Hanuk asked. "That she just left it lying here?"

"It means they're not friends anymore," Broddmar said, sheathing his knife.

Juva looked at him.

"Yes . . . and that he's the one who has the girls."

A prolonged sound rang out in the distance.

Dead Man's Horn . . .

"The last thing we need now," Broddmar said and turned around to go.

"Wait!" Juva held him back. "Listen . . ."

The note was not the single one they were used to. This was something else: two notes, one long and one short.

"Not someone with wolf-sickness?" Muggen asked.

Juva took her crossbow back from Nolan and hooked it onto her back.

"Worse. The ships are here."

THE SHIPS

Juva ran as fast as she dared along the top of the city wall. It was a treacherous path to follow, old and cracked. Stones had toppled out in several places, which had never bothered anyone before since no one in living memory had ever threatened Náklav.

The rocky cliffs were steep, impossible to break down. No army could conquer this city unless it was welcomed with open arms, like now.

The ships were nothing other than a crowd of small lights out on the pitch-black sea. A glowing strand of pearls in the gray of day-break. When the Dead Man's Horn rumbled its welcome, the city had awakened. People hammered on the doors and called to each other from the windows. The streets were busy, and by the time the wall ended by Kistestikk, they were full of people streaming toward the cliffs and the docks to celebrate, to see.

Juva jumped down from the wall to the shelter of an old stable and waited for the others. She felt powerless. She should have had the girls already. Eydala should be dead, and she realized that she had hoped *he* would be, too, Silver Throat. All she had was the likeness.

Muggen thumped down next to her, with Broddmar and the others behind him. She waved them into the stable, where they fought for space with a cart like the pullers used.

"What are we going to do?" Muggen asked. "We can't just search for the girls at random. We have no idea where they are."

Juva peeled off her suit. It wasn't going to help her in the daylight.

"No," she replied as she changed. "But we know where *he* is. Drogg said they would have a reception, and Silver Throat will be where he'll be seen."

"She's right," Nolan said. "This changes nothing. We need to stick to the plan."

Juva rolled up her suit and stuffed it in her backpack.

"Yes, we need to find Nafraím and find out what they've done. Then we need to get down to the docks."

They looked at each other. The sounds of a celebration springing forth through the wall.

"That might be easier said than done," Lok mumbled.

They set off along Kistestikk and crossed Ringmark through the quietest streets, which there were fewer and fewer of. Students and teachers flocked out of the colleges and pushed their way down Professor Dolg's Vei toward the cliffs, where there was clear view of Nyhavn.

She ducked into a side street and waved for the guys to follow her to Florian's. The place was packed. The city's most fortunate stood in clusters with wineglasses in their hands, more elaborately dressed than she would have thought they had time for so early in the day. Some of them were on their way to the docks. Others were already too drunk to try.

Juva walked up to the man at the door and whispered Nafraím's name. He looked around as he let them into the already full hall. She crept along the wall and heard Lok swear behind her. He had probably never seen such affluence before. Eyes lingered on them, following them, and she hurried up the stairs, aware that they stuck out as if they were wild animals.

Juva saw the red door and knocked. Nafraím opened it and let them into what looked like a dark reading room decorated in red and black. She saw flames licking up the wall and jumped before she realized there were cutouts in the chimney with ornate glass tubes emitting the glow of the fire. It made them look alive.

Vamm was sitting at a table with Seire, Faun, and Domnik. He stood up and ran over to Juva.

"The girls?"

"No," Juva said, shaking her head. "Not Eydala, either."

His face wilted, and she felt like a part of herself did the same. Nafraím locked the door, and the guys sat down on the upholstered chairs. Lok sat down hesitantly on the edge, as if he didn't feel like he could sit on these chairs.

Vamm pushed a teacart over with cakes, apples, and leaf-thin cups with gilded handles. Steam from a teapot curled toward the ceiling. No one touched anything. They seemed to lack energy, sleep deprived, just like her. But they could sleep later.

She opened a window. The old panes rattled. The cliff edge was visible over the low row of buildings just below, and it was packed with people. It had stopped raining. Some people were waving torches at the ocean, and she could hear them singing. Two guards kept watch, nowhere near enough. She hoped it was because the rest of them had better things to do.

"Where do we stand?" she asked. "What did the queen say?"

"She said he should stop by more often," Seire grinned.

Nafraím ignored her.

"The rumor has already reached them, fueled by the old skepticism of Undst, which runs deep here. The images have also been a topic, but they couldn't reveal that they were suspicious, so it was advantageous not to intervene. All they've done the last several days has been in secret: guards at Naar, at Nyhavn, and by the bridge. Klemens has control of Silver Throat, and Náklaborg is on high alert. The city is armed to the teeth under the pretense of the festivities.

"They took over the ships anchored for the Dragsuget Regatta, too," Seire said. "Dressed as sailors, to avoid a . . . diplomatic crisis." She nearly spat those last words out, leaving no doubt as to how she would have tackled the problem herself.

"And Drogg has done his part," Juva said.

I hope . . .

She looked out at the sea. The ships had moved closer, driven by the Floa wind; they would dock before long. There were a lot of them, but that didn't matter. Even if there were a hundred of them, they wouldn't take Náklav by surprise. The city had been warned, but she had no time to feel relieved.

"Good," she said, turning to go. "Then we can go find the girls."

Nafraím stopped her and handed her a cup of tea.

"Sit down, Juva. We'll find the girls, but no one has any idea what's on board those ships. And whatever it is, they think it's enough to take Náklav. We need to make sure before we do anything else."

Juva stared at the teacup Nafraím held out to her until he set it down on the windowsill. How could she sit down now? She felt like she was on fire, consumed by the glowing snakes arcing in the chimney. Something was pulling her, an intense restlessness beyond the girls, but she couldn't put her finger on it.

She walked to the door.

"I refuse to wait. I intend to find Silver Throat before he can hurt the girls. I'm going down to the docks."

"Juva, he's not there," Nafraím said, following her.

"What do you mean?" Juva stopped. "He's at the reception with Drogg and the others."

"Yes, and the Hallowed. But they're up in Nákla Henge, and Klemens has things under control up there. We can wait."

Juva stared at him.

"Silver Throat is at Nákla Henge? Right now? When the whole city is meeting the ships. What kind of reception is that?"

"He's probably afraid of having to use his fists," Nolan said, and chuckled.

Juva felt the heat seep out of her body. This wasn't right, not at all. Silver Throat loved an audience. He would have been at the docks no matter what kind of victory he awaited. Whether it was a war or a cure. And she had hunted vardari with him. He was not a man afraid of a battle.

No one has taken Náklav from the sea.

"The gates . . ." she whispered. "They're not coming from the sea. They're coming through the gates!"

Nafraím put his hands on her shoulders, as if she needed support.

"Juva, we have guards in Kreknabork, Skippalun, Haeyna . . . every single henge city. We can rest assured that we can rely on them. No one can come through the gates unseen. We will find the girls, I promise, but first, we need to make sure we don't have an attack to deal with."

Juva leaned against the wall, suddenly unsteady.

"There's going to be an attack, yes, but not at the docks."

"What are you thinking?" Broddmar stood up, seemingly the only one who didn't think she had lost her mind. Even Hanuk looked worried.

Understanding dawned, a point of clarity in a chaos of thoughts. It had been there all along, right in front of her eyes, if only she had been looking. But she had filtered everything she had seen through faith: his faith, the rites held at the henge, the sepultures. Why?

Silver Throat wasn't a man of God; he was a man of . . .

Conquest.

His obsession with the dead stones wasn't about Drukna or about gods. It was about something far simpler than that. The dead gates weren't dead. There was something on the other side, and he knew what.

Nafraím tried to guide her down onto a chair, but she pushed him backward, and he almost tripped.

"The dead stones . . . They don't go to Drukna, do they?"

"Yes, they do. Well, as good as," he replied. "The stones connected to them are drowned, flooded eons ago."

"In Undst, right?"

He looked at her without responding, more uncertain now. Juva fought to remain calm, but she couldn't. Damn Nafraím and his secrets! If she caught his heart now, she would crush it.

She shoved him again. He backed up, lost his balance, fell onto a chair, and sat there.

Juva was seething.

"You say they want to conquer Náklav because they've never had a henge, but that's not true. You lied to me. Again!"

"Juva, I never said they *hadn't* had one, but they don't have one now. History has made sure of that."

"We have erased it from time," Seire said, as if that were the most natural thing in the world.

Juva bared her teeth.

"Not carefully enough because he knows about it. Silver Throat holds death rites at Nákla Henge!"

The warow exchanged uncertain glances.

"That doesn't make any difference," Nafraím said, but she could hear the hesitation in his voice. "The stones in Undst are on the bottom of a lake. They're not active, and they can't find them."

Juva braced her hands against the table and leaned toward him.

"Unless a bunch of dead bodies float up there, tethered to branntang lanterns."

Nafraím stared at his hands, his eyes wandering.

"Lanterns . . . You should have said . . . Why didn't you . . . ?"

"I *told* you that! I told you he sent Haane to Drukna at Nákla Henge!"

"Sent to Drukna . . . I thought . . . I assumed you were speaking figuratively. That he killed her." Nafraím looked at her, and for a second, she thought he was going to lose his temper, but then he wilted again and remained silent.

Domnik shook his head.

"The guy is a measly priest. He's not even an official in Undst. You expect me to believe that all this depends on *him*? And what about the ships? What are they doing here if they're not going to . . . No one would sacrifice a war fleet to . . ."

"Win control over the henge?" Juva completed. "You said it yourself, Nafraím, Náklav cannot be conquered from the water, but that was never his plan. If they have the stones, they have everything."

The room seemed to freeze in time. The warow looked at each other. The guys looked at each other. The silence brooded over a certainty that dawned abruptly. Then they exploded into motion. Nafraím stood up and threw on his jacket.

"But . . . it's not possible," Seire protested. "You can't use a gate that's underwater! They need to be bound with blood and that can't be done as long as—"

Nafraím pushed her toward the door.

"If you can break rock and create a lake, then you can probably empty it, Seire!"

Juva unlocked the door and rushed out. She heard Nafraím shouting commands to Domnik. She ran down the stairs with the guys, and the others thundered after them, throwing open the doors and pushing their way past the guests who gasped indignantly in the line outside.

Dead Man's Horn was still sounding, a macabre salute to all the ships that had never had any other goal than to lure everyone away from the henge.

FROM DRUKNA

Juva fought her way through the crowd, squeezing between what must be every single soul in Náklav. They were celebrating a cure. They were celebrating the Dragsuget Regatta with a party they thought would last for days on end, but they didn't know . . .

Her heart hammered with the knowledge, stronger with every beat. Nákla Henge . . . an impenetrable castle with doors to all the cities of the world. The source of all that was Náklav: money, power, knowledge, freedom . . .

People thronged together, dancing, laughing, without caution, and she lifted her elbow to protect herself in the crowd. Professor Dolg's Vei was a sea of people, sweaty from a pure, uninhibited joy that cut right to her heart. None of them had a mass murder to avert.

Juva ducked into a calmer side street and took off running again, stumbling forward. She tasted blood.

Drogg . . . The girls . . .

She should never have gotten them mixed up in this. They could be dead now.

Her heart lost its hold of the warow, and she knew Nafraím was struggling to keep up. She glanced back over her shoulder and saw Seire, Faun, and the guys coming right behind her. Hanuk caught up to her and ran into Brenntorget behind her. Someone had started a ring dance, and they needed to push their way through until Nákla Henge towered up ahead of them.

With its doors closed.

Juva stopped, gasping for breath. Despair welled up and made her legs weak. Closed doors could mean only one thing. That she was right.

"I'll check the other gates," Hanuk yelled in passing, and he continued around the ring wall. Juva wanted to reply that that was a waste, but her lungs were burning, and she knew he would go anyway.

Seire and the guys caught up to her, and she saw the same discouragement hit them as they stared at the weathered copper gates.

Seire's eyes wandered over the enormous ring wall.

"It's too late . . ."

"It doesn't necessarily mean anything," Nolan tried. "They're supposed to hold a reception. Maybe they're just getting things ready."

"Ready for what?" Seire asked. "A bloodbath?"

Juva gulped. The word reverberated in her head like the Dead Man's Horn. A bloodbath . . . Memories of deaths she had seen and caused melted together into a nightmarish picture of horrible possibilities. Knives, bolts, teeth, poisonings . . . What would they find in there?

Nafraím and Faun came running. Faun with his arm around Nafraím as if he needed to push him along.

Broddmar spat and caught his breath.

"What the hell do we do? We can't get in. We can't pound on the doors, either."

"There's always a way in," Nafraím said, wiping his sweat on the sleeve of his jacket. "Come on!"

They followed him past the buildings clustered outside the wall until he stopped by a solitary oak door squeezed between two businesses. The shop windows were filled with curiosities that reminded her of death: petrified shells, snakes in pots, and decorated animal skulls. But the simple door had no signs, no windows.

"Do you have a key or do we need to break in?" Nolan asked, glancing around at the hectic street.

Juva looked at Nafraím. He had lost everything when Eydala captured him. If he owned the key, he certainly didn't have it.

"If time has been merciful, yes." He pointed up. "Under the third shingle."

Juva prodded Muggen, who bent forward and clasped his hands together so she could put her foot there and climb up. She clambered up until she was sitting on his shoulders, and then she reached up toward the roof. She pulled up the third shingle and stuck her hand into a hollow space below. Grabbed cool metal, an unmistakable shape. The key! She tossed it to Nafraím and let herself down from Muggen's shoulders.

Nafraím unlocked the door with a wonderful click and hustled them into a hallway, barely wide enough for Muggen. Hanuk was last. He closed the door, shutting out the light and sounds from outside. Juva drummed her fingers against her thighs. She felt a strange hovering, a weightless sense of excitement. She heard a new door screech on its hinges, and they made their way into what must be an opening in the ring wall itself, a cold, stagnant darkness that smelled of dust.

Juva pricked up her ears, listening feverishly for sounds. Anything at all that could tell her what was going on inside, but all she heard was the guys' breathing. Nafraím led them up several flights of steep, creaking stairs until they came into a low attic. He opened another door, and they made their way onto what she first thought was a balcony, but it was a kind of gallery, a narrow ledge that seemed to run the whole way around, just under the wooden dome.

She crouched behind the railing so as not to be seen. She steeled herself against what awaited, peeking over the edge and down at the public square around the circle of stones.

It was full of the Hallowed: small talk, a pleasant atmosphere in the glow of the huge lanterns that hung along the wall. She could make out a couple of Silver Throat's initiates, but otherwise, just ordinary believers, regular Náklavites following him because they didn't know any better.

Officials and familiar faces from the city council stood in the arcaded galleries on the second floor, and faint music was coming from King Aug's waiting room, the grand hall with the modest name. A harp and a singer—beautiful, delicate notes reached the balcony through an open door.

No screams, no death, none of what she had pictured.

Muggen slumped down with his back against the brick wall, curved and strong as a mountain but clearly relieved.

"Maybe there won't be a war."

Hanuk craned his neck from the back of their single-file row.

"Or maybe they're attacking the docks after all?"

Nolan looked into her eyes with an unspoken question, and she was asking herself the same thing. Had they run in the wrong direction?

"Ul Fero is here," Nafraím whispered. "And Maina."

Juva followed his gaze toward the arcaded galleries. "Who?"

"They're on the national council, from Fimle and Skaug. They're not just anyone . . ."

"What does that mean for us?" Nolan asked. "That they're enemies?"

"Or victims," Seire said with a shrug. "Everyone wants a cure for wolf-sickness."

Drogg!

Juva saw his outline in the window. He came out onto the gallery, and she let out a sigh of relief.

"Isn't that the one with the grandfather clock?" Lok said, squinting at him. "The one that Skarr smashed to smithereens up on Kingshill?"

He was right; it was Hjarn Gisting. The man had probably been one of Silver Throat's targets, but his cook had drunk the wine and paid the price. Now he stood chatting closely with Drogg, furtively glancing around. His wineglass caught the light as he tilted it over the railing and imperceptibly poured out a splash.

Seire nudged her and winked. Finally something was going the right way.

A line of servers came out an open teahouse and crossed the square with platters heaped with ham, cheeses, and cakes. They made their way through the Hallowed and disappeared in the door that led up to King Aug's.

Juva followed them with her eyes.

"Poison?" she asked.

"Hardly," Seire replied, wrinkling her nose. "Then they'd have to sacrifice everyone, including their own. Either way, Drogg has obviously warned those he trusts, so if poisoning were the plan, it would fail."

"What about the others?" Muggen asked bitterly. "The ones he doesn't trust?"

Juva swallowed. The question stung. She had risked Drogg's life by keeping quiet about the wine, because she wasn't sure where his loyalties lay. If he had been a drinker, he would be dead, and it would be her fault. Doubt could exact far too high a price.

"Come," she whispered. "We have to warn them."

"About what?" Hanuk asked. "The worst thing happening here is that they eat and drink."

"Damned right," mumbled Lok. "They're obviously in the best of health, and if there's one thing I know about the bigwigs, it's that they watch each other's backs rather than stab them."

"More often than you think," Nafraím said.

The guys fell silent and stared at him, but it didn't seem to bother him. His eyes roamed along the walls, studying.

"Juva has good instincts. That's how I would have done it, gathered the elite and incapacitated them. But that wouldn't make a conquest here easier."

Muggen chewed his underbite for a bit before he ventured to ask, "Why not?"

"The crossbows," Broddmar replied.

Nafraím pointed to the arrow slits in the top floor, just below the gallery.

"They're not like any crossbow you've had in your fists, Muggen. These are powerful, and there are a lot of them, the whole way around. Even the first ones installed here were something completely different than the world had seen before. They were built for . . . worse things than men."

Juva looked at him.

The wolves, Gríf's people.

She caught his eye, pained with worry, an unfathomable fear she knew he had always lived with. It hit her that he had probably planned Nákla Henge's defenses personally, in his day, driven by fear of wolves seeking revenge, the ones he had defeated.

And held captive.

Broddmar patted the back of Muggen's head.

"So if anyone were to come through the gates uninvited, the square would look like a pin cushion before you had a chance to blink."

Seire put her hands on her knees as if she were going to stand up.

"Juva, if we're needed anywhere, it's at the docks. The fancy folks up here have heard the rumor. Worst case scenario is that they go home thirsty. The Ring Guard has this under control. We're wasting our time here."

Juva pulled off her backpack and found her crossbow.

"And how many of the Ring Guard can we trust, eh? They're young and swapped out all the time, and everyone knows it's hard to find people. Many guards have run off to other cities because of the wolf-sickness. They'd rather work in Kreknabork. We at least need to find Klemens."

She didn't have time to change into red, but she strapped the backpack to the harness, rolled up as tight as she could, and hooked the crossbow onto her back. She looked at each of them in turn, searching for support. They needed to understand she knew she was right. She could feel it with every nerve.

Am I crazy?

She stared up at the ceiling. The enormous wooden dome arched over her with an endless series of ribs that seemed to flow into each other. Her tongue found her teeth, sharp as a wolf's, and she had an intense feeling of being alone.

She put her hand to her chest to feel the vial, but she had given it to Drogg. It couldn't comfort her.

What if this had all been a feverish hallucination? Nafraím and the first ones, Broddmar and the guys. What if she was actually wolf-sick and none of them were here? No threat, no invasion from Undst. Maybe she was fighting alone, against what she needed most of all: a cure.

No! No one is going to die because I have doubts!

Juva clenched her teeth until it felt like she was snarling.

"Go if you want," she said. "I'm staying here until Nail Throat has given me the girls!"

She leapt to her feet and walked toward the stair niche, crept down the worn stairs until she came out into a dark corridor with bare stone walls. It crawled in a gentle arc, broken up by stripes of light that fell in through the arrow slits. One of them was wider than the others, and a Ring Guard stood there at attention behind one of the massive crossbows. Nafraím hadn't exaggerated. Her own was like a toy in comparison. These were built on stands that she'd never seen, until now. She had only stood down in the square and seen the bolts all the way around.

Seire is right. They are in control.

The light enveloped the Ring Guard as if he were blessed by the gods, and she felt her anxiety dwindling. Juva walked toward him and raised her hand to make herself known, but at the same instant, he turned away with a little jerk, as if he flinched. He stood with his back to her and his hands hidden in front, as if he were peeing.

Not in here, surely?

She stopped. He staggered backward and keeled over. Another Ring Guard stepped out of the shadows. He bent over the man who lay motionless on the floor and wiped a dagger on his trouser leg.

Juva heard a muffled sound from her own throat. The corridor narrowed. Her thoughts narrowed. Everything she had imagined, everything she had feared, gleamed in that dagger that caught the light coming through the arrow slit.

The traitor looked up and saw her. For a brief instant, he hesitated, but then his eyes narrowed and waved her over with a creepy sneer. She realized that he didn't think she posed any danger, expected her to freeze in fear. He didn't know her, an advantage she needed to seize before she lost it.

Juva pulled her knife and rushed toward him. She heard Broddmar yell, and the others came storming up behind her. The murderer's smile faded.

He's going to run away!

He whirled around, and she ran as fast as her legs would carry her. It was sickeningly clear that he was going to alert Silver Throat, get help, and destroy their chance of averting what had been set in motion.

Juva lunged forward and drove the knife into his side, through the black suit he disgraced by wearing it. The blade sank in until her knuckles hit his ribs, and she yanked it out before he had time to fall. His knees buckled and he tipped backward with his eyes open wide. He lay there on the floor, gasping for air, head-to-head with the guardsman he had murdered.

"Who else?!" Juva screamed. "How many of you are there?"

He didn't respond. The white ring, the seal of the Ring Guard, rose and fell on his chest until he stopped breathing.

The others arrived with Hanuk and Seire in the lead.

Juva stared at the gaping wound in the side of the dead traitor and glimpsed something golden through the torn suit. She split it open over his chest to reveal a fiery yellow sweater with a symbol in a dirtier yellow.

Seire scrunched up her freckled face in a sudden epiphany.

"The fire from Undst!"

Nafraím cocked his head to the side until his neck made a cracking sound.

"The crossbows . . ." he snarled. "They want to take the crossbows!"

A spark ignited in his eyes, and Juva suddenly remembered how it had felt to fear him. He opened his mouth to say something but was interrupted by a distant shriek.

Juva jumped over the bodies and stared out through the arrow slit.

There was a commotion on the balcony outside King Aug's hall. A woman hung limply over the railing, as if she had thrown up. She wasn't moving. The Hallowed crowded together in the square and stared up at the lifeless figure. The music stopped. Drogg and the others on the balcony were all struggling to get back inside at the same time, through the far-too-narrow door. The panic seemed unavoidable, and it rubbed off on her. She summoned up Grif's command from her memory.

Breathe!

"We have two fronts!" Juva declared, grabbing hold of Seire. "We need to split up!"

"And do what?" Lok asked, pointing at the dead people as if he were the only one who saw them. "We're blind here. We have no idea what or who we need to fight. We don't even know where!"

"We never have," Broddmar said, unhooking the crossbow from his back and handing it to Lok. "Not with the wolf-sick, either, but we do it anyway, man!"

Juva felt her fear easing. The power in Broddmar's voice brought back memories from the woods and gave her solid ground under her feet. She wasn't alone. She had a hunting team. She had the warow.

She wiped the knife blade on the traitor's thigh, mirroring the last thing he had done before he died.

"Seire," she said, "you all need to secure the crossbows! We have no idea who's manning them, whether they're friends or foes."

Seire drew her knives with a chilly smile.

"We'll find out quickly enough." She waved for Faun, Muggen, and Nolan to join her and set off at a run. Nolan looked back over his shoulder. He and Juva exchanged a glance, and she saw his silent prayer that she would be careful. That was a promise she couldn't make.

Juva ripped the crossbow off her back, unfolded the bow, and set off running in the opposite direction.

"Down!" she yelled. "How do we get down to Klemens?!"

Nafraím pointed as he ran. His heart was a thudding warning in his chest. He had little to run on but nothing to lose. A wall appeared, blocking the corridor; the only way out was an opening smaller than a door.

"Through!" panted Nafraím, and she proceeded into a tunnel of dark woodwork. The sound of their feet took on a completely different tone as she ran, a hollow echo, and she realized she was in an elevated walkway that crossed the north gate, past the massive copper doors.

She made it across to the other side and into the stone corridor again, relieved to find stairs. She thundered down and came out into the gallery on the second floor. Nákla Henge opened out before her, and she could see the whole square again. The crowd of believers was worked up and had evidently realized the woman over the balcony railing was dead. A couple of Ring Guards tugged on the door that led up to the hall, but it wouldn't budge.

He's locked them in . . .

Silver Throat had isolated Náklav's most powerful, and it was impossible to find a single, well-meaning reason for that.

Juva looked around in despair for the quickest route. She was on the right floor, but the hall was on the far southern side. She needed to get around nearly half of Nákla Henge. Every second she hesitated would cost lives, and she couldn't wait for Nafraím.

"Come down!" She bundled Nafraím and Broddmar toward the stairs. "Get hold of Klemens! Tell him what we saw!"

Juva turned around to proceed toward the hall, but an eerie sound stopped her. A mechanical ratcheting, which sent a cold certainty through her.

The crossbows . . .

"Jufa . . ." Broddmar braced his hands against the railing. She followed his eyes toward the Ring Guardsmen. One stood nailed to the door, a bolt sticking diagonally out of his back. It seemed grotesquely large. The guardsman collapsed but remained hanging, like a black bundle propped against the door.

Juva felt a twitch through her body, as if she were falling asleep into a nightmare. She fought the nausea. How many of the big crossbows had been lost to the enemy? One? All of them?

Nákla Henge erupted into complete chaos. Ring Guards shouted and hurried along the balconies to the sound of another crossbow shot. Stunned Hallowed observers suddenly snapped out of it, as if it had taken a minute to understand what they had witnessed. They scattered in panic like ants under a rock someone had lifted, away from the bolt-impaled guardsman, away from the dead. They fled toward the balconies, pounding on locked doors, forcing their way into the open teahouses.

Juva scanned for initiates; they must have been in the hall with Silver Throat and the officials.

She was startled as a young guardsman came racing up the stairs behind her. He was of slight build, in a suit far too big.

"Why are we shooting?" he gasped. "Why are we shooting our own people?"

"The crossbows!" Nafraím said, pushing him along. "We have traitors at the crossbows! Stop them!"

Juva was suddenly aware of the sound of the Dead Man's Horn, the last thing she had time for. She listened. It resounded in the distance, but it sounded different than usual.

"War horn," Nafraím said, growing pale.

The signal was completely alien, and she knew it would be to the rest of the city as well. A gloomy wail that no one had heard for centuries.

"The docks . . ." Broddmar growled. "They're attacking the docks, too."

The world is coming undone.

The Hallowed pushed in groups, fighting to take cover in the already overfilled teahouses. The square lay almost deserted. The stones towered up, silent and untouched, while a handful of Ring Guards ran by. They split up at the Witness, barking commands. One of them held a shield at an angle over his head, as if that could ever protect him against bolts powerful enough to nail a man to a door.

Juva spotted a waiter come out of a teahouse carrying a cask of wine on his shoulder. He walked across the square, seemingly unafraid, as if he were blind to what was going on. The cask slipped and crashed to the ground by the pair of dead stones. He fumbled around, clumsily trying to grab it like a drunk man as wine glugged into the blood gutter.

Wine . . . There's blood in the wine!

Juva stared in disbelief as the certainty dawned. He had dropped it on purpose. A Ring Guardsman yelled that he should get to safety. The man nodded, stumbled through the stones, and disappeared.

Juva's body tensed. She managed to keep her eyes on the stones, all too aware of what was coming.

She heard Klemens shout from down by the iron door to the office. He was distributing crossbows to the guards. Three men lay down there. The balcony was empty of officials. The dead woman hung alone over the railing, and in the distance, the Dead Man's Horn announced the end of everything.

Broddmar tugged at Juva to go with them, but she couldn't move. Her hands clutched the railing.

"They're coming . . ." she whispered.

She stared down at the square as they streamed out between the dead stones. Many battle-ready men, wearing yellow and steel with the fire from Undst on their broad chest plates. Soaked up to their waists, as if they had waded through Drukna. They were dripping mud.

An army from Gaula, with shiny helmets and long swords. Unreal, like a painting. A nightmare. There were far too few Ring Guards against an army that just kept coming. Men fell. Some in silence, others screaming. Red blood rained onto the cobblestones. The army from Drukna spread across the square, and some disappeared up the stairs, as if they knew exactly where they were going.

Náklav is falling . . .

Nothing could stop Gaula. Was this what she looked like, the goddess with the tentacles? The monster comprised of every single dead body in Drukna. Juva felt paralyzed. All she saw was the fire sign from Undst, more and more of them. Time stood still, and suddenly she was a little girl in a boat on a mirror-smooth sea. She could see seaweed and rocks on the bottom. And the yellow keel. Yellow, because the only thing Gaula was afraid of was fire.

Fire!

Juva ripped herself out of her trance. Nafraím and Broddmar stood by the stairs, their faces weary with loss, with the end-time. She shook some life into them.

"Oil! We need oil!"

"In Klemens's office . . ." Nafraím stammered. Then they disappeared down the stairs. Juva hustled Hanuk after them.

"And the lamps in the teahouses! All you can find! Run!"

She set off running down the gallery, encountering panicked guards, new ones and experienced ones alike. One of them saw her crossbow and yelled after her, but another recognized her and let her run.

Raw, pure fear coursed through her body with every heartbeat. Bigger and colder than anything she had felt before. She feared for infinitely more than her life: the girls, the guys, Drogg, Náklav.

She stopped before she reached the south gate—as close as she could get to the pair of stones—and stared down at the battles. No one was shooting from above anymore, but it was impossible to say whether that meant Seire and the others had succeeded in securing the crossbows. It could just as easily be traitors up in the arrow slits, who didn't want to hit fighters from Undst.

And there were a hell of a lot of those. The stones spat out half-drowned men who slashed their way through the guards. A gruesome torrent she needed to stop.

Juva folded her crossbow and hooked it onto her back. Then she jumped up on the wide stone railing and reached for one of the enormous lanterns that provided light and heat through the freezing cold winters. It was bolted to the wall between the gallery arches. The lantern was taller than she was and hung from the jaws of a snakelike wrought-iron dragon. A nest of mythical creatures surrounded the white-hot glass. The heat made her sweat.

Corpsewood—nothing burned like corpsewood.

She put her foot in the ornate wrought-iron bracket and climbed up. She clung tightly and glanced down. She spotted Hanuk running back from the Ring Guard office, his arms full of bottles. Broddmar was right behind him with a barrel on his shoulder.

Jól, let that be oil . . .

Juva inched her way farther out on the dragon, wedged her knife into the iron animal's jaw, and pried. The steel scraped the iron, but the lantern didn't budge. She gritted her teeth and tried again. She groaned and pushed the blade in with as much of her body weight as she dared.

Please . . .

A sob grew in her throat. She lost her balance and leaned on the lid of the lantern. It burned her hands, and she snatched them back. Neither the lantern nor the dragon budged. But she felt herself swaying.

The mountings . . .

The middle of Nákla Henge was a battlefield. The guys stuck to the outer edges, outside the stones, and avoided the fighting with protection from Klemens and a flock of Ring Guards who seemed to have some insight into what the men were doing. Hanuk came so close that she was almost looking straight down at him. He started throwing the bottles so they broke against the stones that were pumping out men. Broddmar pulled the stopper out of the barrel and rolled it toward the stones as oil glugged out of it.

Juva crawled on all fours and turned around to face the wall mountings. She stabbed at the wall around the bolts with her knife over and over again. It was going too slowly; this wouldn't help. She stood up and then roared as she dropped heavily back down, sitting astride the dragon's back. She rode the animal until the mountings creaked free. It sounded like the dragon was screaming, and she could feel herself starting to sag. She fell, losing hold of the dragon, which fell faster than her. The lantern shattered on the ground beneath her, exploding into fire and glass. She was going to land in the middle of it. She was going to die.

Roll!

She hit the ground as the thought came. She curled up and rolled over glass and stone. The pain burned through her legs, her shoulders. She looked up, staring right at a bolt protruding through someone's back and a snake of fire that stretched toward the dead stones. The gate to Undst was on fire. The flames licked around them. Corpsewood lay strewn across the cobblestones, glowing white dots between running warriors, and it seemed strangely beautiful.

I'm alive...

Ring guards, Hallowed volunteers, and servers from the teahouses heaved anything that could burn into the flames: oil, liquor, tablecloths, and sweaters.

Burn them. Burn the wolves.

Dead men lay on the ground around her, frozen in a horrible moment in time. The smell of oil and ash thick in her nose.

The stones from Undst stopped spitting out men, as if the rumor of defeat had crossed the gates, and she saw warriors in new colors. Green from Kreknabork, blue from Skippalun, white and silver from Haeyna...

Náklav had never been alone.

Juva got to her feet and plucked the glass shards from her fist. The pain felt distant, but she knew it would awaken with full force if she dwelled on it. She had her harness, the belt with the knives, and her hip bag. Her crossbow was unscathed.

Bless Agan Askran, the city's finest weaponsmith.

A group of the Hallowed stood in the doorway to the teahouse next door: a young man sobbing out a prayer and an elderly man with a nail band around his neck staring at her in horror.

"It's God's army," he said feebly. "His punishment for our sins. We can't win."

Juva gaped at him. After everything he had just witnessed, he was still a believer, poisoned by Silver Throat's lies. She growled, limping a few steps before her legs worked again. Then she bounded up the nearest staircase. This wasn't over until the last wolf burned.

ORIGINAL SIN

Juva feared a massacre, but inside King Aug's waiting room, the Ring Guard had taken control. That didn't make it any easier to understand what had happened.

A guard gestured to stop her at the door before he recognized her and let her in.

The room was full of officials and elites; some were furious at the guards, demanding they be allowed to leave, but the guards stood their ground. Others had given up and were sitting on the floor. A man comforted a woman next to the harp while she cried. She was more simply dressed than the others, in a black dress.

The singer.

One of the enormous paintings had fallen on the floor, and the curtains had sprinkled decorative beads by the balcony. Juva counted what she at first thought were seven dead, but four of them were Hallowed initiates and officials from Undst, gagged by the Ring Guard. A long table at the end of the room was piled high with untouched food.

Silver Throat was nowhere to be seen.

Juva looked around and realized how infinitely worse it could have been.

Where is he? Where are the girls?

"Juva!" Drogg ran past a group of men and women still clutching glasses of wine they hadn't tasted.

"Juva, blessed woman!" He embraced her before he took a step back and regained his dignity with an *ahem*. "You were so terribly right, Juva! Undst had horrendous plans. I can't believe anyone could . . . Imagine wanting to kill so many people. I'm so glad that—"

"Drogg, have you seen the girls?"

His joy seemed to fade for a moment.

"No . . . no, but we lost a city councilwoman from Baugur, who drank before I had a chance to warn her. I couldn't—"

"You warned people, in here?" Juva stared at him.

"What else were we supposed to do? We didn't know who we could trust, so . . ."

"You and Hjarn Gisting?"

"Yes, you said you thought he was an intended victim for the blood wine and, well, one tries not to kill one's co-conspirators, right? So I talked to him first. After that, I spoke to the people I trusted most on the city council, of course, but we were gripped by the knowledge! We couldn't warn everyone not to accept wine from someone from Undst. We would have had a diplomatic crisis on our hands, not to mention it would have given away that we'd caught onto Silver Throat's plan. I felt like a spy, Juva!"

He put his hand on his chest.

"My heart has been racing like never before. We actually had to keep the secret until we were here, but then we couldn't keep our mouths shut! We went around to everyone and whispered that they could be poisoned. I don't think I've ever mingled so fast in my life."

Juva smiled and felt the fatigue hit her.

"And even if any of the people you warned were traitors, they couldn't do anything since the reception was already underway. You're a pro, Drogg!"

"Well . . ." His cheeks flushed. "The disadvantage, of course, is that we still don't know who we can trust. I don't think this is over."

He was right about that. The most important part remained.

"Drogg, where is he? Did the Ring Guard take charge of him? Did you give him the blood?"

Drogg fished the curved vial out of his pocket and cast a stolen glance around before he handed it to her. It was empty. Juva turned it over; it was so incredibly beautiful without the red contents. It glowed of victory in her palm.

"It was easier than I had feared," Drogg said. "He became increasingly nervous as he realized no one was going to eat or drink. Then I felt certain you were right. I could see it on him, Juva, that something had gone wrong. He kept peeking out the windows and whispering to the initiates. Then he tried to lure everyone into saying a toast together! That was my chance, terrified as I was, but he was nervous and distracted. He wasn't paying attention to his glass, and he emptied it in an instant. He looked bad right away. And then the city councilwoman from Baugur died, right out on the balcony. Then he ran off and locked the doors behind him! I have no idea where he is, but he can't have gotten far. Was it . . . What did I give him? Is it something that's going to kill him?"

Juva stuck the vial in her bag and smiled cuttingly.

"Sooner or later."

Hjarn Gisting walked over and nodded to Juva with a respect that had not been there when Skarr had smashed his big clockwork.

"They say there were skirmishes down at Nyhavn, too. Did you hear that? One of the Ring Guards here says no one would leave the ships. It was as if they were waiting for a signal they never received. Finally, they were boarded and the madness ensued. But they didn't stand a chance, surrounded as they were. I shudder to think what could have . . ."

Juva left them in the silence that followed Hjarn Gisting's half-finished sentence. She had enough to do, thinking about the things that could still happen.

She stepped out onto the balcony and looked around. Silver Throat must have known he had been outmaneuvered when he left the hall. What could he have done? Where could he have fled to?

Home to Undst . . .

Down in the square, the Ring Guard had gathered people around the Witness, and it looked like they were interrogating every last person who could crawl or walk, including the Hallowed and the teahouse employees. She saw Seire and the guys helping grim guards carry the dead. Fewer than she had feared when things were at their worst, but still far too many. They lay them in tidy rows along the wall by the office, where Klemens and Nafraím sat on a bench drinking from a shared flask.

In a bit, she would be doing the same.

Small flames were still flickering around the stones. Silver Throat wouldn't have made it there unseen.

He's waiting . . .

He must be here. She had to find him. If he disappeared, she would never find out where the girls were.

She walked along the balcony and stared up at the arrow slits. Could he have hidden them up there? Or on one of the galleries? She would have to search every corner of Nákla Henge, every single—

She stopped.

An irregular pulse drummed within her, unruly, searching, a rhythmless heart, finding solid ground. A new-born warow.

Where?

Two doors hung open in the wall, leading into storerooms she guessed the Ring Guard had already searched. She felt the weight of her crossbow on her back, but she wasn't going to need it. She had a completely different weapon now.

She peered inside, but no one was there.

"I know you're here," she said and slowly walked on. The gallery was dark and hazy with smoke. Through the arches, she was looking right out at the stones. There was nowhere to hide there. But on the far side, there were plenty of doors to choose from.

Juva felt her way using her heart. She opened her own and let his in, squeezing it until she heard a muffled sound behind one of the doors. She pressed down on the door handle and, judging by the sound, he was dragging himself farther away on the inside.

She opened the door and stepped into a hall far more modest than King Aug's. At the far end, she saw another door that must lead back out to the galleries again, and there he stood.

Drogg was right. Silver Throat looked anything but healthy. His face glistened with sweat, and he was clutching his chest. His other hand was hidden behind his back, and she didn't need to be a blood reader to guess that he had a knife.

Fear darted across his face, and he craned his neck as if to make sure she was alone. He grabbed the door handle but hesitated enough that she knew what he was thinking. He could confront her right there or out on the balcony, but the Ring Guard would see him out there . . .

She approached him and caught herself smiling at how long it was taking him to decide. He lunged at her, sweeping the knife in a wide arc.

Juva took a step back and strangled his heart. She poured her heart into it until she was breathing heavily and heard her pulse running in her ear. He staggered backward and made it out the door. She followed him as he crossed the gallery and stumbled out onto a balcony. He stared down at the henge, clearly aware that it didn't belong to him, that it never would.

The Ring Guard had put out the fire. The cobblestones were stained with ash and blood, the marks of a barely averted atrocity. His followers stood in shivering, dejected clusters, waiting for permission to go home. Maybe they were also waiting for an explanation of what had transpired while they were hiding in the teahouses. The Dead Man's Horn had stopped.

Juva went out to him on the balcony, the same balcony she had stood on for her speech during the Yra Race. She had told Náklav about the warow here, declaring war and shocking them all. It was here that she had opened the doors to him, and it was here that she would close them.

"Where are the girls?" she asked tersely.

He smiled, crooked and mocking, the way he always was, and put the shaft of his knife to his own chest, as if to show that when he used it, it would come from the heart.

"If I die, you'll never find them," he said, creeping along the railing. "So I have a suggestion that will benefit us all. Allow me safe conduct through the stones, then I'll tell you where they are."

Juva got a bitter taste in her mouth.

"Running home, huh? Was Náklav too much for you?"

He looked away with insufferable arrogance.

"Think carefully, Juva Sannseyr. I can take your likeness with me. No one else needs to see it if you choose the wise solution."

Juva took a step closer and took pleasure in seeing him pulling away.

"Do you think you're the first person to throw me to the wolves, Lodd? Many have tried, but the thing is . . . I know wolves far better than you ever will."

She smiled, revealing her fangs. He couldn't hide his shock, but it quickly faded to doubt.

"You're not sick . . ." he said, but it sounded mostly like he was trying to convince himself.

Juva chuckled.

"Because no one gets sick without your blessing? Not without drinking the filth you give them? And when members of the Hallowed got sick, you pulled their teeth and removed their collars so they would continue to cling to a cure that didn't exist, to *your* answer and your salvation! You spread wolf-sickness and for what? For *this*?" She pointed out at the square. "To see your own people bleed out between the stones?"

He wrinkled his nose as if he had eaten something bad.

"You know nothing about this, girl. What are a few paltry men . . . The stones are worth more than any of them, and you took them from us!"

"Ah, the sacred robbery." She rolled her eyes. "Poor Undst, which never found its own henge because it was underwater. Are we meant to shed a tear for you?"

"Don't talk to me about tears!" he hissed and reached for his throat. He pulled the nail out of the neck collar and held it up to her like a trophy. "You poor thing. While you were suckling at your mother's breast, I was spending my days pulling this out of my body. Pain is supposed to drive away the devil. That's the price of coming from Undst. The legacy behind closed doors, and what we could have been spared from. We could have opened our doors as well and grown up as damned happy-go-lucky as you. But they drowned our gates, condemning us to a millennium of darkness and isolation. Ask the fangs you love how that happened."

Juva hesitated. Was he lying? Was he trying to confuse her? No . . . no blood reader would find lies in that desperate face. He was the victim of a violence he had never been able to get away from, but he continued to inflict on others. The nail at his throat seemed more grotesque than ever, and she fought against feeling compassion, against the knowledge that she would no longer be able to bring herself to kill him.

He seized on her doubt with unconcealed desire.

"You need the cure . . ." he said, silky smooth. "It exists, and it can help you, Juva."

"Nothing can help me," she let out a short laugh. "I'm something you've never seen before. All of Náklav is something you've never seen. It was your mistake. You thought we were defenseless and weak, but Náklav has always stood and will always stand. You can put nails on a few, but never on all, Lodd. Náklav is free."

He chuckled, but his eyes were drawn to the square and the crowd of the Hallowed there. He had nowhere to go, and he knew it.

"You're not going to kill me," he said and brought his hand to his jaw as he felt what appeared to be a sudden pain.

"I don't need to kill you. You're dying. Can't you feel it? Someone who poisons people should keep a closer eye on his own wineglass. You're growing fangs, priest. You're one of the ones I hunt now, a warow. And I can sense you."

She saw his tongue searching his teeth, and he dropped the dagger, which clanged against the stone floor. Juva opened the bag at her hip and pulled out the image.

"I'm not the only one. Your god can see you, too." She mimicked the resounding voice he himself used when he preached. "God has seen the evil, and in his infallible care, he has given us his vision! We bear our punishment with us. We forge our own death."

Silver Throat stared at his image. His body seemed to weaken until he was propping himself up on the railing to stay on his feet. It was painfully obvious he hadn't known Eydala had had an image of him.

"You created your own downfall," she said. "So I have a counterproposal for you. You tell me where the girls are, and I let you keep the likeness."

His gaze wandered over the square, where the Hallowed had spotted them, unsure of what they were witnessing. They massed together below the balcony with vacant stares, totally devoid of the reverence she knew he was used to.

"They would never touch me . . ." he said, but doubt made his voice falter.

Juva strode to the railing and held the image at arm's length over the edge.

"You should have more faith in the weapon you created. This will do more than touch you. It will destroy you. You, your god, and any chance that someone like you could come here again."

Juva looked up as she saw something move out of the corner of her eye. A rope dangled from a narrow opening up by the arrow slits. No . . . it wasn't a rope. It was too colorful, too . . .

Clothing . . .

Someone had tied several items of clothing together, which were swinging back and forth from the opening. The colors were bright and familiar, and a memory popped into her head as if tossed down to her. Tokalínn, wondering what they would do if they got caught by warow.

Then you'll have to make a rope out of your clothes! And climb down your underwear!

Relief brought tears to Juva's eyes, as if they had been waiting for a reason to overflow. The opening was too small to escape through, but now she knew where the girls were. And that they were alive.

Silver Throat followed her eyes. His fear vanished into sudden and fervent contempt.

"You will never be safe," he snarled. "We don't need the gates to come here. We're here already. You have no idea where we are or how many of us are hiding in Náklav. Everything that has happened here is your fault! You sowed the seeds for me!"

Juva looked at him, feeling nothing but relief.

"And now I'm scorching the earth."

She threw the image over the edge of the balcony. It sailed over the square and fell among the Hallowed.

Silver Throat was breathing hard as he wriggled away from her.

"You can't touch me," he hissed. "The order has already been given. If anything happens to me, the girls die. Listen, Juva! Maybe you'll hear them screaming."

Juva stiffened.

No! He's lying!

She caught herself listening all the same, but all she heard was her own heart, which felt cold with fear, solitary, unable to hold on to his.

Silver Throat found his way along the railing, slowly as if testing her limits. Then he turned around and made a dash for the stairs.

Kill him!

Juva felt her body move purely instinctively. He was the prey. She was the hunter. That was all she knew, all she had ever been. Her heart hammered out the rhythm of who she was, beat by beat.

Hunter ... hunter ... hunter ... teacher ... mother ...

She let out a scream through clenched teeth and let him run. She set off running in the opposite direction. Up! She had to go up. She had to find the girls before it was too late!

She grabbed a Ring Guard and pointed up at the little opening, where the clothes were still hanging.

"There!" she shouted. "Under the arrow slits! How do I get there?!"

"That's ... that's the half floor," he stammered. "There's only closets and storerooms up there. You go in the door in the stairwell ..." He pointed, and she raced off, following the rope of clothing with her eyes. It hung still now. It had stopped swinging.

She took the first part of the stone staircase in three leaps and yanked open the wooden door on the landing between the floors. It was so simple and unimpressive that it would have been easy to overlook. She entered a low, attic-like hallway, where she could barely stand upright.

"Kefla!" She ran down the hallway, yanking open the doors of storage rooms with no one inside, one after another: bolts, shoes, whetstones, bottles ... no girls.

"Kefla!" Her voice broke, hoarse with worry.

Her shout was answered by a squeaky voice and energetic pounding on the door at the end of the hallway. Juva felt around for the key in the lock, half-blind from tears she couldn't stop. She flung open the door and walked right into Tokalínn's naked arms, which closed around her thighs. She could hear her own name, drowned in sobs. Noora, Syn, and Ulie sat on a crate with their arms around each other, wearing just their underwear.

In the doorway at the other end of the room lay a dead man, Tord, the Hallowed man she had hunted with. On the floor below the window, where the rope of clothing hung out, sat Kefla. She was clutching a dagger in her lap. Her knees were scraped, and her bare legs seemed too thin for her boots.

Juva stifled a sob.

"Come! We can't stay here. It's not safe. We need to get down to the others."

The girls seemed to shake off their paralysis and get to their feet, but Kefla remained seated.

Juva walked over and knelt down beside her.

"Kefla . . . Kefla, what happened?"

Kefla's smile was so strained it tore at Juva's heart. The freckles on her nose wrinkled. Her lips trembled.

"I stabbed him," she said and tossed her black bangs. The dagger shook. Juva carefully loosened Kefla's fingers from around it and wiped the blood off the girl's thumb.

"It gets sticky so quickly, doesn't it?" Juva's voice was close to failing. *Don't break, not now. Get them to safety!*

She wrapped her arms around Kefla and helped her to her feet.

"It okay, Kefla. Everything is fine. We need to get the clothes back inside. Can you help me?"

Kefla nodded, and together, they pulled the rope of clothes back in. Juva had the girls untie the clothes as she led them down the hallway and down the stairs. She stopped out on the gallery with a feeling of safety she would never have thought a battlefield could provide. A heaviness let go and made her numb, weak, and weightless, like a hot bath after a frozen hunt. The girls got dressed while she looked down at the square.

Something was happening down there. There was pushing and crowding near the Witness. Had the Hallowed had their fill and started a fight? A couple of visibly weary Ring Guards halfheartedly tried to disperse them. Juva instructed the girls to wait and went down. She strolled toward the noise.

The Hallowed saw her coming and quieted down. She walked in among them, and they let her through, silent and staring. They withdrew to the sides, like ghosts in the haze from the fire.

A figure came into view on the ground. Juva walked over to him. Silver Throat lay on his back, and he would never get up again. A multitude of nails pierced through his gray suit to his chest and neck. He stared up with a dead, terrified look, as if he had seen the devil.

THE HOWLS

"It fell out, Juva!"

Tokalínn reached behind her head and grabbed her own braid. She made a show of holding it up, as if the bow had insulted her by coming undone.

"It's because you're always tugging on it," Juva said, retying it.

"It's got to be able to withstand that kind of thing!" Tokalínn snorted.

Juva glanced at Kefla, the likely source of the girl's newfound self-confidence, but she merely shrugged.

The girls were barely recognizable. They were dressed as if they had inherited a kingdom, which was entirely appropriate for going to Náklaborg for the first time in your life—a first for Juva as well.

Juva squatted down, and the skirt of her red dress spread out around her, flowing over the mirror-smooth stone floor like a pool of blood. She wasn't used to dresses and had picked red to feel more at home in what was reputedly the ugliest castle in the world. A blatant lie, because she had never seen a more gorgeous place.

She leaned forward and tightened the knot on Tokalínn's shoe, which was also in danger of not being able to withstand that sort of thing.

The girl stared at the shiny shoes.

"If only my mom could see me!"

Juva swallowed the lump in her throat, unable to respond.

Tokalínn's mother was lying drunk at the Rafts, so much so that Ofre had just shaken his head after a brief visit. The world was still full of pain.

The unwelcome thoughts pained her, would ruin the party. Images of what would have become of the girls if Silver Throat had succeeded, and of Heimilla, who should have been alive to see them now. Wide-eyed, their cheeks flushed, speechless at surroundings they had never seen the like of. Syn in a green dress that brushed the floor as she walked and made her red hair sparkle. Noora in sea blue, the only one who had her parents with her. Juva had given them a roughly summarized version of what had happened.

Juva brushed the hair off Tokalínn's face.

"Remember to call her Your Highness."

"That's nonsense!" Kefla said. "I asked, and she said we could call her Drøfn."

Juva stood up and shuffled them along in front of her.

"Go on now," Juva urged, "so you get to be in the picture."

Tokalínn ran over to Nafraím and the others, while Kefla tossed her black bangs and made a show of calmly ambling over there so everyone would see how blasé she felt about the whole thing, but Juva knew better. Kefla had spent the most time getting ready that morning, as her ruffled black skirt attested. The raven skull around her neck was the result of having turned her mother's old jewelry box upside down. The girl had a newfound urge to explore, maybe that had to do with her age.

Or an urge to forget.

The guests flocked around Nafraím, bathed in the light from the tall windows and sparkling chandeliers. He had set things up to demonstrate how the images were made. Silver plates, clips, and tubs of stinky liquid covered a table far too nice for the purpose. If he spilled anything, it would probably cost a fortune, but apparently there weren't any plainer tables in Náklaborg.

He pointed to the black tent that rose behind him and gesticulated eagerly. Juva couldn't hear what he said, but the guests nodded politely and pretended they understood. Broddmar, Muggen, Nolan, and Lok were smart enough to keep their distance, while Hanuk leaned forward to smell the tubs. He immediately regretted it and slapped his hands over his nose, much to the amusement of Klemens, who seemed strangely out of place in a black suit.

The room seemed elated from the victory, a glow that washed the weariness and blood off them. Drogg was there with several members of the city council. They had lost a few members, who had been arrested. The clean-up had been merciless, and it would continue for a long time.

Silver Throat's final words had been his truest: *You will never be safe. You have no idea where we are or how many of us are hiding in Náklav.*

Juva snuck into the adjoining room, a blue lounge with a fairytale view of the city. The buildings crowded together below her as if they had grown right out of the sea. Several of the ships from Undst were floating in the harbor down below, the biggest of them on fire. Either it had been burning for two days or they had just set fire to it recently. So many dead, and all for the stones.

She put her hand between her breasts and found the vial. Caressed its curved form hidden inside her dress. It was empty but reassuring, an anchor to the truth.

Her tongue felt its way to her sharp fangs but found only the flat artificial ones Nafraím had fitted over them. Molded from the finest clay, but they still felt lumpy. Convincing, though. The guys claimed they made her look totally normal, but they had chuckled when they said that. As if they also knew she could never be normal. Nothing could hide the wolf in her.

Grif . . .

He had turned her into something unfamiliar, but whatever she was, she would never be able to forget him. And of all the things she had experienced, that was the most merciless.

Juva heard footsteps behind her, and something told her it was the queen. Maybe you walked in a particular way when you were royal? Or you could just afford expensive shoes?

"I haven't seen Eljas play so well in a long time," Queen Drøfn said, coming to stand beside her. "My son is really enthusiastic about the girls."

"I do believe it's mutual, Your Highness," Juva replied.

The queen regarded her as if she were a mystery.

"They tell me Náklav would have fallen and we would be dead now if it weren't for you."

You would never have been threatened if it weren't for me.

"For us," Juva corrected her. "I've never accomplished anything on my own, Your Highness."

"You'll never need to with that attitude, either," the queen smiled. She was a beautiful woman, seemingly plain except for the small, jewel-encrusted antlers that held her black hair in place. No crown but close enough to evoke one.

The queen glanced out the door at Nafraím, who stood crouched under a black blanket to protect the silver plates from light.

"He's naïve for someone so old," she said with a warmth that revealed more than she had probably intended to.

Juva didn't dare respond, unsure of how much the queen actually knew.

"My family has had the honor of serving Náklav and Slokna for generations, by his grace," she continued as if to spare her from doubting. "And he thought I didn't know. I assume it's easy for a warow to forget that all families have memories. I thought . . ." Drøfn looked down. "I thought he was gone for good. It seemed like such a waste, once you finally meet someone."

Juva swallowed and clutched the vial.

"Yes, Your Highness."

Drøfn raised her chin again and smiled infectiously.

"He says you saved his life. I cannot thank you enough, but I can assure you that I'll try. You run a home for the girls, I understand, so naturally we must . . ."

A woman in a double-buttoned blazer appeared in the doorway.

"Your Highness, they're ready."

Drøfn put her hand on Juva's arm.

"Come, we don't want to keep an extremely old man waiting."

Juva followed her into the hall and allowed herself to be drawn into one of the groups getting their images made. Nafraím and the woman, an estate manager at the castle, herded people back and forth until they eventually appeared to be satisfied. The queen stood in the middle with Klemens and the Ring Guard behind them and off to one side and Juva and the hunting team to the other.

They were instructed not to move. The words brought back memories of Eydala, who had said the same thing, although Juva hadn't had any idea what was going on at the time. She took a deep breath to calm her rising anxiety. Too much was unknown. Too many unpleasant things had happened—and would happen. Eydala had disappeared, only Gaula knew where. The image of Juva had been stolen from Jólshov, and Náklav hid spies from Undst.

"Smile!" Nafraím commanded, and she obeyed to the best of her ability.

After them, it was the girls' turn. They seemed to suddenly change their minds, unsure what they were getting into. But Tokalínn went first, and the others didn't dare refuse. Then it was Drogg and a group of officials. Juva hardly had any idea who they were. Drogg tried to lure Nafraím to stand in one of the images.

"Next time," Queen Drøfn said. A subtle rescue that was rewarded with a rare, genuine smile from the warow man. Juva felt his heart beat faster against her own, and the budding love was as painful as it was warm.

Nafraím held up the dripping-wet silver plates so that everyone could see for themselves. They let out a collective gasp before the applause began.

"That's what I've always said!" Sjur Skattanger boasted. "If it exists in the world, it's here in Náklav!" The chairman of the city council's words were clearly an excuse to launch into a pompous tale that, strangely enough, felt right. The queen was more elegant in her approach; her short speech of thanks was sincere.

A line of women and men in double-buttoned jackets came in with large trays heaping with cakes, and the room flocked around the treats. The girls were practically hopping up and down. Juva walked over to Nafraím and looked at the images. He carefully rubbed them with a handkerchief.

"They're not entirely good," he said apologetically. "But I think it's the amount of sea silver in the coating. Maybe I can . . ."

"Maybe," Juva mumbled, not understanding what he was talking about. She stared at herself in the colorless picture. She looked like a blood reader, like her mother or Solde, in a dress with a wide skirt and a smile that didn't seem genuine. How could success feel so heartbreaking?

It hit her that this miracle would always be exploited. Silver Throat had called it the voice of God, the proof of evil. Now they were proof of who was ruling, who had won.

Nafraím looked around as if he wanted to say something, but his eyes suddenly welled up. Juva caught his eye, and he jumped, as if his mind had been somewhere else entirely.

"I just . . ." He cleared his throat. "I once thought I would never see another party." He started packing up the equipment, a bit embarrassed, and the servants carried it away.

The cakes floated through the room on familiar hands, and

the world was a living painting of chandeliers and dresses, bows and shiny shoes, girls with blueberry cream around their mouths. Vamm shook his head and brushed crumbs from their skirts, as if it had become his life's work to keep them presentable.

The queen quietly retreated, and Juva felt relieved to be able to leave.

They left Náklaborg as a group, and Juva realized they looked like the fancy people who usually hung out at Florian's, expensively dressed, some slightly drunk. Hanuk a little more so than Broddmar and the other guys, of course; he had never been able to hold his liquor.

The queen paid for their three carriages, which brought the whole herd of them to the Sannseyr home. Hanuk sang like a magpie as Juva unlocked the door and let them in, to Skarr's great delight. The house was full of people: Nafraím, Broddmar, Hanuk, Nolan, Muggen, Lok, Vamm, and the girls, the blessed girls—Kefla, Tokalínn, Ulie, and Syn. Ofre was waiting in the library along with Seire and Faun, who wanted to avoid attracting attention from the city officials.

Juva stood by the raven cabinet watching them all, this unlikely blend of orphans, warow, and hunters. The youngest almost seven, the eldest over seven hundred. The pale Náklavites and the dark Ruvians, faces freckled like the night sky. And everything in between. Náklav in a nutshell.

Her heart started beating faster, and she looked at Nafraím. But it wasn't his. Nor was it Seire or Faun. Juva put her hand to her chest. A tingle spread through her body, as if she were being plunged into ice water. She heard something that sounded like a howl.

The conversations and laughter died away around her. Everyone had heard it, including the kids. The three warow leapt to their feet and looked at each other, perplexed. Then they heard it again. An eerie, gaulish howling. Skarr began to bark.

"What is it?" Juva said, grabbing Nafraím. "What is that sound?!"

Nafraím closed his eyes, suddenly seeming as tired as a dying man.

"The end of the world," he whispered.

She let go of him, hiked up the voluminous skirt of her dress, and ran out onto the street. Lykteløkka filled as people swarmed outside, standing mesmerized as they listened to the howling, a devilish sound that chilled her to the bone.

It mixed with sounds of screaming, and people pulled away from the streets just as suddenly as they had come. Some ran, others went back inside and closed their doors. Juva stood alone in Lykteløkka and watched them come.

The wolves. Big, wild wolves chasing through the streets. A man pressed himself against the wall of a building but was ripped down by the pack. He did not get up again. They got everything in their path. They approached, and she knew she needed to get away, but her feet wouldn't obey. She stood as if petrified, clutching her red skirt.

We're dead.

She heard yelling from the stairs but couldn't move. The wolves came at her like a snarling, black river. They slowed down as they neared, and a couple of them circled Juva and sniffed her before they ran on. The pack divided into two and continued chasing past her on both sides. She stood untouched in the middle of a river of fur and teeth.

Then a heart hammered against hers, so familiar and all-consuming that she thought she would burst. Her knees buckled, and she fell to her knees.

Gríf was here.

© Julie Loen

ABOUT THE AUTHOR

Siri Pettersen made her sensational debut in 2013 with the Norwegian publication of Odin's Child, the first book in The Raven Rings trilogy, which has earned numerous awards and nominations at home and abroad. Siri has a background as a designer and comics creator. Her roots are in Finnsnes and Trondheim, but she now lives in Oslo, where you're likely to find her in a coffee shop. According to fellow writers, her superpower is "mega motivation"—the ability to inspire other creative souls.

www.siripettersen.com

© Libby Lewis

ABOUT THE TRANSLATOR

Tara Chace has translated more than fifty books from Norwegian, Danish, and Swedish. In addition to Siri Pettersen's first Vardari book, *Iron Wolf*, her other recent translations include books by Lina Areklew, Sara Blædel, Katrine Engberg, Anne Mette Hancock, Edvard Hoem, and Jo Nesbø. An avid reader and language learner, Chace earned her PhD in Scandinavian languages and literature from the University of Washington. She lives in Seattle with her family and enjoys translating books for readers of all ages. She just might be the only Norwegian translator who grew up in Hawaii.

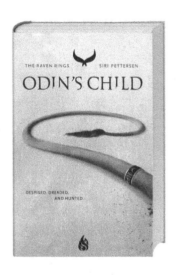

Discover the thrilling fantasy adventure series
WHISPER OF THE RAVENS

Malene Sølvsten
Ansuz (Book 1)
On sale now!
ISBN 978-1-64690-026-8

Malene Sølvsten
Fehu (Book 2)
On sale October 2024
ISBN 978-1-64690-027-5

Malene Sølvsten
Mannaz (Book 3)
On sale Fall 2025
ISBN 978-1-64690-028-2

Arctis

Anna can see events from the past, and the dream-like visions suddenly become very real when a series of murders of young girls take place in the area where she lives. Murders that she has seen in her dreams. She soon learns the murders are linked to an ancient prophecy of Ragnarök and supernatural forces are at work because her new friends are directly connected to the Norse gods, and all carry a knowledge of who she really is.

Discover the exciting Rosenholm fantasy trilogy!

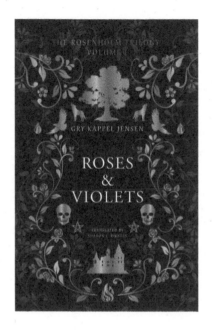

Gry Kappel Jensen
Roses & Violets
(The Rosenholm Trilogy Volume 1)
On sale now!
ISBN 978-1-64690-012-1

Arctis

Four girls from four different parts of Denmark have been invited to apply to Rosenholm Academy for an unknown reason. During the unorthodox application tests, it becomes apparent this is no ordinary school. In fact, it's a magical boarding school and all the students have powers.

Once the school year begins, they learn that Rosenholm carries a dark secret—a young girl was murdered under mysterious circumstances in the 1980s and the killer was never found. Her spirit is still haunting the school, and she is now urging the four girls to bring justice and find the killer. But helping the spirit puts all of the girls in grave danger . . .

AURE

tengnok

SLOKNA

Ulfherred

NORRANA

Steinnhed

Baugur

SKORT

Hølne

Preik

Hjóljav

UNDST

Haeyna

Baupa

Tjærvik

DUGE

Maethey

GRIMSE

Thexvia